AMARNA

NEPHILIM QUEST BOOK THREE

LEENA MARIA

Leena Maria

ISBN (paperback) 978-952-7250-10-5

ISBN (EPUB) 978-952-7250-08-2

ISBN (MOBI) 978-952-7250-09-9

JOIN LEENA MARIA'S NEWSLETTER

Leena Maria's Newsletter subscribers are always to first to hear about Leena's new books and publications.

You can sign up for the newsletter at www.leenasbooks.com

1

DESERT-BORN

Our son was born in the middle of the desert, under the stars. At the very moment Seth lifted him up into his arms, the moon rose to greet the son of the Moon Daughter.

"He is so beautiful..." Seth whispered, his voice filled with wonder at the perfection of a newborn. His loving touch examined the tiny limbs, toes and fingers.

I lay exhausted on the cloth that had served as my birthing bed. There were no birthing bricks here and I could not squat in the way a woman usually did. So I had laid down on a cloth on the ground, supporting myself on my elbows to push our new life into the world. The pain made me dizzy.

Seth was on his knees, having helped our son enter into life. He was gently drying him before wrapping him in a special cloth Mut-Bity had given us. When he was ready, he placed the baby on my stomach.

When I looked at our beautiful child, I felt my heart bursting with unimaginable joy as I saw the moonlight reflecting from his eyes. I couldn't tell whether he was pale like me, not by moonlight. Tears rose up – my love was too great to be contained. Gently I touched his cheek with my finger. I had never felt anything so soft and wonderful in my life.

Then came fear.

"Do you see them?"

Seth rose to his feet and looked across the desert.

"No, I see no one."

"They can't be far. They may have heard me..."

I had tried to be silent but when the pain was at its worst, I hadn't been able to help crying out.

Seth stood listening.

"I hear no one. I see no one. I feel no one. I am sure the wind took your voice and carried it away so they could not hear it."

"Quickly, use the knife!" I felt panic rising. "We need to go."

Seth knelt down and took an obsidian knife from a small bundle. He tied a linen string around the umbilical cord and cut it with the knife. Mut-Bity had explained how he should do it while she led us away from Mi-Wer, away from the Pale Man, the Nephilim lord who wanted us and all our kind... dead.

"We have to wait for the afterbirth," Seth gently pushed me back when I tried to rise.

"We can't. We have to be far away before the sun rises!" My voice was high-pitched with fear.

"We have no choice – if we leave now, you're risking not only your life but also the life of our son. Mut-Bity explained it all to me."

The tiny baby moved and primeval instinct rose from within me. I would do nothing that would endanger our son. So I remained there, lying still.

Seth walked to the little donkey we had with us. The patient animal had carried me and my heavy belly until the pains of birth began. Now it stood quietly while Seth took a large cloth from one of the sacks hanging on both sides of the animal.

It was Mut-Bity's tent. The old, worn tent she had used for years on her walks through the desert. With experienced movements, Seth raised it to shelter the baby and me. We were on the north side of a big stone boulder, hoping it would give us shade once the sun rose.

In time the afterbirth came, but then the sun had already risen. I could not move from under the canvas or the rays would have burned me. I was still so weak and the heaviness of my limbs kept me in place. Knowing we should be on the move, I cursed my feeble state, and just lay there enveloped in the heat of the day.

Seth kept guard, constantly watching the surroundings. The little donkey stayed in the shadow of the boulder as best it could. It had patiently walked for days and nights under the scorching sun and the cold stars that showed us our path westward towards the secret valley. The stars were a map written in the sky, Mut-Bity used to say. It was never written down in words or as a drawing, so the location of the valley of the good Nephilim could never be revealed by accident. Those who could read the night sky taught the way to anyone who needed to know it, during long trips to the desert.

The warmth of the day and giving birth not only made me tired, but filled me with concern about how our son would survive this blazing heat. I poured some water on a cloth from a leather flask and placed it over him while I tried to make him suckle my breast. I was worried when he didn't. He just lay there in my arms, eyes closed, but I could feel his breath on my skin like the touch of a butterfly's wing.

And then, when the sun had already begun to descend towards the west, I felt them. My back began to buzz in the familiar way that told me our kind were near. I had sensed them during the days we had been walking through the hot desert, knowing they were hunting us, but they didn't seem to know where we were headed and soon circled away from us.

"Seth..." I whispered.

"I feel it too," he said quietly from outside the tent. "Stay as quiet as you can... I'll try to find out how close they are."

I had to force myself to breathe calmly. That was the only way I could hide myself from other Nephilim, to keep my force hidden from them. Strong emotions would make me hum, and they would feel it in their bodies and discover where I was.

So I concentrated on breathing deep from my belly, forcing down my anxiety for Seth and the baby and hoping our child would be silent. He lay there with his cheek against my skin and slept.

Seth was away for so long, I began to fear something terrible had happened to him. Then I heard steps. I grabbed the obsidian knife lying next to me. When Seth's legs appeared, I started breathing again. Silently, he bent down and crawled into the tent, next to me. The tent was barely high enough for us to sit inside it, and was meant for one person only. Seth lay on his side and bent his knees so that his feet were inside the tent. I did the same.

"Dark ones," Seth breathed into my ear, "flying. Coming this way."

The sensation grew stronger by the moment. We lay still, waiting for the sign that would tell us our pursuers were close. And then someone spoke nearby.

"See anything?" It was a male voice, above us. Despite the fact he wasn't speaking in a loud voice, we heard him clearly. He would also hear any noise we made. That was the blessing and the curse of the Nephilim senses.

He must be standing on top of the boulder. Our little tent was under a thin ledge of the mushroom-shaped stone, in a depression underneath. Seth had thrown off stones to make the surface more level so we could make the best of whatever shelter was available. The mushroom shape of the boulder kept us out of view of our hunter.

But they might see us anytime. And what about the donkey!

"No. I do not see them. But I can smell blood."

Seth and I looked at each other. The blood from giving birth! Seth had buried the afterbirth in the sand, but the wrapping I had worn on our journey, and had been lying on to give birth to our son, was soaked through.

I formed the word "donkey" with my lips but Seth could not answer. He just nodded and I had no idea what the nod meant.

"Maybe an animal has died nearby. I have seen lions around here before," another voice said.

"Maybe... but they can't have gone far! There was no scent of them in the mists. Also she was heavily pregnant, the lord said. So they will not be flying. If they have walked or have a donkey, this is about as far as they could go. Perhaps she has now given birth and it's her blood we can smell?" the voice above said and my heart gave a heavy thump. Seth squeezed my arm. Sweat trickled down my face.

"True. And that means they are somewhere nearby still... What can you see from up there?"

"Nothing..."

So they still hadn't seen our little tent. Our only hope was that they would not come down to our side of the boulder.

"Let's circle around here for a while..."

They would find us. They would kill us. Bile rose into my mouth. We should escape to the misty world...

"No," Seth formed the word with his lips, guessing my thoughts.

Falling into the mists behind our world would be our only way to escape, but to do so I would have to use the power of my wings. And they would feel that, and would follow us there immediately. There would be no boulders in the mist to hide us.

"What is that?"

"What?"

"Over there! Is that... a donkey?"

"Yes it is... It has to be them! They must be near!"

I did not hear anything but knew they would now land on the desert floor and see us. Seth took the obsidian knife from me. I closed my eyes and cried silently, holding our child. This is how it would all end.

2

LORD OF VAMPIRES

Forcing his anger back, Daniel moved on, his senses sharpened by the urgency of the hunt. He flew quietly, like a ghost, feeling the dry mist against his skin telling him how fast he was moving, conscious of its absence whenever he stopped.

The vampire had Dana and Diana had said he intended to kill her.

Part of his mind warned him that Ambrogio was the most dangerous prey he had ever tracked and would be the hardest to catch. The First Vampire. The most lethal of all of Cain's servants, the lord of all vampires. A hunter like no other, his immortality making him infinitely patient in his own pursuits.

Ambrogio had eternity on his side. Cain's personal hunting hound, sent to seek and destroy all Cain's enemies. Angel's private assassin. Cain's daughter wanted Dana dead so she could have Daniel to herself; and Ambrogio was Angel's right hand.

The thought brought anger flooding back so he had to fight it again. Now was not the time or place, going into the unknown. There had never been a vampire who could move into the buffer zone unaided, so there had to be another with him. Who – or what? Was it a shadow? Or – another Nephilim?

What mattered was that he had to stay as silent as possible. Rising anger would set the buffer zone humming with the power of his wings, warning whoever - or whatever - lay ahead of him.

It had to be Cain who had sent Ambrogio back in time to catch Dana. Why, then, hadn't he taken Dana back to his master? Was he following Angel's orders instead of Cain's? Or did he have his own agenda? An unknown agenda that threatened the life of Dana...

As if in response to his thought, as insubstantial yet compelling as an old memory, her faint scent came to him. Dana. His twin soul, his love. The reason he had fought his way back to health after the shadow attack on the Time Walker Centre. So many had died – but he had survived and he intended to make sure it was not in vain. He would save Dana even if meant death for himself.

Once he saw movement in the mist, something heading towards him, but it was only a fleeting glimpse that vanished immediately. He did not doubt he had seen it, though. He trusted his senses. Whatever it was, it had seen him and hidden itself immediately.

After what felt like an eternity of flight, Dana's scent grew unmistakably more intense. She *had* to be near. He slowed down, preparing himself for the fight he was sure was approaching.

Someone was nearby in the mist. No, there were two of them, keeping completely still. Dana's scent surrounded them - but Dana was not there.

Daniel stopped, protecting himself within the cocoon of his blue wings, and waited.

"Welcome." The voice was soft and hoarse, unsurprised. They had known he was coming. Daniel did not move.

"Who are you?" he asked, trying to see who was standing before him.

"I am the one you are chasing," the voice said matter-of-factly. "I - am Ambrogio."

Rage threw Daniel forwards, uncontrollably, the strength of his force field enveloping the figures, forcing them backwards.

"Wait!" Ambrogio's voice betrayed no emotion. "Let me speak before - "

Daniel saw the linen cloth he was holding. The scent of Dana surrounded him. Ambrogio's eyes followed his gaze. He lifted the scarf.

"Yes, I have her. And no, I am not giving her back."

Daniel stared into the face of the First Vampire. The first and only time he had revealed himself to Daniel. Any Time Walker who had encountered Ambrogio had not survived the confrontation.

He knew Ambrogio's reputation, and had even seen his hooded figure from a distance while fighting his soldiers. Now, here he was for the first time, fully visible without a hood concealing his features. The First Vampire whose word was law to all the others of his kind.

His odd golden-tinged skin was very much like the skin of the dark Nephilim. His eyes were unblinking. His black glossy hair fell down onto his shoulders. He was the image of a Mediterranean artist's antique figure, come to life in front of Daniel, ancient, burdened with knowledge.

"You are wondering how I came to meet you here, and why I made your hunt too easy for you," Ambrogio said.

Daniel waited, his wings rumbling, saying nothing. That new emotion clawing at the back of his mind. Fear.

Not fear, not now. It was anger he needed, anger to make him able to function. He concentrated on all the anger this creature had ever caused him to feel. All those dead team members - friends he had known, people Ambrogio had killed, directly or indirectly. He thought of their deaths, lives that had ended before their time. The burials and grief he had witnessed, observing the hate and desperation growing in his own heart at his incapacity to prevent all these losses.

His heart obeyed his mind. Fear fell back into the darkness it had risen from, and anger took its place.

Ambrogio observed him silently while he fought his emotions, and the expression in the vampire's eyes did not match the anger in Daniel's. Daniel sensed weariness, infinite horizons of stale, deathless fatigue.

"No matter if you have no desire to talk. I have tasted Dana's blood and seen you there in her memories. So I know you are the one she loves."

Tasted her blood? What did he mean? Had he bitten her? Daniel's hands rose instinctively, reaching for the cursed vampire.

"No, I have not bitten her," Ambrogio looked at his hands. "I drank her friend Diana dry. Well, almost. And so Dana gave her a blood transfusion to keep her alive. That blend of Diana's blood, mingled with Dana's, was enough to show me many of Dana's memories. The strongest ones were of you. And - ah, the taste… the exquisite, unique taste..."

Ambrogio's voice was playing him, testing his reactions. Other than the rumbling of his wings, nothing revealed Daniel's anger now. His face was set, and he observed the vampire without apparent emotion.

"You'll never escape me." Daniel's voice was controlled. "I know your scent, now."

"And I yours. So we are both capable of following each other's trail. Only you won't follow mine."

"I don't have to obey your orders." Daniel moved forward, forcing Ambrogio to take a step back. The vampire did not seem alarmed by this.

For the first time, Daniel looked at the other form standing next to Ambrogio. The Egyptian-looking man with the strange cloudy eyes.

"Ah, yes, this is my servant. I sent him back to get Diana from the tomb, and he saw you and returned to warn me. That is how I knew to meet you here."

So - this servant was the fleeting form Daniel had seen earlier.

"The eyes. Unusual, are they not? He used to be my shadow, but I gave him independent existence through a human form. He uses the man's senses and body now, but cannot hide his true nature completely."

What was this creature saying? He had created a fresh horror?

"Shadows can't have independent existence." Even as he said it, Daniel knew Ambrogio had not been lying.

"Oh, but they can. I have found a way to make it possible," Ambrogio's voice held no emotion. "Now. Here are your instructions. You will not follow me. You see, my servant and I are the only ones who know where Dana is. If we don't return to her, she will die. I have left her tightly bound and she has lost a lot of blood and is weak. If you attack me, I will fight you to the death. That will probably be *my* death, knowing your power. But I do not fear death. I would welcome it. Living forever - when you have witnessed the ages that I have, there are precious few things that make life worth living."

Ambrogio's voice kept its emotionless tone, yet Daniel sensed something there, something he could not fathom.

"And once I am dead, you will never know where Dana is. I know Nephilim can live for centuries, longer even. But a Nephilim weakened with blood loss, without food or drink, will eventually die. My demise would bring about Dana's death. And you will never find her on your own. She is well hidden in a place you cannot discover in time."

Daniel looked at the servant who stared back at him with those dark, cloudy eyes. They seemed to be of the same material that formed shadows. The human eyes were underneath, but the shadow-stuff swirled on the surface, sometimes hiding the pupils completely.

"He obeys me unquestioningly. And should you kill him, his essence will simply disintegrate back into the mist he was formed from. If I die, he is to kill himself. And he will. Even shadows have no wish to disintegrate, though, so he is motivated to protect me. And - I can see your thought - you won't find him easy to destroy."

Daniel saw the glint of a blade in the shadow-man's hand. Whatever Ambrogio said, he was sure he could kill the physical form of this creature.

There was no fear in the shadow- man's posture and expression. Daniel could see that Ambrogio had created a being who was loyal to the bone to his master. And that was hardly surprising - the first shadow ever to be given independent life in a physical body. For that, any shadow would be fiercely loyal forever to the one who had given solid form to his existence.

Kill the shadow - and lose Ambrogio? No, that he couldn't do. Ambrogio would drop out of the buffer zone and hide in the physical world. Daniel knew he needed to keep the First Vampire in sight as he racked his brains for a plan.

"Why do you need Dana?" he asked, playing for time.

A flicker of emotion crossed Ambrogio's face. His eyes darted briefly away from Daniel, as if he had not expected the question and was no longer fully in control. Daniel sensed an internal struggle. When Ambrogio finally spoke, his voice was hoarser than before.

"You do not need to know that and I am not about to tell you. We are leaving, now. All of us, together. Back to the physical world where you will remain while my shadow and I return to the buffer zone. My shadow will return to make sure you have followed my instructions. If you have vanished when he comes back to you, I shall kill Dana immediately."

Daniel said nothing, but when the shadow-man took Ambrogio's hand and began to descend through the mists, he followed.

They landed in a desert wadi. Daniel had no idea where it was – east or west of the Nile. The sun had set and all that was visible was the Milky Way stretching across the heavens between the dark mass of the craggy walls rising upwards on both sides. The wadi floor was scattered with heavy rocks, brought there by the deadly floods that filled these ravines unexpectedly when heavy rains fell far away.

"Stay here and keep your wings open. My shadow will watch from a distance to make sure you are doing just that. They give enough light during the night to show where you are, so my shadow won't need to come near you again. Knowing your reputation, that seems to me to be wise. When the sun rises, you may leave. I have no issue with you. Not anymore."

The last words were barely audible, and again there was that flicker of emotion in Ambrogio's cold eyes when he looked into Daniel's. For the briefest of moments Daniel felt a curious sensation as if he was looking into a mirror - the anger and longing matched what he was feeling.

With these cryptic words Ambrogio and the shadow-man fell back into the buffer zone. Daniel noticed the scarf on the ground and picked it up. He pressed the soft cloth to his face and breathed in deeply.

The fear he had held back burst out and clouded his mind. He knew enough about the horrors of vampirism and had witnessed the results too frequently himself. His fear showed him all the bloody, tortured forms he had ever seen, and placed those wounds on the image of Dana he carried in his heart. He fell onto his knees, barely able to breathe.

No. Fear only had power over him if he allowed it. No! Concentrate on a plan, that was what he must do. Dana was still alive. Ambrogio had told him that if Daniel didn't obey orders, he would kill Dana immediately. That meant he hadn't been planning on doing so - yet - and that meant there was still time.

If the vampire thought he wouldn't hunt him down, he was wrong. The only reason he had obeyed the vampire's orders was to make sure Dana survived. He was going to find him and he would find Dana, alive. This was only a temporary setback.

Daniel thought deeply. Whatever Ambrogio needed Dana for depended on how soon she would recover from her blood loss. Nephilim healed quickly and time was what Daniel needed. Now his only hope was that Dana, who was already weak from being forced to time-time travel to the past before she had fully healed, might recuperate more slowly than usual. But the fear in his mind whispered that Dana was herself a healer. Her blood would restore her too - maybe even more quickly than would normally be expected.

Daniel forced himself to stand up. Ambrogio's shadow was not going to see him remain on his knees, beaten by desperation. Fear in his stomach tried to pull him back down, but he straightened his back with force and again concentrated on drawing on his reserves of anger.

It wasn't easy. The fear in him was so powerful. Only by forcing his attention through memories of episodes from the past could he do it. He concentrated on one name at a time, one face, one life story, one death. And then moved to the next. A string of faces floated to the front of his inner vision, rising from his memory, and slowly his anger, his hatred towards the servants of the enemy Nephilim built a wall that contained the fear.

His wings open, he stood in the night, listening for signs of life. When the sun finally rose above the craggy mountains, he concentrated his energies backwards into his spine and entered the buffer zone.

He recalled the vampire's odd dusty smell and the scent of the shadow-man's human form. He wouldn't forget them now. Staying in the place he had entered, he concentrated on finding them, but too much time had passed. There was nothing.

"How?" he challenged himself.

Not wanting to leave the place where Ambrogio had landed, he returned to the desert wadi and closed his wings. Kneeling down he touched the footprints Ambrogio had left, as if that would help. When he arose, his mind was still whirling, without any idea of the next step. The arid desert mountains were all around him – a vast area he could not search on his own.

In rage, he roared his anger to the air, fists clenched. He would never give up. He was going to search every inch of the desert for her. The whole world if need be. And if he found Dana too late...

Daniel stopped the thought before it took hold. He needed his anger now more than ever, but as a tool, not as a master, clouding his judgement. He would fetch Elijah and together they would find Ambrogio and Dana. There was still time

He turned around, imprinting the place onto his memory so he could return to the precise location. That was when he noticed the three men standing next to the rock wall of the wadi, staring at him.

3

CAPTIVE

I woke up with black dots swimming in my field of vision. The sides of my mouth hurt like hell and there was a bundle of cloth drawn tightly across it - a gag.

Memory came flooding back along with pain, unbelievable pain.

Ambrogio's shadow had tied me to what felt like a long piece of driftwood. Its curving lumpy form pushed into my back and there was a stump of a branch scraping the floor of the cave close - too close - to my right eye. My brain began to work despite the pain - it immediately started puzzling over where on earth he had found a piece of wood, rare as it was. Perhaps we were close to the Nile. Or the sea.

Then, the pain again. The shadow had forced my heels up to my buttocks and then yanked my hands back and tied my wrists to my ankles. After that he had fastened my elbows close together - it was the throbbing pain in my knees, ankles and arms that had brought me back to consciousness. It even felt as if my fingers were tied up tightly like bundles of sticks, making it impossible for me to move them.

Tied like one of the enemies of Egypt, captive in front of the pharaoh. That's how they were depicted in ancient Egyptian art. Lying there in the dirt and dust of the cave, I experienced some of the pain and fear they must have felt, visualising them lying under the burning rays of the sun and the gaze of the king. The shadow had made use of the memories of the man whose body it now inhabited, and had tied me accordingly.

I felt as though I had been unconscious for a long time. Eyes closed, I breathed as slowly as I could, tasting sand and dust despite the gag, listening for any noises. This was survival mode. I almost hoped to hear the voices of Ambrogio and the shadow discussing me, giving some hint of where we were, any clue as to what was happening, the reason Ambrogio had brought me here. If he wanted to kill me, why wait? Why not do it right away?

After listening to the silence for a while and hearing nothing, I lifted my head to see better, even though the dry branch stuck into my cheek painfully, undoubtedly leaving a mark.

The cave was small and I was lying in the middle of it, staring at the entrance. Through the opening, I could see rocks and the blinding light of day, but not a single living thing. On the ground in front of me, I could make out footprints - they'd kicked up the dust that was blocking my nose. I couldn't see behind me, but I could sense there was no one there. My ears were ringing in the absolute silence and knew I was alone. They had gone and I didn't know if they were ever coming back or had just left me here to die.

Fear for Diana's safety made my heart beat more quickly. Ambrogio had forced me to leave with him - or, he said, he would hurt Diana. Nothing stopped him from doing it anyway - maybe that's where he had gone with his shadow now, to kill her. Ambrogio would drink her blood until there was nothing left. What the shadow in his physical form might do to her... I didn't want to think about it, pushed the thought away.

That strange musty taste lingering in my mouth. I tried my damndest to push away the next memory as well, but couldn't.

Ambrogio's shadow had left us as soon as he had tied me and removed all the silver rings from my fingers and taken my silver necklace. These went straight into the pouch he carried on his waist, just before he disappeared from the cave into the buffer zone. After he left, Ambrogio sat still like a statue, observing me without a word.

I tried not to look at him, but as he was right in front of my field of vision, it was impossible. I had seen him cutting the palms of his hands with a knife, ignoring the little pieces of flesh that fell on the cave floor with his blood. Through my nausea, I realised why he was doing that. He was cutting his connection to a Weaver, the one who had brought him back in time to find us. Someone under Cain's command. And if Ambrogio had severed that connection, it meant he did not intend to return to the future with the Weaver. It could also mean he was no longer following Cain's orders.

For some reason, that thought made me even more scared than the idea of being taken back to the future, to Cain. But I had said nothing. I was petrified by despair and fear and couldn't see any way out. I hated that feeling of helplessness and I knew my voice would betray my fear to him. Yet I also knew he could sense my fear easily - like any vampire, any predator, he could smell it.

After Ambrogio and I had been observing each other for a while in silence, the shadow returned and Ambrogio turned his cold eyes away from me. It felt like pressure was released in my pancreas and I had to fight both fear and the urge to vomit that accompanied it. There was no way I was going to give him the satisfaction, the enjoyment of witnessing my emotions.

The shadow had spoken quietly to his master - so quietly that even my enhanced sense of hearing could not make out what he was saying.

Ambrogio had risen, holding the same knife he had used to cut his palms. Then he cut his left wrist with it as if he felt no pain at all. I had seen thick dark blood welling out of the slit. The blood was almost black and flowed like syrup. He'd yanked my head back with his right hand and placed the bleeding wrist against my lips. That was before the gag went on...

"Drink."

I wouldn't. Like a child avoiding something it hated, I had closed my mouth tightly and shut my eyes, refusing him. I didn't have to breathe through my mouth or nose. I could breathe through my wings, even if they were inside my back, and so no need for oxygen would force me to drink a vampire's blood. I had kept my lips closed, fighting nausea, feeling his cold blood making the skin around my mouth burn.

His response had been to drag my head back, pulling my hair harder until tears ran from my eyes.

"Drink. It won't turn you into a vampire, not with your silver blood. Not when I have not bitten you to replace your blood with mine. It will only make you sleep. I need you to be unconscious so you won't try to escape," Ambrogio said with cold logic.

I had looked into his dark unblinking eyes and said nothing. Thinking of my friends - and Daniel - gave me the courage to not drink even as I felt the cold blood dripping slowly down from my closed lips onto my chin, burning my skin as it trickled. The shadow man took a step forward, eagerness showing on his face, but one look from Ambrogio made him step back. The vampire then looked me directly in the eyes again.

His eyes - they were mesmerising. He didn't look evil. And the expression in them… there was the briefest hint of emotion there…

"I need you alive and I need you to heal. I need you for a purpose. And so you will do exactly as I tell you. Your friend Diana will be kept alive as long as you do - is that clear? If you refuse me anything, I will kill her. I have not eaten in a long time, and she could satisfy my hunger. But - her blood told me how close you two are. And so, I will keep her alive - but only on the condition that you obey me. I trust I will not need to ask you again."

He had pressed his wrist against my mouth once more and I had opened my lips, almost sobbing, and drank his black blood. Darkness covered my mind like a cloak, pushing me below the surface of consciousness and I finally vomited from disgust. But by then the blood was already having the effect Ambrogio wanted. I fell into a sleep so deep it was like a coma. The last thing I had felt was someone wiping the vomit from my face.

Now I had woken up and no one was here. I could try to escape into the buffer zone…

Stupid. What was I going to do when I got there? Lie there like a caterpillar, wrapped like a living mummy, waiting for them to come and drag me back? Not to mention Diana - he would kill her, I knew he would. If anything, I trusted Ambrogio to keep his word, as long as I did. I had never met a vampire face to face before - and I had never met anyone who was so... cold. So empty of feelings. I must have imagined the glimpse of emotion I had seen... sadness. Must have been all the romantic stories of vampires I had read before I knew they were real. Gosh, how wrong those books were. If only people knew the truth, no one would have written such nonsense.

Something at the edge of my memory tried to show me something... I concentrated. This could be important.

All I could feel was - a sadness that wasn't mine. Loss. And a... sudden sensation of... hope?

I could not grasp the elusive emotion and it vanished.

Kitty? Could I reach my dead friend somehow? So she could tell the Time Walker team where I was?

I screamed Kitty's name through the gag, but to no avail. She did not appear.

Exhausted, I stopped. All I could do was to lie still and wait for Ambrogio, his shadow and Diana to return.

4

THE MIRACLE

Then, the miracle.

I could hear little stones crunching under the feet of the two Nephilim men as they approached. I closed my eyes tightly only to open them again. I did not want to see them, yet I had to know who they were. I would not wait for death with my eyes closed.

Seth rose to a sitting position next to me, quietly.

Someone moved past our tent. A pair of dark, tanned legs. Then another pair.

"Stop!" the voice of the Nephilim man said.

The pair of legs stopped and turned to face someone.

"Greetings," a man's voice said in an accent that was strange to me. "What brings two such mighty lords this deep into the desert?"

"We are searching for two of our kind. A woman without colour, either heavily pregnant or having just given birth. And a man with red hair. Both are very tall. Have you seen them?"

Seth and I stared at each other, not believing our ears. A figure walked right up to our tent and sat down in front of it, filling the opening. A woman. She did not look into the tent, but her dark skin and dusty clothing revealed what she was. A desert dweller, member of a tribe of nomads that had walked the deserts for innumerable generations, somehow managing to survive in the harsh conditions.

"No, my lord, we have not seen them. We took shelter here by the rock when my wife gave birth. She will soon have recovered enough for us to continue our journey."

Now we saw the bundle in the woman's arms. A little arm moved. A baby.

"Is this your donkey?"

"Indeed it is. A good animal - the best! It doesn't need much water, never runs away and is used to the desert."

The wind was getting stronger, and the woman's robe billowed about her, filling the opening to the tent. A cloud of sand blew inside and we had to cover our faces to be able to breathe. I pulled the cloth over our son's face and forced myself not to cough.

"A sandstorm seems to be rising," the man's voice said. "It might be wise to search for shelter."

I saw a pair of legs appear as shadows on the tent fabric. That was when our son began to cry. The woman began to rock the bundle in her arms right away, murmuring softly. I could not move, for fear that the Nephilim would hear there was someone inside the tent. I put my little finger in the baby's mouth and he went silent.

For a while, the Nephilim man stood still, then he turned and walked away.

"If you see the ones we are looking for, send us word. We live in the oasis far to the west and north. I see you are of the desert tribe and can easily walk to us if need be. Tell us where they are, or bring their severed heads to us, and you will be richly rewarded."

"I shall remember," the man's voice said, "and will send word if I see them."

"You do that."

And then the buzzing feeling in my spine stopped, They were gone.

The woman turned now, and we saw her dark eyes and almost black skin.

"We reached you at the last moment," she said.

The man bent down to look into the tent.

"Mut-Bity sent word to us right after you left. She said it was important

to send a couple with a baby. You had half a day's head start. You moved fast despite not being able to fly, so it took us this long to reach you." Then, looking directly at me, "If you had not given birth, we might not have found you in time."

All I could do was to stare at them.

"Who... who are you?" Seth asked.

"We are desert dwellers. We owe Mut-Bity many favours. She has helped us in the past, brought us food and honey. Mut-Bity knew our kind were near, at the edge of the desert near the king's palace, and came to meet us after you had escaped. 'Find the Moon Daughter and take her and her family to safety. The winged ones are on their trail and must not catch them,' she said."

"And you know of... our kind?" I asked.

"Many in the desert know of the winged ones. And we know there are good and bad kinds. The ones after you were of the bad kind. They have killed our people in the past, bitten them, drunk their blood. We know them by their smell. They aren't necessarily aware of how much we watch them, though. They always try to do their killing when no one can see. But the desert has many eyes," the man said.

"It is true a sandstorm is approaching," the woman now said. "We will put up our tent next to yours and wait it out. Also - your donkey needs to be protected."

She put her baby down between Seth and me and arose. Seth hesitated a moment and then took the baby into his arms, earning a smile from the woman.

Quickly the couple erected their tent next to ours so that they touched one another to form one bigger tent. The man brought the donkey alongside the tents and pulled a coarsely woven sack over its head. The surprised animal shook its head but the sack was tied around its neck and would not fall off.

"It will keep most of the sand out," the man explained, putting a heavy stone on the other end of the rope that went around the animal's neck. He pushed it up effortlessly despite his small frame, and dropped it over the rope, fastening it expertly at the top. "And now the donkey won't wander away from you either."

Then he crawled into the tent and the woman secured the tents to each other with coarse cords the man had been carrying. Now I understood why Mut-Bity's tent had little holes carefully cut and strengthened with stitches. Probably they were meant for a cloth to close the entrance to the tent, but now they were used to keep us all secure and together in a single space.

Even inside, we covered our heads tightly against the sand that would inevitably get inside the tent.

"They will keep on searching for you," the man said, his voice rising over the sound of the increasing storm. "Mut-Bity told us how her bees destroyed all the winged ones that attacked you. All but the Pale one. He is their high lord, and he wants you dead. He will stop at nothing, Mut-Bity said. And so we'll take you through our secret ways back to the valley of the winged ones. We can only pray we make it. I have never seen so many of the evil winged ones flying around in bright daylight, not caring who sees them in the desert. Stories of winged gods are already spreading. This sandstorm is a blessing - it will wipe away the traces you left on the desert floor - the same ones we followed to find you - and will make it even harder for them, for they are not as good at following tracks as we are. They trust their sense of smell and keen eyes and ears, and their ability to observe from above. This disrespect for our ancient skills will work to your advantage now. They were searching for you all over the desert, flying high above the earth, ignoring the small traces of your steps; we followed the path directly to you. It was clear enough to us."

"You speak eloquently," Seth said, "I had always thought your tribe didn't talk much, or so well. And I mean no disrespect by saying that."

"We have no need to let others know who we are. Just because we don't read and write or live in houses doesn't mean we are stupid or can't speak eloquently, as you put it," the woman said.

"We are honoured to meet you, and will be forever in your debt for saving our lives," I replied warmly.

They both nodded solemnly, accepting the debt.

"Has your baby fed yet?" the woman asked.

"No, not yet. I am worried," I said.

"Don't be. Once the sandstorm has finished, I will help you teach him how to suckle. Some newborn babies need to be shown how it is done. And I

saw the baby accepting your finger in its mouth so I don't think you will need to wait long," the woman said. "Do you have a daughter or a son?"

"A son," Seth and I said at the same time and could not help smiling at each other.

"You are blessed," the woman smiled back at us and then fell silent.

The wind was now howling so loudly it was pointless to try and speak. So we sat there, huddled together, waiting for the storm to pass.

5

DESERT HUNTERS

The three men looking at Daniel held spears in their hands, but they were carrying them loosely by their sides. Their stance was relaxed and not threatening in the least, but this could be deceptive; Daniel knew they could throw their spears instinctively and accurately in the blink of an eye at the first sign of a threat.

They wore very little clothing, were small and sinewy and their skin had been baked dark by the sun. Desert dwellers, nomads, at home and at ease in their natural environment.

Daniel acknowledged them with a nod of his head and they answered in kind. Their expressions revealed nothing as they took in his height and his odd clothing. Then one of them stepped towards him, still holding his spear. Daniel stood with his hands down, ready to open his wings again, unsure of what to expect.

The man who was coming towards him was approaching old age. His hair was already white and he had deep, sharp creases in his cheeks. He stopped about ten strides away and inhaled deeply. Daniel's own face betrayed his surprise. Why would they *smell* him?

And then he got it. They had seen his wings. And the only reason he could think of for smelling him was that they already knew the scent of Nephilim.

The man was checking to see what kind of Nephilim they had encountered.

After a while the man smiled and gestured to his two companions to approach.

"I give you greeting," Daniel said as calmly as he could, keeping his voice friendly.

They looked at each other, not understanding his language. Of course they wouldn't! He tried to recall what he'd learned during lessons in the ancient Egyptian language at the Centre... how did the Egyptians greet one another? How did one say "Hello" in ancient times? Then, in an instant, it came to him.

"*Nyny*!" he said.

The men's brows furrowed as they repeated his words, and then they all laughed.

"*Nyny*!" they said, pronouncing it slightly differently.

Daniel smiled back. The oldest of the men pointed at Daniel's chest and said a word that Daniel had never expected to hear, not over three thousand years in the past. He said the word in an unusual way, but there was no mistaking it.

"Nephilim?"

Not being sure if a nod meant yes or no, Daniel answered in the clearest way possible. He opened his wings.

The men stepped back. Then they spoke to each other in an odd language, clicking their tongues against their palate, glancing up and down the length of his wings. They seemed to come to a conclusion as one of them stepped forward, past Daniel and pointed down at the ground.

Daniel turned to see what he was pointing at. The footprints of Ambrogio and his shadow were clearly visible in the dust.

The man indicated the footprints, inhaled audibly and placed his hand across his forehead to shade his eyes, before turning his head this way and that as if in search of something. Then he bent down, examined the footprints, took a few steps, observed the ground again, straightened himself to look around once more... and raised his eyebrows questioningly. He pointed at the footprints, then at Daniel, and made the universal sign of walking with his fingers.

Daniel understood. Maybe they had seen Ambrogio, even witnessed what had happened.

"Yes! Yes! I need to find them!" he said out loud, though of course they couldn't understand.

He lifted Dana's scarf and pressed it to his heart. Then he bent down and traced the outline of a winged female figure in the sand and dust. He raised the scarf, and indicated the picture, taking in Ambrogio's footprints with a sweep of his hand. Finally, he repeated the man's gesture of walking with his own hand.

The men spoke together again, before one of them left at a relaxed jog along the wadi. The others squatted down on the ground and indicated that Daniel should join them.

6

SPYING

From a high vantage point next to a vertical spike of stone, Ambrogio observed the little camp on the desert floor. Wrapped in a long cape, with his face shadowed by a cloth pulled low over his forehead, he was certain they were invisible to anyone below.

"Who are these people?" Ambrogio asked his shadow. "Desert dwellers?"

He could only see women and older men. A few children were there too, doing some minor chores, or playing. The younger men must be out hunting. Despite its arid appearance, he knew well that the eastern desert had plenty of animals. Hunger assailed him.

His shadow hesitated, exploring the memories of the man he now inhabited. Finally he replied "Yes. Desert people. They do not want to live by the River. No one knows why they choose to live in the desert. They have done so always, and hunted their food."

The shadow's strange accent twisted some of his words so badly that Ambrogio barely understood them. The man's tongue was not used to speaking English and struggled to make the right sounds.

Discovering people so near their hiding place annoyed Ambrogio. The cave the shadow-man had found was small, but gave good shelter from the heat of the sun, and he had no doubt that anyone who lived in these harsh conditions would know of its existence. He had to make sure these people didn't make their way towards it. He had forced the silver girl into deep sleep with his blood, but they would have to return to her soon. He didn't trust Dana not to try to escape, especially now that they did not have her friend Diana - a fact he thought Dana would guess soon enough.

As he watched, a man appeared from behind a boulder and walked into the camp. He spoke to the oldest woman, clearly identifiable even at this distance by her white hair. After a brief exchange, the man turned and left.

The people began to dismantle the camp immediately and were soon walking in the same direction the man had taken, away from the cave. Good.

"We are going back now," Ambrogio said, stepping away from the stone finger pointing at the sky. He faced his shadow. "I may return to feed from them later if I cannot find a big enough animal to satisfy me. But now we need to return before Dana wakes up. She must not realise we no longer have her friend under our control. If that were to happen, I am sure she would do her best to escape. So you are not to speak about her friend at all. Not a word. Understand?"

The shadow said nothing, but bowed his head respectfully and took his master's hand. As they sank away from the physical world, they missed what was happening below them.

There below, on the desert floor, one little figure stared up intently in their direction before running after the rest of the group. And not far from where they had been standing the translucent form of a young woman faded out of sight.

~

Daniel fought his impatience. His mind told him it was a waste of time sitting still in the shade, while the sun climbed ever higher. However, at the same time, he knew instinctively that the desert dwellers equalled some kind of hope, perhaps his only hope in his search for Dana. They were the experts in this environment. If she was here in the desert at all, might they have some idea of where Ambrogio had taken her? That was if they had understood that he was looking for a woman, if he'd managed to communicate with them...

So he forced himself to be silent, and sat still, waiting. The two men said nothing, sitting with the relaxed patience of people whose lives were not ruled by time.

Daniel thought of Lilith and Elijah, and Diana. They must have waited for the shadow to return – but were they still in the tomb of Sithathoriunet? Perhaps they were wondering where he was. His active brain played scene after scene, running over the possibilities.

Had the shadow-man returned to fetch Diana? If so, Elijah would have attacked and destroyed him. How likely was it that Ambrogio would send his servant back to fetch Diana, though, guessing that if Daniel had appeared here in the past, Elijah couldn't be far off? For surely Anna must have told Cain that both brothers had survived, and it would make sense that this knowledge had been passed through time by Anna to Ambrogio. There was no reason for Angel not to share the information.

There was something more, though, a thought that unnerved him. As a hunter himself, Ambrogio would know Daniel was following Dana's scent – which he could only have found in Sithathoriunet's tomb where Ambrogio had imprisoned the girls. So logic dictated that would be where Elijah was waiting for them to return. If Ambrogio really had found a way to give a shadow an independent existence by embedding it somehow in a living human, it was not likely he would jeopardise his creation by sending him straight to Elijah. Trying to mesh his own hunting instincts with those of Ambrogio - it was unnerving, attempting to enter the mind of the First Vampire.

After about two hours, the man who had left the camp returned. He talked briefly with the other two and they got up and gestured to Daniel to follow.

They were soon met by a group of women and children and some older men. Daniel counted just eighteen people. They carried everything they owned on their backs and all had the same slender build and sun-baked skin.

The children stopped when they saw Daniel, and then ran to him, giggling. They pulled at the fabric of his jeans and looked at his striped T-shirt, mesmerised. One little girl squatted on the ground next to him and poked his trainers with her finger, saying something in an excited tone. Daniel wasn't sure if the children had ever seen shoes or sandals, for the whole group was barefoot. And no one here could ever even have imagined something like the modern trainers he was wearing.

He smiled at the little girl, who grinned back, revealing a gap where her front teeth had been. The women smiled at them, looking at him approvingly.

The man who had returned talked to everyone and indicated a place on the ground where a faint impression of footprints still remained. It was hot and still down here, so the wind had not erased them.

One of the children, a boy, said something, pointing back towards where they had come from and lifted two fingers. The man asked him something and after hearing the answer, turned to Daniel.

He bent down and with his finger, he drew a group of stick figures on the ground, pointing at the people. Daniel nodded. Then he drew what looked like a mountain behind the stick figures, pointing at the cliffs that surrounded them after drawing the ragged line. Again Daniel nodded, looking the man directly in the eye, trying to make it clear that he understood.

Then the man drew two more stick figures above the mountain, pointed at the boy who had spoken to him, placed his hand so that it shaded his eyes and looked upwards, towards the cliffs.

The child had seen two people nearby.

Excited, Daniel took a few involuntary steps towards the man, who said something that caused the other two to lift their spears and follow. The boy came too, jogging alongside them as the hunt for the First Vampire and his shadow began.

7

PURSUIT

The sandstorm lasted the whole day. During that time, we made fast friends with our rescuers, while the wind moaned and flung sand against the walls of our tent.

The woman spread a fine linen cloth over me and our babies once the worst was over to shield us from the men's eyes. Safely hidden from view, she then taught my son to suckle milk. I was so relieved when he fed for the first time that I pulled down the cloth to show Seth. He smiled broadly as he observed us. The woman did so too, showing good teeth, which was usually the case amongst the younger desert dwellers.

"What is your name?" I asked her, as we sat next to each other, feeding our babies.

"You can call me Ibah," she said, laughing.

Ibah meant laughter and she laughed a lot.

"I am called Nu," the man said.

Nu, the hunter. We guessed these were not their real names – the desert people were elusive and Mut-Bity had told me they believed names had magical power. They thought that if someone knew their true name, that person had a hold over them.

"What is your baby's name?" I asked Ibah.

"We call her Asule."

Asule, a butterfly. I looked at her delicate features, long limbs and dainty fingers. The name suited her well.

We left as soon as it was light enough to move.

"It is not safe for us to move at night any longer – your kind have very keen eyes and can see living things in the cool of the night from a much greater distance than we can," the man said, "so it would be best to travel by day, if possible. Even those who can fly dislike the hottest part of the day in the desert. But for now, we can't stick to moving at night. We have to take you away as quickly as possible."

Ibah looked at me.

"Mut-Bity told us you are a Moon Daughter, and I can see she was speaking the truth. You must not be touched by the sun. She sent this to you."

She gave me the fine linen fabric that had sheltered us.

"She wove it herself. It is big enough to cover your baby too. Also this..."

Ibah took another piece of cloth and wrapped it around my upper body so that it formed a small pouch in front of me to put our little boy in. Having done that, she got out of the tent. We followed.

I had not been on my feet for over a day and was still weak. Seth supported me until vertigo no longer made me sway.

"Here, you sit on the donkey," Seth said.

"She has just given birth," Ibah said. "You need to make sitting down easy for her! Let me help."

She swung down her bundle from her back and placed it on the donkey's narrow spine. With a piece of rope she tied the bundle around the little animal.

"If you seat yourself carefully, you won't slip off," Ibah said.

I was so tall I got on the back of the donkey almost by sitting down. I was so thankful to Ibah for making a pad for me to sit on instead of the patient animal's bony back. Wrapping the linen scarf securely around me and our son, we set off on our journey.

Nu and Ibah walked with a steady rhythm that brought Mut-Bity to mind. The linen cloth was so fine I could see through it, and while the hours passed, I began to wonder whether the sand people were related to the inhabitants of the secret valley. Both wanted to live away from other people, both knew of the Nephilim. If not related, at least they had been in contact with each other. How else would Mut-Bity have known the tribe of Ibah and Nu was nearby? And they had told us they owed Mut-Bity for favours done and so were willing to help us.

The day was uneventful, but very tiring. When the sun set, we had to erect our tents under the sky as there were no boulders nearby.

"I'm worried about the donkey," Seth said. "It needs water."

"We will get water in the morning," Nu said, "we'll reach the watering place then."

Despite being desperately tired, I could not sleep, because I was not used to sleeping at night. Because of my colourless skin, I had spent most of my waking hours in the shadows, or on the rooftops of the royal court by night. And now I had our beautiful baby to admire. How could I have slept?

"He looks strong," Seth whispered to me, though he could barely see our son's nose and eyes in the bundle of cloth.

As if in response to his father's voice the baby moved, letting out a little cry. A tiny hand stretched from under the fabric. Seth touched it and the little fingers grabbed his finger and held on tight. Seth smiled and we spoke no more that night. There was no need – our hearts were full and we sensed each other's happiness without words.

I heard Ibah and Nu moving outside long before sunrise.

"Time to go," Nu's voice said. "We have to follow the stars as long as they are visible."

And so we continued our journey. I felt sorry for the tired little donkey and chose to walk instead. The air was cold and I kept my arms around the baby. I enjoyed walking with my head uncovered, watching my old friends, the stars. The night wind caressed my hair, which had grown to below my shoulders during the seven months since it had been shaved off.

When I had learned the ways of preparing bodies for eternity in the tent of embalming, all my bodily hair had been removed. I sometimes thought about the little girl who had been prepared there after her death. I had been certain I had felt her near me during the seventy days of beautifying her body for the afterlife.

I had been able to see the dead before I was pregnant with our son. But not now, not anymore. I wondered if I would ever see the dead again and my feelings were mixed. The Great Royal Wife Tiye had given permission – no, an order – that I must be allowed into the tent of embalming after she had been told that I could see the dead. Probably she wanted to know if I could see her eldest son, Prince Thutmose, the one who should have been king. He had died from the foreign disease that had also taken so many others, and now Prince Amenhotep would be the next king when the old king joined his ancestors.

Ibah began to hum a tune. It was a simple tune, and catchy. I soon found myself humming along. It was as if the stars hummed with us, and I sensed it like a buzz in my body. I had been listening to the stars all my life, certain I could hear them singing at the very edge of my hearing. Now it felt stronger than ever before.

And then I understood. It wasn't the stars that I could hear - I felt the presence of Nephilim.

"They are near!" I whispered. "I sense them."

Ibah and Nu did not question me. They sprang into action immediately.

"Quick! Give the child to me," Ibah said and she had taken the baby from my arms before I had time to answer.

"Give me your wrapping. Lie down on the ground. Over there, with your feet in that hole," Nu said, pointing at a narrow depression in the ground. The sandstorm had piled a lot of fine, dust-like sand next to it, against the rocks that surrounded the depression.

We had no time for questions and did as Nu asked. We lay down on our backs so that our feet were at a lower level than our heads. Nu snatched the material from my hands and covered our faces and upper torsos with it, tucking the ends of the fabric under our shoulders. Then he took the little basket Ibah had carried and started ladling sand over us with it, starting with our feet.

"Protect your nostrils with your hands," he whispered.

I sensed sand flying from another direction – Ibah was now helping her husband. Quickly they covered us up, and all the while, the sensation of Nephilim approaching grew stronger. They put a thinner layer of sand over our faces so that we could breathe through the linen cloth.

"Keep calm and stay absolutely still so the sand won't fall off you!" Nu whispered. "Ibah, take the babies. We have to get as far from here as we can in the time we have."

We heard them leave, taking our child and our donkey with them. My whole being was screaming silently. I could not be separated from my baby! Panic took over and I felt as though I was suffocating.

It was the hardest thing I had ever done, to stay completely still, buried in the sand. I could barely breathe and my wings inside my back were surrounded by sand as well, so they couldn't help me breathe as they would normally have done when closed. The sense of paralysis was terrifying.

Again I used the breathing Mut-Bity had taught me – under my fingers, which were covering my nose, I breathed slowly through my nose into my belly, held my breath for a short while and then let the air out by relaxing my stomach and waiting for a few heartbeats before beginning to inhale again. I concentrated on sensing Seth's warm body next to mine. Probably that feeling was the only thing that kept me from giving in to the sharp claws of fear.

Slowly my panic ceased. I felt the familiar buzz of approaching Nephilim intensify in my spine, demanding recognition from my body. Controlling my breathing, I kept my wings in check and I felt Seth do the same.

They must have flown very near – it created a roaring throughout my whole body, circling around us in sweeping curves, but it did not stop directly above us. Just as I thought I could not take any more, the unbearable feeling began to weaken. And then it was gone, and we lay there, under a layer of sand, not knowing what had happened to our Ibah, Nu and the babies.

8

ESCAPE

I must have dozed off again, weakened by blood loss, and lack of food and drink. When I finally opened my eyes, as before, little black dots surrounded by bright rims were dancing in the air. I felt weaker than ever and my ears were ringing, or –

Had someone spoken?

"Dana? Can you hear me?"

My mouth was dry and I had a pounding headache. The disgusting aftertaste of something strange was in my mouth. I did not want to remember… but the thought of Ambrogio's wrist on my mouth was too close to the surface of my mind and it all came back. I retched but thankfully did not throw up. Being able to breathe through my wings, that wouldn't have caused me to suffocate, but there would have been no way to clean my mouth. So I breathed slowly and deliberately until I felt a bit better again.

"Dana!"

I turned my head, remembering too late the driftwood I was tied to. The branch stuck into me under my right eye and the pain yanked me fully awake.

A see-through figure was floating in the air in front of me. Kitty!

“Kitty! Oh, Kitty! Where have you been?” I tried to speak through the gag, but my words came out as incomprehensible panicky noises.

“Don't try to talk now. We need to get you out of here!” my dead friend said. She looked at me.

"I can't become physical and untie you. You'll have to do it yourself. Use your fingers!”

I looked at her. How did Kitty think I was going to do that? I was wrapped like a mummy, and fastened to this piece of wood for some reason. My fingers were tied fast too. I tried to look behind me in a meaningful way to make her understand.

Kitty floated behind me.

“Yes, they've certainly fastened you up securely. But I'm sure your strings can get through those bandages around your fingers.”

How had that not occurred to me? I couldn't even wriggle my fingers, but I focussed my mind on my fingertips and outwards, trying to force the strings out. And then I stopped. I couldn't escape. Concentrating all my willpower, I pronounced the word as clearly as I could.

"Diana."

"You think Ambrogio has Diana?" Kitty asked, and I nodded, so that the branch poked my cheek again, barely missing my right eye.

“That’s just it - they don’t have her! When I finally managed to find my way out of the buffer zone again, I searched around to see where I was and happened to see Ambrogio and some Egyptian man standing on mountainside, watching a group of people in the desert…”

Hope raised its head. I tried to form the word "team" and luckily Kitty understood.

“No, not our team. It looked like a desert tribe. But the point is, I heard Ambrogio and this odd-looking man talk about how you should be kept unconscious so you don’t work out that they don’t have Diana anymore.”

I didn't understand. How was that possible? She was left alone in the tomb of Sithathoriunet and she didn't have the skills to enter the buffer zone. She had been left a prisoner in the tomb.

"Now, you need to concentrate on getting yourself untied. They could be back here any time!"

This might be my only chance. I closed my eyes and concentrated – not only on my fingers but on my back as well. I was feeling really faint, but didn't give up. I forced my wings to recognise my will and then directed their energy backwards from my spine – through the driftwood, and into the buffer zone.

With my eyes still closed I felt the strange echo-less fog enveloping me. I opened my eyes and saw nothing but grey mist. I had made it!

"Quickly, your fingers!" Kitty would not let me rest for a moment.

I lay there in the odd softly yielding surface of the buffer zone, and concentrated again. My back hurt, with sharp spasms of pain all along the spine. I had no time to think what kind of damage I had done to myself this time. All I knew was that I had to get the strings out of my fingers to open the ropes the shadow had fastened round me so tightly.

My fingertips felt raw, but then I became aware of them responding – the tips of my fingers grew longer and started to weave strings – I could see them around me, weightlessly floating in the air.

"Good, they are coming out!" Kitty said from behind my back. "Untie your hands now."

I closed my eyes so that I could feel the strings better. Previously, I had always been able to see them when I… they… *something* inside me healed Elijah, or Jonathan who had turned dark months before. When I had given a blood transfusion to Diana so she would survive, I had also seen the strings puncturing her veins. But I had never tried to use them as fingers without seeing what I was doing.

I felt the tips of the strings, and stroked the rope around my wrists, locating the knot. I mentally pushed them inside the knot and after a while got the hang of it. By pushing and pulling the rope, I felt it loosen, then fall off and I finally managed to move my hands. I shook my hands as circulation returned, my eyes watering because of the pain.

I had no idea how long my hands had been tied, but my whole body was protesting at moving my limbs.

"Hurry – I think I feel them approaching!" Kitty whispered.

Frantically, with my strings, I tore into the linen strips that had tied my fingers together. Then I had to strain my arms backwards to reach the knots behind my back. My fingers were still too stiff to work properly so I pushed the strings out and used them once more.

I could hear them now too, Ambrogio's raspy voice saying something, and his shadow's quiet answer. I attacked the ropes tied around my ankles and tore them free, more tears running from my eyes because of the pain. I untied the gag and threw it away.

I felt Kitty's touch – here she was half-solid. Quietly, she pulled me backwards. I kept my wings silent and took wobbly steps, led by my dead friend. I would only have a few precious moments.

My breathing sounded so loud, even though I was trying to breathe with the help of my wings. I only hoped Ambrogio's discussion with his shadow, and his certainty I was still in the cave, would distract him from listening for sounds in the buffer zone.

A vain hope. There was only a short moment of silence, and then I felt an outburst of emotion so strong that my wings responded like scanning radar, sending shockwaves through me. A horrifying howl, full of rage and longing, pierced the buffer zone. A flashback of the night we had arrived in ancient Egypt chilled my blood – we had been sitting on the rooftop of Thomas's house in Deir el-Medina and from a distance had come a similar wild, nocturnal sound. Had that been Ambrogio?

"Move!" Kitty tried to drag me further, but she did not have any real strength.

"Where can we go?" I whispered. "He'll catch my scent in a second and I can't outrun him."

"Try to fly!" Kitty said. "Quickly!"

I forced my wings open, almost passing out from the pain. But they did open - my black wings with silver veins. With great effort, I stretched them out fully, directing my thoughts to the tips of the wings. They lifted me up and I started flying, enveloped in weakness and pain. My vision turned black. It was as though my wings could no longer breathe...

Breathe... from the depths of my mind rose another memory, one I had tried to catch earlier. When I had first realised Daniel was breathing with his wings... what was it that I had heard... wondered... almost asked a dumb question about...

"Get up!"

I had not even noticed I was no longer flying but was on my knees. I got up and forced myself to continue. The dead silence of the buffer zone enveloped me, the silence of the hunter and the hunted. Ambrogio could catch me at any moment.

And then I remembered. When I had understood how the Nephilim breathed, I had almost asked about...mermaids?

"Kitty, you said you've been around this area – lead me to water. Deep water!"

Kitty did not ask why, she simply took my hand and we began to descend towards the physical world.

"No, don't take us right down," I whispered, "he'll outrun me on the ground!"

We emerged from the buffer zone into blazing sunlight, but Kitty had not brought me down to the ground. We were high in the air. Ragged, dusty mountains spread out in every direction around the plateau of rubble that lay straight underneath us.

Kitty pointed down and I was not surprised to see two figures running below us.

"Where do you see water?" I asked. "I am too weak to fly for long."

"There." Kitty held my left arm and pointed towards the horizon. A bright light behind the mountains. I looked up to the sun. The bright stretch of light was to the east. We were in the eastern desert, and I was looking out at the sea. "You'll have to make it there without falling to the ground. Come on, Dana, you must do it!"

My heart sank. I felt just as weak as I had when I was forced to heal Jonathan, the Nephilim who had been infected for months and was on the verge of turning evil. It had almost killed me, burned me to the core. Only Daniel's love had kept me alive.

Daniel... He was still alive in the future... A picture of him made all the difference. I would do anything I could just to see him again.

So I concentrated on keeping myself in the air, silently, since speaking took too much energy. I simply flew forward, at a fraction of the speed I knew I was capable of when healthy. The figures below me did not even have to run fast while we were still above the plateau. They were jogging in a mockingly relaxed fashion, like predators who knew their prey was hurt and the hunt was coming to an end.

They were right.

Then we reached a mountainous area again and I hoped that would slow our pursuers.

Only - I was too tired to fly any higher. The sharp rocky peaks loomed over me. I had to land, right on a sharp point jutting out of the crumbling mountainside.

"Two breaths," Kitty said, pointing back.

I looked over my shoulder, on all fours, too tired to turn fully. The two small figures were now running at an impossible speed. The predators had seen the prey fall.

"Up, Dana, up!" Kitty did not let go of my hand.

I crawled on all fours to a ledge and let myself fall, forcing every ounce of energy I had left into my wings. And so we continued, the sun scorching my skin, flying only a few metres above the ground, towards the sea. My field of vision contracted into a tunnel and the sea seemed to retreat, further and further away, a mirage, escaping me.

We crossed ridge after ridge. When I looked down I saw Ambrogio and the shadow man running, climbing, not giving up. I had never known how fast vampires could be, or how strong, and now I understood the terror installed in everyone who had encountered Ambrogio. His speed was almost inhuman, and his shadow did not lag behind him. The feeling of Ambrogio's eyes on me from a distance was like the touch of frost on my burning skin.

And then the last of the mountains were behind us. My feet were scraping the ground. I could not fly any longer.

"Only a little more, Dana! You can't give in now! They are running right behind you!" Kitty almost screamed at me.

But I could not fly, not anymore. I could not look over my shoulder, all my energy went into trying to keep upright. One tired step after the other I stumbled towards the waterline. I saw the waves touching the rocky shore and headed towards them.

I could hear their steps now, feet kicking the stones of the beach, and feel the sea spray on my cheeks.

"Run, Dana, run!" Kitty shouted.

And I did. I ran into the sea and fell on my stomach just as a hand grabbed my hem.

"Catch her!"

Ambrogio's voice. So it was the shadow who had grabbed my garment.

The cold water brought me to my senses. I kicked back as hard as I could and felt my foot land on someone.

"Ooof!"

I must have kicked the shadow-man hard in the stomach for he let go of my clothing. I turned onto my back and saw him kneeling in the salty water, holding his belly with both hands. His eyes were on me, swirling dark abysses in a human face. Behind him stood Ambrogio, his eyes like piercing black fire, not able to step into the water.

He did not say anything as I swam further out, still on my back. When the water was deep enough, I stopped moving.

I sank into the depths of the sea, still looking at Ambrogio, the salt burning my mouth and eyes. All the while he stood still, the sun making his golden skin shine as if he were a statue. The look in his cold eyes meant certain death if we ever met again.

The water closed over me, and I sank into the depths of the Red Sea.

9

LITTLE BUTTERFLY

We lay still under the sand and waited. The wind had risen again and that was all we could hear. My heart almost stopped when I felt the sand shift beside my body from the weight of someone's step. Almost immediately, the cloth was lifted from our faces and to our relief we saw the worried face of Nu.

"We have to escape now. Those were two new Nephilim, both evil. They asked about you and were very threatening."

We got up, shaking sand off ourselves, and followed Nu. Ibah stood next to the donkey, her expression concerned. She held only one child in her arms – I could see it was her own daughter. Alarmed, I looked around to see where our son was.

"He is here." Ibah tenderly raised a sack hanging off the donkey's side. "I wrapped him well and had just enough time to put him in before they arrived. Thank the gods he remained silent so the abyw *paid no attention to him. He is too young to have the scent of your kind so they did not smell him either."*

Abyw, *the gods who slay. The word that described the enemy Nephilim.*

"I said we had already been asked about you and I had promised to send word should we see you. They threatened us, demanding that we look for you," Nu said. "We have to leave now. There are too many of their kind

around here. They may draw the conclusion soon that since we are the only living people they have seen here, we must be suspect. They will know how far it was possible for you to reach without flying, and they found us right there... So now, we're going into hiding. Underground."

I took our son to my arms, relieved beyond belief that he was safe.

"Underground? As in under the ground?" Seth asked, looking around. "How?"

Nu did not answer, just took the donkey's rope and started walking. The exhausted animal followed, its head low. Nu walked determinedly across the sand and stone surface as it led up hills and alongside peaks of rock, Ibah falling in step with him while we followed last.

"Here, let me carry him for a while," Seth took our son into his arms. I hung the linen cloth around his neck and he placed the baby safely against his chest. Then I covered myself with my own linen cloth as the sun rose. Our long shadows hurried before us towards the west, becoming shorter as the sun climbed higher.

When the sun was high in the sky, Nu approached a boulder that didn't look too different from others we'd seen.

"We have arrived. This is where we have to leave the donkey," he said.

"How will it ever survive here?" I felt sorry for the animal.

"It is a hardy animal. And we'll give it water first," Nu said. "It has a chance..."

He took two steps forward – and disappeared into the ground. Seth and I let out a surprised yell, Ibah only smiled.

After a while Nu's head appeared again. His hands lifted up a large leather pouch – it was dripping with water. Ibah took it, and opened it enough for the donkey's muzzle to fit in. The donkey drank deeply.

"Get in here. Give me the baby first," Nu said.

We stepped up close and saw he was standing in what was an opening in the ground that led under the boulder. Sand had almost covered it, forming a slope that led into darkness.

"Where does this..." Seth began.

The presence of Nephilim hit us suddenly. My spine began to hum so that I could actually hear it. They were very near.

"They are here!" I whispered.

"Now!" Nu extended his arms and took our baby. "Follow me!"

We had no time to hesitate - we rushed onto the narrow sandy slope with such speed we fell on our backs and slid down into the darkness, hitting our shoulders on rocks in the narrow passageway. Even before we were back on our feet, Nu had placed the baby on my breast.

"Feed him. Keep him quiet. Move deeper into the darkness and be very still. If I don't return, wait until you feel they are gone and then start walking in that direction."

Hastily, he pointed behind our backs and left us. We saw him climb up the slope towards the small opening into the sunlight. Very quietly, we walked into the darkness, and found a fold in the stone wall to stand behind. I could only hope our footprints were not visible to anyone looking through the opening. As far as I could see, the sand Nu's feet had kicked down had covered our steps.

The baby was now awake and moving in my arms. I placed his mouth on my breast and he settled.

We heard words. At first normal, then angry. Then – a scream. Ibah... Another scream, this time a male voice. Nu...

My limbs trembled as I tried to calm my wings and waited for the Nephilim to attack us. But no one came. And then the feeling of Nephilim presence got weaker, and finally, disappeared altogether.

"I'll go," Seth said, "you stay here."

He walked to the opening and climbed up. Small cascades of sand slipped onto the stony floor and then he was gone. I did not dare move. Our baby felt my tension, let go of my breast and began to make little fretful noises, weaving in the air with his tiny fists.

Then Seth slid back down. When I saw that he was carrying Asule I knew what had happened. Without a word Seth walked up to me.

"We shall have to go on alone from here." His voice was shaking.

I smelled blood on Asule and felt as if I would choke.

"Is she all right?" I could barely speak from the shock.

"As far as I know. They didn't even bother to attack her. She would be dead in a few hours, anyway, left there in the desert. And she was too tiny to feed on or else they weren't hungry. Also – " He paused "they did not feed on Ibah and Nu, which is a good thing."

Mut-Bity had explained how the dark Nephilim could read their victim's memories from their blood. They had used this to their advantage since time immemorial when hunting our kind.

"Nu said we should keep on walking here, underground," I said, forming the words very carefully through numb lips. Concentrating on practical things meant I wouldn't lose control because of the horror of what had happened. I wanted to go and see Ibah and Nu. They had given their lives to protect us.

I touched Asule's cheek. The girl looked at me, eyes fully open, serious. She was maybe a month old.

"We shall take care of you, little butterfly," I whispered with trembling lips. "Because of the sacrifice your parents made, you are our daughter now."

Seth placed his hand on Asule's head.

"Our daughter," was all he said.

We looked into the darkness, from which came the sound of water. The small puddle near the opening to the cave was part of a little underground stream that flowed into the darkness.

"We should follow the water, I think," Seth said. "Mut-Bity told us the senses of the enemy Nephilim get dull over water."

"Is that light ahead?" I looked into the darkness.

Indeed the darkness was not absolute; we could see the stone walls.

"Yes, we'll follow the water and the light," Seth said. "Let me carry Asule; you carry our son."

And so we continued our journey underground, escaping from the dark Nephilim, carrying our son and daughter with us.

10

"YOU HAVE A SON"

"You have a son," Mut-Bity said, lifting up the little boy, who had just entered the world from Meryt-Neith's womb, so that all could see him.

The women around them murmured contentedly, and smiled at the new mother. They were poor, but their joy in a safe birth was clear as they stamped the ground and clapped their hands in a celebratory dance.

"Give him to me…" Meryt-Neith whispered.

She lay back down on the floor of the mud hut, on a coarse reed mat, next to the birthing bricks that she had been squatting on moments before. Her beautiful wheat-coloured hair had been braided to keep it out of the way, and it was wet with sweat. The birth had been long, but not too difficult. Experienced hands had been ever-present to support her when she needed them.

Mut-Bity placed the boy on Meryt-Neith's belly and tied and cut the umbilical cord. Then, with gentle hands, she lifted the child up higher so that Meryt-Neith could hold him. Meryt-Neith began to sob.

A woman bent down to wipe the baby clean and a welcome breeze filled the little hut through the open doorway. Naked children were peeking in – seeing a child being born was nothing strange to them.

"He will search for the length and breadth of the whole land to find you. You have given him a son, and he will want to have his heir," Mut-Bity warned.

The Pale Man, the great dark Nephilim lord who had fooled Meryt-Neith into becoming his mistress, just so he could get closer to Shuet, the silver Nephilim he wanted dead, together with Seth and their baby.

Meryt-Neith had almost died when the Pale Man attacked them, and only because he could smell that she was pregnant had her life been spared. The difficulty he and his kind had in conceiving children meant that when they were successful, the mothers were kept out of harm's way. Meryt-Neith's broken arm had healed in time, despite the fact she could no longer turn to the physicians of the royal court for help.

Meryt-Neith's tears were spontaneous as she watched the new son she had wanted so much. This baby should have made it possible for her to be even with Shuet, to have the same admiration and love her sister had. That had been before she learned who the Pale Man really was.

The shock of the deception and the knowledge of her own stupidity were so great it had broken her. She had been lying on the floor of their house when Mut-Bity returned, having escorted Shuet and Seth on their journey. Without speaking Mut-Bity had tied two flat pieces of wood tight around Meryt-Neith's arm for support.

"And now we're taking you to safety too," Mut-Bity had said. "We're leaving by boat as soon as I have dealt with them..."

They were the three dead Nephilim that had been lying on the floor, covered in the dead bees that had destroyed them. One was already in a big woven basket. Mut-Bity disappeared for a while and soon there was a rapping on the door followed by servants delivering two more enormous baskets to the entrance of their house. When the servants were gone, Mut-Bity quickly brought the baskets indoors.

Meryt-Neith had been whimpering with shock and pain, caressing her broken arm, while her mother and Mut-Bity managed to cram the two tall remaining Nephilim men into the big round baskets, tying the lids in place. The little room was almost filled up with baskets and it was claustrophobic.

"These can't be hidden - they have to be carried away before sunrise," Mut-Bity said. "We need two strong men. I'll have to tell Tiye what is inside them and ask for her guards to help – I'll come up with a story, some reason for the attack..."

She left, leaving Meryt-Neith alone with her mother.

"I hope you understand now why you need to be responsible for your actions," Merit said quietly. "Your jealousy and selfishness have caused all this. Your sister has had to escape into the desert heavily pregnant. If she gives birth there, she and the baby may both die. You are carrying the child of the most evil Nephilim there is – and do you think he will leave you alone? He only saved your life so you can give birth to his child. He will come after the baby and take it from you. After that you'll be of no further use to him – unless he chooses to keep you as his mistress. And you'll have no say in that either. He can bite you and turn you into his likeness whenever the mood takes him. Your old life is gone forever, and I see your future filled with darkness."

Meryt-Neith cried silently, from pain, humiliation and fear. She had carefully painted her eyes before meeting her lover and her cheeks were now streaked with green. With her shaking good hand she tried to wipe her face.

"He is after me too, and one day, no doubt, he will reappear to take his revenge on me and Mut-Bity as well," Merit continued. "If your sister survives, she will be hunted till the end of her days, as will Seth and their child. If you manage to escape from the Pale Man now, the same fate awaits you. Forever hunted."

Finally Meryt-Neith raised her eyes and looked at her mother.

"The best thing I can do is kill myself. That way the child will never be born, and you will have one less thing to worry about."

Merit stepped closer and squatted next to her, looking into her swollen eyes.

"Never. You are carrying new life. The child is not to be blamed or taken revenge on for the actions of its parents."

"But it will be evil!" Meryt-Neith whispered. "Like its father!"

Merit touched her shoulder gently.

"The children of the enemy Nephilim are not born evil. They are made that way through the passing of the venom into their bodies. This is done through biting them. Somehow the unborn child is protected from that venom until birth. All life is sacred. You will carry your baby to term and give birth to it. And despite all you have done, we will protect you."

"How can you protect me?" Meryt-Neith asked. "He can appear out of thin air, anywhere he likes."

"You saw what Mut-Bity's bees do to the dark ones. As long as you stay near them, you can live. It won't be a life without worry and fear, but you have a chance of survival, you and your child, even if he finds you. So flee while you can. The future may yet bring a solution."

"But all the bees are dead..." Meryt-Neith whispered, looking at the insects on the stone floor. She knew how important the bees were to Mut-Bity. And they had all died because of her.

"She will get new ones. But before that, you need to be taken to safety."

"To your secret valley?"

"I don't think you will be taken there," Merit said.

"Because we cannot trust you," were the unspoken words that hung between them.

Meryt-Neith did not blame them for thinking that. She had been stupid, childish and irresponsible and was not deserving of anyone's trust.

Mut-Bity returned with two soldiers. They looked at the hundreds of dead bees on the floor but said nothing, just lifted up the first basket and carried it out.

"What did you tell Tiye?" Merit asked quietly.

"I told her that these men had come to take you. They had heard of your beauty and wanted to sell you and your daughters to Mitanni, as the wife and daughters of the king of Kemet. The foreign kings desire nothing more than one of the pharaoh's womenfolk as their wives. This raises their esteem not only in the eyes of their own court but in the eyes of neighbouring kings as well. It was a believable explanation, as Tiye has seen correspondence from kings asking for Amenhotep's daughters as their wives. When the king answered that no daughter of the king of Kemet would ever be given away in marriage to any foreign country, one king had the nerve to write back and say the king could send any pretty lady and he would just tell everyone that she was the daughter of Amenhotep. This attack so soon after that correspondence makes my story all the more believable."

The soldiers returned, lifted the second basket and carried it out. Mut-Bity waited until they were out of earshot.

"I told her that Seth had taken Shuet away to his own family to give birth in safety. And I said that I needed to take Meryt-Neith away as well – I lied and said she was promised as wife to a nobleman of the north and it would be best to take her there so that she would be safe too. I said I was going to escort her and we were leaving immediately. We'll be going to a safe place where I can send word for more bees."

Mut-Bity looked at the hundreds of bees lying on the floor, her expression stony.

"What about me?" Merit asked. "Shouldn't I leave too now that the bees are dead?"

"Tiye would never let you go. And here, you will be safe. Tiye has ordered two soldiers to guard your door. It's not likely the Pale Man will attack you in the near future. He will need time to heal and does not know that all our bees are dead. Now, gather up Meryt-Neith's belongings. We are leaving soon. There is one message I still need to deliver, to make sure I've done everything I can to ensure Shuet and Seth make their way to safety."

Mut-Bity was gone for a few hours before returning for Meryt-Neith. They walked through the gates of Per-Hai to the harbour, leaving the royal palace.

And so Merit remained alone in her house in Per-Hai, worrying whether either of her daughters would escape the dark Nephilim who would be hunting them from now on.

Mut-Bity and Meryt-Neith sailed away on a little fisherman's boat, as far out from the shoreline as the boat could go.

"That's the best way to hide your scent from him," Mut-Bity said to Meryt-Neith who sat still, biting her lip so she would not reveal how much her arm hurt.

After several days they had reached the great lake and sailed across it to a small fishermen's village. Meryt-Neith had never been to such a poor place. These people had nothing. Meryt-Neith had been so used to her life of luxury, she felt she was now living in an odd dream.

"You are to remain here now," Mut-Bity said after they had stayed there a few days and nothing had happened. "The villagers will not tell anyone else about you, they have promised me that. They know they will be well rewarded for taking care of you. My most important task now is to get more bees to protect your mother." She looked at Meryt-Neith. "I will return before it is your time to give birth."

Meryt-Neith waited for months for Mut-Bity. She wanted to punish herself for her actions and so, as soon as her arm had healed, took part in all the village chores. She had always had servants to fetch and carry for her and never had to look after herself, but now she washed clothes, cooked fish, took care of babies and cleaned the house where she was given a mattress to sleep on.

No outsiders ever came to the village – the men fished and dried the fish for their own use. They had plenty of grain to make bread and beer.

Meryt-Neith's belly grew heavy with the child and life became uncomfortable in the heat. Soon she stopped going out during daylight hours at all.

As if she knew that her labour was imminent, Mut-Bity returned by boat a few days before Meryt-Neith's son was due to be born, just as she had promised.

"How is Mother?" Meryt-Neith asked.

"I wrote to her and she wrote back to me. She is safe with the Great Royal Wife," Mut-Bity said. "She sends her love and wishes for your safety. Yours and your child's."

"And Shuet? Seth? How is their child? Did it survive?"

Mut-Bity looked at her.

"I will not speak of Shuet to you, Meryt-Neith. If you are ever... caught... you will tell him everything you know, *he* will make sure of it."

Meryt-Neith lowered her eyes. She could not blame them. And they were right – the Pale Man was after her and if he ever caught her... Mut-Bity had told her how the bite of a dark Nephilim changed the victim, how they lost any of their nobler feelings and only wanted to please their master. They had no secrets of their own any longer. They gave all and told all to their lord when he ordered them to.

Mut-Bity observed Meryt-Neith right up to the moment the pains of birth began. The girl seemed genuinely changed. There was nothing left of the selfish, pleasure-seeking young woman who only wanted to be admired and loved by all. A humble posture, downcast eyes... and depression. Mut-Bity felt sorry for Meryt-Neith, but was not prepared to trust her anymore, nor tell her what she knew of Shuet. And so the events of the past separated the sisters from each other forever.

11

ROYAL ANNOUNCEMENT

Merit was aware of his presence long before the Pale Man showed himself. Forcing herself to be calm, she intended to reveal nothing to him even though he was a permanent, maddening presence on the edges of her perception. He must have been at the very edge of the buffer zone, circling, observing, careful not to be seen. Perhaps he did not know she could sense how close he was, or so she tried to reassure herself.

Mut-Bity had not come back yet from her journey to take Meryt-Neith to safety. Merit spent all her time with the Great Royal Wife now, trying to hide her fears for her daughters, but Tiye knew her well enough to see her concern.

"It's best that you stay with me, at least until Mut-Bity returns," Tiye said to Merit the morning after the attack. "It is unthinkable that anyone would attack a royal residence to get wives for a foreign king. The rumour of the pale beauty of you and your daughters has spread, and I will not take the risk of anything happening to you again. Mut-Bity told me that the leader of these three dead criminals escaped. Is that so?"

"Yes, Great Royal Wife, he did," Merit answered.

Tiye's eyes under her heavy lids were sharp and intelligent and

Merit guessed she suspected she had not been told the whole story. It was typical of Tiye not to ask directly in front of others; the Great Royal Wife was doing what she had always done - gathering information behind the scenes. When she had all the information she needed, she would ask Merit directly what she knew about the attackers. Unsurprisingly, Tiye wanted to learn how four men could possibly have entered the royal residence without being seen or heard by anyone.

"As long as he remains free, you will sleep in my palace, with my women. My guards will be nearby all the time, to make sure you stay safe."

Merit agreed and so she moved into Tiye's southern palace in Per-Hai, the great compound built by the pharaoh Amenhotep the Third on the western bank of the Nile. Two soldiers were still guarding the little house Mut-Bity and Merit shared within the palace area, in case there was another attempt to get Merit.

The days were busy now, as Tiye met with diplomats and noblemen and effectively took care of the governance of the land.

After his great heb-sed celebration, it seemed the king had given in to old age. Merit remembered what she had read about him in her own time three thousand and three hundred years in the future. Art had shown the king as overweight, his posture slumped, his back curved by age. His mummy had revealed he had bad teeth – abscesses in his jawbone must have made his last years agonising.

Long gone was the dashing man in his prime who had made a move on her so many years ago in Inbu-Hedj, the later Memphis. An ageing, over-weight man indulging in sweet wine and beer and honeyed foods had taken his place. The country was at peace with its neighbours, too powerful for any foreign king to seriously consider attacking, and there was no need for the pharaoh to stay fit for battle. The king's military officers were charged with keeping the peace and left alone to get on with it.

Amenhotep's lifelong love of gold was now shown in the decorations he wore from head to toe, as if being covered in gold could replace his waning physical authority. Gold, the symbol of solar power, reflected his divine status. He spent more and more time in his own private quarters, entertained by his many wives, and being treated by his doctors for the increasing pain in his jaws. It was clear to see that the ruler who had proclaimed himself divine, together with his Great Royal Wife Tiye, was succumbing to old age.

Majesty did not slip away from him entirely though. Tiye took the reins of power tightly into her hands and no one questioned her right to make decisions. The less time the king spent on his throne, the more Tiye occupied it.

Today Tiye was expected to meet the priests from the temple of Ipet-Isut, or Karnak as it would later be known. The power of the Amun priests was of concern to Tiye and she opposed it. Ever since Amenhotep had chosen to build his palace on the west bank of the great river – away from the great temple of Amun on the east bank - Tiye was aware of the priesthood's anger at events; a discontent that had now turned to plotting. Also, after his self-proclaimed divinity, the king had turned more and more towards worshipping the sun god Aten. Amun, the Hidden One, was the god of Ipet-Isut and his golden statue was kept behind locked doors at the darkest ends of the great temple on the east bank, only accessible to an elite few amongst the priesthood. Aten, the old god now rising in importance, however, did not hide inside dark temples and was visible in the sky for all to see.

This was the first real check the Amun priesthood had known. Ever since the expulsion of the Hyksos, the foreign rulers who had taken over northern Egypt, the priests of Amun had been gaining power with every reign. The Hyksos had been defeated by Ahmose the First over a century and a half earlier and all the kings after Ahmose had shown their gratitude to the state god Amun for each military victory since then.

Every ruler had kept in with the priesthood for this reason, or simply bought the support of the priests to justify their rule, as the female king Hatshepsut had done. Quantities of gold and land had been granted to the great temple. Used to having the power even to dictate who inherited the crown, the Amun priests were now facing a situation where their power was slipping away.

"They have heard that the great king is not well. Vultures gathering to see if there is a carcass to be picked over!" Tiye said. "And they are trying to re-establish their control over the royal house by subtle means. That endeavour I shall certainly nip in the bud."

There was bitterness in Tiye's voice. Merit followed her outdoors to her lush garden, joined there by Prince Amenhotep who would be the next king. A little altar was built there, in the open, under the sun, next to the pool in the middle of the greenery. Tiye walked to the altar, where one of her maidens gave her a bouquet of lilies and a small basket of dates. Tiye placed them on the altar, lifted her hands in the air and recited:

"You appear in the horizon, oh living Aten, the beginning of life! When you rise on the eastern horizon, you fill the land with your beauty. You are gracious, glistening, and high over all the lands. Your rays encompass the lands to the limit of everything you have made. As you are Re, you reach to the very end of them. You subdue them for your beloved son, the king. Though you are far away, your rays are on earth. Though you touch everyone, no one knows your path."

Merit looked at the heir to the throne. She knew, of course, by what name he would be known in the future. Akhenaten, the king who would banish all other gods and who hated the god Amun so much he would have the god's name hacked off all the temples. The extent of his revolution was revealed in the fact he would do so even within the names of his own father. Some conflict would happen between him and the priesthood, serious enough for him to change his name and move the capital from Thebes, the city dedicated to Amun, to Akhetaten, on virgin ground where no god had ever been worshipped before.

Merit knew the young prince looked up to his father with great respect. He sat with the king often, listening to him. And he was clearly worshipping the power and light of the sun that the Aten represented. He was often present when Tiye gave offerings to the god. To Merit, it seemed the most dedicated worshipper of the ancient god in the family was Tiye, who was passing her religious sentiments on to her son. The boy was very interested in divine matters and wanted to discuss them with his mother. And Tiye was learned in the ways of religion in general, and of the Aten in particular.

Now, while Tiye was still giving her greeting to the light of the sun, the prince approached the altar, poured scented oil over and around the bouquet and the fruit, and with a burning stick given to him by a servant, lit the oil. He then used his hands to encourage the fumes to rise towards the sky. It was an odd sight - the fresh flowers burning almost without a visible flame under the bright morning sun, the skinny young prince in his teens solemnly performing priestly duties.

"You will follow me today, my son," Tiye said to him, "for I need to make an announcement regarding you, and you must be present."

"Yes, mother," Prince Amenhotep said, obedient as always to his mother's requests.

Leaving Tiye's palace, they walked to the king's palace with its audience chambers, offices, library and gardens. Merit followed close behind them, with Tiye's maidens, many of them princesses fathered by the king, following on last of all.

"Wait here," Tiye ordered her maidens and servants when they reached the entrance to the king's private chambers.

Merit stopped too, but Tiye gestured her to follow.

The king had barely risen from bed. He was wearing a long garment that hid his round form and had not put on his heavy golden jewellery or had his eyes painted yet. His jawline was sagging and there were dark circles around his eyes. The stink of his breath reached all the way to the entrance of the room.

"Greetings, my favourite and most beloved wife." The king smiled at Tiye so that his bad teeth showed.

Merit never ceased to wonder how attached these two really were to each other. The king had allowed his Great Royal Wife to rise to a position of near equality with him. And she had been a great asset to him, helping him rule, asking her trusted servants to tell her every piece of gossip they heard about the goings-on in the palace and temples. A tough and demanding mistress, she rewarded her informants well. And so, through the years, she had developed a whole network of spies and people who were loyal to the bone to her. This had helped the king greatly when he was younger. And now, when he was old, he was effectively letting her rule in his name.

Merit stayed outside the room. The king always greeted her with respect - but then again he was the only one of the royal family who had seen Merit's wings. He had considered her a goddess ever since and was so humbled by the experience he never tried to make another move on her. Also he had promised never to tell anyone what he had seen, and he had kept his word.

As Merit had not visibly aged during all these years, she often found Tiye looking at her with an unfathomable expression. Women aged quickly because of their many pregnancies, lack of proper medicine and modern cosmetics, but Merit looked exactly like the young woman she had been when giving birth to twins after arriving at Mi-Wer, Tiye's palace near the Fayum.

"Today, I have an important announcement," Tiye said. "It is time the prince was given a proper wife."

Prince Amenhotep swallowed, and kept his head high. He already had a few wives, as it was the king's duty to give him his own 'harem'. But these were all minor wives and servants, considered to be more of an education for the young man than actual marriages.

"Very well. Do I need to be present?" the king asked, already knowing the answer.

"No need. It is only one announcement among many," Tiye said. "You rest. I'll take care of everything."

"The priests too?" chuckled the king, reaching for the cup of sweet wine a servant was offering to him.

"Especially the priests," Tiye smiled, amused. "They have come to see if you will die soon, having heard you were ill for a few days! Such concern, husband. They would love to have the prince under their influence and I know the First Priest has formed his own plan to give his daughter to our son in an effort to seize power. My informant in the temple told me all about it and he intends to make his suggestion today. During the royal audience, of all places, to make sure everyone hears of it!"

"He may give his daughter in marriage if he likes," the king sat down on his bed, "but he should not expect her to be the Great Royal Wife."

"Oh no. That place is already decided - for someone else," Tiye said matter-of-factly. "Now, let us go."

She turned and walked out of the room, Prince Amenhotep and Merit in tow.

The audience hall was still empty when they arrived. Tiye sat on the king's chair with the prince standing next to her. Merit withdrew towards the wall and covered her head, hiding behind the fabric so that only her eyes showed.

The vizier gestured to the officials to let the first people in.

The long line of petitioners and officials began to present their cases to Tiye. She handled their issues with the expertise gained from years of practically co-ruling with her husband. Merit followed the discussions for a while in case Tiye would ask her to look into the future of any of the cases. Fortunately her good memory meant that she recalled much of what was going to happen in the king's reign. After so many years, she could adopt the role of seer to the Great Royal Wife with ease.

Merit sometimes wondered what Tiye thought of the divination Shuet had given her when still a child. Tiye knew the year when the king would die but had never told anyone else. Maybe it was for this reason she wanted to secure the reins of power for herself and prince Amenhotep long before the king would die in his 38th regnal year? For now it was his 34th year as a king.

When the matters handled seemed trivial, Merit concentrated on feeling the presence of the Pale Man. With closed eyes, she listened for any reaction in her spine and wings. A faint buzz told he must be in the buffer zone. Not close now, but still circling the palace.

"Is he near?" a familiar voice asked quietly next to her.

It was the scribe Ahmose, who knew about the attack and that Shuet and Meryt-Neith had been taken into hiding. Merit had felt she needed to warn him of the Nephilim presence, since the Pale Man might attack Ahmose as well. Ahmose had been Merit's constant companion ever since they stole the clue to the whereabouts of the forefathers of the Nephilim from the House of Life of Hut-Ka-Ptah, the great temple of Ptah in Inbu-Hedj, soon after the birth of Shuet and Meryt-Neith.

After all, this was the main reason the Pale Man was still pursuing them. He wanted to discover the path that led to their origins, to find the lost knowledge of the Watchers, the angels who were the ancestors of the Nephilim.

With that knowledge, called the Scroll of Thoth in this time and age, the Pale Man hoped to gain power over life itself, to bend all creation to being his servant. Ahmose understood full well the danger and took care never to be alone if at all possible.

Merit looked at her trustworthy ally.

"He is still circling the palace, unseen," she said quietly. "I suspect he will let himself be known soon. I do not know if he will kill me straight away or - whether he aims to talk to me first."

"There are no bees yet?" Ahmose whispered.

"No. I hope Mut-Bity comes back quickly with new bees," Merit whispered, "until then we will not be safe."

Months had passed and they were still without the protection of the bees.

"And now, I have an announcement..." Tiye stood up. "I have chosen a wife for the prince. She will be his Royal Wife. Nefertiti, come here."

A slight figure approached from the back of the room.

Nefertiti had grown in beauty since the heb-sed last year. She was still very young, but you could see the first roundness of her breasts and her hips were no longer boyish. Merit knew her period had begun for the first time a few weeks ago, so she was now of marriageable age. She was a relative of the Great Royal Wife from her home town of Khent-Menu and Tiye had had her brought to the palace before the king's jubilee. Tiye had been pleased with her character and the respect Nefertiti showed to the royal family. The girl never said anything without being asked, and when she responded to anyone her voice was beautiful and soothing. She spent endless hours in Tiye's company without complaining. Being called to the royal court by the Great Royal Wife was a stroke of luck for any young girl, so it was no wonder she was constantly on her best behaviour. Still, she gave the impression of sharp intelligence just as Tiye did.

"This is Nefertiti. She comes from my own family. From now on, she is the main wife of the prince and will give him an heir. No one is to dispute her position and she is to be shown respect," Tiye said, and without further ado took the hand of the young girl and placed it in the hand of Prince Amenhotep.

Red spots burned on the girl's cheeks, but she raised her head and looked straight at the people in the hall. She's already aware of her position, Merit thought, and intends to hold it.

She was not the only one with colour in her face. The First Priest of Amun stood at the back of the audience hall, flushed with rage. Tiye had not shown him any attention and had let everyone else of lower status come to her instead. She had not even given him the chance to offer his daughter in marriage to the prince, as no one could address Tiye unless the vizier had first invited them to approach the throne.

It was clear that the First Priest had taken this as an insult. He must have known that Tiye was aware of his plans to give his daughter to the king-to-be, even if the matter had never been discussed openly.

He stood there, wearing a huge decorated wig that looked ridiculous to Merit, dressed in his finest for the occasion and covered in gold. The priests around him kept their expressions in check, staring coldly at the young girl next to Prince Amenhotep. Was Nefertiti aware of the First Priest's plans for his daughter, wondered Merit, and Tiye's own plan to frustrate them? But the slight young thing stood there proudly, regarding the priests with a similar look on her face as her husband, an expression that could only be described as contempt.

Merit was glad the First Priest had not brought his daughter with him. She pitied any young girl having to bear so great an insult when she did not even have any say in the matter of her marriage.

For with this announcement prince Amenhotep and Nefertiti were officially married. She was now the prince's main wife and would later perform the religious duties expected of the Great Royal Wife, four years from now when the king would die and Tiye, the former Great Royal Wife would become the King's Mother and step aside from the duties of her previous life. Knowing this, Tiye had done wisely to keep the girl close to her, teaching her to respect and regard Tiye and rely on her advice.

The marriage would be celebrated that evening, and then the prince would take his new wife to bed. From that moment on, everyone would be waiting and watching for signs of pregnancy and the birth of the new heir to the crown prince.

Merit sighed.

"She is too young to marry…" she said quietly.

"It is as the gods wish it to be," Ahmose the scribe said. "As the wise men of old said: you should marry young and have many children to be your security in your old age."

"A girl that young will have trouble giving birth," Merit said. "Look at how narrow her hips are..."

Ahmose said nothing to this for there was nothing he could say. The deed was done; the girl was married, and would fulfil her duties. She would never refuse her new husband, as only a live birth would ensure her position. It was the way of things.

Tiye did not sit down after her marriage announcement, but gave the vizier a signal instead.

"The royal audience is over," the vizier said.

The First Priest of Amun turned his back and stalked out of the room before Tiye had done so - an open insult and a sign of disrespect. Tiye looked at his retreating back with narrowed eyes but said nothing. Then she turned and left through the door leading to the king's private quarters behind the throne. Behind her, Prince Amenhotep and his new royal wife Nefertiti followed, hand in hand, and behind them the rest of Tiye's entourage.

The wedding banquet that evening was a lavish one. The new bride smelled of expensive oils and wore a heavy wig on her head, decorated with golden pearls. Her eyes were painted with beautiful green malachite, and her lips and nails were red. She wore a see-through linen dress that showed every line of her lower body. On her arms and ankles were rings of gold and around her neck hung heavy golden necklaces with nefer-beads that hid her budding breasts.

Still, despite her youth she was already living up to her name. Nefertiti. The beautiful one has come. Her beauty outshone many of her peers, and her new husband could not keep his eyes off her. They talked only to each other, and forgot themselves in one another's eyes.

At least their marriage would be a happy one, Merit knew. And she would outlive her husband, maybe even rule as pharaoh after he had died. So Merit decided not to impose her modern moral values on these ancient times.

When the young couple had been escorted away to fulfil their marital duties, people started to disperse. Merit stayed with Tiye until she too went to bed. Merit, wanting some air, walked towards the garden, and sat just outside the door, near the guards.

The voice whispered in her ear out of nowhere.

"You will tell me where Meryt-Neith is."

Merit jumped to her feet, her hand flying to her throat with shock. How had she not felt the presence of the Pale Man at all? He must have understood that she could feel his approach and had hidden his energies. She couldn't see him either. No, of course not; he wouldn't come out of the buffer zone in front of the guards. Merit's sudden movement had already alerted them and they were looking in her direction keenly.

Merit took a few slow steps to assure the guards everything was all right. A sense of fatality came over her. This meeting had to happen - and this was as safe as it could be before Mut-Bity and the bees returned.

"I will never tell you," she said quietly. "You will have neither one of my girls."

"Then I shall have to kill you."

Now Merit saw movement - the Pale Man had stepped closer to the veil between the buffer zone and the visible world. The effect was as though a shadowy figure was pushing through a plastic film that was glued to his outline and reflected the scenery around him. One of the guards took a step closer, frowning, trying to make sense of what his eyes could not comprehend.

"Killing me will only make it harder for you to find them," Merit said in a low voice. "If you think Mut-Bity will ever reveal where they are, you are wrong. If you attack me now, those guards will thrust a spear right through you in an instant."

"I am faster than they are," the whispering voice told her.

"That may be. But all it takes is one scream from me. And I will fight you. It will give them enough time."

A silence.

"Do not think I have forgotten you, or will ever forget you. Or your daughters. They will be mine. As will be the secret you stole from the House of Life of Hut-Ka-Ptah. I know you read it. You can tell me by choice where you hid the scroll, or I will make sure by other means that you give up the information. You will not always be guarded."

"Your desires will never come to anything," Merit said, as calmly as she could. "And you'd better leave now. The Great Royal Wife has given your description to all the soldiers. Should they see a tall colourless man anywhere nearby, they are to kill first and ask questions later."

Tiye had given no such order, but he could not know it.

Merit turned and walked inside the palace without waiting for an answer, shaking with shock. How had he managed to approach her undetected?

The rest of the night, Merit sat in the bed chamber surrounded by the queen's sleeping maidens, feeling him circling the room so close that her spine buzzed.

12

THE UNDERGROUND STREAM

We walked into the darkness of the cave, with no knowledge of what lay ahead of us, heading in the direction Nu had indicated. Stepping carefully on the uneven surface, we concentrated on finding good footing. Seth was carrying Asule and I held our son. Simply moving silently helped me stay calm, but I was still listening for any noises behind us. When none came, I prayed the dark Nephilim had not realised where we were.

The broad walls of the cave soon drew together and we had to step into the little stream to keep on following it. I lost track of time, wading cautiously in the running water, trying not to slip and fall because the stone underneath our feet had been smoothed by the stream.

Then Seth stopped and looked around us in the increasing light.

"This is manmade..." he said

I had been concentrating so hard on finding my footing and listening for noises that I had not even glanced around me. Now I stopped and looked up.

Our eyes were sharper than ordinary people's, and the sunlight seeping in through a crack in the rock a bit further up gave ample light for me to see that Seth was right. The walls curved around us in a slim oval – narrow at the bottom and the top, slightly broader in the middle. The walls clearly bore the marks of stone-workmanship and their surface had been shaped more evenly, allowing enough space to walk through.

"What is this place? I have never heard about anything like this before," I whispered, still reluctant to raise my voice.

"I have heard stories of underground canals that the desert tribes created, but never met anyone who had seen one..." Seth said. "This is their closely guarded secret – until now it's remained unknown to anyone else..."

His voice echoed from the walls, waking Asule who started to cry.

"Maybe we should stop so I can feed the children," I said. "There seems to be a broader space ahead where I could sit down."

It was clear that the natural widening of the passageway further on had a drier stone surface on which to rest, and we waded through the water to reach it. I sat down on the stone floor wearily and Seth placed Asule in my arms.

The babies were hungry and their eagerness to suck the milk made me smile despite our situation. I felt deep pride at being able to feed both of them. When they were satisfied, I placed our son on my shoulder and patted his back the way I knew it should be done. He belched a little milk up, but not much.

Seth took Asule and did the same. The little girl let out such a loud burp it made us laugh, echoing back from the walls as if unseen people laughed with us.

But there was more than just the sound of our laughter. We heard the unmistakable splashing sound of footsteps wading through water. Someone else was approaching along the underground canal.

Seth grabbed the long knife he was carrying on his belt – it was made of bronze and had a decorated handle. Mut-Bity had given it to him when she left us at the desert's edge and Seth had put it in the pouch hanging from the donkey's side. It was similar to the weapons Tiye's private guards used and was not only valuable and decorative but a dangerous weapon as well.

A shadow was blocking the faint light that had been showing us our way. It swayed along the walls, filling the space with darkness.

Should I get up and stand beside Seth? No, the children would be in danger... Hastily I took off my covering, put it on the floor and placed the sleepy babies on it. The tiny contented noises they made multiplied from the stone walls.

Then I stood up to face the danger side by side with Seth.

In my state of fear, the figure against the faint light seemed huge. Then, from the way it moved, I realised that it was quite a small person after all. It stopped when it saw us and raised a hand in greeting.

Seth sheathed his knife.

"Greetings," he said. "Who are you?"

"I could ask you the same," a man's voice said, "for your kind should not know of our secret ways."

"We were shown the way here to be safe."

"Who showed you?" the man kept his distance.

"Nu and Ibah of the sand people," Seth said, "and in so doing they lost their lives."

The man bowed his head and placed his hand on his heart.

"Where are their bodies for us to perform the rites of death?" he asked.

"They are at the entrance to this place, under a big rock, where there is a small pool."

The man nodded his head several times.

"When did this happen?"

"Not long ago. It is hard to know the exact time in here."

"We will send for them," the man said. "Was it the winged ones, the gods who slay, who killed them?"

"Yes," Seth answered.

"Why?"

"Because Nu and Ibah stopped them from killing us and our baby."

"Why do they want you all dead?"

A silence. Then I decided to tell the truth.

"They call us the silver ones. And there is an old legend of the desert saying that the silver Nephilim will be the doom of the dark winged ones."

"But there has never been a silver one," the man said. "Can you prove this? How are you silver ones? You don't shine. Come towards the light."

He turned away and walked back towards the distant ray of light.

We looked at each other.

"I suppose we need to convince him," Seth said, "so that he'll help us."

We lifted the babies up into our arms and followed the man to the place where a thin sliver of light touched the stone floor.

"You talked of a baby. But I see that you have two."

"This is Asule," I pulled aside the scarf hiding the little girl's dark delicate features. "She is the daughter of Nu and Ibah. She is unharmed."

"We have taken her to be our own daughter to pay our debt to her parents," Seth said.

The man looked at us keenly – the light reflected from his eyes but other than that, he was shrouded in shadow. He squeezed an amulet hanging from his neck on a leather string and mumbled quiet words in an unknown language. Then he let go of the amulet.

"If you have promised that to the spirits of her parents, the promise is binding," the man said.

"That is how we wish it to be," I said. "Asule will be brought up as the sister of our son. A full daughter in all but blood."

"Then she will remain your daughter, even if she is of our tribe," the man agreed. "Now; show me in what way you are silver."

I stepped into the light and the man took a step backwards.

"You are a child of the Moon!" he whispered. "A daughter of Thoth!"

"I am," I said, opening my wings.

The sunlight reflected from them, colouring the stones around us red. The man observed my red wings with silver veins silently and then looked at Seth. He stood behind me and I could feel it in my body when he too opened his wings.

"You're speaking the truth," the man said. "Nu and Ibah saved you because of the ancient legend. I know of it too, and I see you have come to help us get rid of those bad spirits. I shall help you reach your valley."

We looked at each other again.

"You too know of the Valley?" I asked.

"All desert dwellers know of it. But we will never reveal its location, because of the prophecy. It is said that if the gods who slay find it, we will never be free again. They would take us as their slaves. We will not be slaves! We are born free. And so, if they attack any of us to drink our blood, we fight so hard they have to kill us first. If we are dead, they cannot learn our knowledge."

He stepped into the light and the shadowy form changed to an elderly man with a wrinkly face and wiry, dry body. He wore nothing but a loincloth of leather, his amulet, and a small sack on his back. On his hips he had a short knife in a sheath.

"Now we need to make the fire," he said.

"The fire?"

We did not understand. He didn't explain, only turned and started walking, and we followed, carrying the children.

Again, we walked in water in the darkness. The man knew his way and we followed him until he stepped out onto dry stone.

"We get out here," he said, "and go up there."

He was pointing upwards.

"Up where?" Seth asked. "We can't climb the wall with the babies. And there is not enough space to fly."

"No need to climb the wall or fly. Follow me."

The man moved up to the wall, took another step sideways – and vanished. There was an opening, behind a ledge, just wide enough to squeeze through sideways. We followed the man, protecting the babies from being scratched by the rough stone, then stepped out into a narrow crevice where an ascending stone path began.

The way led us out and, after squeezing sideways through an opening that was just wide enough to let us through, we found ourselves standing on the side of the oddest shaped boulder. The opening to the canal below ground was only visible if you stood right beside it, as another ledge hid it from any passer-by – as if anyone would ever walk past this boulder in this vast emptiness that was the desert...

More time had passed than I thought – the sun was already setting on the horizon. Nervously we looked around, but the only thing visible was a hawk high up in the sky, still searching for prey in the diminishing light.

The man bent down and dug something from the sand. Dried dung and plants. These he placed against the rock surface and then squatted down as if there was no hurry in the world.

"If the abyw *are after you, it might be best that you don't come out here in the open," he then said.*

We moved back into the stone corridor and waited. The sun set and when the darkness was complete, we heard the man moving again. After a while, a glow of light revealed he had lit a fire.

"Is that wise?" Seth asked him from the doorway. "Everyone will see the light and the winged ones may come and inquire about it."

"If they come, they'll find an old man roasting a rat," he answered.

I peeked out too. I had no idea where he had got the rodent, but indeed there was a skinned rat in his hands.

"Also, if you look closely, you see the fire is lit between stones so that it only shows in one direction. An answer should come soon enough."

The dung fire was burning in a naturally formed recess in the stone boulder. It did not show upwards or sideways – only in one direction as he had said.

I looked into the darkness.

"There!" I pointed.

"I can see it too," Seth said.

A tiny light burned in the distance.

The man unceremoniously removed his loincloth and placed it in front of his little fire - covering and revealing it in a way that showed he was sending a message. The little light in the distance flickered out of sight in a similar manner.

"Good. Help is on the way. Let us go inside."

He extinguished the fire with sand, put the loincloth around his hips again, and we all went back into the cave.

"Go down to the water," the man said and we made our way back to the underground stream. "You must be tired," said our guide. "We'll only walk a short distance and wait there."

Reaching a small cave, we left the water again. It was then that exhaustion hit me. Leaning back against the cave wall, I closed my eyes.

I fell asleep and only came to when Seth gently touched my shoulder.

"Shuet – they have arrived."

Three figures were standing talking with the man who had been our guide. They spoke the same strange language as he had done, with clicks of their tongues. Our guide pointed back to where we had come from and two of the men departed.

"They're going to bring back the bodies of Nu and Ibah," our guide explained. "We'll take you to your valley, going as far as we can underground."

I scrambled to my feet right away and felt so dizzy I almost fell.

"You're not well," Seth said. "Here, let me carry both babies."

"No, I will manage," I said, still trying to stand erect, "I'm only tired, as I am sure you are too."

The third man turned his back and disappeared into the darkness.

"He's going on ahead of us to alert the Valley of your arrival," the man said. "You are not out of danger yet – the dark demons don't give up their hunt easily. We're going now."

More walking. The weight of our little boy grew heavier by the hour, but I would not give him to Seth – I could see how tired he was.

Losing all sense of time, it seemed hours before our guide finally stopped.

"From this point, we're going up again. The stream turns away here from the way we need to go. Then we'll be walking above ground."

"We have to rest," Seth said. "My wife can't walk any further. She has just given birth and has not had a chance to rest since."

"Then we'll stay here, underground. You have not eaten either?"

"No. Not since... Nu and Ibah..." I said and sat heavily down on the nearest rock.

"Eat this," the man put something in my hand – a piece of dried meat. "Soften it in the water if it is too hard. You too." He handed a piece to Seth.

I did not ask what kind of meat it was, but the thought of the skinned rat made me suspect this wasn't anything we would have chosen to eat voluntarily. But we needed the strength food would give us so we thanked the man and ate. At least the water of the underground stream was pure enough to drink. Afterwards, I took the babies and fed them too – thankfully my milk was flowing easily now and the children were soon asleep with full bellies.

Too soon, the man told us it was time to get up, adding "We have to be fast crossing the open space so your hunters don't see you."

With heavy limbs, I got to my feet and we followed our guide once again. This time the entrance to the pathway that he led us along on our way to the open air was wide, but at the other end we had to squeeze through sideways again.

We were out under moonlight in the middle of sand dunes. It was eerily beautiful – the soft dunes lying like still waves in the cold light. I breathed in deeply – the sense of freedom was wonderful.

Our guide looked up at the stars and started walking.

We had only taken a few steps when I felt them. A painful buzz in my back made me turn. Two Nephilim were standing on top of the nearest dune, staring straight at us. One had black skin, while the other was paler.

"If my eyes aren't deceiving me, it appears we have found what we were looking for," the one with the lighter skin said.

His companion didn't reply; he simply opened his wings with a loud crack and rose into the air.

13

THE CAVE

Daniel and the three hunters lay flat on the mountainside above the camp where the child had seen the two strangers. When the men spoke to the boy, he pointed upwards to indicate the place where they had stood.

Daniel had automatically opened his wings to fly there, but the leader of the men held up a warning hand, stopping him. There was no fear in the eyes of other two who had been observing his wings, simply the same curiosity they had shown when they had first met. Clearly, they had seen Nephilim before - and if the sniffing earlier had revealed anything, they knew how to distinguish between threatening and good Nephilim.

Daniel accepted their judgement. Of course, they were right - if the two figures the child had seen were Ambrogio and his shadow, they might still be up there. Ambrogio had threatened to kill Dana if Daniel followed them. Daniel closed his wings and followed the men, although it took them over an hour to reach the place the child had indicated.

No one was there, but the men pointed out some barely visible footprints to him. They were just a shallow depression in the dust, with a few small pebbles pushed forward by the toes, but it seemed that two people had been standing here.

The men walked around, looking at the ground, frowning. It was clear they couldn't find what they were looking for.

Daniel understood. He drew two stick figures on the ground, pointed at them, and then entered the buffer zone in front of the men. He returned quickly, finding them in discussion with each other. It was clear they had taken in what had happened. Ambrogio and the shadow had not walked away from this place in the physical world they inhabited.

Should he follow Ambrogio into the buffer zone now that he knew at what point they had entered it? There was always the possibility that Ambrogio had left his shadow on guard, to make sure Daniel did not follow. But that might be his only option. These men couldn't follow Ambrogio into the buffer zone anyway.

The men seemed to have come to a decision. The eldest gestured him over, bent down and with a stone drew the outline of a mountain. On the side of it, he drew a half circle. Daniel understood. A cave. He pointed at the drawing and then gestured around in a wide sweeping motion.

"Where?" he asked aloud.

The man pointed to the east. And then in two other directions.

"Three caves?" Daniel lifted three fingers up, questioningly.

The man did the same. Three caves. He said something to the two other men and they walked away, each in a different direction. Then the remaining hunter, gesturing to Daniel to follow him, began walking across the rubble-strewn mountainside.

He moved surprisingly fast, and Daniel had to work hard to keep up with him, not being as used to walking on this rough terrain. Using his wings would cause a detectable electric atmosphere; even visiting the buffer zone briefly had been a risk.

The man kept on walking and climbing, only stopping for brief moments to rest. Once he stopped to listen and Daniel heard the sound of footsteps walking on small stones too. It could not have been

Ambrogio, for he moved so silently even the Nephilim had trouble hearing him.

It turned out to be one of the other hunters, who simply made a silent gesture with his hands that was clearly negative – there was nothing in the cave he had searched.

The sun set and still his companions gave no clue as to where they were headed. Daniel could have continued through the darkness as well, but the three hunters could not. They were in need of rest. But before curling up to sleep, wrapped in thin blankets they carried like belts on their waists, the youngest one of them lit a small fire.

Daniel pointed at the fire, looking worried. Surely it would show for great distances?

The man pointed to a far off point where a tiny light twinkled back – another fire. It vanished suddenly from sight in a way that was not natural - something was blocking it so that it only became visible at intervals.

The hunter waited for the flickering to end and then took his blanket and drew it across their little fire three times, holding it for a few seconds. The third hunter, Daniel assumed, was producing the far-away twinkling light.

Daniel sat in the darkness while the men slept. He couldn't sleep. Knowing that Dana was in Ambrogio's hands made his stomach curl into a knot. Why did Ambrogio want to kill her? *Did* he want to kill her? Daniel tried to make sense of it, knowing Ambrogio had some private agenda that he had revealed to no one else.

Daniel stared into the darkness, listening to the sounds of the night.

"Where are you, my love?" he whispered, not allowing the fear to take control of his mind, refusing to give in to it.

The Milky Way travelled slowly across the silent sky and then, finally, the sun began to rise.

The men got up as soon as it was possible to see the ground, sipped a little water and chewed on dried meat, offering some to Daniel as well. He took a sip and chewed, showing his gratitude to these three strangers whose life had now entwined with his. And then they were off again at the fast walk that the three hunters made look so effortless.

The edge of the plateau in the middle of the mountains at which they finally arrived revealed a lighter streak on the far horizon, starting to shine in the morning light. The sea!

The two men stopped. The oldest pointed downward. It took Daniel a while to spot the narrow opening into the mountainside. The wind circling the mountain wafted towards them, bringing the faint scent of cinnamon.

Dana's scent!

The instant Daniel knew Dana was in the cave, he calmed down. Careful planning was what counted now. Ambrogio was a killer who knew how to kill Nephilim - quickly. Daniel wasn't going to give him that chance, not with Dana.

The men read the change in Daniel's posture. The oldest pointed at the cave entrance again and Daniel nodded.

The men lay down on the ground and Daniel did the same. With every muscle ready to spring into action, he fixed his gaze on the entrance, trying to catch any sign of movement.

There was none. Also, there were no noises - no voices, no sound of anyone moving inside.

Dana's scent was fading rapidly. Daniel got to his feet and sprinted down to the cave. He had to bend and squeeze sideways through the horizontal opening to get in.

No one. The cave was empty. There were footprints in the dust and he could see where Dana had been lying.

Where had Ambrogio taken her?

14

RAMOSE

Meryt-Neith awoke suddenly one morning to the sound of her son's cries. Instantly alert, she saw a familiar figure seated on the earthen floor of the mud hut, holding the baby.

"Your son is healthy," Mut-Bity said quietly and smiled at the baby. "You have plenty of milk, then?"

"Mut-Bity! How glad I am to see you!" Meryt-Neith whispered and sat up, not wanting to wake up the other women who were still asleep.

"Motherhood suits you," Mut-Bity looked at her approvingly.

"Have you seen Mother? And Shuet?"

"Your mother sends you her love," Mut-Bity said.

"And Shuet?"

Mut-Bity did not answer and Meryt-Neith sighed.

"I understand. You are still not sure whether or not I can be trusted."

"Not quite," Mut-Bity said. "We might trust you now, but if the Pale Man ever finds you and changes you, you'll willingly tell him everything you know. And so there are some things that we can't speak about with you, to keep others safe."

Meryt-Neith wrapped her arms around herself, suddenly feeling cold.

"So he is still after me..."

"He is. He approached your mother and threatened her life if she did not tell him where you were."

"Is she...?"

"She is fine. She moved in with Tiye's household immediately after we left, and he knew better than to attack your mother when there were soldiers everywhere. I sent new bees to her and now she is protected again."

Meryt-Neith took her son from Mut-Bity's arms and placed him on her breast. The baby began to suck with such vigour that both women laughed.

"Hungry little thing. Funny how dark his hair is..." Mut-Bity's dark hand gently touched the baby's black hair.

The baby's father was colourless, like Shuet, and Meryt-Neith was blonde so the dark hair of the child had come as a surprise.

"Are you sure of the father?" Mut-Bity asked, her hand still stroking the soft baby hair.

"Yes," Meryt-Neith did not look up.

The days of passion in the arms of her lover seemed to have happened in another lifetime. The spoiled, selfish young girl who had so willingly given herself to the handsome stranger had gone, never to return. Instead, she was now a young mother whose life's purpose was her baby, sitting in the poorest mud hut, as far away from the splendour of the royal court as possible.

But there was no question about the father. He had been Meryt-Neith's only lover.

"You said you sent bees to mother... but you did not go yourself?" Meryt-Neith asked. "You have been away all these months..."

"Yes. I need to make sure you will be safe before I return to the court. He would surely follow me if I visited your mother and then returned to you."

"You mean I'm not staying here?" Now Meryt-Neith looked at Mut-Bity.

"No. I would not have you and your baby living in a mud hut, as much as I like these people. I have arranged a place for you. I shall take you there and then return to your mother. You'll have to manage on your own from then on, with the help of those I have asked to protect you, as I can't return easily for fear of leading him straight to you."

"Where are you taking me?"

"I'll tell you on the way so no one else overhears. Now, you need to gather your belongings and... no, no, not right away. We're leaving tomorrow. I have things to arrange here with my old friends."

Meryt-Neith sat back down on the floor - there were no chairs here, only reed mats, rolled open for the night as mattresses.

Mut-Bity spent the day meeting her old friends in the village. After a night during which she slept very poorly, Meryt-Neith was ready to depart. She hugged the village women she had become friends with, put her little son in the linen sling in front of her body and followed Mut-Bity to the shore of the fishermen's village at the western edge of the great lake. One of the fishermen was waiting there for them.

"Have you given your son a name yet?" Mut-Bity asked when they had settled into the small fishing boat.

"Yes. He is Ramose," Meryt-Neith said.

Ramose, born of the sun. She had chosen the name as a spell against the child's father who was as far from the light of the sun or any light as she could imagine.

"Ramose. It's a good name," Mut-Bity said. If she saw any irony in the choice, she did not show it.

The little fishing boat was old, but made of wood, not from reed bundles tied together. It had a real sail and the fisherman skilfully sailed close to the northern wind. Meryt-Neith kissed the top of Ramose's head as he looked about him with round eyes.

"Don't you worry, my little one. I'll never let him find you," she whispered.

Mut-Bity hid the sadness in her eyes by looking away across the lake.

15

MARINERS IN THE DESERT

There were ships in the desert, but they didn't look like ships. Dismantled in Coptos, just to the north of Thebes, they were carried in pieces through the Eastern Desert by their crews, using the dried-up riverbed later known as Wadi Hammamat.

There were no waterways between the Nile and the Red Sea, and no wood available for ship building near the shore of that sea. So, from time immemorial, Egypt's sea-going ships had been built in the Nile valley, disassembled, and then carried overland to the sea. There they were reassembled using ropes and left in the water, so the ropes and wood swelled up and sealed all the openings until the vessel was watertight.

From here, the trading ships headed to Punt to get exotic goods: animals, ivory, and the incense that was in great demand in the temples. Many pharaohs had tried to grow the trees that produced the fragrant resin used as incense to communicate with the gods, but with little success.

Punt was the destination of the ship that one weary crew was working on as the sun slipped towards the western horizon. By evening, the men were tired from the assembly work and fell asleep almost right away after having their evening meal of coarse bread and dried fish. All of them were looking forward to the following day, when they would try to catch fresh fish from the sea.

One of them was sleeping a little apart from others, in the open under the night sky, wrapped in a blanket. "You chatter too late and then snore too much!" he had grumbled at his companions, who had laughed at him.

He was easy prey. Ambrogio slashed his throat with his sharp teeth so quickly the sailor did not even have time to open his eyes. The vampire's hand pressed down hard over the man's mouth to muffle his screams, which soon died away. Ambrogio drank deeply, almost killing the man in his voracious hunger. After that, he chose another victim. Both were young and strong men.

How hungry he was! All the time he had hunted for Dana he had not eaten, to sharpen his hunter's instincts. He had drunk some of Diana's blood but refrained from taking all of it and that had increased his hunger rather than sating it. The girl's memories revealed much of their plans, telling him they needed to get to Amarna and find someone. Vague images floated in his mind, glimpses of some wall relief. The girl had fought his will fiercely, which always muddled his ability to read memories. He had let a lot of her blood fall to the floor without attempting to drink it, holding her still until she lost consciousness, just to stop her resisting him. Tasting her blood had almost made him lose control, his body screaming for more sustenance. But he had not given in, in case he needed to continue to hunt for Dana. Now he had secured her, and could finally have the nourishment he desperately needed.

So he gave in to the cravings of his body. The blood of healthy strong men sated his thirst and he drank them dry almost to the brink of death. But not quite… no, he would not do that while he still had a use for them.

Dana had escaped to the only place he could not follow her, lost in the depths of the sea. Furious, Ambrogio had waited on the shore but she had not surfaced again.

"Jump into the water and see if she is there!" he had ordered as soon as the shadow-man managed to breathe again from the kick the girl had given him, a strike that had sent him reeling and gasping.

Ambrogio had been unconvinced they would find Dana, but in his enraged state of mind it was better if there was no one he could kill nearby. And now all he wanted was to kill. Kill anyone; the sheer lust for violence was upon him. It was best that there was some distance between him and the human form his shadow now inhabited.

The shadow had walked into the sea, and had only swum a few strokes with his head under the water before starting to howl like an animal.

"The water hurts! I can't see, I can't hear!" he wailed.

Of course. The man was now filled with both human blood and that of Ambrogio. He was both shadow and vampire. He couldn't cross water. While water wouldn't kill a vampire, it heightened all the senses that were already so much sharper than those of an ordinary human being, until there was a sensory overload that drove them to madness. The sounds attacked their ears, their eyes were blinded by colours and light, and their skin became so sensitive it felt as though it was being torn from them while they still lived.

"Come away," Ambrogio said.

The shadow crawled out of the water, towards his voice, unable to see anything. He fell on his side on the shore and shivered there, under attack from his own senses. When he finally calmed down, he opened his eyes.

"I am sorry, master. I failed you," he said.

"The fault was not yours. Our kind cannot tolerate water. But - did you see her anywhere below the surface of the sea?" Ambrogio asked.

"No, master, there was nothing as far as my eyes could see… for as long as I could bear to look for anything! Nothing on the sea bed."

Perhaps Dana had drowned right in front of Ambrogio, to be carried away by the sea currents? But so quickly? All the Nephilim Ambrogio knew disliked water. Creatures of the air and the buffer zone, perhaps they couldn't tolerate water either? Maybe they couldn't swim – or perhaps the water had the same effect on them as on Ambrogio and other vampires, causing a sensory overload?

The age-old knowledge Ambrogio had acquired in his long years of existence warned him not to fall into the trap of drawing quick conclusions. There was much he didn't know about the Nephilim, especially the unspoiled kind. The Nephilim held their secrets close – Ambrogio had only learned by accident of the fatal effect that bees had on the evil Nephilim.

It was logical – in certain circumstances, bees could kill vampires, he knew that from experience. Layla, whether by silver, sunlight or bees, had killed many of Ambrogio's children. The Nephilim though; Ambrogio had considered them to be a master race, practically immortal and so strong that no small creature could ever harm them. But then again, he saw a logical thread. It was the blood of the evil Nephilim that created vampires from humans, and so any weakness these Nephilim had would transfer to their blood servants. Ambrogio hadn't drawn the obvious conclusion before now. The weakness came from the Nephilim: they had passed it on.

Having existed for almost two and a half thousand years without knowing this, he recognised the futility in drawing yet more instant conclusions now that Dana had drowned. *If* she had drowned; he wanted to see proof of it. He couldn't follow every movement of the sea currents, nor observe the whole shoreline to see where Dana's body would wash ashore. He needed help for that. Loyal servants of his own who knew the sea and its ways...

He had sprinted along the shore towards the north, his shadow heading southwards. He had found no one, nothing. No trace of anyone getting out of the water.

Once more, his shadow had proved his usefulness; on his return, he told Ambrogio about the group of men that he had seen approaching the seashore from the desert, carrying their ship with them.

A ship's crew, sailors who had travelled these shores and knew the ways of the sea. Perfect.

During that night, Ambrogio learned from drinking the blood of the sailors that they were experienced men who had sailed along the coast on earlier expeditions and had knowledge of the sea currents and especially the shore. Egyptian ships always stayed close to shore; the vessels were not designed to be seaworthy in deep water.

Ambrogio needed the two young strong men, as he couldn't use up any more of his own blood, despite the fact that his body healed quickly. All vampires needed fresh blood to function properly. One after the other, he poured his blood into the two sailors' mouths and veins, and, with his shadow, led the men away from the rest of the sleeping crew.

He couldn't let them return to the ship. They were too new, too ferocious, wanting to kill too much. Their bodies had not gone through the necessary changes yet. It was better if their fellow crew members thought they had run away or been taken by animals.

So, he and the shadow took the new vampires to the desert to hunt. Ambrogio didn't spare them; ruthlessness was needed to make them obey his rules. After he had broken one arm, several fingers and a leg, they accepted him as their sire. Then they had to wait for two days for their bones to heal. The men sat wrapped in their blankets, hiding their skin from the sunlight. Ambrogio left the shadow to guard the men and hunted a gazelle for them to feed on.

Only after their skin was strong enough, would they be able to hunt gazelles themselves. This was an important part of the process, teaching them to hunt and kill with their bare hands and teeth. The blood of the animals made the men grow even stronger and once they had drunk blood, they calmed down enough for Ambrogio to talk to them in the ancient Egyptian language that he now spoke fluently due to his time with the Pale Man. He remembered his first discussions with the sculptor Thutmosis, a lifetime ago it seemed, back in ancient Greece, before Artemis had turned him into a vampire.

The men understood his orders easily enough and that was all that mattered.

"You are to constantly scout these shores for a sign that someone has risen from the sea. A tall, blonde woman. She may have wings. Ask anyone you encounter, but avoid bright light when you do so. Your skin will look strange to them and if they fear you, they won't talk to you. If the one I am seeking has drowned and washes ashore, you are to bring her head to me."

"How will we find you?" the sailor with the longer beard asked.

"I shall send my trusted servant to you after a while," Ambrogio pointed at his shadow. "Until then, you are to run tirelessly. You can feed on animals, but on animals only. Do not enter any water!"

The men were eager to please him, happy with their newly gained strength. Never before had they felt so strong, so passionate. The hunt and bloodlust now governed their existence. It was often so with newly born vampires – the irony was that they felt more alive than they had ever done before, because of their enhanced senses. It was only later, when years had passed and everything that happened to them began to be repetitive, that they began to decline. First mentally, then physically. The ones who kept the lust for hunting and killing lasted longer. But eventually even they would weaken and die. Thus it was with the children of human vampires; the ones created by Nephilim were much stronger, imbued with the superhuman strength of their makers.

But the day of decline was far in the future for these two, maybe even hundreds of years ahead. Ambrogio's blood was still strong and his direct children lived longer than his grandchildren.

They ran back to the shore where they had left the ship. There was no sign of either ship or crew.

"Go now, and begin your search," Ambrogio said. "I will send for you in a few days."

The men turned and began to run in opposite directions. Ambrogio watched them heading off at supernatural speed and did not move. His shadow waited patiently for orders while his master stayed deeply wrapped in his thoughts.

Watching the sea reminded Ambrogio of his journey from Kirrha to Ephesus with Selene. The love of his life; the woman he had killed. He remembered how Selene's blood in him had whispered words of love to his mind, how he had tried to recreate her by giving his own blood mixed with Selene's to other women. How through the centuries the blood of these other women he had consumed had slowly, steadily silenced Selene's presence in him. And now – maybe the only hope he had ever had of bringing Selene back had slipped from his fingers for all eternity.

If Dana had drowned, he would not be able not drink her blood. The only hope he had had was gone, the belief that the silver blood of the healing Nephilim would wash him clean and erase all the tainted blood of the women he had taken as his wives. He had imagined it destroying all those whispering voices, carried by their blood into his mind, an endless choir that stopped Selene from speaking to him. He had yearned to be returned to his original state, to bring Selene back.

Desperation hit Ambrogio so strongly he swayed. But he did not say anything.

Dana had to be alive. Had to be.

He turned and took the shadow's hand. Together they entered the buffer zone and the shore was empty once more.

16

TO THE VALLEY

The bright cold moonlight left us nowhere to hide. We stood still, holding the babies tightly, watching the two Nephilim approaching. One was flying, the other walking. Even before he landed, we could make out the dark skin and yellow eyes of the Nephilim who flew towards us. Our guide kept still by our side. His posture was alert, but calm and he showed no signs of fear. Had he been in league with our enemies all along?

"Maybe we could fly away?" I said.

"Maybe..." Seth said, considering my suggestion with his hands clenched into fists.

"Yes, we have to fly," the yellow-eyed Nephilim said in a deep voice, landing in front of us. "Your pursuers are not far, and we'll need all possible speed to get away."

That hadn't been what we were expecting to hear.

"Who... we thought you were the ones who are after us," Seth stammered.

I just stared at the yellow eyes. The Nephilim looked back at me.

"Don't be deceived. Our kind can have yellow eyes, especially if the skin is dark," he said.

I still didn't trust him.

"Do I smell like the other kind?" he asked, seemingly used to distrust.

I breathed in. There was a spicy undertone but it was not the scent of rotting fruit. It was a scent I had smelled in the Nephilim of the secret valley. But I did not remember seeing him there.

"No..."

"Well then. Isn't that sufficient proof?"

The other Nephilim, a tall man with black hair and blue eyes, had also arrived.

"You were the one who sent word to us?" he asked our guide.

"Yes."

"We give you thanks. These silver ones need rescuing now. There's no more time. You get into hiding and we'll take them to safety."

The man lifted his hand in greeting, slipped through the opening in the rock and vanished from sight.

"Now, can you fly?" the yellow-eyed one asked.

"Yes, but we are very tired. Shuet has just given birth, we have been walking for days and have not eaten much," Seth said. "Also, we have the babies to carry."

"We will help you," the blue-eyed one said and moved up to Seth. "Here, take my arm."

"And you hang on to me," the yellow-eyed one said.

Together we all lifted up into the air. When I opened my wings to help, I found my strength was almost gone and I could offer very little assistance.

We had been flying over the moonlit dunes for quite some time when our escorts suddenly swerved down into the middle of nowhere.

"What is it?" I asked, alarmed.

"Dark ones. We may have been seen."

We looked in the direction of his pointing finger. Two Nephilim were approaching, fast, their wings glowing in the moonlight.

"Both of you, take my arms," the blue-eyed Nephilim said. "We'll use the mists to get away. There's no point in avoiding it any longer – they know about us now so the mists will only be telling them what they already know."

"I'll stay and fight them," the yellow-eyed one said, "I may gain some time because I have yellow eyes. Get away, now. I'll try to keep them off long enough to give you time to reach the safety of the Valley."

My mind went almost blank with fear. I was tired beyond belief, but I grabbed the Nephilim's arm. I felt it resonate in my spine as he concentrated on his wings and we fell backwards. Then the mists enclosed us.

I had often wondered why entering the mists seemed to be something many Nephilim could do - yet some not. Why Seth couldn't do it on his own I did not understand. And why was this knowledge not shared until long after a Nephilim had opened their wings? Mother had told me about the mists only when I was pregnant with our son, and had been surprised to hear I knew of them already.

We flew as fast as we could. The texture of the mist against my face felt odd and dry. Like smoke without the scent.

A strong buzzing feeling suddenly filled the strange echoless world. Our escort said nothing, just kept on flying forward. We knew what the sensation meant. I kept on staring into the grey mist, expecting the inevitable.

And then – the mist was alight with wings. Ochre, grey, bluish, green... They shot towards us like arrows from a bow. Four Nephilim warriors met us - and passed straight by. They did not acknowledge our presence with a greeting. I only saw their eyes measuring us as they flew by. Our kind of Nephilim.

When the fighting started far behind us, we continued until the mists no longer carried the presence of Nephilim. Only then did our escort step out of the mists with us. I looked around us and could have cried with relief when I saw the familiar stone walls of the secret valley.

17

FLIGHT

"Is this how we are to travel?" Meryt-Neith looked at the merchant ship suspiciously.

"You are. You are not safe in this land. The ship is going to Gubla, where there are other blond people like you. You won't draw so much attention to yourself there. The owner of this ship is a person I trust who has traded with the people of the Valley for a long time - though he does not know about our secrets nor the exact location of the Valley. He will give you and little Ramose a home in his own house. You are to work for your upkeep, but you will not be considered a servant. You know how to weave, so that is the work you are to do there. My messages can reach you in his house."

Meryt-Neith looked at the ship nervously. Like everyone else, the thought of going to the sea on a ship scared her. She looked at Mut-Bity, wondering how the old beekeeper knew any foreign merchants.

"Come," Mut-Bity approached the ship. "We can't stand here where everyone can see you and the baby."

Meryt-Neith pulled her head covering across to hide her hair and face, wishing she were shorter, before stepping carefully onto the plank leading to the deck of the merchant ship. Both she and Mut-Bity were hoping that the hubbub and noise of the harbour of Inbu-

Hedj would be enough to hide them from prying eyes. It certainly felt as if the whole world was pushing and shoving its way onto the docks.

Meryt-Neith could not help turning to look back. Never before had she been in such an enormous city. Mi-Wer or Waset were nothing compared to this. The king's palace, the temples, the diplomats' quarters, the gardens, the harbour... It was mesmerising.

For a while her features were clearly visible when the wind blew the covering from her face, and she quickly drew the cloth back. A loud bang nearby woke Ramose and he began to cry. Meryt-Neith turned her back on the docks, shushing the baby, and followed Mut-Bity.

A tall figure standing under the canopy of a merchant of the harbour observed the ship's departure for a long while before leaving.

"He was an odd one," the merchant said to his son, who was arranging the wine jars in the little storehouse they had.

"How so?" the son counted, "...twenty, twenty one... yes, all here."

"Didn't you see his eyes?"

"No, I was working," the son said a little self-consciously. "What about his eyes?"

"I have never seen eyes like them..." the merchant shook his head. "He must have come from some very far country. Or – well, have you ever heard of men with yellow eyes? Not light brown but pure yellow, I tell you!"

"Can't say that I have..." the son said and saw movement near the sacks. "Damn, there is a rat here, between the grain sacks!"

"Kill it!" the merchant said.

In the following rat-hunt they soon forgot about the yellow-eyed man.

18

MERMAID

The sea water enveloped me as I let all the air out of my lungs and sank towards the sea bed. I watched the sun reflecting through the waves, too tired to do anything but let the water take my body. Would I die now, in the ancient past, by drowning in the Red Sea? A school of little fishes swam by and disappeared. My hair floated up, past my face, streaks of gold reaching for the sunlight.

The cold water against my hot skin finally shook off my stupor. A tremendous need to breathe took over, and my body reacted by jerking into action. My limbs started to move in an effort to swim back up towards the air. But I was too far gone, too weak. I would never reach the surface. All I could do was watch my hands against the light, moving as if trying to climb from thc dcpths.

Then I gave in and let myself go down again. It was not dark, the sea was clear like glass and the sun above me created a liquid mosaic from the ripples on the surface. It would be a beautiful surrounding in which to die...

My vision began to fade. I opened my mouth and let the water in. It was saltier than anything I had ever tasted. The bad taste shook me back to life. Why had I wanted to get into the water?

Mermaids. I had been thinking about mermaids. How they breathed in water. How the Nephilim were supposed to...

I remembered. With my last strength, I concentrated my thoughts into my wings and opened them underwater, just as my knees hit the sea floor. The silver veins in the black wings made me look like part of the coral reef that was all around me.

My wings pulsed once, twice, reacting to the electric sensation of water that seemed to enhance all my senses almost painfully – and then the wings breathed in. Deep breaths through their whole surface that shook my body – as if my wings were giant gills. Oxygen filled my blood even though my mouth was still filled with salty water.

It was true. We could breathe underwater.

I sat on the sea floor, mesmerised by this strange turn of events. I lifted my hands in front of my face and they were covered in tiny bubbles that broke free and rose towards the sun. Was I breathing in through my wings and out through my skin? It appeared to be, as all the skin that was exposed directly to the water was covered with these tiny, living bubbles that fizzed upwards.

I was surprised at how clearly I could see underwater. It was as clear as if I was wearing swimming goggles, not at all like my memories of diving underwater with my eyes open, when everything was a blur.

What would it be like to move in the water? I got to my feet. The water resisted my movements at first, but when I moved my wings I felt lighter. I hopped upwards with my wings open and they gave off a distinct humming tune that resonated throughout my body. I remained floating in the water. I moved my hands first, trying to swim a few metres. That felt quite similar to diving in my human form. Then I decided to try my wings. I concentrated my thoughts into my wing tips as I always did when I wanted to fly.

Something surprising happened. Before, whenever I had opened my wings, they had opened behind my back, their tips reaching upwards and their lower parts wrapping around my legs. They did the same now too, only the wings continued to turn, up over my head and in front of my face and at the same time, the edges of the wings turned from my sides and closed in front of me. Daniel's wings had done the same when he had saved me from my dangerous encounter with Angel. The lower part of the wings closed around me too and I found myself inside a cocoon created by my wings. There was seawater inside the cocoon as well. When I looked down, the part of my wings covering my feet had lengthened underneath me and formed a horizontal extension that looked like… the tail of a dolphin.

"Holy shit…" I breathed out. My words bubbled around me in the cocoon and were then absorbed through the wings and into the sea.

Maybe the stories about mermaids weren't fairy tales after all. What if *we*, the Nephilim, were the mermaids?

Keeping my knees together, I kicked with both legs – and the tail shot me forward in the water like a missile. It felt to me like I was moving much faster than when flying.

I scooted around for a short while but had to stop when my body reminded me how weak it was. What should I do – I couldn't waste my energy like this. I stopped to think, swaying in the water, watching, absorbed by the bubbles that continued to rise from my skin .

Ambrogio would be waiting on the shore if I returned to the same place now. He would want to be sure I had drowned. I wasn't going back. I couldn't stay in the water indefinitely either. The logical thing was to get out of the water so far away that Ambrogio wouldn't see me, and then head back to the Nile to try to find the Time Walker team again.

I didn't want to leave any footprints on the shore. So what I needed to do was to fly straight out of the sea without touching the shore, and head directly towards the Nile.

Undulating my tail like a dolphin, I journeyed north for about half an hour, and then stopped to catch my breath. Concentrating all my power into my tail, I kicked myself vertically out of the water. All I could hope was that my wings would recognise the changed circumstances and carry me up into the different element.

I shot out of the water like a bullet. The sun hit my eyes; my wings gave an electric crackling noise as they opened. Silver sparks flew all around me, water fell shimmering down – and I was airborne.

I had no idea how far the fireworks my wings had created had been seen, and looked south along the shoreline.

There was no visible movement. I was sure Ambrogio would never simply accept that I had died, though. He or his shadow would be bound to run along the shoreline soon, to see if I had emerged from the sea. I didn't know whether Ambrogio was aware of the ability of the Nephilim to breathe in water, so I did not linger, but headed straight towards Egypt's eastern desert.

Making it to the top of a jagged hill, I landed, breathing heavily. Those black dots swam before my eyes again. I was so thirsty… My tongue was swollen from all the salty water, and it appeared that my stomach couldn't even feel hunger anymore. The last time I had eaten food and had a proper drink had been on board the Great Royal Wife Tiye's ship before Ambrogio had lured me into his trap.

The thought suddenly came to me – he had been using an odd silver-coloured device. What if it still had an effect on me? Even though I knew to be wary of it now, I might be too weak to resist.

I lay down so I would not be visible against the sky and observed the shore. I had been right – after perhaps half an hour, a small figure ran along the beach with impossible speed.

"Ambrogio…" I breathed quietly.

"Ambrogio?" a deep voice said behind me, and then ancient Egyptian words I did not understand.

I turned onto my side and stared at the yellow-eyed Nephilim standing behind me.

19

BETRAYAL

Meryt-Neith settled quickly into the routines of the merchant's household in Gubla, the City of the Goddess to the northeast of Kemet. The months she had spent in the fishermen's village by the great lake of Mer-Wer had taught her humility. She wove cloth without complaining, and took care of little Ramose who flourished among all the attention he received from the women of the household. He was given treats so that his cheeks became chubby and he charmed everyone with his infectious giggle and zest for life. As soon as he learned to stand up and began to walk, he was inseparable from the other children of the household.

The household knew her language and she soon learned theirs. They liked her and she liked them. With a sense of relief, Meryt-Neith felt her life settle into peaceful routine. Twice, she received a little note from Mut-Bity telling her everyone was safe. There was no mention of Meryt-Neith's name nor any signature, but she knew who had sent them.

The day it all changed began as usual. Meryt-Neith rose at sunrise and helped to prepare breakfast with the other women. The merchant had returned the evening before and so the breakfast consisted of bread, dates, meat and beer. His trip had been successful, trading cedar trees for gold, ebony, ivory and papyrus.

"And how have you been?" the merchant asked Meryt-Neith.

"I have been fine, thank you for asking," Meryt-Neith smiled.

"Do you not long to see your own family?" he asked, biting into the fresh bread.

"Of course," Meryt-Neith said, but did not offer anything more.

Mut-Bity had told her that the merchant didn't know about the Nephilim. All Mut-Bity had told the merchant about Meryt-Neith was that she was a widow, and someone was harassing her into marriage so that she had to flee. According to this story, Meryt-Neith had inherited a little wealth, and the man in question was a threat to Meryt-Neith's son. By her deceased husband's will, two-thirds of his possessions went to their son and one-third to Meryt-Neith. Should the child die, Meryt-Neith was to inherit everything. Moreover, Mut-Bity had told the merchant, she had heard the troublemaker speak to someone about marrying Meryt-Neith and getting rid of Ramose so that he could get the whole inheritance into his hands.

"Perhaps you should consider remarrying?" the merchant asked Meryt-Neith.

"Perhaps at some point, if I find a good husband who cares for my son." Meryt-Neith said what she expected he wanted to hear. She had decided she would never become involved with a man ever again but kept her thoughts to herself.

The merchant smiled and took a long sip of the good beer and gave a loud burp. His wife smiled, proud of his appetite.

"Which brings me to the issue. I think I may have found you a husband."

Meryt-Neith almost dropped her cup.

"I see you are surprised," the merchant smiled, pleased that his surprise had been successful.

"Yes... yes, I am..." Meryt-Neith stammered.

"I thought you might be lonely, away from your own people. And seeing you are a beautiful young woman – if a little too tall for many tastes – I thought what a shame it would be if you would have to spend the rest of your life on your own. A beauty such as you needs a man. So I kept my eyes open to see if I might meet someone who would wish to marry you and give a secure home to your son as well. And on my last visit I found one."

The merchant's wife clapped her hands together in joy.

"Do tell, husband!"

"I sailed to Inbu-Hedj to sell cedar wood. It's in great demand in your country. And there on the docks I met a man who came to purchase some wood from me. To have a coffin built for himself, he said. He told me that he had paid attention to my ship when he saw it in the dock after an earlier voyage and thought he would approach me directly instead of buying his wood through someone else. He looked very much like you. He was very tall, though strangely colourless. And he had the most remarkable eyes. Yellow."

Meryt-Neith froze. The merchant took her blank expression the wrong way.

"I *knew* you would be interested. Too happy to express yourself with words, I see." He patted his round belly and burped again. "Now, I asked him where he came from. He said he lived in the west, in an oasis to the west and north. He must have meant the great oasis many days walk from the great River. I asked if it was not a lonely place to live and he agreed. Not many beautiful women there, he said, and asked if I might have seen any women like him. He was looking for a wife, one who would be able to bear many children for him – can you believe it? He told me he was very rich and the wife would lack nothing. Ha! I knew exactly what to say to him. I told him all about you. How you had escaped a man who was a threat to your little boy – I mentioned the child as his existence proves that you can conceive and carry children, which is what every man wants. I described you to him. He wanted to know how old Ramose was and was very happy to hear his age. Of course, I take it he likes the idea that the boy is weaned and you are not tied to him as much as you would be if the lad was still a baby. A new husband wants to enjoy the company of his wife without disturbances, as you know."

The merchant chuckled and his wife slapped his back amicably.

"Did you tell him where you... where I live?" Meryt-Neith's lips were stiff with fear.

"Of course! I told him we live in Gubla and how he can find my house, and he promised to pay me... and *you* a visit soon! To see if you were the one he is looking for, were his words. Now, what do you think about that?"

The merchant's wife was more skilful in interpreting emotions and looked at Meryt-Neith with concern.

"Is everything all right, dear?" she asked."You look...".

"No. Everything is not fine..." Meryt-Neith got to her feet, "I have to leave, I have to leave immediately."

The merchant's smile died.

"Why? Do you not wish to marry?"

Meryt-Neith took a deep breath.

"The one you described... Very tall. Colourless... His hair was white? And his eyes bright yellow?"

"Yes, that was how he looked..." the merchant stared at Meryt-Neith.

"He is the very one who threatens my son. I escaped to another land because of him, and now you have told him where we are. He or some of his servants must have seen and recognised me at the harbour of Inbu-Hedj before we left. They knew your ship and waited for you to return to find out where you had taken me."

The merchant said nothing for a while.

"I... I didn't... I'm so sorry..." he finally stammered.

"I have to leave now. He must have followed you," Meryt-Neith took a few indecisive steps.

"But he couldn't have. I came back home with my ship, and he was not there. There is no way he could have reached here before me by land."

"He does not travel by land..."

"There were no ships coming from Kemet behind us. And we arrived late in the evening. If there was a ship coming this way, the earliest they can could dock would be in the morning. It will take him a while to find his way here..."

"He does not need to travel by sea either."

"Well unless he can fly I don't think there is any way he could have followed me," the merchant said, "But – I'll take full responsibility. We'll send you to my cousin in the mountains. And if he comes calling, we'll tell him you left a long time ago."

"He will know I have been here. He can smell my presence after I have left."

"Smell you? But you don't use perfume. What is he, a dog?"

"I might object to being called a dog…" a cold voice said from behind Meryt-Neith.

Meryt-Neith felt her blood turn to ice. A hot hand landed on her shoulder. The merchant and his wife were up on their feet so fast they fell against each other and onto the floor. They stared with round eyes at the man who had appeared out of thin air.

"Well, my dear. It has taken me so long to find you. You managed to slip though my fingers once, but you will not do that again."

Meryt-Neith turned around and looked into the oily depths of the Pale Man's yellow eyes. She could not speak.

"It would greatly amuse me to kill these people for hiding you from me, but I will give them a chance. If you obey."

"They have done nothing wrong!" Meryt-Neith's voice was barely audible.

"They have done everything wrong in hiding you, but as you are of the weaker breed, you would feel compassion towards them for helping you that way. Now, here is what we'll do. You have given birth to one son of mine. You are rare in that respect. It took you only a few months to get pregnant. My other wives did not manage to breed with me. I want more children and you are going to give them to me. You will surrender to me willingly. If you do not, these people will die. And you know me well enough not to expect an easy death for them."

"He is… the boy is your son?" the merchant managed to pipe up. "I did not know! I would have brought you here myself if I had known she had taken your child from you! We were told she was a widow!"

"Silence!" the Pale Man said quietly and so coldly that the merchant and his wife could do nothing but stare.

Meryt-Neith stood still, petrified with fear.

A little giggle from the doorway revealed Ramose. The Pale Man turned to look.

"Is this my son?" he asked.

"He is, my lord, he is!" the merchant whispered. His wife whimpered and pressed her hands over her face.

"A handsome little fellow. I am pleased!" The Pale Man smiled, bent over and touched the child's cheek with his finger. "And you are going to have siblings soon."

The child smiled back at him.

"Now, take him away. And stay away for as long as this takes. Unless you like to watch, of course."

The merchant's wife got up and snatched the little boy into her arms. The merchant was already out of the room.

"Now, my dear..." the Pale Man said, lifting his hand, and with one swift movement tore off the clothes Meryt-Neith was wearing, "get on your back. Or knees. Whichever way you prefer."

"Never!"

"My, my... what is this? As far as I recall, you enjoyed me greatly in the past. What has changed? I can give you great pleasure. Or pain. Your choice. Whichever way, you will give me more children!"

The merchant and his wife pushed the curious servants and children ahead of them, away from the dining room where Meryt-Neith's screams were starting to rend the air.

20

YELLOW-EYED NEPHILIM

His ochre wings were open and the veins pulsed with a slightly darker brownish colour. His yellow eyes stared at me with an unfathomable expression. His skin was almost black, and his features reminded me of the Somali girl who had been in my class in another time and place. She had been so beautiful, the blonde crew had to make a serious effort to compete with those naturally high cheekbones, huge eyes, sensual mouth and thick, shiny hair.

When I made no reply, he said something again and pointed at me, raising his eyebrows. I couldn't answer because I didn't understand. I was too scared to even move. Clearly he was not the pale Nephilim we knew about, but I knew what those yellow eyes meant.

Then he said a word I did understand.

"Nephilim."

It was more of a statement than a question. Carefully, with slow movements, I stood up, searching for any signs of aggression in him. There were none. He was clearly curious about me, but not aggressive. He did not lift his hands, and just stood there, looking back at me.

I opened my wings. He stepped back - I could not tell if he saw the opening of my wings as a threat or whether he was just surprised by the sight. Then he bent forward, squinting his eyes, and looked at my wings for a long while. He straightened and smiled. A genuine looking smile.

I kept observing him warily. He pointed at his eyes, slightly amused. I nodded; clearly he knew I was suspicious of him because of his eyes. He tapped his nose and inhaled deeply. I understood and did the same. A faint scent of cinnamon, without any trace of rotting fruit.

Surprised, I let out a little sound. This time he laughed aloud. And now I was no longer in a state of shock, I did remembered that some Nephilim could have yellow eyes. Also, his eyes seemed brighter in colour somehow than Angel's eyes were. And when I looked into them, the slow oily pulse I had seen in Angel's eyes was missing.

His smile was catching and I smiled back. Then he opened his mouth and out came a surprising word.

"Merit?"

He pointed at me. Surprised, I shook my head in denial and made gestures with my hands to try to make him understand I was not Merit. He raised his hand, bent down and with a stone scratched a stick figure on the rock. From this stick figure he drew lines downward, each line ending with another stick figure. And more lines down from these. Then he tapped the upmost figure.

"Merit," he said.

Then he pointed at me and showed the lower stick figures. I understood. He wanted to know if I was related to Merit. I looked at him, perplexed. Did he actually mean Elijah's wife, the Merit who had fallen through time to this ancient past?

But I was not related to any Merit as far as I knew. I made a gesture of denial with my hands. For the briefest moment, I thought that if I had married Daniel, or even been engaged to him, I might have agreed I was related to Merit. But the thought of Daniel was too painful in my weak state. For all I knew he was 3,300 years in the future, and we might never see each other again.

The Nephilim looked away from me and towards the shore. He pointed. I turned to look and saw a tiny figure approaching from the north, running along the waterline. Quickly I withdrew my wings, dropped down and gestured urgently for the yellow-eyed Nephilim to do the same.

He did not hesitate but closed his wings and lay on his stomach by my side, keenly observing the tiny figure until it disappeared from sight. He then pointed at his nose again and inhaled deeply. I nodded. Ambrogio was not Nephilim, but if his gesture meant the enemy, then yes.

He got up and extended his hand to me. I took it and he helped me up. I lost my balance from weakness and almost fell on my knees. Quickly his hand was round my waist and he lifted me again. Then he took a flask that was hanging from the belt on his side, placed it in his hand on my side, and removed its wooden stopper with his free hand.

I reached for the bottle even before the stopper was out. Staggering from exhaustion, I lifted the flask to my lips and drank, water pouring down over my chin. In my eagerness, I stepped backwards and he took his hand off my waist.

Nothing could have tasted better than the warm water. I could not stop drinking until the flask was empty. I closed my eyes to savour the bliss of water. When I opened them again, the yellow-eyed Nephilim was waiting, with his hands folded over his chest. I sighed contentedly.

He offered me his hand again and I took it. When the world around us began to become misty, I dropped his hand and stepped back. He looked at me questioningly. I pointed towards the now empty beach and tapped my nose, hoping he would understand. I could not go to the buffer zone for fear of Ambrogio's shadow finding me.

He opened his wings in answer and again offered me his hand. I could only hope he had understood I did not want to enter the buffer zone.

I took his hand and opened my tired wings. Unceremoniously, he put his hand around my waist and we lifted up in the air.

Now I had time to watch the scenery underneath my feet. It was beautiful in a rough, broken way. But it was hot, so hot, and I was grateful that our speed raised a wind that blew against our skin.

I was too tired and let my escort take care of the flying, giving myself over to his supporting arm with relief. I didn't know him and I could not understand him, but I trusted him.

The sun began to descend, its blazing red disk blinding me. Then the dark blanket of the night rose from behind, curving over us and pulling the stars with it. As always, the beauty of the stars enchanted me. The water had given me some strength but I still felt weak, as if I'd been through a serious illness, entering into a strange state without any real thoughts. I didn't even wonder about the fact that I could clearly hear a distinct sound that seemed to come from the stars, reflecting back from the earth below us. Absentmindedly, at one point I wondered how I had managed to survive this long – maybe Ambrogio's blood had given me strength. Then the memory of the taste of his blood made me nauseous and I concentrated on looking at the scenery.

We reached the Nile valley much sooner than I had expected – my escort was a fast flyer. The song of the stars changed when we flew over water, as if there was an extra layer of sound below a basic melody. I found myself weakly humming the tune while the little villages appeared and disappeared under us so far below I couldn't see anything other than the little specks of light from the doorways and windows. I had no idea in which part of Egypt we were.

Only when my escort looked at me curiously did I realise I was humming and stopped.

We landed at the edge of the western desert, beyond the villages and fields. The yellow-eyed Nephilim put his finger on his lips to make sure I would stay quiet. I just looked at him, exhaustion meaning that I was past the stage where I could have expressed myself in any way.

I was sitting there, slumped against a small tree, when he retreated to the buffer zone. He was not gone for long and returned with a loaf of bread, some eggs and a new flask. Food! Finally!

I attacked the bread while he peeled the eggs for me. I stuffed them in my mouth almost without biting. The flask was full of beer so thick

I would not normally have drunk it, but for now, it was enough that it was liquid.

My escort observed me with a worried look. After a while I realised why. My stomach protested at the sudden influx of food after being starved. I had to concentrate on not throwing up, and after a few nauseous moments with my hand pressed to my mouth, managed to keep the food inside.

I sat on the ground a while longer, my escort standing next to me, constantly looking around. He was nervous of us being seen. So I got up and smiled at him. He took me by the waist again and we rose into the air.

Now we were flying across the western desert. I looked around curiously, feeling my strength returning slowly. I wondered where Kitty was – the last time I had seen her was before I reached the sea. Could she follow us? I didn't know how quickly the dead could move in the land of the living – or the buffer zone for that matter. Kitty had simply appeared wherever I was on the occasions that I had seen her. The only time she had actually moved with me in the buffer zone was when she helped me escape from Ambrogio's cave; and then we only spent a short while in the mists before she escorted me out above the desert floor. I remembered how slow-going it had been, because of my exhausted state.

I fell asleep in the air, trusting the strong arm of the Nephilim man. When I woke up, I saw only mist. We were in the buffer zone! Scared, I turned my head to look over my shoulder. No one, nothing...

My escort said a few words and I thought I understood part of it. His words were to calm me down, to tell me all was well.

Maybe we were far enough from Ambrogio's shadow by now. After all, they had no idea where I had gone.

When nothing happened, I calmed down. After an eternity of flying, we finally came out of the buffer zone, our feet almost touching a rocky formation in the middle of a vast expanse of sand and stones.

We landed at the bottom of a valley, whose dry stone walls reached to the sky.

I took a step to feel my legs again, and kicked at a small stone. It bounced against another with a clack.

Immediately the echo repeated the small sound. Clack clack clack… it must have been a dozen times. How could anyone move here without being detected immediately?

Someone approached us. I heard the footsteps echoing against the walls of the narrow valley. A tall woman in a reddish dress appeared and spoke a few words. My escort answered and again I heard Merit's name. The woman looked at me and smiled.

"We Merit's friends. Come," she said. In English.

I stared at her open-mouthed. My ears had not deceived me. My escort nodded once and then rose back into the air.

The woman gestured me to follow.

21

THE KILLING

"He should not treat you like that... you have given him a son, he should respect you for it."

The merchant's wife brought Meryt-Neith's food into the little room she was held captive in. Its door had been bolted from the outside. After raping Meryt-Neith, the Pale Man had made it abundantly clear that if Meryt-Neith was not in the house when he came to pay her a visit, the merchant, his wife, and their children would die.

The merchant was so scared he had practically pushed the bleeding Meryt-Neith into one of the storage rooms and bolted the door behind her.

The merchant's wife came in later with water, a washcloth and some new clothes. Meryt-Neith sat expressionlessly in a corner, hands around her knees, rocking herself back and forth. Her eyes were swollen almost shut, the side of her mouth was torn and her arms were bruised. There was a bald patch on the side of her head and blood matted the hair around it.

Meryt-Neith said nothing. She had not reacted in any way when the woman spoke to her.

"Here, dear... I am so, so sorry for this... but if he is the father of your child, it was not right for you to take the baby away from him… that's what my husband says… " the wife whispered.

She took a wet cloth and gently wiped the blood from Meryt-Neith's face and from the side of her head. It hurt but Meryt-Neith did not react. It was like washing a statue.

"But I do not agree… I will help you… if a man treats a woman like that, no child is safe with him."

Now Meryt-Neith turned her head, but could not look at her properly because of the swollen eyelids.

"You need to heal first. I don't know how I can help you, but I will try to assist you to escape," the wife whispered as if afraid someone would hear.

"Ramose?"

Meyt-Neith's whisper was hoarse, her swollen lips barely moving. Thankfully, it appeared she had not lost any teeth during the attack.

"Ramose is fine. He is asking for his mama all the time, but we told him that you would be coming back soon. That… monster…" the merchant's wife's voice broke and she had to search for words. "He said that if a hair breaks on the boy's head, he will kill us. Also, if you escape, he will kill us."

"How… then… help?"

Bloody saliva ran from the corner of Meryt-Neith's mouth when she spoke and dripped onto her arms, still tightly wrapped around her knees.

"I do not know. But I will try to find a way to help you. Now, let me clean you up…" the wife whispered.

Meryt-Neith did not move, did not let the merchant's wife touch anything but her face. Finally the wife lowered her hand. Her expression was shocked, and tired.

"I will leave this cloth and water for you. Clean yourself when I am gone. It will make you feel better. And put on the dress I brought you. I will bring you a blanket and a mattress to sleep on later. My husband says I am not to let you out of here."

She got up and left, opening the door just enough to squeeze through. Meryt-Neith could barely see through the eyelids of her right eye, but it was enough to reveal the form of the merchant right behind the door. The door shut quickly behind his wife, and Meryt-Neith heard the bolt being shot home again.

How could the merchant's wife ever help her? She couldn't assist Meryt-Neith to escape because in doing so she would kill her own family and household. She was feeling sympathy towards Meryt-Neith, as any woman would towards any other woman who had been raped. But she would want to keep her own family safe. Their whole life was here, in Gubla, and they would not want to leave the comfort of their home just to save Meryt-Neith.

"I'll come back when you look presentable again," the Pale Man had said as as she lay bleeding on the floor, half-conscious with fear and pain. "Do not resist me again."

Meryt-Neith could not even think about him touching her, not ever. She would never let him touch her again.

Finally, the numbness began to recede and she felt rage rising inside her. How she hated the merchant now, that stupid, fat little man who had brought this horror upon her! How he had grovelled in front of the Pale Man, ready to please him, to offer him whatever he wanted. How wrong Mut-Bity had been to send her here.

She forced the eyelids of her eyes open with her fingers and looked around. The water jar the merchant's wife had left was heavy. She made an effort to move it. Her bruised arms hurt, but the good thing was that no bones seemed to be broken. Then Meryt-Neith looked at the cloth the wife had left behind. It was long enough.

She knew what to do.

The next morning, a servant woman ran out of the merchant's house, screaming. The merchant's next-door neighbour, also a merchant, ran outside to see what was going on.

"What is it?"

"Murder, murder!" the servant woman screamed, pointing at the house with a shaking finger.

"Who has been killed?" the neighbour asked.

But there was no way to get a coherent word out of the servant.

The neighbour went inside his own house and returned with a long knife. Curious people had already begun to gather.

"Show me!" he said – but the serving woman refused to go back inside.

The neighbour's wife appeared as well now, and seeing the hysterical servant gestured to her own servants to come and escort the woman indoors.

"Come with me!" The merchant ordered two male servants to follow him.

They entered his neighbour's house, looking around. It was deathly silent.

"We heard screaming from here yesterday, master..." the older servant told him.

"When?"

"In the morning when you were at the harbour, master," the younger and more nervous-looking servant answered, "a woman was screaming."

"Did you go to see what it was?" the merchant asked.

"No, master, of course not. It was none of our business," the servant said, "and we saw the master of this house later. He was alive then."

"Look!" the older servant pointed.

The door of a storage room was ajar and a woman's feet were visible in the doorway. The merchant stepped forward and saw the body of his neighbour's wife. Her lifeless eyes stared at the wall. Her dress was above her knees – she had been kicking, resisting.

"She has been strangled..." the older servant said, looking in from behind his master. "See those marks on her neck? Done with that, probably."

A long cloth lay on the floor next to the wife. It was covered in blood.

"Why is she lying on a mattress? Did she sleep here?" the younger servant asked.

"Of course not! But someone must have done. Maybe there was

something of value here and a servant was ordered to sleep here to make sure it wasn't stolen," the neighbour said, looking around.

His eyes took in whatever was on the shelves. Trade goods, but nothing so valuable a servant would have needed to stay inside the room to guard it. Or maybe indeed the valuable thing had been stolen, and they would have no idea what it might have been.

"Yes. That must be it. But did that servant then strangle the woman? Whatever for?" the older servant asked. "I know all the servants of this house and they are loyal to the family. They were treated very well and it was in their best interest to take good care of their master's property. Everyone knows whose servants they are, so they would have to escape far and fast with any stolen property to use it without being caught."

"An outsider then…" the younger servant said.

"But where is the master of the house?" the neighbour asked, fearing the worst.

They walked towards the next room, keeping close to one another and looking over their shoulders. It was the room where the merchant conducted his business and was empty.

"Everything seems as it should be…" the neighbour said. "Search the rest of the house."

The servants walked out, more relaxed now when no sound was to be heard.

"There has been a fight," the younger servant shouted from the dining room. "The table is broken like someone had jumped on it. It has been wiped but there is some blood. And on the floor too!"

"You'd better come and see this…" the older servant yelled from the back of the house. There was fear in his voice.

The merchant and younger servant hurried to the private quarters of the house.

"By all the gods…" the neighbour whispered.

The merchant lay on the floor with his throat cut. A sharp-edged piece of smashed ceramic jar lay next to him and he was surrounded by a dark pool of blood.

"Where are all the servants?" The younger servant's concern was not all for the family – he had had his eyes fixed on a pretty girl that had joined the household not long ago.

They searched the rest of the rooms. Nothing. Then they went to the enclosure at the back and there they were, lying on the ground towards the rear of the small garden the merchant had been so proud of. An unconscious male servant who had clearly been hit on the head. Two women, gagged and tied. And two small boys, similarly gagged and tied. All but the unconscious male servant were looking at them with round scared eyes. On the ground were strips of torn cloth – the bindings of the servant who had run for help.

Quickly they untied the servants.

"What happened here?" the neighbour asked.

"Rape... he came for Meryt-Neith..." the oldest of the female servants said.

The neighbour remembered the tall young woman with blonde hair. Quite pretty but far too tall for his taste.

"Who came?"

"A tall pale stranger – he came to get Meryt-Neith. He said she was the mother of his child. And she had taken the child away without permission."

"Little Ramose?" the older servant asked.

"Yes. He raped Meryt-Neith in the dining room..."

"But if she was his wife, how could you call it rape?" the neighbour asked.

"He beat her till she bled, tore off her hair, cut her and raped her. She was bleeding like an animal at the slaughter when he finished... and he said to our master that if Meryt-Neith escaped, he would kill all of us. Master put her in the storage room so she would not try to escape."

So it was Meryt-Neith's mattress in the storage room.

"Those must have been the screams we heard," the older servant said. "The man disciplining his wife."

"Was he coming back to take her with him then? Why did he leave her behind?" the neighbour asked while his servants freed the rest.

"I... I heard him say that he would come to... to meet Meryt-Neith here in our master's house whenever he wanted. And master was ordered to keep her here and not let her escape."

The neighbour understood a husband would want his escaped wife back, but this kind of brutality... tearing her hair, and raping her in another man's house. And to expect them to then keep the wife in their house so he could come and visit her whenever he wanted? Why had the merchant agreed?

"But what happened to you then? Why are you gagged and bound here? Why are your master and your mistress now dead?"

The other servant woman and the children looked at him, horrified. The children started crying and ran to the older servant woman. Maybe they were old enough to understand their parents were now dead. The older servant had her hands full, comforting them, and the young pretty one answered in her stead.

"Meryt-Neith ran to us in the middle of the night. She said he had come back, and had killed master and mistress. They must have opened the door for him because we did not hear him knocking on it. Meryt-Neith said that he had left again, in a rage, and said he would soon return to kill her and little Ramose too. She said he no longer believed Ramose was his son and accused her of having lain with another man. She and Ramose would have to leave. She said that if we would allow her to tie and gag us, it would be clear we did not help her escape and that would save our lives. He had only threatened the lives of our master and mistress, not us, so we might have a chance. We decided it was best she tied us up."

"What about him?" the neighbour nodded towards the servant lying unconscious on the ground.

"He refused. He said Meryt-Neith's husband had every right to do what he did. He said he would have done the same if he had a wife and she had been unfaithful."

"But how did he end up unconscious? Surely no woman can knock down a grown man like that?" the neighbour asked.

"Oh but she could! We didn't believe it possible, with her being so assaulted and injured, but she had a broken jar in her hands and she is very tall and she hit him on the side of the head when he turned away to get help. He didn’t believe Meryt-Neith’s husband would kill us. But he was away when her husband raped her. He didn't witness it, so he couldn't know how evil the husband was or the state he left her in. He thought Meryt-Neith brought it upon herself.”

The neighbour was inclined to be of the same opinion, but this was not the time to discuss the morals of the matter – least of all with servants.

One thing he had to ask.

“Was there blood on Meryt-Neith?”

“No, not anymore. The mistress had washed her after he… the husband raped her.”

“No blood on her dress?”

“No,” the servants said in unison.

So, the killer could not have been Meryt-Neith. There was so much blood around the merchant, she would have been soaked in it if she had killed him.

“We need to make arrangements for the burial of your master and mistress. And we need to send word out that there is a murderer about. Do you know where Meryt-Neith has gone?”

“No. She said it was best none of us knew where she was going. She gagged and tied us and then took little Ramose and left. Before she left, she said we would be able to open our ties if we tried, but it would have to look real which is why she tied us so tightly. And finally…”

“Yes, we were alerted by the servant who freed herself. That is how we knew to come looking,” the neighbour had talked enough. “You,” he pointed at the younger male servant, “go and take a message to the mayor of the city about this murder.”

“What should we do?” the older servant woman asked.

“Take care of the children. Your master often talked of his brother. Do you know where we could reach him?”

“Yes, he lives just near the shrine of the Lady of Gubla. He has a small shrine of the Goddess built next to his gate.”

“I know the house,” the older servant said.

“Good, go and fetch the brother quickly so he may come and

secure the house and the goods here. He is now the guardian of these boys; they are the heirs of their father. Word is spreading quickly about these killings and some may try to get in here to steal now that the master is dead. I'll stay here until the brother arrives."

The older servant left.

The neighbour walked back in, and looked more closely at the body of the merchant. The sharp shard of pottery was clearly the weapon that had caused the death-blow. There was blood everywhere, the jagged cut was not neat and had required considerable force. For a while he thought of the broken jar in Meryt-Neith's hands but dismissed the idea. She may have been able to swing a heavy jar to hit the servant, but there was no way a woman could have done this deed. It would have required strength and the mind of a killer. Only a man could have done it. Also, the mistress's dress had been pulled up; he may have raped her too. And that was something he could not accept – touching another man's wife.

If Meryt-Neith's husband came back, they would be ready.

22

THE UNDERGROUND VILLAGE

I looked around at the underground village carved inside the rocky hills, not believing my eyes.

The doorway was partly hidden behind a vertical ledge. Once we walked through, the woman turned and easily rolled a big round stone from the side of the doorway to cover up the opening completely. That she could do this single-handed was amazing in itself. My yellow-eyed escort had not come inside with us.

The first thing that I noticed was the smell of dung and animals. After a few steps the source became visible too – little donkeys were standing in their stall made of stone. A few goats were there too – one of the donkeys had two cute baby goats standing on its back but clearly didn't mind.

We walked past the animals and descended a few steps. I saw that there were smooth corridors, from which rooms opened. Steps led from one level to another, up and down – there must have been over ten storeys but no clear main thoroughfare to walk along. The paths twisted and turned, rose and fell, sometimes with stairs, sometimes without. Corridors opened on both sides of our way. I caught glimpses of figures in the rooms on either side. Depressions in the stone steps revealed that this place had been inhabited for a long time.

The larger rooms had pillars supporting the roof. The air was always fresh and I noticed ventilation shafts cut into the ceilings of the corridors and rooms we walked through. Even in my tired state, I had to admire the skills of the people who had constructed this strange place. How had they been able to carve it all out without causing the rock to collapse? How had they managed to arrange the ventilation so skilfully?

Little oil lamps gave enough light for my Nephilim eyes. There were openings allowing in outside light as well, and out of curiosity, I peeked out of one to see the view. All I saw was a natural rock wall right in front of me, but by twisting my neck, I could see a thin crack that showed a sliver of sky above. The crack was only slightly wider than my head.

"We hide," said the woman who had taken me into her care. In English. "Bad Nephilim," she explained.

I nodded, too tired to show how surprised I was at this sudden knowledge of a future language. But if Merit had lived here, she might well have taught her language to others.

"Old place?" I tried to keep my sentences simple.

"Old," she agreed.

"Merit teach you this language?" I asked.

"Merit. Shuet."

"Shuet?" I remembered my pendant. "Is she here?"

I was eager to see the person whose pendant had found its way into my hands in the future. Grandma had said it had been passed down through my family line from mother to daughter through the ages. Could it be this Shuet was my kin? An ancestor? Had the pendant belonged to her originally?

"No, not here. Gone. Merit gone."

She continued walking and eventually we found ourselves in a bigger cave. Many people were there – and many Nephilim too. They did not have their wings opened, but their height revealed them – along with the sensation in my spine. Among them were several much smaller figures. The only word I could come up with to describe them was dwarf. I had never seen so many dwarfs in one place. To be honest, I had only seen little people only a few times in my future life. My mother quickly taught me not to stare at them.

Here, no one stared at them; they were talking with the tall Nephilim like there was nothing special about either one. And the humans around didn't seem to think that being Nephilim or dwarf was anything out of the ordinary either.

When we walked into the cave, everyone turned to look at us and silence fell. The woman I was with spoke to them, and I caught enough words to understand she explained where I had come from. There were several nods, a few questions, and the overall feeling was that of kind curiosity.

"We welcome you," the woman said, "tired?"

"Very," I said.

My eyes felt dry and hot, and my whole body ached.

"Come. Rest," she said and gestured me to follow. We walked back the same way we had come.

She took me to a room where a bed had been made into a niche in the rock wall. It was well padded with blankets. She gestured to the bed.

"Food," she said and walked out.

I could only see the bed. I bent down to avoid hitting my head and climbed into the niche.

By the time she returned, I was fast asleep.

23

ON BOARD

He had made her pregnant.

When Meryt-Neith understood what had happened she decided to kill herself.

He would never leave her alone now. He would keep her prisoner, keep raping her, forcing her to have his children. The long lifespan of the Nephilim she had thought of with joy was now a cause of panic. The man she had so wanted in the past was nothing but a monster who willingly tortured those who disobeyed him. And now he considered her to be his own property, to do with as he pleased.

That was the only reason he had not bitten her, he had said. She had proved she was fertile, capable of giving him what he most wanted – his own offspring.

"They shall carry on my legacy. Through them I shall recreate the master race that will rule kings," he had said to her when she lay on the floor, bleeding.

Now she had proven him right – she could be the one who could carry his offspring, something he had not been able to do with others yet. He had confessed that to her too, that horrible morning.

"You are a miracle, my darling. I intend to use you as long as I want. As long as you can give birth. If I can't make you pregnant again... well, we'll see."

No, she would never submit to that! And so, she had killed the merchant and his wife. She felt sorry for the wife, who had shown sympathy for her, but the merchant... no, she would never feel sorry for killing him. Furious over what the merchant had done, Meryt-Neith had walked into the bedroom where he was just about to lie down, and cut his throat with the shard from the water jar she had smashed. Then she returned to the storage room, took the wet rag she had used to kill the wife, and wiped herself clean. Some blood had splattered on her, even though she had tried to keep the merchant still until he had died, standing behind him. It had helped that she was so much taller than he was. She had never imagined she could have enough strength to keep a man firmly locked in her grasp until he was dead. She could still feel the fabric of his clothes against her own naked, battered body, the movements of his body when the spasms of death took him.

Then she put on the clean dress the wife had brought her. And when she ran to the servants, there were no tell-tale signs of the merchant's blood on her.

The servants were not to blame, so she didn't kill them. They bought her story that the Pale Man had returned and killed their master and mistress. All but that stupid manservant. She had knocked him unconscious before he could do anything to endanger her, such as run out of the house calling for help.

She knew she would have to leave immediately. *He* had said he would return when she was presentable again. He had always loathed people whose looks were less than perfect. In her old life, she had taken pride in the fact that she was beautiful enough for *him*. When he had revealed his dislike of ordinary-looking people, she had found nothing wrong with it. In fact, she had joined him in mocking the ordinary-looking people around them. But she now knew he really despised physical imperfection, and because of this she understood the amount of time she had before he came after her again.

Bruises and cuts like hers would take two to three weeks to heal at least. She would have that long to escape, and he could no longer follow her scent then.

She had tied and gagged the servants in the garden, and then gone through the house as quickly as she could, collecting every piece of jewellery she could find. There was a little wooden box filled with small expensive perfume bottles. She took that too. They would be easy to use as payment for the services she needed.

Then she went through the mistress's coffers in search of clothing to wear. She was much taller than the lady whose dead eyes now stared at eternity in the storage room, but the mistress of the house had fine long lengths of fabric in her boxes. Meryt-Neith wrapped them all around her, and they reached down to her ankles. The cuts in her skin were still bleeding, but she would not wait. She hoped the layers nearest to her skin would absorb the blood. She pulled two fine linen veils over her face to hide not only her features but also the damage that had been done, and put on the woman's sandals. Thankfully, Meryt-Neith's feet were small, and the sandals fitted her perfectly.

She then took a long knife from the merchant's bedside – he had been prepared for attempted robbery, but not for an attack by a woman seeking vengeance. She attached the little hilt to her hips so it was clearly visible. Then she snatched a piece of papyrus with writing on it from another coffer.

Finally, Meryt-Neith went to wake little Ramose who had slept the whole time. Meryt-Neith was glad of that. She would not have wanted her son to witness the killings, necessary though they were for her – and his – safety.

The little boy climbed into her arms sleepily. She wrapped a cloth around him and then slipped through the door into the street. Standing, listening intently for a while, she waited for the smell of rotting fruit, or that telltale sensation in her spine that would reveal the presence of Nephilim.

Nothing. He had indeed gone, certain of his power over the merchant's household. He would expect them to keep her prisoner for him.

Meryt-Neith had then walked down the street and on to the harbour. The moon had risen, lighting the hill of the Baalat Gubla temple and its sacred pool. How the presence of the temple had brought her comfort during her months of exile. Kings of Kemet had sent offerings to the Lady of Gubla for hundreds of years, and the fame of the temple as the mansion of the goddess Hathor had spread far and wide. Obelisks were erected in honour of the Goddess here.

Now she turned her gaze away. Hathor, the goddess of love. She had once dreamt of being a dancer in the temple of Hathor in Iunu. She had once believed in her existence. Now she would never believe in love between a man and a woman again. That was only about domination, violence, total disregard of the woman's wishes. The only love she would recognise from now on would be her love for little Ramose.

There was a ship in the harbour, ready to leave at first light. Sailors were still moving on the deck, even though it was the dead of night, making everything ready for departure at sunrise.

The ship was big, one of those that took on board valuables such as tin and copper for bronze making. Spices, wine, resin and barley were loaded in the hull. Ivory and jewellery would be carried too, no doubt.

Without hesitation, she walked up to the ship and asked to see the captain. The small, dry man looked at the fine veiled lady carrying a child and a bundle of possessions. She had hidden her face, wrapped it round completely with a long piece of fabric, but her slender, tall form revealed that she was young, even if the only things visible were her feet – and beautiful feet at that, dainty in exquisite leather sandals. The embroidery on her garments was of the finest quality.

"My lady. How can I help you?" he asked.

"I am to meet my husband in another country. Where are you headed?"

"We are going to the land of Keftiu," the man answered, "as soon as the sun rises."

"That's good. For that's where my husband is too," the woman said quickly. "He sent me a letter asking us to join him as he is now settled there and wants his family with him. I would like to travel on your ship."

She raised her hand and he could see a piece of papyrus there. The letter the husband had written, no doubt. The captain looked at her with respect. A woman who could read? She must be from a very fine family, then. But she had no servants with her. The whole thing was odd. Still, every chance to earn an income was welcome.

"Can you pay for the journey?" the captain asked.

"I can. He sent me valuable perfumes from the land of Kemet to pay for the journey."

The captain noticed the angular shape of a box inside her bundle. Fine perfumes were worth a fortune. The captain's ship also carried also terebinth resin from pistachio trees for perfume making, but ready-made perfumes were too valuable to pass over.

"Is that all you are carrying with you? That bundle?"

"It is. I have everything I need for myself and my child for the duration of the journey. Our new home has everything I'll need in Keftiu. I assumed my payment would include meals with you, so I did not bring any food with me. I have left the servants to take care of my husband's house here. I heard your ship was leaving and that the winds will turn soon, so that travelling to Keftiu won't be possible for months. There is no way of knowing if another ship heading that far would come to the harbour in time. So I quickly gathered my belongings and came here as soon as I could."

The captain did not trust the woman entirely, but who was he to argue? Maybe she was escaping someone. But he wouldn't take sides in any quarrels. The woman was well off, and had the means to pay for the journey. They would have sailed on their way before anyone knew enough to come after her.

"Very well. Come on board. You may sleep in my cabin with the child."

"Thank you. I trust we will be the only ones sleeping in the cabin."

After seeing the fine perfume bottles, made of real Egyptian glass of yellow, white and blue, the captain was more than ready to give up his cabin for the lady's use.

"You shall get these after we have arrived in the land of the Keftiu." His new passenger snapped the lid shut and skilfully tied the strings holding the lid around the knobs on the sides of the box, even though she was still holding the child in the crook of her arm.

"Of course."

She couldn't give the perfume bottles away to anyone else, not once they were out to sea, so the captain wasn't worried he would be cheated out of his payment.

"How long do you think it will take us to get there?" she asked.

"Well, we'll travel up north first, as the winds are blowing that way now. Carchemish and Qode will be our first ports of call, before turning west and following the coast of Arzawe. Then we navigate south to south-west for Keftiu. So a few weeks with all the calls to port. It will be a long journey. I hope you don't get seasick easily."

The ship had left the harbour before the merchant's servant had a chance to alert the neighbour about the murders. Meryt-Neith could only hope that this time, no one had paid attention to her in the harbour. But even if they had, she had covered herself from head to toe. Women carrying small children were not an out-of-the-ordinary sight. Only her height might have given her away, but she hoped anyone who had seen her would not remember where she had gone when the Pale Man returned for her.

Despite the captain's kind wishes, Meryt-Neith was violently seasick. Or so she thought until she counted backwards and realised she had missed her monthly bleeding. She sat in cold horror for hours, trying to tell herself she had to be wrong. And when she finally understood that the worst had really happened, she made the decision. She would not give herself or a new child to the Pale Man. Ever.

Waiting for rougher seas, she went and stood on the side of the deck, gathering the courage to jump into the churning waves. She could feel the men's eyes on her body when the wind pressed the fabric around her – she still had not revealed her features to the men, even though the bruises had already vanished.

Then little Ramose ran to her, giggling as the ship swayed in the deep blue waves. He had developed his sea legs quickly, and the sailors had taken to him almost as a mascot and kept an eye on him all the time so no harm would befall him.

Meryt-Neith looked at the little boy grabbing her leg, and her heart felt heavy. What would become of him if she killed herself? Surely, they would sell him into slavery. There would be no one to tell him of his heritage, to explain who he was. And if the transformation to Nephilim was as painful as they said, she could not bear the thought of him going through that alone. She would have to arrange for Ramose to be taken to safety at least.

"Land ahead!" a sailor shouted.

The captain came to her and pointed. She saw clouds first, and then underneath a darker sliver. Land.

"That is the land of Keftiu."

She stood there, looking at the big island in the middle of the sea and then at little Ramose.

No. She couldn't kill herself. She would have to make another plan. She had heard stories of the great palace of Kunusa where they danced with the bulls, and would head there. Maybe she could find some position for herself. Not as a dancer as soon she would be heavy with child. But something...

The captain was observing her. She straightened herself, looked at the man and managed a humourless smile.

"Thank you for bringing me here," she said. "As soon as we are standing with our feet on solid earth, I shall give you your perfumes."

"Hope your husband has sent someone to meet you," the captain replied.

Meryt-Neith did not answer. It seemed to the captain that she paled at the word "husband."

24

NEWS

The cup Merit was drinking from fell from her hand. She stared at Mut-Bity.

"Dead? Murdered? By whom?"

Mut-Bity's slumped shoulders indicated her despair.

"It was my fault. I took her there. To a merchant who happily revealed her location to the very person she was trying to escape. My contact – another contact, not the trader – told me what had happened. It seems the merchant came back here on business and met the Pale Man at the harbour of Inbu-Hedj. That suggests to me that someone spotted us going on board ship – and he must have had his men keeping an eye on merchant ships ever since then. And as soon as the merchant reappeared in Egypt, the Pale Man came to talk to him. The story he told the merchant was that he was searching for a wife. Or for *his* wife, it's not entirely clear. The merchant told him there was a beautiful tall blonde woman in his household, and thought they might be a good match, or so it seems. The servant who overheard this discussion was not in the dining room, just overheard the conversation from outside..."

"And the Pale Man must have known the merchant was talking about Meryt-Neith..." Merit whispered.

"Yes. He trailed the man all the way to Gubla, to his house, and found Meryt-Neith. There, he raped her. Beat her brutally and raped her."

"No..." Merit's hand flew to her mouth.

"The next thing anyone knew was that Meryt-Neith and little Ramose had disappeared. Lots of valuables had vanished too. Jewellery, perfumes... the thief had not found the gold, though, as the merchant hid it and never told anyone where it was. But the merchant and his wife were murdered. The wife was strangled and maybe raped, and the merchant's throat was cut..."

"He came back. He came back and has taken her..." Merit pressed her hands on her eyes and drew a ragged breath, rocking back and forth. "Taken Meryt-Neith and Ramose. We have lost them."

"So... it would seem. I have asked my contact to ask if anyone has seen a tall blonde woman and a small boy. There may be hope yet, if Meryt-Neith managed to escape."

"But the murders – she couldn't have killed anyone!"

"It is unlikely," Mut-Bity agreed cautiously. "So, the most likely explanation is that he came back for her, killed the merchant and his wife and took Meryt-Neith. But the story the servants told doesn't make sense, in that case..."

"What do you mean?"

"Meryt-Neith told the servants he had come back for her and killed the couple. And then, for some reason, he went away again. This is when Meryt-Neith, to save the servants' lives, tied them up so it would look like they weren't responsible for the fact that she was missing, because he had said he would kill those who let her escape. But – why did he not take her immediately? Why kill the merchant and his wife, and then leave Meryt-Neith and his son behind?"

"Perhaps he went away only for a short while? And then came back for her?"

"What I heard is that she walked out of the house alone, with Ramose. The servants heard no sounds from the house that would have indicated anyone else was there. So she may have used the short time he was away to escape."

"Did the servants hear noises when the murders were committed?"

"No, it seems they heard nothing. He must have killed them quickly. If…" Mut-Bity did not finish the sentence.

"If he was there at all…" Merit finished the sentence for her.

"He was there. They say there was no doubt that he raped her. It seems he did it almost in front of them. And they saw Meryt-Neith afterwards. She was brutally beaten, they say he had even pulled torn off part of her hair…"

Merit kept rocking back and forth, pressing her eyes with the palms of her hands.

"My poor daughter…" she whispered, "my poor daughter…"

"But if he did not come back for her that very evening, it can only mean that… that she was the one who killed the merchant and the wife. Also… the merchant's throat seems to have been cut with a sharp piece of pottery… that isn't the way the evil ones would kill. They would use their teeth or rip the person apart with sheer force."

"So it may have been Meryt-Neith after all… desperate to escape…"

"After being raped she may have panicked and done everything necessary to ensure her escape. And if the Pale Man had said he would kill anyone who released her… well, they were not going to let her go, that's obvious," Mut-Bity sighed.

"Or did he… maybe he… bit her and she changed…?"

Desperation showed in Merit's eyes.

Mut-Bity reached out and took her hand.

"I don't think that happened. Firstly, the change wouldn't be immediate. It can take months. And secondly – if he were to bite Meryt-Neith, she might lose her ability to carry children. And he wants children. That is why he raped her too, I am sure. And intended to keep on doing it until she was pregnant again. This isn't just my belief, the servants heard him say so to Meryt-Neith before he left."

"So my daughter is not an evil Nephilim, but may still be a murderer…" Merit said.

"If so, she was protecting not only herself, but also her child. I saw her with the baby. She loves him and would never give him to the Pale Man voluntarily. If there is a threat to her child, any mother turns into a lioness, ready to kill anyone who threatens her family."

Merit didn't answer. She stared at the wall with unseeing eyes. Her world had darkened and was closing in on her.

25

SUMMONING THE NEPHILIM

Daniel walked back and forth restlessly outside the cave, barely able to contain his anger. The three hunters who had escorted him there talked quietly to one other, watching him pace up and down.

One thought occupied Daniel's mind, which naturally turned towards action. Which way to go now?

The men came to some conclusion and the oldest one approached him. Again he used a stick to draw in the dust. This time he drew stick figures with wings. The man pointed at Daniel and then at the winged figures. He then turned his back on the drawn figures, looked back from over his shoulder and made a gesture of invitation. As if... asking the figures to follow. Then he pointed at Daniel, repeated the inviting gesture towards the drawing and again pointed at Daniel.

"Are you asking if you should... invite someone who is... like me to come here?" Daniel asked aloud though they could not understand him.

Then he pointed at his nose, inhaled deeply as if smelling something and pointed at the drawn figures. The hunters made denying gestures. They must be talking of his own kind of Nephilim.

"What the hell... it's not as if I had anything to lose..." Daniel said to himself.

He pointed at the drawn figures, made the inviting gesture and looked at the hunters. The oldest one nodded but did nothing more. One of the other men disappeared, only to return shortly thereafter, carrying dry sticks and dung to light a fire. Where they came from, Daniel had no idea. Perhaps they kept firewood and dung hidden in the desert...

They stayed near the cave the whole day. Daniel's impatience drove him almost to the point of leaving because nothing was happening. All he could do was pace inside the cave, staring at the place where Dana must have been.

The sun set and still there was no sign of movement, of action. Daniel's patience now ran out. He must have misunderstood the meaning of the men and the stick figures. Making the decision to leave on his own, he stepped out of the cave, and saw the men were making fires. Not one, but three, each at an even distance from the others so that they formed a triangle.

The oldest of the men took the horn he carried at his waist and from it, he carefully took out a glowing piece from last night's fire. With it, he lit the first fire. When the flames were well established, he took a burning stick from it and, sheltering the little flame with his hands, he walked to the second fire and lit that. And after that, the third one.

Each hunter remained standing beside his own fire, looking... upwards.

Daniel looked up to the darkening sky as well. Nothing happened, but the men did not stray from their fires. They only added some more sticks and dung to the flames.

And then he felt it: the familiar buzz in his spine that told him a Nephilim was approaching. He kept absolutely still, ready for anything.

A shadow appeared in the sky – a darker form surrounded by a glowing yellowish circle. It flew from the west, approaching quickly.

The Nephilim was a dark-skinned man with ochre-coloured wings. He landed outside the ring of light and said something in a deep, booming voice. The oldest of the hunters answered, pointing towards Daniel and the cave. After a few more words, the Nephilim stepped into the light of the fire.

Daniel's senses revealed two things at the same time. The scent. He could smell Dana's scent all around the man. And the eyes. They were yellow.

Daniel did not give time for the other Nephilim to react. His wings opened with a whip-like crack and he attacked.

The Nephilim was ready. His wings instantly formed a shield around him. He stumbled backwards as Daniel's wings slashed at his protective cocoon, but he did not fight back.

The three men started yelling and ran up to them. Daniel had to take a step back to avoid hurting the hunters.

The oldest of the hunters ran between the two Nephilim, though his eyes were wide with fright. He lifted his hands in the air in an effort to block Daniel's way. When Daniel hesitated, the hunter quickly tapped his nose and drew air in through his nostrils.

Daniel would not have survived for so many years if he could not control his emotions, but this was the biggest challenge he had ever faced. This was about Dana! But he forced back his anger and fear, shaking with the effort. The yellow-eyed man stood still, alert, his hands down, palms open, making no attempt to attack. His still posture and the white-haired hunter standing in front of him, arms spread protectively, told Daniel to retreat.

He did as the old hunter suggested and breathed in. There was no scent of rotting fruit. Only the fragrance of Dana and... a slight scent of cinnamon.

The yellow-eyed Nephilim slowly raised his hand and pointed at his eyes, lifting his eyebrows questioningly. Daniel stared at him. The eyes were yellow but brighter than those of the enemy Nephilim. Also they did not have that oily pulse he had seen too many times before.

Daniel understood he had almost made a fatal error. He stepped back, and to make his changed intentions even more clear, closed his wings. Placing his hand on his heart, he bowed. When he did that, the amulet he had hanging on his neck slipped out from underneath his shirt.

It was the sign of the Nephilim Council that he had been given in London. The one that every Nephilim obeyed.

The other Nephilim also closed his wings and then reached for the leather string around his neck – and drew out a similar amulet.

Another Nephilim in the ancient past – and he was the leader of a Nephilim council. One who had met Dana...

Daniel reached for the scarf he had tucked into the waist of his jeans. Dana's scarf. He put it against his face and inhaled. Then he extended it towards the Nephilim leader who took it from his hands. He smelled the scarf – and his lips spread in a wide smile. He pointed at the scarf and then Daniel, nodding eagerly.

Daniel's relief was such he had to sit down on the ground. He placed his head between his knees and breathed deeply so he wouldn't start to sob. It took a while for the constriction in his throat to disappear.

"Dana is safe?" he asked, not expecting an answer.

The man smiled and answered.

"Dana safe. With us. You go to Dana?"

Daniel's jaw dropped.

"You speak my language?"

"I speak little. Merit taught. Shuet taught."

"You took Dana to safety?"

"Dana safe. You go to Dana?"

"Yes..." his throat refused to let the sound out but his lips formed the words.

"Then come. We fly."

Daniel stumbled to his feet and opened his wings. Before getting up, he turned to the three hunters.

"I thank you with all my heart. If ever you need my help, send me word and I will come."

The yellow-eyed Nephilim listened, and then said a few words, no doubt translating what he had said. The hunters placed their hands on their hearts as Daniel had done and nodded their heads solemnly. Then they unceremoniously turned and sat down on the ground, taking dried meat out of their leather pouches.

Daniel and the yellow-eyed Nephilim rose into the air, heading west. In a matter of moments, they had disappeared from the gaze of the desert hunters.

26

THE LAND OF KEFTIU

Meryt-Neith gave birth to her second son in the palace of the king of the Keftiu. This time the birth was easier and took a much shorter time than with Ramose. The midwife smiled broadly when the baby began to cry in a loud voice as soon as she lifted him up.

"Healthy boy! You will be proud of him!" she said.

Meryt-Neith barely looked at the baby. She had made her decision as soon as she had paid the merchant with the perfume bottles. While the midwife cut the umbilical cord and cleaned the child, she looked away, thinking back to her arrival in Keftiu.

"It's important you don't tell anyone where you have taken me," she said to the captain. "There is... someone who would have me killed if they found me. For revenge. I embarrassed him by managing to escape."

"Who?" the captain had asked, eyeing the box of perfume still in Meryt-Neith's hands.

"He was someone who tried to take advantage of the absence of my husband. He tried to..."

Meryt-Neith paled and looked ill. Her pregnancy wasn't showing yet, and so the captain was easily convinced she had bad memories of a man who had tried to rape her.

"That is why I appeared at the harbour without much else but my son and a few valuables," Meryt-Neith said. "I had to escape for the safety of myself and my son. I was going to join my husband here later, when the little one was bigger and travelling with him would have been safer. But as it was..."

She looked so sad and so beautiful that the captain believed her. Those valuable perfumes, too – yes, he was inclined to help this lovely woman.

"Very well, I swear I shall not tell anyone about you."

"And your men?"

"I'll give orders that anyone who mentions you is to be thrown overboard."

"How can you be sure you've stopped them from talking?"

"That's easy. I'll tell them that if anyone should ever mention to me that they've heard about a beautiful noble lady on our ship I'll know right away that someone has disobeyed my orders – and I personally will throw them all overboard."

Meryt-Neith did not believe this, as the captain could never sail his ship alone, but she would have to trust that the men feared their captain enough to keep their mouths shut, at least for a few months. Then she would be gone.

Her situation was desperate. She knew no one. She had valuable jewellery with her, but could not waste any pieces on small things such as buying food. So she made a daring plan and decided to follow it through immediately.

"Show me someone here who speaks my language," she said to the merchant, "after that you shall have the perfumes."

"Gladly, my lady," the captain bowed.

"Now leave," Meryt-Neith said and the captain left the cabin.

Meryt-Neith took every piece of the stolen jewellery she had with her and put it on, avoiding Ramose's hands as best she could. The boy wanted to play with the shiny things and cried when his mother refused to give the trinkets to him.

There was a real golden chain with a pendant of glass. Bracelets, rings, ankle bracelets. A sash with turquoise beads sewn into it with gold wire. After having put on everything she had, she combed her hair and lifted it up into a big bundle atop her head. She used the ivory pins and combs the merchant's wife had been so proud of to make the hairdo of a married woman, managing to cover the spot where her hair had been torn off. Thankfully, it had begun to grow again – she wouldn't be left with a bald spot.

Then she took the sheerest cloth of the ones she had stolen and placed it elegantly on her head so it framed her beautiful face, which had finally healed. On her feet, she wore the fine leather sandals. She checked her reflection in the little bronze mirror that had been a source of envy to the women friends of the merchant's wife. Then she took a deep breath and straightened herself.

"Come, Ramose," she took the little boy's hand, "let's go ashore. We are going to see a king and queen."

When she stepped down from the ship, everyone turned to gape at her. The captain's eyes almost popped out of his head when he witnessed all her finery. For a fleeting moment, he thought himself silly for not having asked what had been in the bundle she was carrying. The perfume bottles were nothing compared to the riches the noblewoman was now wearing.

"Now, take me to someone who speaks my language and who also has access to the royal palace of Kunusa," Meryt-Neith ordered.

"The royal palace?" the merchant looked up towards the mountains.

He had not heard anyone call the old palace royal for a long time. In the past, a great volcano eruption of the circular island to the north had blown out a great pillar of dust and rock that rained down on the lands in and around the Great Green sea, leaving just a circlet of land like a crown where the island had once been. Later earthquakes had stripped the great island of its power, making its rebuilt palaces crumble into dust. But the great palace of Kunusa was still there, a remnant of its ancient power. Its inhabitants still ruled parts of the island. Maybe they could be called royal. The captain decided it was not his place to correct his beautiful passenger. If she called the palace royal, then by all means it could be just that.

Meryt-Neith turned to look, trying to see where the palace was.

"That's where your husband is?" the merchant asked

"Yes, he will be there."

Meryt-Neith hoped she sounded convincing.

"Yes... yes, of course..." the captain believed the noble lady when she said that her husband was someone of influence, if he was in the Kunusa palace. There was no way she could have carried riches like the ones she was wearing if her husband was not connected to the highest echelons of society. "I do hope you'll put in a good word for my trading services?"

"Indeed I will," Meryt-Neith nodded her head gravely. "You have saved me from a terrible fate. I won't forget, but in return you have to keep your promise that you won't let anyone know you brought me here. That... man may try to follow me otherwise. He is... obsessed with me. And he will not be kind towards anyone who has helped me escape. Also, I am afraid he may send someone to harm my husband so he could have me."

The captain saw nothing unusual in this. She was so exquisite he thought he had never seen a more beautiful woman. The only flaw in her looks was that she was too tall. No man liked their woman to stand taller than they were.

He indicated with a gesture that she was to follow him. They walked together among the merchants of the harbour of Amnisos until he saw a familiar face among them, whom he greeted.

"My lady here is expected at the Kunusa palace," he said to the trader, "and needs someone to escort her there. She may need someone to speak for her if no one there speaks her language. She comes from Kemet."

The merchant stepped up close to see Meryt-Neith – he was near-sighted. His expression changed to respect.

"My lady. You may travel with my cart up to the palace. My servant, who will accompany you there, speaks your language too. Honoured to be of assistance."

"You shall be rewarded," Meryt-Neith said, deciding to give one of her cheapest rings to the man if she arrived safely at the court.

The prospect of being paid by the wealthy lady made the merchant move fast. While he ordered his servant to fetch his donkey cart, Meryt-Neith handed the perfume box to the captain. She had taken one bottle for herself, but there were still five to give.

The captain bowed low, already planning where he might sell the perfumes. Maybe somewhere here in Keftiu. Glass bottles were rare and worth a fortune, as were perfumes.

In a matter of moments, Meryt-Neith and little Ramose were sitting on two coarse pillows in the merchant's donkey cart, heading for the hills behind the Amnisos harbour.

The sound of the cicadas in the trees was deafening and Meryt-Neith's acute sense of hearing made the noise painful to her. Little Ramose turned around, trying to see where the odd noise was coming from. The trees themselves were a great wonder to the small boy, who had never been in a forest before.

The trees growing in the dusty ground along the road leading to the palace gave welcome shade in the heat of the day. The servant leading the donkey did not speak to her once. He was a thin little man who seemed almost scared at the responsibility of getting the noble lady and her son to the royal palace. Meryt-Neith saw him as no threat. After a while she dozed off, still sitting.

Then – a familiar sensation, a buzzing in her spine. For two heartbeats, Meryt-Neith remained immobile. Then she pulled sleepy Ramose next to her and placed her hand on the dagger she had been carrying throughout the journey. The boy leaned against her side. Meryt-Neith pulled the cloth over her head so that she could see through it but her features were still hidden. There was no point in trying to escape. If she could sense the Nephilim, they could also sense her presence.

A tall figure was walking among the trees, coming towards them from the direction of the palace. Meryt-Neith's fingers squeezed the handle of the dagger more tightly.

Then the figure moved out onto the dirt road and Meryt-Neith breathed out. A woman. So it was not *him*. She breathed in deeply, now searching for the telltale scent. But there was no sweet, sickly smell about the woman. Instead she caught a familiar spicy scent – much like her own and that of her mother and Shuet.

The woman carried a jar on her head and walked with a balanced step. She did not look at the servant, but when she passed the cart, her blue-grey eyes turned to Meryt-Neith and she smiled. A friendly smile, to acknowledge one of her own kind. Still, she was not about to draw attention to herself, that was clear.

Meryt-Neith turned her head and looked back, following the form of the woman as long as she was visible. Just before she turned around a bend in the path, behind the trees, the woman turned to look back and raised her hand slightly.

Meryt-Neith had had no idea there were Nephilim in Keftiu. She decided to change her plan accordingly.

27

TOGETHER AGAIN

I had the most wonderful dream. I was in the underground town, sleeping in the niche, utterly exhausted, when a warm hand touched my face. Gentle fingers drew back my hair and someone kissed me lightly on the cheek.

It was such a wonderful dream that I smiled. Then I felt lips touching mine. How real that felt…

And then I understood it was not a dream. I jerked upright so fast I hit my head on a low bit of the stone ceiling above my bed.

"Ouch!"

I opened my eyes and Daniel's blue eyes looked back into mine.

Time stopped. It took my brain a couple of seconds to catch up with what I was seeing. But then the love shining from his bright blue eyes convinced me I had not lost my mind.

"Daniel…" I whispered, unable to move.

He only smiled, took my face between his beautiful, warm hands and placed another trembling kiss on my lips.

"Daniel!" Now my voice obeyed me and I almost screamed his name.

I didn't even have time to put my feet on the floor – his hands were around me and he lifted me up from the bed as if I weighed nothing. We must have kissed and cried for several minutes, me in mid-air with my feet dangling.

"How did you find me?" I asked. "How did you get to the past? Was it Lilith? Did you see Diana? How is everyone else? Is Elijah here? Does Elijah know he has two daughters? Does he know Merit has been here? She must have taught them English!"

"Slow down, slow down..." Daniel smiled so that the dimple that used to turn my knees to putty in the past... no, the future... became visible.

He lowered me so my feet touched the floor again. I saw the same yellow-eyed Nephilim who had brought me here. He was leaning on the wall across from the room I was in, his hands folded across his front, smiling broadly.

Daniel looked at him.

"Thank you," he said, "I'm in your debt."

"You lovers," the man chuckled. "Happiness."

I stared at him open-mouthed. I had no idea he spoke English. I should have added my words of thanks, but I was in such emotional turmoil I turned my attention back to Daniel, afraid he would disappear if I glanced away from him for so much as a second. From the corner of my eye, I saw our helper walk away.

How can I describe my feelings? I had had no idea Daniel had managed to get back to the past. All that time I had been Ambrogio's prisoner I'd been afraid I would die without seeing Daniel ever again. When we flew over the desert to reach this strange underground village, all I could think of were the thousands of years separating us. And now he was here – flesh and blood, real.

I had to touch him again just to make sure he was really real. His cheek, his hair, his lips...

"Oh, Dana..." he could not keep his hands still either and his arms wrapped around me again.

I pressed myself tightly against him, breathing in his scent, sensing his warmth, wanting to melt into him. I could not speak for a long while, I thought I would die of happiness. He pressed his face into my hair, breathing in, moving his hands only to squeeze me even tighter.

His love enclosed me in a world where no one else existed but the two of us.

Finally, I had to move.

"I'll get bruises soon," I half– laughed, half– cried, pulling backwards a step.

Reluctantly, he let go. We sat on the bed I had been sleeping on.

"How did you get into the past?" I asked. "I thought you were stuck in the future."

"Lilith was the only weaver strong enough to even try to reach for this time and distance. She needed an anchor. So we stole one. And we had to do it in such a way that neither Cain nor Angel could track us down."

"Stole an anchor? What anchor? You must have had something from the right time period?"

"It was the head of Tiye from Berlin. Remember? The tiny stern-looking queen?"

"Wow. Yes, I remember her. The statue. And the living queen too. We were travelling on her ship when Ambrogio kidnapped me."

"You have met Tiye?" Daniel looked surprised.

"Yes, she is on her way to Amarna now as were we. Maybe she has already arrived. Probably has… everyone else in our team is on her ship, except Diana. Ambrogio almost killed her! He kidnapped her, took her from the ship and then he used some strange singing device to hypnotise me, to bring me to Diana and get me under his control… I think that's what it did… I couldn't resist the music."

"What device? What music?"

Daniel may have been in emotional state, but he was as sharp as ever.

"It was some kind of silvery… thing. He had it wrapped around his neck so that the device touched his throat and when he sang it was as if he was drawing my soul to him. I really can't explain it better than that. It was as if I had no will of my own. And Daniel… it was Ambrogio who killed all the silver Nephilim, long ago, in the ancient past. Or rather, the future from where we are now…I think this device has something to do with it. It seems the silver Nephilim can't resist its sound, its voice..."

"Is he *that* old?" Daniel looked genuinely surprised.

"Well they call him the First Vampire... and didn't someone say that the first human vampires appeared about 400 BC in Turkey? Which is about the same time when the silver Nephilim were killed... am I remembering correctly now?"

Daniel nodded, pushing my hair behind my ear, thinking.

"Yes, you remember right... so he has been a vampire ever since then... He is over two thousand and four hundred years old. That's even older than many of the enemy Nephilim. The blood of the Nephilim who created him must been very strong to pass on that degree of longevity – probably something to do with his own genes as well. There are very few stories of him feeding on humans – it's as if he doesn't really need human blood. Some people seem to be natural-born vampires, who keep their strength even when not able to feed for a while - and some can barely stay alive as vampires without feeding constantly. But if he came into possession of this device that no silver Nephilim can resist, I wonder why Cain let him keep it. Or no – they didn't realise that there still was a silver Nephilim alive. That must be it. So if that thing was created to call them, they didn't need it any more. They hadn't heard of you way back then, of course. They may even have forgotten about the device by now."

"Where is Diana?" I interrupted him.

"I left her with Lilith and Elijah. They must have taken her out of Sithathoriunet's tomb ages ago by now. They stayed there to wait for Ambrogio's shadow to reappear so he would lead them to you. And I left to follow your traces as soon as I arrived."

He then told me all about his search for me. And I in turn told him everything that had happened to me.

"So it was Kitty we have to thank for your escape..." Daniel said.

"Yes, if she had not told me about overhearing Ambrogio and the shadow-man talking about not having Diana anymore, I would have waited for them to return. And I might be dead as a result."

"He actually made you drink his blood?" Daniel asked, worried.

"Yes, and it only made me fall asleep."

"Yes, quite… he did not inject it into your veins. Vampire blood numbs the skin if applied externally, and makes you sleep if ingested… if it gets into your circulation at the same time as you drink it, you turn into a vampire. But he didn't do that to you. He probably knew your blood would heal itself even if he tried. But why did he kidnap you? Why did he want to taste your blood? What's his plan? I don't get it."

"I don't know. I only know he wants my blood. For some purpose he alone knows."

A memory surfaced.

"Wait – he did say something strange after tasting my blood from the cup… mine and Diana's, to be precise. He said something like *yes, I can hear you."*

"Hear whom?" Daniel asked.

"I have no idea… maybe he meant he could read my memories. From my blood."

"Yes, that could be it… they can read the life of their victim in the blood they drink, if they drink enough of it. But he only tasted a drop of yours."

"But he almost drank Diana dry… so he got access to her memories. That means he knows where we are headed. Where we need to go…"

"And that means he doesn't need to follow us. He can just go straight to the destination and wait for us in Amarna," Daniel said.

"So there's no point in hiding anymore, then."

"I still don't think it wise to show ourselves to him unless we can't avoid it. It is best we get going as soon as possible, and find the others. If Elijah and Lilith have managed to get to them with Diana, they'll probably have drawn the same conclusions as we have. But if not, we need to let them know."

"We have to leave as soon as possible…" I said.

"Yes, but I can see you are not well. You need to rest."

"No time for that. We must go!"

I got up. My limbs felt like lead.

"You look like something out of the London Dungeon," Daniel commented, not very flatteringly. "You'll need a few hours of rest at least."

"A few hours... When Ambrogio is after our team? No..."

Daniel reached for my arm when I tried to get out of the room, pulling me back to the bed.

"Our team is well prepared to meet Ambrogio, if he approaches them. What do you think Time Walkers have been doing all these years? They can't be taken by surprise, not anymore. They know Ambrogio is here, they know he has this shadow with him. And they have Elijah now. If Ambrogio or the shadow try to get through the buffer zone, Elijah will be onto them right away. It won't make any difference if you get some much-needed rest for a few hours. I would leave you here for weeks to recover, if I didn't have the feeling you'd escape the minute I turned my back. So humour me – a few hours of sleep. Then we can go, I promise."

To be honest, I did not need much persuading. The emotional turmoil of seeing Daniel again had made me even more tired.

"Ok. But once I wake up, we're going."

"Yes, of course..."

Daniel pulled me closer and kissed me tenderly.

"And this time nothing will separate us again."

He pulled the blanket over me and sat by my bedside until I fell asleep again, his hand holding mine.

28

NEPHILIM COUNCIL

Daniel sat for a long while, watching Dana sleep. Relief flooded through him and he felt no desire to move. She was alive. They were together. That was all that mattered right now. For the first time in weeks, he could relax again.

But he couldn't forget his duty towards all the Time Walkers – both the living members of the team and those who had died. They were fighting an unseen war that ordinary people didn't know about. If Cain had his way and found the ancient knowledge of the Watchers, the forefathers of the Nephilim, unimaginable things would happen...

No one knew what that knowledge was, but Cain seemed to believe it would give him dominion over everything, his belief being based on an old Nephilim prophecy.

This prophecy was the reason he had carefully bred his line across the centuries – he wanted to create the perfect Nephilim Time Weaver so he could reach back to ancient times and find the Watchers. Why he should think he needed to reach so far back into antiquity was a mystery known only to himself. But he had succeeded – Dana was the living proof of his success, the only Nephilim who could travel back through time. A Time Walker and a Weaver: Cain's granddaughter by his son, who escaped his dangerous father and met Dana's mother during the Blitz in London.

Daniel leaned back, thinking hard. They would have to get to Amarna soon, to find the first clue that would lead them to the path towards the knowledge of the Watchers. If Ambrogio knew where they were going, it followed that he would head there too – and if he knew they were searching for the two dwarfs in the retinue of Mutnofret, Nefertiti's sister... he'd try to get there first and take the clue. And he'd have no intention of letting the dwarfs live. The knowledge they had was too valuable to be shared – owning it would give Ambrogio power even over Cain.

But had Ambrogio been able to read Diana's memories from her blood clearly enough to be able to see the dwarfs? Daniel moved restlessly at this new thought. After all, the team had not met the dwarfs, only seen a picture of a wall relief where they were depicted standing next to the royal couple and their retinue.

Also, there were those strange names. *His Mother is Re* and *King's Wives Live Forever.* Diana had read books about Egyptology continuously after arriving at the Centre from her previous existence in the 19th century, which meant her mind was full of little details, images and knowledge of ancient Egypt. That was the danger; but with luck Ambrogio hadn't been able to isolate the key pieces of information he needed from Diana's memories. Diana must have fought him, and active resistance would have muddled the vampire's ability to read the memories and detect what he needed.

A discreet cough came from the doorway. The yellow-eyed Nephilim leader was standing there. Daniel made up his mind. With one last glance at Dana, now sleeping peacefully, he stood up, took the amulet into his right hand, placed his left hand on his heart and bowed three times. The ancient signal that meant that one Nephilim council leader had official matters to discuss with another council.

His guide took his amulet and repeated the same movements.

"Follow," he said, turning to walk away.

They entered a round chamber, with stone-carved benches that could seat a dozen or so. A single oil lamp gave some light to the chamber, but that was all Nephilim eyes needed.

"Wait," the council leader said, gesturing for him to sit on a stony seat in the middle of the round room.

Daniel didn't have to wait long. One after another, the Nephilim arrived, looking at him with open curiosity. Six men, six women. The council leader took his place opposite Daniel and spoke to the others in their own language first. Then he pointed at Daniel.

"You... Name?"

"Daniel."

"Daniel," everyone greeted him with his name, one after the other, placing their hand over on their hearts as they spoke.

"You want help?" the council leader asked.

It was clear he had not been using English much because the words came slowly.

"Yes. We need to get to Amarna... I am sorry, I mean Akhetaten. As soon as possible."

It seemed Daniel managed to pronounce Akhetaten correctly, as no one seemed to have trouble understanding the word.

"You need us?"

"Yes. Our enemy is strong. He is a..." Daniel searched for a word for vampire. They would not know that term. "He is blood-drinker. Not Nephilim."

"Nephilim servant?" council leader said.

"Yes."

"They drink blood," he nodded and then talked to the council in their own language.

More nods and quiet discussion.

"This one drinks human blood. And he creates blood-drinkers himself by doing so."

The brow of the council leader furrowed.

"He makes children like him." Daniel tried to think of a different way to explain it.

"He... has children? Nephilim servant drinks *people*?"

"Yes. And in doing so. he makes them like him."

"He makes blood-drinkers?" the man's eyes rounded with surprise. "Nephilim servants... not do so... Nephilim only do so."

"*He* does. And this is why our friends in Akhetaten are in danger."

Daniel hoped the man understood. Now the council members talked passionately with each other, but not for long

"We help," the council leader then said. "We take you."

"I thank you," Daniel bowed to each of the council members in turn and they acknowledged him in kind.

"I need to know one more thing..." he said, "if I may...?"

They looked at him curiously.

"Merit..." Daniel said, and they clearly knew her name. "Is she here?"

"No, she go."

"When?"

"Before you come. Soon."

Soon... he must mean that she had left shortly before Daniel and Dana arrived.

"She was here just before we came?" Daniel asked.

"She. Yes. Go soon before."

"Can you tell me where we can find her?"

"She go to... Mi-Wer."

"Mi-Wer?" Daniel thought for a while.

Gurob. It was the palace of queen Tiye. The... the very place where Dana and the team had left for their journey on Tiye's ship. Sounded like they had just missed each other. Daniel almost groaned aloud.

And Merit had found information about the knowledge of the Watchers. Her notebook that had somehow managed to travel through time to the library in the City of Immortals had revealed it.

It was nothing short of a miracle that the head librarian of the City of Immortals, Mr. Donnelly, had found her notebook hidden behind books there and had it in his pocket when Daniel and Elijah kidnapped him for the very purpose of asking him if he knew where it might be.

And the clue that had led the brothers to the library of the City of Immortals in search of information about Merit had been waiting for

Elijah in the Turku Cathedral in Finland. He had gone there to say his goodbyes to his wife who had vanished on their honeymoon in Egypt. No one else could have known of their agreement to say their final goodbyes on their wedding day in the cathedral, on that very spot, should the other one die. Only Merit.

A note, Merit's wedding ring, and an ancient mirror with Queen Tiye's face had been waiting for Elijah there. They must have been sent by Merit, to let Elijah know where she'd gone after she had vanished. And now – she was here. Alive. And she knew of the secret Cain was so desperately trying to find. If they found her, there would be no need to search for the clue in Akhetaten. What was that clue? Who had written it? Merit?

"I need to reach her," Daniel said.

"You... family?"

"Yes, I am the brother of her husband. I need to tell her that her husband is here!"

That created a bit of a turmoil among the Nephilim after they heard the translation.

"Merit husband back? Come back?"

"Yes, the father of her children."

"Shuet? Meryt-Neith?"

"If those are their names, then yes. We need to go to Akhetaten first to take my people to safety. But could you send a message to her in Mi-Wer that Elijah is here? Is that possible?"

"Tell... Elijah? Husband?"

"Yes, Elijah, her husband."

"We take you to Akhetaten and tell Merit," the council leader said.

"Thank you!"

Others would have told Elijah about Merit already, that she was alive. But they had no idea where she was! She might have arrived in Mi-Wer right after the team had left it.

"We need to get to Akhetaten soon," Daniel said. "We should use the buffer zone... the misty way. To travel fast."

"Not good." The council leader's jaw tightened. "The dark ones search us. Too near. If many go to misty world, they hear. We hide here. Other way. So, they not see."

"The dark ones don't know where you are? Where this place is?"

"No. We hide. Secret place. Long time we hide."

The enemy Nephilim did not know the location of this place? Daniel would have to respect their choice not to travel as a group in the buffer zone. He had seen adults and children here – he knew all too well what would happen if the other Nephilim found them.

"I thank you. And – we need to go as soon as we have rested," Daniel said.

"We go, yes."

The council leader rose. The meeting was over.

29

HIS MOTHER IS RE, KING'S WIVES LIVE FOREVER

Nefertiti was proud of her first pregnancy and she let the world know it. So soon after the wedding – what queen would not be gratified to show she was carrying the king's child right away? – she walked around wearing an almost see-through dress that revealed her rounded form. Her hands were constantly on her belly, pressing the fabric so that no one was left in doubt that the new child was growing inside her.

"I am worried about her ability to give birth," Merit said to Mut-Bity in the garden. "She is so tiny!"

It seemed Mut-Bity did not want to leave her newly acquired bees which had only arrived that morning. She walked around the beehives humming to the little creatures and they hummed back in answer. It was as if they were having a conversation, getting to know each other.

Mut-Bity then took out the linen plugs that had kept the bees inside their hives during the journey to the king's gardens, so that the air could flow through.

The bees flew out of the hives and immediately surrounded the women. Merit did not feel threatened by them. These special bees had been bred to protect the Nephilim - the unspoiled kind. So the insects went around her as if to make her acquaintance and then spread out into the garden like little warriors. Merit didn't know how they differentiated between the unspoiled and dangerous Nephilim, but suspected it probably had to do with scent. They could probably distinguish between the slight cinnamon scent of Merit's kind and the sweet rotting fruit smell of the evil ones.

"You have told me Nefertiti will have many daughters, and this is only her first pregnancy," Mut-Bity said. "Don't let her small size fool you. Look at Tiye. She is related to Nefertiti and they are both small. Yet Tiye has given birth many times and is flourishing."

"Yes, I know she will survive the births... but I feel giving birth that young will be difficult and there's a risk for the baby that she might have avoided if she'd become pregnant later."

"But this child will survive?" Mut-Bity looked around with her hands on her hips, doing a final check on the location of the clay hives.

"I don't know. I'll only know when I hear the name of the child whether she is going to survive or not."

"You know it will be a daughter, then?"

"Yes."

Merit did not say anything more.

Mut-Bity observed the bees, and seemed happy with what she saw.

"Well, there's nothing anyone can do now. She will carry the child and give birth and gods will decide if the child will live," she said.

Merit couldn't add anything to this and they returned to their little house, which they'd moved back into after Mut-Bity had returned with the bees.

Tiye had certainly been delighted when she heard the news of the pregnancy.

"It shows the gods are pleased with my choice of First Wife to Prince Amenhotep. Khnum was ready to create the soul on his potter's wheel the moment Prince Amenhotep took her to bed," she said to Mut-Bity as they sat together in her suite of rooms drinking beer during the hottest time of the day. Merit was sitting nearby.

Tiye's straw was made of metal and she used it with skill to get below the thick surface of the beer. Her beer was sweetened with honey. She loved honeyed treats, as did the king. Maybe that was one of the reasons Mut-Bity was so special to her. The bees – and something that had happened in Tiye's childhood.

"Indeed, Great Royal Wife," Mut-Bity answered.

"I have decided to invite Nefertiti's sister Mutnofret to join us as well," Tiye continued.

"As another wife for the prince?" Mut-Bity asked.

"No, that is not my plan. She may marry someone else who is of use to us," Tiye drank deeply. "She should be of marrying age soon, she is already ten. All the better to bring her in and teach her obedience before she gets ideas of her own. You know what young girls are like – ready to fall in love with any young man, not understanding what's best for them."

And so Mutnofret arrived at court. Nefertiti could not hide how pleased she was to see her sister again, even though she tried to behave with dignity, in accordance with her new position.

Mutnofret was not as beautiful as Nefertiti. Her face was rounder. She had pleasing eyes and beautifully arched eyebrows, and her lips were thinner than her sister's. She was pretty, but would not be a mesmerising beauty like Nefertiti.

"Nefertiti seems to be pleased to see her sister," Merit said to Mut-Bity.

"She would be... she needs someone to talk to who knows her well. Also – Mutnofret is not a threat to her."

"Threat?"

"Surely you have noticed that Nefertiti chooses her maidens from the plain-looking ones? That's typical of beautiful women – they are very aware of their looks and always afraid someone is more beautiful and could steal their husband's attention from them."

"Ah, quite..." Merit smiled. "At the moment the young husband seems to be completely besotted by her, so I wouldn't worry, with her pregnant and all. And Mutnofret certainly poses no threat. She is too young for a start. Though she might become more beautiful once the roundness of childhood goes away."

"Soon the pregnancy will make Nefertiti feel uncomfortable and she won't be as eager to accept the prince's advances. Then the prince will turn to other wives, of course. It's only natural. She is worried about that," Mut-Bity said.

"But that's the way things are. A prince has many wives and will father many children. He likes some wives more than others, but only one will be his Great Royal Wife," Merit replied.

"Yes, and Nefertiti has secured that title. Still, she is very young and uncertain of her position, no matter how confident she looks or how proudly she behaves."

The women had now moved up onto the rooftop, where they were enjoying the breeze.

"Any message from Shuet?" Merit asked quietly. "They are still safe?"

"You don't feel him around?" Mut-Bity whispered.

"No," Merit answered.

Ever since the Pale Man had threatened Merit, they had spoken of Shuet and Meryt-Neith quietly, and only when Merit had been certain he was nowhere near. Hearing about Meryt-Neith's fate had made them even more careful not to be overheard.

"The young family is safe. Their son is healthy. I received word today when the bees arrived," Mut-Bity whispered.

"I miss them. I wish I could visit them," Merit sighed. "Not to not be able to see your own daughter and grandchild! And not knowing whether your other daughter and her son are even alive anymore..."

Merit closed her eyes. The feeling of longing and fear made her whole being ache.

"You will see Shuet, when it is safe to do so," Mut-Bity said.

Neither commented on when that might be.

"And Meryt-Neith? No news? Nothing at all?"

"Nothing," Mut-Bity stared sadly over the rooftops towards the western desert.

They heard someone's steps on the stairs leading to the rooftop and turned to look.

It was not one but two figures who emerged from under the rooftop canopies. Two short figures.

"Iahmesu, Seshat, come, join us!" Merit managed a smile.

The dwarf couple usually lightened her burden. They seemed to be able to read the mood of other people and encourage them to see the good in any given situation. They excelled at making people laugh.

"Here, wife, come and sit on the pillow. Not that you would need one, with your beautiful bottom..." Iahmesu slapped Seshat on her behind with an affectionate gesture.

Seshat smiled over her shoulder and sat down next to the women.

"We have been busy entertaining the young First Wife," Iahmesu smiled. "She does love to see us dance. Tiye had to tell her we can't go on for hours without stopping."

"And a good thing she did," Seshat smiled. "My legs are not long, but I felt them getting even shorter by the moment from all that dancing."

"Mutnofret was there too?" Mut-Bity asked.

"Of course. She had never seen dwarfs in her life and was clapping her hands and singing along. She liked us so much Nefertiti said she could have us if we made her that happy."

Iahmesu laughed his deep bellowing laughter. It was a surprising sound, coming from such a short figure.

"Really? Did she believe her?" Merit smiled, letting his laughter shake off the shadow of worry about her daughters.

"Oh, she believed her all right! She jumped to her feet and ran to hug her big sister and thanked her profusely. You should have seen Nefertiti's face when she understood she had given us away."

"But you were not hers to give," Mut-Bity said. "I think Tiye considers you hers."

"The Great Royal Wife gave us to Nefertiti when she heard of the pregnancy. She was certain we knew spells and dances that would protect the pregnant young wife and the unborn child. She said we were Bes and Beset to Nefertiti."

Bes, the ugly dwarf god who scared demons away by showing his tongue to them.. who protected the household and pregnant women and children. And his wife Beset, who had the same role.

"And you know what Mutnofret said?" Seshat giggled and

answered her own question. "She said she would give us funny names because we were so funny. So that every time she said them aloud she would laugh."

"And did she do that?" Mut-Bity asked.

Now both dwarfs were laughing.

"Oh yes, she did. I was renamed *His Mother is Re*," Iahmesu said, "And Seshat became *King's Wives Live Forever*".

Mut-Bity smiled and shook her head.

"No sense in those names at all... Re is male so he is not a mother."

"Maybe Seshat's name makes more sense – if as Beset she makes sure the king's wives won't die in childbirth," Merit said.

"And is everyone now calling you by your new names?" Mut-Bity said.

"Gods, no. Tiye, who was there, laughed and said that we will remain Iahmesu and Seshat as no one will ever learn to remember such strange names that make no sense."

"Mutnofret pouted for a while, but then she said that a time will come when everyone will know us by our new names. At that point Nefertiti, slightly sour at having given away two valuable dwarfs, decided she was feeling nauseous and everyone's attention turned to her," Seshat said, "which is when we left. Before she decided watching us dance again would make her feel better."

"And now we are so thirsty from all the dancing and re-naming, that we wouldn't mind a jug of beer." Iahmesu patted his stomach.

Mut-Bity clapped her hands and a servant girl appeared.

"Bring beer and food for us all. And some more pillows so everyone can be comfortable here."

The servant girl did as asked and they spent the rest of the hottest part of the day on the rooftop, enjoying what little breeze the north decided to send their way.

30

MERITAMUN

Merit was right – Nefertiti's labour was long and painful. Her narrow hips meant the baby was struggling to get out and everyone was worried both mother and child would die. When the labour had been going on for two days, Tiye sent for Mut-Bity.

"You have knowledge of childbirth. Help Nefertiti!" she ordered, but her voice betrayed her fear.

Mut-Bity had been expecting this and already had her potions and oils ready.

"Come with me," she said to Merit, "I may need your help. The girl trusts you."

Nefertiti's rooms were crammed with people. Servants, her maidens and even a priest of Amun who was burning incense and reciting spells. The women cast sour looks his way when he tried to peer into the room from which Nefertiti's wails were coming. Mutnofret stood in the corner behind the priest, looking terrified. It was obvious she had not witnessed childbirth before.

"He has no role here," Mut-Bity said aloud, pointing at the priest. "Leave us!"

"I am here to bring the protection of Amun to the new child," the priest replied, looking down his nose at Mut-Bity. "The First Priest of the God sent me and I will stay to do his bidding!"

Mut-Bity did not like wearing any jewellery, was barefoot and her skin was baked dark by the desert sun. In the priest's eyes, Mut-Bity no doubt looked like a mere servant woman who should hold her tongue in the presence of a servant of Amun.

"If she says you are to leave, you are to leave. Now. And don't come back. This baby does not belong to Amun."

Tiye's voice from the doorway to Nefertiti's rooms made it clear she would accept no objection.

The priest, trying to keep his dignity, left the room, but slowly, and throughout his exit he chanted his spells. When he reached the doorway, he bowed deeply to Tiye, but he was stony-faced.

Tiye was fuming, but as soon as the priest had gone, she turned to Mut-Bity.

"Most likely he was here reciting spells so that Nefertiti would die, enabling the First Priest to offer his daughter to the Prince again. Now, you must help Nefertiti to deliver this baby," she said.

"Very well. But I want everyone else out of here, only two strong women can stay," Mut-Bity moved to the doorway of Nefertiti's room.

"You heard her. Everyone get out, now. You, and you, stay."

Tiye pointed at two strong-looking female servants. They stepped inside the chamber where Nefertiti was struggling with the birth of her first child. She had not wanted to give birth on the rooftop where the air was cooling, nor in a birth house erected in the garden. The windows high up near the ceiling let in some air, but the room was hot and smelled of sweat and fear.

Nefertiti was lying on her side on a bed. Her hair was braided – she had never wanted to shave herself bald, just as Tiye had chosen to keep her heavy locks of hair despite the lice. Her servants combed her hair daily in an effort to control them.

"Now, you need to get up and come over to the birthing bricks," Mut-Bity said matter-of-factly.

Nefertiti looked at her with her eyes glazed with pain.

"I can't move. I will die!"

"Nonsense, young woman. You are giving birth. This is what it is like. Your hips are narrow and this is your first child, so it will take some time. But I will help you. Unless you come to the bricks, the pain will not get better."

Nefertiti was silent for a while, concentrating, and then a thin cry escaped from her lips, the sound of a woman who had suffered pain for so long she no longer had the strength to scream.

"Now, this way. This is how we do it. First, you will drink this. Merit, give her a cup."

Mut-Bity poured a herbal drink from the jug she had carried with her. Merit held the cup for her until it was full to the brim. Then she carried it to Nefertiti. The girl grabbed the cup and tasted the drink. She cringed.

"Bad!"

"It's not supposed to entertain your palate," Tiye said, "it is to speed up the delivery. You need to push the baby out or it will not survive. The labour has already lasted far too long."

Tears were streaming down Nefertiti's cheeks, and her hands shook, but she drank the potion in long, determined gulps. Merit took the cup from her and wiped the sweaty strands of hair from her face. Nefertiti's jaw muscles moved as she gritted her teeth and then sat up slowly, pushing her weight up with her hands.

"She has great courage despite the pain," Mut-Bity said approvingly.

"One of the reasons I chose her," Tiye said, "the future king's wife has to be strong."

"Now, help your mistress over to the bricks."

Mut-Bity gestured to the servants. They crossed over to Nefertiti and helped her stand up.

She looked pitiful with her huge belly, thin childlike arms and legs, her hair glued to her back. Pregnancy had rounded her breasts, but they were still small compared to the enormous belly. Merit felt a surge of sympathy and a thought came to her.

"What will be the name of the child?" she asked.

"If the baby survives and is a boy, he will be Thutmose. If a girl, she will be Meritamun," Tiye said.

Meritamun. Beloved of Amun. Illogical, considering how much Tiye disliked the priesthood of Amun. But a traditional name as such. And a good name to help Merit identify her, confirming what she knew of the history of the royal family. Meritamun's name would be changed to Meritaten soon. Beloved of the Aten. And she would be the eldest daughter of Akhenaten and Nefertiti, one that would survive. No one knew of any male children being born to Nefertiti and Akhenaten.

It wasn't customary in ancient Egyptian art to show the royal heir as a child, though. All of Akhenaten's six daughters would be shown, but a son… never; unless the baby carried by a servant in a scene in a royal tomb in Amarna was Tutankhaten. And who was his mother? Another wife of the king? Or his full sister? Merit had read the DNA research about Tutankhamun's heritage before falling into the past and it had seemed to indicate Akhenaten had taken his own full sister as his wife and she had given birth to Tutankhaten. But which sister?

"What do you see?" Tiye asked. "You have that look on your face that tells me you are seeing what will be."

"The baby will be a girl, and her name will be Meritamun," said Merit.

"You are sure? This is what you can see?" Tiye asked.

"I have seen this," Merit said, hoping that Nefertiti was not about to give birth to a dead baby girl and then reuse the name when a living girl was born at some point in the future. But she knew that King Amenhotep would soon die – in less than three years – and that Meritaten would already be born by that time. Was it possible this could be a baby boy that would die, though? But no. Merit put her trust in her memory and instincts.

Nefertiti looked at her with hope in her eyes.

"She will be born alive? And I will live too?"

"Yes. You will live and give more children to your husband. I have seen this," Merit said.

Hearing her words seemed to give Nefertiti strength. She stepped onto the birthing bricks. Now Merit was watching the same scene she had gone through herself. Mut-Bity took some oil from a tiny jar she was carrying, spread it on her hands and then between Nefertiti's legs.

"This is to soften your skin so it won't tear..." she explained.

She then walked behind her and reached for the big stomach from behind, placing her hands on top of it, palms down.

"You – keep her up," she said to the servants.

They moved either side of the girl and slid their hands under her armpits. When they had taken a good grip, Mut-Bity breathed in deeply and started pushing down.

Nefertiti's screams were so piercing that Merit almost felt her pain in her own body.

"Push!" Mut-Bity said in Nefertiti's ear. "Help the baby out with me!"

And Nefertiti pushed, together with Mut-Bity. Screamed and pushed. Everyone was sweating, even Tiye. They knew the young mother would have the strength for just this one try. She was exhausted.

And then, suddenly, her hips opened and the crown of the baby's head appeared.

"Merit!" Mut-Bity ordered.

Merit dropped to her knees to take hold of the baby's head. Another push and suddenly the child slipped out of the womb and into Merit's hands in a gush of fluids.

"A baby girl," Merit said.

"Is she alive?" Nefertiti said faintly.

Mut-Bity let go of her and bent down to see the baby. She wasn't moving.

"Quickly, knife," she said.

Tiye saw the obsidian knife on a table and passed it to Mut-Bity, who tied and cut the umbilical cord with experienced movements and lifted the baby up by the legs. One pat on the back – and a thin cry relieved the crackling tension in the room.

"Alive she is. Little Meritamun."

Neferiti stood there, shaking. The servants led her back to her bed where she lay down, eyes closed, breathing heavily. Then her eyes opened.

"Show her to me..." she said.

Mut-Bity had already wiped the baby clean and wrapped her in a soft cloth. She carried her to the new mother. Like every mother, Nefertiti lifted away the cloth to see all of her baby.

"She is perfect," Mut-Bity said. "A beautiful daughter you will be proud of."

And proud she certainly was, taking pleasure in her role from the start. She did not breastfeed her child so as not to ruin her figure. Because of the valuable oils her servants had applied to her skin all throughout the pregnancy, she had managed to avoid pregnancy scars and was soon even more beautiful than before the birth. The roundness of motherhood suited her well and her young husband seemed pleased with the change.

"He has started taking her to bed again," Mut-Bity commented, when three months had passed from the birth.

"I hope she doesn't get pregnant immediately," Merit said. "Her body needs to rest."

"I have helped her there. Discreetly. Even the Great Royal Wife doesn't know," Mut-Bity smiled. "I gave her pomegranate grain powder mixed with beeswax. Also, crocodile dung, mixed with honey and dates – she is to soak this into a cloth and linen. Either way – when placed inside her when her husband comes to visit, she is unlikely to conceive. Of course, this is between the two of us. Tiye might not understand, but having seen how difficult the birth was, I agree with you – it's best to let her body rest for a few months at least."

They were on the rooftop at the end of the day again. Absentmindedly, they looked towards the lake that had been dug between Per-Hai and the River. A vessel that looked like a fishing boat was approaching. Merit followed its movement, letting the breeze lift her hair. It seemed there was a woman with equally long hair on the boat. A woman with... long blonde hair? A woman holding the hand of a young child who stood beside her!

She was on her feet in an instant, bending forward as if that would help her see better.

"What is it?" Mut-Bity asked.

Merit could only point. Then she turned and ran down the stairs, out of the house and towards the harbour. She did not stop to wait for Mut-Bity but heard her steps pounding down the stairs behind her.

By the time Meryt-Neith's boat landed on the pier, Merit and Mut-Bity were already waiting for her.

31

RETURN

"And the baby died after birth?" Merit asked, wiping away her tears.

"Yes – it did," Meryt-Neith said quietly. "It survived for two months and then it died."

Mut-Bity's eyes were wells of sadness.

"I can't find the words to express how sorry I am... This is all my fault. I chose the merchant, because I was certain he would keep you and little Ramose safe. I had no reason to doubt him, as we had known each other for years," she said quietly.

Now was the moment Meryt-Neith should have told her it was not Mut-Bity's fault.

The silence stretched uncomfortably. Then little Ramose ran laughing into the room, followed by a servant girl, still not much more than a child herself. The following fuss eased the situation somewhat, but it was clear Mut-Bity was not forgiven.

"He never found you again after the... attack?" Merit found it hard to use the word "rape". Looking at the delicate beauty of her daughter it was too painful to think of what the Pale Man had done.

"No. He is vain, and does not like ugly women. I was ugly after what he did to me. He said he would return to me when I was... presentable again."

Meryt-Neith's hand made an involuntary movement, pulling her hair behind her left ear. The hair growing there was shorter than rest of her locks. Merit noticed the left side of her mouth seemed to be hanging down slightly. But then again it might have been her joyless expression.

"So I ran to the harbour, and paid for my travel to a... safe place."

"Where did you go?" Mut-Bity asked.

"I won't tell you, or anyone else either. He might cause trouble for the people there who helped me during my pregnancy if the word spreads."

Again unspoken words hung in the air. If she wouldn't tell her own mother and Mut-Bity, it meant she didn't trust them, just as they did not trust her enough to tell her the location of the secret valley and Shuet's fate.

"We are so happy to have you back," Merit touched her daughter's arm gently, "and if there is ever a way to make retribution for what he did... you can be certain it will be done."

Merit's eyes were hard behind the tears.

"When did you decide to come back? And... why? You know he will search for you here at some point," Mut-Bity's voice was lacking its normal strength.

"When the baby died, I did not want to stay in... where I was. Before that, I didn't want to leave, he was too young. I knew you would have your bees here by now. They seem to be my only protection so I had to come back. Neither people nor Nephilim can protect me from *him*," Meryt-Neith turned her head and finally looked Mut-Bity in the eye.

It was Mut-Bity who first lowered her gaze.

"That was probably the wisest decision," she said. "Let my bees do the job that I could not. Eventually he would have found you even if you went to the ends of the earth. Your looks are too distinctive to go unnoticed. And men talk of beautiful women. Something I should have thought of."

"You couldn't have known the merchant would be so stupid that he would talk so freely about Meryt-Neith… he knew she was in need of protection," Merit said, throwing a look in her daughter's direction.

"True. But I cannot help thinking I should have told him outright never to talk about Meryt-Neith to anyone. That, I didn't do. I thought he would understand. And he didn't," Mut-Bity said.

"Meryt-Neith… I have to ask…" Merit looked around to see if any servants were around.

Ramose's laughter came from another room where he was running away from the servant girl who pretended not to be able to catch him. The boy never tired of the game.

"Yes?" Meryt-Neith lifted her chin, clearly having expected the question.

"Who killed the merchant and his wife?"

Meryt-Neith looked at them both.

"I did."

Merit swallowed. It was as she had feared.

"There was no other way I could take Ramose to safety," Meryt-Neith said, staring at the wall. "I admit I acted in anger. No, more than anger. Rage. I was hurting too much, too scared to be sane. I had to get out. I… I don't remember much about it… How I did it… Only she was suddenly lying on the floor. I think I strangled her… And then there was… blood…"

Meryt-Neith got to her feet and ran to the little room where they bathed. They could hear her throwing up.

"So she is not a cold-blooded murderer. Just as I said. She was protecting the child – and herself," Mut-Bity said. "You shouldn't condemn her."

Merit sat without speaking.

"And of course we can never tell anyone about this," Mut-Bity continued.

Meryt-Neith returned to the room, looking ill.

"Tiye will ask why you have returned," Mut-Bity said to her. "We'll tell her your husband died and you returned with your child to your mother after having sold your share of the inheritance. We'll say your husband's brother got most of it. Nothing needs to be said about what really happened."

"That seems wisest, yes," Meryt-Neith sat down on the mat on the floor, "but I do not want anyone to start finding me a new husband. Ever. From now on, it will be me and Ramose alone."

"There is that danger... especially if Tiye gets that notion into her head, as you'll be living here as one of her ladies," Merit said, "but there is one role you might take on that would give you a position and keep you here for some months at least until we come up with something better..."

"What is that?" Meryt-Neith asked.

"Your baby died a month ago. Is your milk still rising?"

"Yes, it is," Meryt-Neith said, "I have to bandage my breasts tightly."

"Good. Nefertiti has a little daughter now. Three months old... the same age your son would have been..." Merit's voice trailed off for a while, "and she does not want any lowly wet-nurse feeding her. She's not breastfeeding the child herself, either, to keep her breasts firm. She is looking for a noblewoman who could start feeding little Meritamun."

"That's an excellent idea," Mut-Bity agreed. "At least for as long as you're breastfeeding the prince's child, no one will get it into their heads that you need a husband."

Meryt-Neith looked surprised.

"You mean I would be the wet-nurse for Nefertiti's and Prince Amenhotep's daughter?"

She felt her breasts ache. It had not been a month, she had lied about that. She had been separated from her second child for a much shorter period. The winds had been favourable and she had sailed in another merchant ship directly back to Kemet and Inbu-Hedj. Carefully wrapped in linen cloths, she had arranged for transportation to a smaller ship that carried goods upriver to Waset. The strong northern winds had pushed the ship towards her goal. Maybe she still could breastfeed, judging by the ache in her breasts.

"Very well," Meryt-Neith said, "will you speak of this with Tiye?"

"I will," Merit replied. "The word of your return will certainly have reached her ears by now. First thing in the morning, we'll have an audience with her."

And so, the next morning, Meryt-Neith was introduced to little Meritamun. The baby sucked her breast easily and her milk still flowed freely. Thus Meryt-Neith became the royal wet-nurse of Meritamun.

32

WEAVING

Soon after I woke up, we left the secret valley. I wished I'd been able to have a better look around as I had never heard of any place like this being found in Egypt in our time. Maybe it was still there in the future – perhaps the descendants of its inhabitants were still living there... but there was no time to lose. Ambrogio was on the move so we had to get to our team as soon as possible.

"I think maybe you should stay here. You still look exhausted," Daniel said to me when I had finished eating a breakfast that mostly consisted of goat cheese.

"I'm never letting you out of my sight again!" I said. "So don't even think about leaving me behind."

"If you are sure..." Daniel said, but I could see in his eyes that even though he was concerned for my safety, he wasn't liking the idea of being separated again.

"I am."

I emphasised my words with a kiss that lasted for a long time.

So, at sunrise, we stepped out through the doorway into the valley. A scout had been sent to check that our enemies were not nearby. While we waited for him to return, Daniel told me that Merit had been here just before we arrived.

"How amazing! So close... now Elijah and Merit will be united again!"

Daniel smiled.

"Yes, that makes my heart so glad," he said. "The Nephilim here promised to send a message to Merit about Elijah once they have taken us to our team."

"You think she arrived in Mi-Wer right after we left?"

"I believe so... if the odds had been different, you might have met her there!"

"Imagine that.... but even so, we'll find her soon. If all goes well, that is," I added cautiously.

"Indeed. We just need to trust it will be so."

Later, our words came back to haunt me again and again. If only things had gone well....

"We go," our yellow-eyed guide said, "no bad Nephilim."

"Wait..." I said, "can I ask your name?"

He bowed.

"My name is Bay."

"Bay... thank you for all you have done. You saved me. And you brought Daniel to me. I am forever in your debt," I said.

"Forever? Long time!" he smiled. "But I remember. Now, we go."

We had decided to fly close to the ground so as not to be seen from afar. I was very tired, so Daniel wrapped his arm around me and we flew with his wings only.

"You are not going to waste your energy any more than is necessary," he said.

I had no wish to resist. I felt his warm body against my side, loving the feeling of his strong arm around my waist. I pressed my cheek against his shoulder and breathed in his scent.

How I had dreamed of being together with him again! My heart was singing with joy despite the danger we were in, despite the knowledge I would meet Ambrogio again soon. Right now that did not matter. We were together.

We flew towards the Nile at an angle, heading southward towards Akhetaten so that we'd cross the river close by. There were five of us,

Daniel and me, Bay and two Nephilim soldiers. We were following the contours of the land, keeping low in valleys of sand and rock. When evening came, we landed and entered a cave so our body heat wouldn't betray us to the enemy Nephilim, if any were nearby.

We flew for two days and then the Nile appeared on the horizon.

"Where to now?" I asked when we landed on the rosy-hued sand at sunset to catch our breath. "Do you think they are in Amarna already?"

"We don't need guesswork. We're going to use your skills for a brief trip into the buffer zone. Here."

Daniel dug something out of his jeans pocket. An enamelled hairpin. I recognised it.

"That's Diana's!"

"Yes, it is. Elijah happened to find it after she had dropped it and was going to give it back to her. He never had the time before the shadow attack. And so, we happened to have our second anchor at hand when Lilith brought us here. The statue of Tiye's head brought us to the right time, and Diana's hairpin brought us to Sithathoriunet's tomb where you and Diana had been held. We were sure that the two of you would be together, so it was enough to find Diana to find you."

I took Diana's hairpin. Immediately I felt prickling in my hands.

"Bay – we need to go our own way now. You return to the Valley and send that message to Merit."

Bay raised his hand.

"No. We take you to friends. Leave then."

"We may be moving in a way you are not used to…" I said, "I'm going to weave our way to our friends."

"Weave? You make cloth?" Bay did not understand.

"No, I make thread. And those threads will take us to our friends."

Clearly, Bay did not understand.

"We come too," he said determinately.

"Why did we not do this in the underground village?" I asked Daniel. "We've wasted two days when we could have done this a lot quicker."

"Because we could not risk entering the buffer zone there. It might have drawn the attention of our enemies. Also, it will be easier if you're as close as possible to Diana's supposed location before trying to weave your way there. We want to keep our journey as brief as we can, both to avoid the attention of the dark ones and to be sure you don't get lost."

I understood.

"Very well, then. Take my arm. All of you – you need to take a hold of my dress or hand..."

Daniel gestured to the three Nephilim to grab my arm. I opened my wings and fell backwards into the mists as fast as I could. I then closed the fingers of my left hand around the hairpin and concentrated my energies into my right hand, trying to ignore the sensation of everyone holding on to me.

The orange strings flew out of my fingers and tested the mists around us. I heard the Nephilim men gasp at the sight, but I concentrated on feeding energy into the strings. I clenched the fingers of my right hand into a fist, collecting all the strings together and then pushed my hand forward, fingers straight. The strings shot out and tightened, and we flew.

No one spoke, but I could sense the surprise in Bay and his soldiers. They'd never have experienced anything like this. I had no idea if time travel was even possible at this time, or anchoring to a destination using the strings of a time weaver. What I did know was that the Nephilim were not supposed to be able to weave. Only I could. I alone had the skill that Cain had wanted to control for his own reasons.

The strings took us to our destination faster than I expected. Suddenly the mists began to thin.

"Stop now," Daniel ordered.

I clenched my right fist intuitively and the strings whipped back into my hand so fast they stung my hand. That had never happened before; it was as if my body and my unconscious mind knew more about navigating with strings than my conscious mind did.

We stood still, looking at the surroundings through the mist. We could all feel the electric presence that told us another Nephilim was nearby.

Daniel pointed at us and lifted his finger to his lips. Then he pointed at himself and towards the scenery looming through the mists. I couldn't object out loud as my words could have been heard in the physical world. Also, Daniel was a Nephilim warrior. He knew what to do if he was faced with the other kind of Nephilim.

He didn't simply step out of the mists. He walked away from us until we couldn't see him anymore. I understood; this was to prevent any potential enemies learning where he had come out of the buffer zone, to prevent them stepping in at the same spot where they could see us. Daniel, I knew, had this skill of sensing where someone had entered or left the buffer zone, so I presumed other Nephilim warriors could too.

We heard voices, and then a familiar figure approached together with Daniel and moved right into the buffer zone.

"Elijah!"

I ran to hug him.

"Dana, thank God you are safe... We thought Ambrogio had killed you!"

He pushed me away and I noticed how tired he looked.

"Elijah! Do you know Merit is here, right now, in Mi-Wer?" I asked.

His expression changed.

"What? Here? Now? Alive?"

Then he looked at our escorts. Bay and the two warriors bowed slightly with their left hands on their hearts. Elijah returned the greeting.

"You Elijah?" Bay asked. "You Merit's husband?"

"Yes... Yes, I am. You know Merit?"

"We know Merit. She go to Mi-Wer. Many days."

"She must have arrived right after we left Mi-Wer," I said, "so that is where she is now. Bay has promised to send her a message that we... that you are here."

Elijah's hand shook as he offered it to Bay.

"Thank you..." was all he could say, his voice breaking.

They were twin souls, Elijah and Merit. Elijah had fallen into such depression after Merit disappeared, that he had wanted to kill himself. Only recently had he gained enough strength to live a normal life again – whatever that entailed to a Nephilim warrior. For a while he had even shown signs of infatuation towards me – it had been a confusing experience as I had already fallen in love with Daniel. And Daniel had seen Elijah kiss me – that was when the brothers were not talking to each other and Daniel avoided me for a while after that. The brothers were united in our struggle against the enemy Nephilim though – that was surely the thing that had given Elijah the strength to carry on.

"Your daughters... beautiful," Bay said.

"My daughters?" Elijah's face reflected the impact of this bombshell. Had the others not told him about his children?

"Shuet. Meryt-Neith."

I thought I might be imagining it – Bay's voice seemed to change when he mentioned the latter name. Shuet's name was spoken with warmth, Meryt-Neith's in a more neutral tone, almost as if he was trying to hide something.

"Twins? Where are they?" Elijah asked.

"Shuet go to Mi-Wer. After Merit. Meryt-Neith... to Akhetaten."

Meryt-Neith was in Akhetaten?

"No matter how happy I am for you, brother, we need to talk about this later," Daniel said and turned to me, "Dana – you need to come quickly. It is Diana. I think she is dying."

33

THE HEALING LAKE

The hut in the wadi appeared to be abandoned. I could see the green shoreline of the river Nile on the horizon. The position of the sun told us we were still on the western side of the river.

I understood now how Elijah had not heard about his daughters – no one could have told him, as the only people in the hut were Lilith and Diana, who was lying under a blanket on the earthen floor, shaking. Her beautiful coffee-coloured skin was now ashen grey. Her eyes were almost closed – from what little was visible, they had rolled up to reveal a glimpse of white. It was clear she was deeply unconscious.

"Dana!" Lilith enveloped me in a hug as soon as we appeared from the buffer zone. "You are alive! Are you well? Did Ambrogio bite you?"

"No, he didn't. But I gave Diana so much of my blood that I am still not as strong as I could be yet... but I will survive. What's the matter with Diana?"

"It may be the blood transfusion you gave her. We know that the blood of the evil Nephilim can cause severe illness, usually transmitted when they try to create a new vampire in their service. They rarely do that, though, having plenty of servants as it is. But then the blood of the human vampires when creating their own offspring has the same effect: severe illness and many of the potential vampires die.

We've never heard of a pure Nephilim giving blood to an ordinary human, so we're not sure if this is the usual effect or whether it relates to blood types or something similar."

Kneeling by Diana's side, I placed a hand on her forehead. I had expected the sensation of fever, but instead her skin was cold and clammy.

"My blood made her this ill?"

"Either that or it's an infection given through Ambrogio's bite. It can't be the effect of his blood as he didn't make Diana drink it – he didn't inject it into her veins either. He didn't, did he?" Lilith looked at me for confirmation.

I shook my head.

"No. The only marks on her were on her neck when I arrived. And then on her wrist when the shadow cut it so Ambrogio could taste our combined blood. Is there anything we can do?"

"We can only wait and hope for improvement. We have no medicine for this," Lilith sighed and stepped into the doorway.

Sunlight revealed her burned cheek clearly.

"No... but you have me," I said. "Maybe I should try to heal her?"

Lilith raised a hand in denial.

"You'll do no such thing. If it is your Nephilim blood that made her this ill, adding more won't help. And you shouldn't take any risks yourself, not until you're well again," Elijah said. "It's a good thing you don't have a mirror. You look like a panda with those circles around your eyes."

I was a bit shocked by his attempt at humour when Diana was so ill. But he had probably seen so many people die during his long life that it wouldn't be so shocking to him.

I turned to Diana again.

"Diana, can you hear me?"

She made a noise that could have been anything – confirmation that she heard me or just a sound signifying pain. Her breathing was fast and shallow.

And then we felt it – the presence of Nephilim. Bay and his soldiers were on the alert immediately. They didn't leave the hut, though, but simply peeked carefully from the doorway, staying in the shadow.

The sensation did not last long.

"Evil ones!" Bay said. "You leave."

"How can we leave? Diana is too weak!"

"Listen," Bay said. "She... sing. They hear."

Sings? Whatever could Bay mean? Diana was not making any sound.

"I think he means that Diana is giving off a vibration that the enemy can hear..." Daniel said. "Can't you feel it?"

We all fell silent and sure enough – there seemed to be a faint echo of a Nephilim vibration coming from Diana.

"That has to be my blood in her veins," I said.

"And Diana has no way of controlling it – quieting it..." Lilith said. "She is like a beacon sending a weak signal for those who can hear."

"Beacon?" Bay asked.

"It means she makes a sound for those who can tune into it to hear."

"Hear. Yes. Bad hear her. You leave."

"But how? Where can we go? We can't fly in the... mists or anything else if the bad Nephilim are gathering. They'll see us however and wherever we go."

"There is... place. We take hurt there. Healing," Bay tried hard to get his message across.

"A place where you take the injured to heal?" Lilith asked.

"Yes, healing place," Bay said, "far."

"Won't the dark ones follow us?" Elijah asked.

"We stop them," Bay said and turned to talk to his soldiers.

They were all muscular and tall, just like Elijah and Daniel. They discussed matters for a while and then the two soldiers stepped out of the hut, opened their wings and rose into the sky. They did not try to camouflage their presence in any way. If anything, they seemed to amplify their energies, so that we felt it buzzing up and down our spines.

"Look," Bay pointed to the sky.

His two soldiers were flying fast towards the desert fast. And from a distance, two other forms were approaching rapidly, high up in the air. Bay's soldiers turned towards them at an angle, leading them away from us. Their plan worked and they turned their backs to us, flying onwards.

"We go now," Bay said.

Elijah bent down and lifted Diana into his arms. We retreated to the buffer zone – Bay holding Lilith's arm, Daniel holding mine and Elijah carrying Diana.

"Come," Bay said, "fast."

His ochre wings were powerful and he flew through the mists like a bullet – we had trouble keeping up with him. We had to trust the fighting Nephilim would not catch our energies and follow us.

They did not.

After hours of flying, we descended from the buffer zone into rugged mountains. This had to be the eastern desert again.

"We rest," Bay said.

Elijah placed Diana on the ground. She was delirious, mumbling words in a strange language.

"What is she saying?" I asked Lilith.

"I don't know… but I know her mother was abducted from somewhere in Africa. This may be her mother tongue that Diana learned as a child before she was sold away from her family? I don't understand it."

Bay rose up into the air and landed higher on the mountain where he had a good view around us. He closed his wings and sat still, watching the sky. His garb was the same colour as the stone around him, so he melted into the background when he didn't move. We were also as silent as possible, so we wouldn't miss any Nephilim energies approaching us.

There were none, so it seemed we had escaped.

Lilith and I sat with Diana and after a while Daniel and Elijah joined Bay on watch, choosing different locations around us. Lilith's head started to nod and she fell asleep, leaning against a boulder. I managed to stay awake longer, as Nephilim usually don't need that much sleep, so I realised I must be recovering. I looked at Lilith, noticing how thin and frail she now seemed. It was such a shock – she had always been so vibrant and strong. The burned skin on her cheek was an angry red colour and I wondered if I should try to heal it. But then she would wake up, and right now what she needed was sleep.

Eventually I also dozed off and woke up after sunset when Daniel gently shook me.

"We need to go," he said.

Lilith got up too, Elijah lifted Diana back into his arms and we entered the buffer zone again to continue our flight.

I lost track of time, but when we finally left the buffer zone, the sun was high in the sky once more. We had entered the physical world by at a narrow lake at the bottom of a gorge. Lush vegetation around the clear lake shaded us. It looked like something out of a Hollywood movie.

"Where are we?" I asked.

"Place to heal," Bay said and pointed Diana. "She. To water."

Elijah was still carrying Diana whose colour had turned to a definite grey now. She looked like... a corpse.

"Oh my God – is she dead?" I asked.

"No, still breathing. Barely," Elijah said. "Take her to the water, you said?"

Bay nodded. Without another word Elijah walked straight into the lake, so deeply that the water reached unconscious Diana. Her long gleaming tresses spread onto the surface and floated around her head like the rays of a black sun. Elijah immersed her, keeping her face above the water.

"Now that is strange..." he exclaimed.

"What is it?" Lilith asked.

"Look at the water..." Elijah nodded.

We all walked to the water's edge. There were odd silver particles in the water. They covered Diana like tiny air bubbles – at first I thought that's what they were. But they seemed to be moving on their own. When Diana's hand moved weightlessly in the water, the silver particles... followed it? If they were solid particles floating in the water, you would expect Diana's hand to leave a trail in it, pushing the particles away. But no – the silver specks seemed to create a trail behind her hand and wherever it moved, they condensed much more thickly, surrounding it in order to cover the skin again.

Without noticing it, I had stepped into the water and only realised I had done so when the refreshingly cold sensation rose to my ankles. I took another step so that the water reached my knees.

For a few moments, nothing else happened. Then I felt a strange tingling in my legs and looked down, lifting my hem to see better. A thick... mat of the silver particles was covering my skin where it was under water. It felt like someone was stroking my ankles with light feathers. It tickled my skin in a gentle way.

"What are these?" I asked.

Daniel turned his gaze from Diana to me.

"She of the silver waters..." he said to himself.

The prophecy Cain believed in in his quest for world dominance. Silver waters. Could this place have something to do with the prophecy?

"Well these sure are silver..." I bent down and put my hand in the water.

The water exploded.

How can I explain... the second my hands touched the water, it was like the whole lake evaporated. Suddenly we were standing in the middle of a silvery glittering mist like little ice specks dancing in the air. The mist was so thick we couldn't see each other.

"Dana! Where are you?" Daniel's voice was muffled.

"Here! Just where I was before!" I said.

My voice also sounded strange as well.

When I spoke, I breathed in the particles but they didn't feel moist. It was like a dry shot of energy, slightly clogging my nose. I raised my hands to cover my nose and they were no longer ordinary hands – they were glowing like liquid metal and silver strings were pouring out of my fingertips.

I felt someone touch me and turned. It was Daniel.

"Dana..." he said, "calm down..."

Why would I need to calm down? Actually I felt like giggling, even though I was stunned by the change in my hands.

I tried to see where the silver strings were headed. The mist was blocking my view so I began to walk, following the strings.

After maybe ten steps, I saw the form of Elijah holding Diana again. She was in his arms still, but I saw no water anywhere. They were completely covered in silver – the particles and my strings both hid them from sight. How could these incredible lengths of silver strands come from my hands? They had wrapped them both like a spider's web and were moving like fine hair in the wind, twisting and swirling, concentrating on Diana's limp form.

Someone moved up next to me. Bay. He looked at me, but his expression didn't reveal any fear, only curiosity.

It was clear my silver strings were healing Diana, but this time they did not puncture her skin, did not need to clean her blood. No, they wrapped her gently, and the silver specks did the same, following my strings so that they looked like thin Christmas tree ornaments. Then it was as if the mist started to sing, an eerie, ululating, beautiful noise, like someone singing endlessly without words.

Elijah was looking at Diana and me, not moving.

"Put her down," Bay said, and the mist borrowed the tone of his voice for a few moments.

Elijah bent his knees and lowered Diana on what had been the shoreline of the water.

I stepped closer to her. She looked much calmer now. And she was definitely resonating with that odd, eerie sound, I could feel it inside me too. It echoed from her as if she was a tuning fork.

I kept my hands in front of me, waiting, wondering what on earth would happen next.

Rain happened. The silver specks collided with each other and formed larger and larger drops until they were heavy enough to fall down. A few drops at first, and then it rained with an increasing speed. The surroundings slowly became visible, the water level of the lake rose, and we could see the sun again.

Then the strings began to withdraw at ever-increasing speed, my hands turned back to their normal skin colour, and it was all over. Diana did not move, she lay on her back, but she was breathing normally now. Her skin was smooth and alive once more.

"Diana…" I bent down to touch her.

"No," Bay said, "she sleep. She heal. Not disturb."

So we sat down too, to rest.

"What was that?" I asked from Bay.

"Healing water. You healer. You touch water. Water stronger. Then water rises."

"You mean that when a Nephilim healer touches this water, its healing properties get stronger?" Lilith asked.

"Water heals always. Healer heals with water. Stronger. Water rises," Bay said.

"Does it always explode like that?" Elijah asked.

"Explode?" Bay did not understand the word.

"Does the water rise into the air like that every time it heals?" Daniel asked.

"No. Strong healer make so."

"How long will it take?" I asked, pointing at Diana.

"Day. Two."

Diana slept, breathing deeply. Evening came, night stars showed high above us, and then sun rose again. Still Diana slept and we waited.

And she did not wake up the next morning either. Bay touched her, looking worried. But she just kept on breathing, even smiled slightly in her sleep.

"We wait," he said

"How long?" Elijah asked.

"Strange sleep. Deep healing. Days. Many days. Change."

It was so frustrating we could not speak normally.

"Should someone stay here with Diana while the rest of us return to Egypt… to Kemet and try to find our team?" Daniel asked.

"No," Bay said. "We wait. She wakes, we go. We guard her."

"I think that is best. If the enemy should appear here, we need all the Nephilim strength we can get."

"Very well, we'll stay," Daniel said.

Elijah said nothing. He was covering his emotions, but having once healed him and knowing his mind, I could sense what he was feeling.

He had just heard his beloved twin soul Merit was still alive, and here in this time with us. He wanted to go to her, but was duty bound to protect Diana. I could sense how passionate he felt, eager to meet his wife again.

But he kept quiet and neither of us revealed what we were thinking.

We settled down to wait for Diana to wake up. Surely it would happen soon.

It didn't.

34

THE KING IS DEAD

"The falcon has flown to heaven."

The message announcing the death of the great King Amenhotep left the palace of Per-Hai to circulate throughout the Two Lands.

When the king's body was taken to the pure place to prepare him for eternal life, the king's women wailed on their knees, throwing ashes over themselves as the canopied stretcher with closed curtains moved slowly past them.

Tiye, who had known the date of Amenhotep III's death beforehand, had arranged for the crown prince to be in the palace at the time, guarded by the most trusted of the Medjay, the king's personal body guards. It was no surprise she had organised this, as the obese king's health had deteriorated to the extent that he spent most of his final days lying in bed drinking cups of wine mixed with pain killing herbs. His bad teeth were coated with honey, which helped with the inflammation, but he had been in agony in the days before his death.

Tiye was sitting by his bedside when his time came. She remained with her head bent for a few moments, then stood up and continued with the affairs of state. There had been great love between her and the king, but it had mellowed into deep friendship with the passing of years. Now, she needed to show her strength and keep the reins of the country in her hands until it was time to pass them over to the heir to the throne.

The gates of the palace were closed and few outsiders were allowed inside. Tiye and the prince stayed in the royal quarters, heavily guarded, where Tiye met with important officials and mayors from different nomes of the realm. She made it clear to them that she was in control and would deal promptly with any other claimants to the throne.

The court went into mourning. Singing and dancing ceased. People talked in hushed voices, and no merriment was allowed.

Shuet had kept her word. She had never revealed what she had learned of what embalmers did to the dead bodies, but in the distant future Merit had read about the mummification process.

She visualised the slitter making the incision on the left side of the king, there in the pure place of embalming. One of the embalmers would then draw out the king's internal organs. The man who had made the incision was chased out of the embalming house, with the other embalmers throwing stones at him as he ran. This was as it should be, for he had injured the body of the king.

Merit recalled that the one thing that was left intact inside the body was the heart. She knew that when the king entered the Duat, the underworld, his heart would stand for all he had done in the ritual of the Weighing of the Heart ritual. During this ceremony, the Egyptians believed that the heart was placed on a scale and weighed against the feather of truth of the goddess Ma'at. If the king's heart was innocent of any wrongdoing, the scales would balance perfectly. He could then proceed from the Duat to the realm of the blessed god Osiris, to the Field of Reeds, the afterlife.

"My heart of my mother, my heart of my forms, do not stand against me as a witness, do not oppose me in the tribunal, do not turn away from me in the presence of the controller of the balance. You are my 'ka', the dweller in my body, uniting and strengthening my members. Thou shalt come forth to the happiness to which we advance..."

The great god Anubis would do the weighing, and the god of

wisdom, Thoth, would write down the verdict. If the king was found guilty of bad deeds, his heart would sink lower than the feather, and would be devoured by the monster Ammit. He would die eternally and exist no more. But everyone knew that would never happen.

After the embalmers had taken out his internal organs, they washed the king's body inside and out with Nile water and sweet wine. Once this was done, it was time to remove his brains. The men used hooks wrapped with linen that they pushed through the left nostril, breaking the ethmoid bone to reach inside his skull. They rotated the hooks repeatedly, until the king's brains were liquified. They then turned the king's body on its stomach so that what was left of the brains would drip out of his nose, until the skull was empty. All the linen used for this was saved and placed in a jar of its own, as it was sacred now and it would receive its own burial.

The cleaning and purification took fifteen days, after which the embalmers sealed the king's bodily openings with resin. They filled his limbs with lichen and linen to round them out again, and then covered his body and his organs in salt to dry them completely. The salt packs placed in his abdomen were changed regularly, as was the salt covering him so that all the moisture was drawn out of the dead body.

After forty days, the salt used to dry the king's body was taken away, and the embalmers washed his body once more. His limbs were still flexible enough to allow the embalmers to bend his hands into the royal position: crossed over his chest, holding the crook and the flail, the symbols of a just ruler.

After this, the embalmers took jars of fine oils, incense and herbs and anointed the king's body with them. Spices and resins would make him smell good for eternity. Thin strips of the finest linen, with sacred spells written on them, wrapped his body completely, held in place with resin. The king's women had been weaving the strips for him in various houses devoted to his harem all over the country. Inside the wrappings were valuable protective amulets to ensure his safe arrival in the afterlife. The most important of all, the heart scarab, was placed on his chest as a replacement in case anything happened to his real heart. The amulet could then take the place of the king's own heart and had a spell written on it to prevent the heart from speaking against its owner during the ceremony. All this took another fifteen days.

Amun's priests now had access to the king in death. Even if they had been out of favour in his later life, they could now take every advantage to show their power over the deceased king. It was their spells, recited during the embalming process that would ensure the safety of the body so that the king's soul, hovering nearby, could occupy its resting place when it became habitable again.

All throughout this time, the palace was in mourning, and people talked in hushed voices. But behind the scenes, Tiye ruled with an iron fist. Her informants were everywhere, listening, reporting back to her what they had heard. The priests of Amun taking part in the mummification process were prohibited from approaching Tiye, the heir to the crown or Nefertiti. The royal body guard never left them unprotected.

By the time the king was wrapped and ready for his tomb, seventy days had passed. Seventy days that symbolised the mourning of the goddess Isis when she gathered the pieces of her husband Osiris's body after Osiris's jealous brother Seth had killed him, ripped him to pieces and scattered every piece throughout the land. Isis collected the body parts together and brought Osiris back to life long enough to become pregnant with their son Horus, the falcon god, the symbol of the living king of Kemet. On his death, the king was considered to become Osiris himself, and his chosen heir continued to rule as the Horus of his people. And so the chain of generations of rulers continued.

Seventy days was also the period when the star Sothis was invisible in the sky. On the seventieth day, it appeared again on the horizon, marking the new year, the return of life on earth when the waters of the great river began to rise with a fresh inundation, bringing in the fertile mud and water that made life possible in the river valley.

And so, on the seventieth day after his death, the king was to enter his life ever after just as the star of Isis marked the return of life in its eternal cycle.

The priests now placed the king's body on a sled pulled by oxen to his magnificent tomb in Ta-Sekhet-Ma'at – the valley where kings' tombs were now built. Milk was poured on the ground so the sled would move more easily.

And there, in front of the tomb entrance, the priests raised his mummy in an upright position so that his heir could perform the Opening of the Mouth ceremony.

This was the moment Tiye had been preparing for, keeping the heir to the throne safe, surrounding him with the most trusted guard of the dead king. For whoever performed this rite to the dead king, was the one who would inherit the crown of Kemet. Tiye was taking no risks – the rulership of the land would now transfer to her son.

A great entourage left Per-Hai on the morning of the burial to the pure place where the king's body waited for them. Tiye and Prince Amenhotep led the mourners in a gilded sedan at the front, following the sled of the dead king on its journey to the valley of the kings. Before them, soldiers opened the way and priests walked solemnly in procession. Behind them, another sedan carried Nefertiti and Meritamun, who was old enough to sit up and look around. Nefertiti's youngest daughter, Meketamun, was still a baby, so she was left behind with a nurse.

Merit, Mut-Bity and Meryt-Neith followed behind among the other people of the court. Little Ramose was now a strong boy who could walk on his own and was very proud of being allowed to join the entourage.

"You must not make any noise, you understand?" Meryt-Neith had said to him as they prepared to leave their house.

"Yes, mother!" the little boy had said.

And he made his mother proud with his good behaviour.

Meryt-Neith had breast-fed Meritamun for months, and when it was time to wean the child, there was no longer any discussion about finding her a husband. Mut-Bity had told the Great Royal Wife that Meryt-Neith wished to continue as a court lady of Nefertiti. Nefertiti had grown fond of Meryt-Neith, and so she found her place in the court.

Meryt-Neith observed the small figure of Nefertiti next to the equally small Tiye. Princess Sitamun was there too – she had been elevated to the position of a wife to her father in his heb-sed festival after his thirty years of rule. Nefertiti was standing near Prince Amenhotep as he performed the Opening of the Mouth ceremony. Touching the upright mummy's ears, eyes, nose and mouth with special tools, he magically returned its senses so that the dead king could again breathe, hear, see, smell, and taste in the afterlife. The dead king now became Osiris, the king of the dead, and his son became Horus, the king of the living.

"My mouth is opened by Ptah, the bonds of my mouth are caused to be unfettered by the god of my city. Thoth comes indeed, fully equipped with his magic, and has released for me the items belonging to Seth, the bonds of my mouth, My hands are moved by Atum, he puts them forward as the guard of my mouth. My mouth is opened, my mouth is parted by Ptah with that tool of iron, with which he has split open the mouth of the gods."

This was the moment when Tiye ceased to be the Great Royal Wife of the living king and became the King's Mother. Her old title was transferred to Nefertiti, the new king's First Wife.

Nefertiti raised her chin a bit higher, aware of her new position. Tiye stood still, her eyes half closed, every inch of her the consummate royal, taking on her new role immediately.

A great banquet was spread out on the valley floor. Those of the court who had been allowed to enter the valley, now sat down and had the final feast with their old king. His mummy was standing next to the doorway to his tomb, and it was believed he took part in the feast, enjoying the essence of the foods placed in front of him.

Then the priests placed his body on a stretcher and carried him inside his tomb carved into the depths of the mountain. Long corridors led to the burial chamber that was already filled with unimaginable treasures. There, the priests lifted the king's mummy and placed it in his innermost coffin, made of solid gold and waiting inside the sarcophagus. A magnificent golden mask hid his upper body. The outer, wooden coffins were all gilded.

Only the king's immediate family followed him on this final stretch of his journey. While there, Tiye and Sitamun observed the rooms reserved for their own burial within the king's massive tomb. The new king and his Great Royal Wife would have their own tomb built for them. The work would be starting immediately, so that they would be sure to have an appropriate place to be buried in when their time came.

Tiye placed a flower garland on the chest of the king and then the lids on the nested coffins were closed one after the other. Finally, the heavy lid of his sarcophagus of red granite was lifted into place. The sarcophagus was named Neb-ankh, Lord of Life, as it protected the king's life in the hereafter.

The priests then left the tomb with the royal family following behind them. After everyone had stepped back out into the sunlight, the door was closed and sealed with the official seal of the valley of Ta-Sekhet-Ma'at – a jackal recumbent over the nine bows, the tied figures of the traditional enemies of Kemet. The guardians of the valley formed a guard in front of the tomb where they would stay until the tomb entrance was properly hidden. There were some who would gladly have taken the riches from the king's burial and this substantial body of soldiers was there to prevent them.

The entourage then turned their backs on the land of the dead and returned to Per-Hai and the land of the living. It was time for the new king to take control of his land, following in the footsteps of his fore-fathers, making sure balance would prevail and everything would continue as before.

The glances the priests of Amun threw towards the sedan of the new king made it clear that they already suspected troubling times were ahead that would risk the authority of the great god Amun.

35

THE SWIMMER

We gave our son the name Sa-Khons, the son of Khonsu. Everyone just called him Khonsu – the Traveller. Khonsu was also the name of the moon god, the child of Amun and Mut. It felt right, considering the way he was born travelling through the desert under the moon, to his mother the Moon Daughter.

He and Asule grew up in the safety of the hidden valley and despite their differing looks were truly brother and sister. When they were old enough to wonder about their different skin colour, we told them about the sacrifice Asule's parents had made to save our lives. Every year, we went outside at the time of Khonsu's birthday, to look at the northern sky,and the children picked out two stars they believed were Asule's parents, now in the afterlife. At first they chose different stars but as years passed, they settled for two stars near the imperishable stars of the north.

Sometimes Seth and I sneaked away to our hidden lake to spend time together. We floated in the silver waters we had loved from the time we were children. The little silver specks gathered around us and hummed pleasantly, just as they had done in the days of our youth.

On the flat rock in the middle of the lake we could make love to each other without being disturbed – a rarity when raising two children. I did not get pregnant again, though. We were not in a hurry. If children came, we would welcome them, but for now, we enjoyed one another's company whenever we managed to get away. It was not only raising children but also taking part in the life of the underground village that kept us busy and so we could not do this as often as we would have liked.

Seth was often on guard duty outside the village, as were many female Nephilim, too, but not the ones with small children. That meant I stayed in the village, looking after the children, weaving cloth, preparing food, reading manuscripts and copying them.

For we had an extensive library – the beekeepers and visitors to the land of Kemet brought with them scripts and papyrus whenever it was possible. Three copies were made of each – one for the library for anyone to read, one for teaching purposes, and one for safekeeping and copying when the other two had had been used so much that they started to crumble.

As I had learned to read and write, I joined the scribes in their work. We sat in one of the caves in companionable silence, painting the texts with our brushes. Sometimes we read excerpts of texts out loud and discussed their meaning. It was a job I loved well.

My writing improved, as I was taught by other, more experienced scribes, and I returned their favour with my own skills – there were moments when I could see glimpses of their future upon asking. I worded my answers carefully so as not to take away their own freedom of choice, for fear I would meddle with predestined things. But they appreciated my words nonetheless and never pestered me with incessant requests about what would happen next.

One particular day, I had finished copying a manuscript that told the story of the shipwrecked sailor who ended up on an island where a giant snake lived. I knew Sa-Khons and Asule would enjoy hearing the tale and decided to tell it to them at bedtime. They were impatient, because Mut-Bity had sent word she was coming to the secret valley soon. The children loved her stories, too, and she adored the children with all her heart. Maybe the story of the shipwrecked sailor would keep the children's minds occupied this evening so they would have the patience to sit still and not jump around our home.

But before evening arrived, Seth and I had planned to go to our secret lake. We went there separately, careful not to be followed as we did not want anyone to find it.

And there we were, floating in the water on our backs, when we heard the sound of footsteps. The sounds were faint but there was no mistaking the fact that they were coming from a corridor decorated with ancient paintings of stylised animals and stylised people.

"Someone is coming here!" I whispered, my voice betraying my disappointment. I had never wanted anyone to discover our secret lake.

"Let's hide behind the rock..." Seth said quietly. "Close your wings."

We both did so, leaving the silver trace of our wings in the water. It would take a while to dissolve. We swam behind the rock with quiet strokes and there we waited silently in the water, holding on to the rock so the current would not carry us away.

We had taken off our clothes and placed them near the mouth of the corridor that led to the lake. They were behind a boulder that had fallen from the ceiling ages ago, and I hoped that whoever arrived wouldn't see them.

The sound of footsteps approached further, and then a familiar figure came into view.

Mut-Bity. She stood at the mouth of the corridor and looked around with such an expression of surprise that it was clear she had never been here before. Thankfully, she hadn't spotted our clothes and since we hadn't left the water there were no wet footprints to give us away.

She took something that was hanging around her neck on a leather string. I recognised it – it was the leather pouch that contained the fish-shaped amulet Seth had brought to her the day we became lovers. I had seen Mut-Bity take it out occasionally and turn it so that the light hit it directly. She was always in a state of deep concentration when she did so. She never showed it to anyone, though, and I never asked what it was all about.

I did know that Mut-Bity never did anything on a whim; and whatever she chose to keep to herself, was not something I or anyone who loved her would ever ask her to reveal. This amulet had been given to her by an old friend before she died. If she had not died, Seth might never have come to me when he did. In my mind, I had felt gratitude for this death, along with guilt about my joy. But it had brought my love to me, and now we were a family. How could I not be grateful?

Mut-Bity stood still, turning slowly, looking at the strange markings on the cave walls. Signs neither I nor Seth could read. As a child, I had convinced myself that one day I would read them, once I learned to read and write. Upon returning to the cave years later, I realised that these were not markings I recognised even after going to the lessons in the kap.

Mut-Bity touched the water with her toe and from a distance I watched the silver specks gather around her foot.

Then she squatted down, put the little amulet back into its pouch, tightened the string and stepped into the water. Where she was, at the mouth of the corridor, there were natural steps leading into the water. She descended until the water reached her chest. Then she began to swim.

I had never known she could swim. But with all the streams and lakes hidden in the rock it made sense she would have learned to do so. She had probably been born here, played as a child with many of the old people still living, and like all children, learned to love the water.

Mut-Bity did not swim towards us, but against the stream that flowed through the lake. She disappeared into the low canal the lake received its water from.

Seth and I had swum in that direction as children, but the ceiling of the canal was so low we kept banging our heads on the rocky surface. The stream became narrow there too, and the stones sharp and close to the surface underfoot so you could not avoid kicking against them. So we'd never bothered to explore further. It was just another stream and the lake was more comfortable to swim in.

We waited, not saying a word, as the water might have carried our voice to Mut-Bity. When you spoke in the cavern, it imitated your tone in an eerie way, like a faint whispering wail. You could almost imagine you heard other words, strange words.

Mut-Bity was gone for a long time, but the water was comfortable, so we carried on waiting, curious as to what she was up to. Seth had wrapped his arm around my waist, to keep me steady, and I loved the touch of his skin against mine so I was in no hurry to leave.

When Mut-Bity finally reappeared, she was swimming more quickly than she had been when she had entered the canal. The stream did most of the work for her. She climbed back up the steps. Something in her body language made me wonder – it was as if she had been scared. No, it wasn't fear, but more as if she was experiencing some inner turmoil.

She sat down on the stone, her hands around her knees. Her wet dress revealed her sinewy, strong form. Her black hair fell down her back and when she looked up at the markings on the opposite wall, she suddenly appeared beautiful to me.

I'd always just thought of her as old, but now I began to wonder what her real age was. She spoke about ageing often, making fun of it and joking that no one knew her anymore when she returned to the great River with her bees, because everyone else had grown so old or died.

But when the late afternoon light hit the water and made it shine like glittering silver, its reflection smoothed away any shadows from her face. She was ageless. Now that I considered it, her skin was surprisingly smooth. Certainly, she had deep lines reaching from the corners of her eyes from squinting in the bright sunlight, but other than that, her skin was not old and wrinkly. Only tanned.

I observed Mut-Bity with new interest for a long time. What was her real name? I knew she had not been given the name Mut-Bity, Mother of Bees, at birth. She had earned that name because of her connection to her bees. She had never shared her real name. Not even my mother knew it.

After a while, Mut-Bity stood up, and walked back along the corridor.

When we could no longer hear her faint footsteps, we quietly swam back to the stairs and got out. When our skin was dry, we dressed again.

"What was that about?" Seth asked.

"I don't know. She hadn't been here before, you could tell that from the way she looked around."

"But where did she swim to?"

"Upstream... but as far as we know, there is nothing there," I said. "She seemed a bit... scared, though, when she came back. Didn't you think so too?"

"Maybe the current was too strong. I didn't know she could swim. It may have been years since she'd last been swimming, and perhaps she got tired and afraid she wouldn't make it back?" Seth wondered.

"Yes, probably. We did swim there as children and there was nothing but sharp rocks."

"I cut my foot on them, remember?"

I did remember. Seth's foot had been bleeding when we got back to the lake. But the silver particles had gathered around his foot and the bleeding had stopped.

"We'll have to get back. Let's not tell Mut-Bity that we saw her," Seth said.

"Yes, that would be best. And in future, we'll have to be more careful when we come here," I said. "We need to make sure Mut-Bity is occupied with something else."

"She's only visiting anyway and never stays long. Let's wait until she has left again before we come back here," Seth said. "We'd better get back now. It's getting late, and Mut-Bity and the children will be waiting for us."

Seth kissed my neck and hugged me from behind.

"We'll go back and get the latest news about your mother, Meryt-Neith and little Ramose," he said.

I gave him a little kiss on the cheek and we returned to the hidden village.

36

FAMILY NEWS

We waited until the children had finally fallen asleep before talking openly about mother and Meryt-Neith with Mut-Bity.

I hated keeping secrets about my family. I was longing for news of mother, Meryt-Neith and Ramose but didn't dare let the children overhear. Children are curious by nature and to allow them to know too much might put us all in danger. We had simply told them that mother lived by the Great River, and that I had a sister who had married and travelled far away to live with her husband.

I longed to tell them that they had a cousin and how much I wanted them to meet... but as long as the Pale Man was after us, I couldn't. He knew where Meryt-Neith was, and if he ever turned her into one of the dangerous Nephilim, she would tell him about us right away. How Meryt-Neith could carry on living in constant fear of him, I couldn't imagine.

Sadly, we had decided that we couldn't ever meet Meryt-Neith again so she would never learn where the secret valley was. Our children were not to leave the Valley until they were old enough to understand the importance of secrecy. They didn't have a sense of danger yet and without thinking, might easily reveal something that could lead our enemies to the Valley.

While I didn't approve of my sister taking the Pale Man as her lover, I couldn't blame her either. She had been young and foolish, intoxicated by her own beauty, easily seduced by flattery and gifts. She hadn't known what the Pale Man was – or rather, she had been naïve enough not to believe what she had heard about the yellow-eyed Nephilim from the rest of us. After learning what she had suffered at his hands, I felt only pity now.

"Who is he really? The Pale Man?" Seth asked Mut-Bity quietly as we sat together, listening to the children breathing, deeply asleep in their little niche.

"The bringer of death, they call him..." Mut-Bity said. "He is their high lord, the one whom everyone obeys. The Pale Man is not his real name, of course. He keeps his true name a secret."

I offered Mut-Bity some bread and a cup of water. She nodded her thanks and took the bread, smelling it appreciatively before biting into it. As the grain had been ground to flour deep inside the mountain, there was no sand in it, unlike the bread from the River valley. Our bread was soft and delicious and not harmful to teeth.

"Has he been around... since the king's death?" I asked.

"We do sense him occasionally, but he doesn't dare come too close now. The bees warn us even before we feel his presence, so then we stay quiet and don't talk about you. It saddens Merit's heart."

It saddened mine too, this unseen enemy forcing us to be silent, constantly seeking to steal our lives from us.

"But we can write," I said, "that's one good thing."

"Yes, that is good. Though Merit destroys your letters as soon as she has read them, so that Meryt-Neith can't get to them. Or the Pale Man for that matter."

I had kept all my mother's letters, but they were not in our rooms. Each scribe had their own private chest in the library in a room that only the scribes could enter. No curious child was allowed in there, and no one ever opened anyone else's chests.

Mut-Bity sipped her water.

"Little Ramose has grown into a handsome young boy, just like Khonsu. They look very much alike, though Ramose's hair is black. Khonsu has lighter hair and paler skin."

That was no wonder – I was colourless, and Seth had pale skin and reddish hair. Still, my sister was very light-coloured too, and the Pale Man was like me. Where did Ramose's black hair come from then? Mother had told me that our father had had dark hair. So maybe Ramose had inherited his darker colouring from his grandfather?

"So, what is happening in the realm?" Seth asked.

"So much I don't know where to begin; and that's why I am here. In his second year as king, the king ordered new temples to be built in Waset. Temples without a roof, with no hidden god in the holy of holies. And by his third year, he had already celebrated a heb-sed. *Or should I say, he and Nefertiti had celebrated one – the Great Royal Wife had a great role in the ceremonies."*

Mother had written to me about this. A king was supposed to celebrate his first heb-sed *after thirty years of rule. Thirty, not three.*

"There is now open hostility between the king and the priesthood of Amun. Tiye told me that her loyal informers enabled her to catch a servant who had put poison in the king's cup," Mut-Bity continued.

"No!" I whispered. "They were ready to kill the king? Did he drink it? Is he dead now as well?"

"No. But the fact he didn't drink it is only because Tiye is ever alert and has her own servants everywhere around the young king. So, when a new servant suddenly appeared in the kitchens, she had him followed right away. He was spotted pouring poison into the king's wine after it was opened. He and the wine were brought to Tiye and she forced him to drink it himself. His death was not pleasant to watch. I was there, as was your mother."

"What happens now?" Seth asked.

"When the king heard of this, he was furious that the servant hadn't been questioned before he died. Still, there was enough evidence that this man had come from Ipet-Isut. The lower crews of priests who serve every fourth month at the temple include loyal followers of Tiye among them. Tiye sent for them to come to her in secret, one after the other, and showed each one the body of the dead servant before it started to putrefy in the heat, until one of them identified him as a servant of the great temple. And not just any servant either. He was a priest known to be close to the First Prophet of Amun."

"Did the king have his soldiers take action in response?" I asked. "Did they attack the temple?"

"No, not yet. But it's clear he is planning something big. The first thing he ordered to be done, though, is that when Nefertiti goes to worship in Gem-

Pa-Aten, and the Hwt-Benben, she is always to be surrounded by a real army of Medjay. They are not to let any Amun priest near her. Nefertiti is now called Neferneferuaten-Nefertiti – Exquisite Beauty of the Aten, A Beautiful Woman has Come."

Gem-Pa-Aten – the great temple of the god Aten. The first construction inaugurated by the king after he ascended the throne. The huge, roofless temple to the east of Ipet-Isut was a slap in the face of the priesthood of Amun. It stood in complete contrast to the roofed, dark temple of the hidden god Amun. The offering tables of the Gem-Pa-Aten stood under the open sky. And most of the time, Nefertiti, the Great Royal Wife, performed the offering rites alone, without the king by her side.

Every day, she was carried in her sedan chair past the ancient temple of the state god of Egypt, not paying her respects, into the new temple. Surrounded by huge statues of herself and the king, she greeted the morning sun in her see-through dress, to arouse him, and to give him sustenance. Great piles of food, flowers and incense were offered to the Aten daily.

The statues... Mut-Bity told us how odd they looked.

"They have round hips, and the faces of the royal couple are elongated and strange. Their bellies are hanging round. They look almost exactly like each other, it's hard to tell which statues are male and which are female, for both seem to have breasts, too. No one has ever seen anything like it before. The wall reliefs are the same too. I have seen some of that art and... well, they have managed to make even Nefertiti look ugly."

"Why are they like that?" Seth asked.

"Supposedly they represent both male and female in the same form. Shu and Tefnut, the first godly couple, given birth to by Amun with his own hand so that he would know himself through his creation. The divine couple from whom all the other gods and goddesses descend from, the fertile god and goddess."

"You said the king is planning something big. What, exactly?" Seth asked.

Mut-Bity savoured the moment for a while. Clearly she had great news to tell. We waited, letting her enjoy her secret a little longer.

"He has ordered a new city to be built. On his journey to Inbu-Hedj, one morning he was standing on the deck of his royal ship, ready to greet the Aten as he rose above the land. There, in that place, he saw how the Aten rose

from behind an opening in the mountains east of an uninhabited plain. The mountains and the sun formed the sign of akhet, *the horizon. He took it as a divine sign that Aten had chosen this place to live in on earth. He has now decreed that his new capital will be built there – a new place where no other god or goddess has ever been worshipped before. Once the city is built, the court will move out of Waset."*

I was shocked. This was indeed unexpected news. Of course the kings had always travelled up and down the River and lived in many royal abodes where they kept their women, and there had always been a capital. Inbu-Hedj. Waset. These had been built in the distant past. But – to build a whole new capital for the land?

"What will happen then?" I asked.

"All the officials and the court and anyone in the service of the king has to move to the new city. I'm not sure everyone will, as they have their own lives and their estates near Waset. And not all are willing to give up the old way, either. The whole city is in turmoil because of this." Mut-Bity said, "and Meryt-Neith is involved in all of it as well. Which is why I am here."

"What do you mean?" I asked.

"Our special bees are now in the royal palace of Per-Hai, in Waset. The Pale Man knows where Meryt-Neith is. When Nefertiti moves to the new capital, Meryt-Neith will have to follow. And to stay safe when she does that, she needs bees to protect her from the Pale Man. I am here to collect a new queen bee for her. There's still time to create a hive for her before the court moves."

The bees were raised in a branch of the Valley close to the water, and in the shadow of the valley walls, flowering plants grew. It was a long and narrow strip of vegetation under a roof of stone – the wall arched over the valley floor forming a ledge and so the plants were not visible from above, and flourished in the shade. There, the beehives were tended. Only for a brief while when the sun shone along the Valley in late afternoon did the plants get direct sunlight.

"Will Seshat and Iahmesu stay in Waset?" I asked.

Mut-Bity rose and stretched her legs. We had been sitting for hours. She walked over to look at the sleeping children, and pulled up their blanket to cover them better. Looking at her and the children, I once more wondered what was the tragedy that had stopped her from having a family of her own. She was so good with children, and clearly loved them. And yet she was alone, without blood relatives.

"No," Mut-Bity answered the question, "Nefertiti gave them to her little sister Mutnofret and she has made her keep her promise. As Mutnofret is in Nefertiti's retinue, she and her own little court will follow the royal couple. Which is just as well. Iahmesu and Seshat can protect Meryt-Neith and Ramose too, and I shall give the bees into their care so they will tend them. People believe they too are beekeepers because they are close to me and I have said that they can take care of the bees while I am away, which is not a lie. It's not the first time they have tended to my bees."

The honey the bees made by the River in Kemet, travelling up and down the River on rafts and boats following the seasons, was not all given away or sold. Some of it was always brought back to the Valley, to be used as food for the hives here. The bees couldn't survive on their own in the middle of the desert, not even with the green strip of plants here. But this was the place the special queen bees were bred, queens whose descendants could sense the evil Nephilim and protect us all. White, with three pairs of red wings.

Just like me.

"And as another blow to the Amun priesthood, the king has decided Amun cannot even be a part of his name any more," Mut-Bity said.

"He is going to use Aten, isn't he?" Seth asked.

"Atenhotep? Aten is satisfied?" I asked.

"No. He discussed this with Tiye. I wasn't present when that happened, but Nefertiti told Meryt-Neith who told me. He will be Akhenaten."

Akhenaten. Effective to Aten.

"The whole country will be in turmoil," Seth said.

"Yes. Probably we have no idea how big the changes will be... Some of the officials have already begun to change their names as well, replacing Amun with Aten. Some temples have begun to be converted to sun temples already and the priests have declared their loyalty to the Aten. They are afraid their temples will be closed otherwise," Mut-Bity placed her hands on the small of her back and stretched her upper body.

"Will Tiye be moving to this... Akhetaten?" I asked.

"She hasn't decided yet. Maybe by the time it is ready, she'll no longer be

in the land of the living. But she has no intention of living in a construction site. Most likely she will return to Mi-Wer and decide later," Mut-Bity answered. "She is a wise woman and likes Nefertiti. Probably she wants everyone to see Nefertiti is now the Great Royal Wife and that she is not her rival. It's important to her that the royal couple stands together strongly. Of course, she will remain the wise woman behind the throne, no one doubts that."

"She won't stay in Waset? In Per-Hai?"

"No. They want the royal family out of Waset, out of reach of the Amun priesthood. And now, children, I think I shall retire to my own bed. You are young and don't need much sleep, but I am exhausted."

She smiled at us, that ageless smile with dazzlingly white teeth.

"I'll walk with you," Seth said, lighting a little oil lamp for her.

"There's no need. I have been walking these corridors for so many years I could close my eyes and still find my way. I don't mind the lamp, though. It's much pleasanter to walk with open eyes."

She took the offered lamp, kissed me on the cheek, patted Seth on the arm and was gone.

37

DEDICATION OF THE ATEN TEMPLE

"Now don't run off anywhere on your own!" Meryt-Neith warned Ramose. "I don't want to see you covered in dust. It's an important day, and you are to stay by my side."

"No, Mother," the boy said, but his eyes were darting in every direction, taking in the shoreline of the River, and the new buildings standing proudly under the sun on its eastern bank. He tried to keep still, but his feet were constantly on the move and his fingers fidgeted on the cloth of his new – and still surprisingly clean – linen kilt. It had just been pleated and was stiff and scratched his skin. He had never been given permission to wear pleated linen before – it was reserved for nobles. But because of Meryt-Neith's position as one of Nefertiti's ladies, they were both given permission to wear the finest pleated linen today. Ramose really was trying to remember his fine clothing, so that he wouldn't ruin it, because it showed everyone his increased status.

He had grown to be a tall, beautiful, boy. His thick black hair needed shaving constantly. His side lock of youth was hanging from the left side of his head, the rest of it had been shaved away. Meryt-Neith found it hard to believe that nearly ten years had passed since his birth. Soon, he would be of age to be circumcised, and after that he would be considered a man. Boys from the nobility were often taken to temple schools at that point, to become officials, but Meryt-Neith would not let him leave her side. Already he excelled in reading and writing, and his teacher could not praise his hard work highly enough. He would surely have a great future in the service of the king.

Which king would that be, Meryt-Neith wondered. They would have to move somewhere else when he came of age and his wings developed. Everyone would notice that he wasn't ageing at a normal pace after reaching adulthood.

If his wings developed, that was. Meryt-Neith's wings had never opened.

"Sometimes they develop much later than usual," Mut-Bity had said, "and there are cases when they don't open at all. Yet the children of Nephilim whose own wings don't develop still usually get their wings after they have reached adulthood. We don't know what causes the wings not to open."

Meryt-Neith had so wished for her wings when she was young. She had her own theory as to why hers had not opened – and she blamed the Pale Man. Maybe the fact that she had carried two children of an evil Nephilim had somehow disturbed her body's normal development.

But what she did not have, she was no longer going to agonise over.

Meryt-Neith touched the back of her beautiful son lightly, as a reflection of her thoughts about the wings. Surely *he* would get beautiful wings. Ones that would make his mother proud.

Sometimes Meryt-Neith could see a glimpse of the Pale Man's features in Ramose, but she had learned to live with that. It became easier as the years passed, with the boy growing into a personality of his own, which did not resemble that of the Pale Man at all. He was polite and cheerful. Also, his darker colouring was so different from his father's, that there were days when Meryt-Neith could almost push the Pale Man out of her mind. Almost.

She never mentioned her other child. The only ones who knew of him were Merit and Mut-Bity. And they never asked her for more information, nor told anyone else, understanding the memory to be too painful for her.

She never as much as looked at a man any more. Passion was dead for her after what she had gone through. She received compliments on her beauty constantly, but never responded to them in any way, and soon earned the reputation of being a cold and proud woman for whom no man was good enough. She didn't mind. It suited her purposes well. Men could keep their violent appetites to themselves.

The city of Akhetaten was still under construction, but palaces and temples had been built for the royal family and now it was time for Nefertiti and the children to move in with the king. A huge flotilla of ships and boats sailed from the old capital of Waset to the new city, leaving the priesthood of Amun behind. Now, over twenty thousand people lived in Akhenaten's shining new capital.

Nefertiti's ship led the way, followed by ships carrying the members of the court – ladies, officials, new priests for the Aten.

The King lived up to his new name. He was effective to the Aten. He often travelled to the site of the new city, living in a tent while it was being built, and walked about with his architects, giving orders about which building should be erected next, and where. Outside the official centre of the city, the houses of courtiers and workers had begun to extend its boundaries. Officials began to move in with their families when it became clear the court really would soon move to Akhetaten permanently. Ships sailed between Waset and the new location, carrying messages relating to the governance of the land, along with people and provisions. Fields on the western shore of the river, opposite to Akhetaten, produced food for the capital and the King's vineyards in the delta area carried on producing excellent wine.

Servants had been sent beforehand to make everything ready. The royal women would be taken to their quarters in a magnificent procession. But first, a fat ox was to be sacrificed to the Aten in his new temple and the King and the Great Royal Wife would greet the god who was now above all others.

Akhenaten stood on the pier to welcome his Great Royal Wife

Nefertiti, the Mother of the King, Tiye, and all the other ladies. Tiye intended to stay in Akhetaten for a while, but had decided to return to Mi-Wer eventually.

"You need someone near Inbu-Hedj," she had said to her son, "and I can travel up here often. I will only stay until you have settled."

And spread out her network of spies, as Akhenaten and Nefertiti knew. No threat to the king would go unnoticed.

Nefertiti was wearing a magnificent wig as well as the headdress of the principal queen: a golden vulture's downward reaching wings framed her beautiful face. Her heavy golden jewellery glistened in the sun and together with the palest see-through, pleated linen dress, accentuated her tanned skin. Her body was clearly visible under the sheer linen. Her sandals were gilded and the air around her was rich with perfume.

It was traditional for noblewomen to stay in the shade to keep their skin as pale as possible. Nefertiti, however, exposed her skin to the sun daily when she made offerings to the Aten. As a result, her skin was the same colour as the king's. Her maidens massaged expensive oils into her skin every day to keep it soft and beautiful despite the harsh sun.

As the royal ship glided into the harbour, the crowd cheered at the sight. The Lady of Grace, Lady of the Two Lands, Mistress of Upper and Lower Kemet. Sweet of Love, Great of Praises – the Hereditary Princess, Neferneferuaten-Nefertiti. For she was no longer just Nefertiti. Her new name meant "*Exquisite Beauty of the Aten, the Beautiful One Has Come*".

Nefertiti's belly was rounded as she had just given birth again. She had five daughters now – Meritaten, Meketaten, Ankhesenpaaten, Neferneferuaten the younger, and Neferneferure, who had been born this year. No one doubted she would soon be pregnant again – the Great Royal Wife had been blessed with great fertility.

Each birth had been easier than the previous one; Mut-Bity was no longer needed to push the babies out of her. Nefertiti did not tie linen around her waistline, though, to hide her sagging belly, though, as was the custom of the noble ladies. No, she showed the signs of motherhood proudly, proving she was a fertile queen to her king. Her breasts were still firm as she did not breastfeed. Other ladies had followed after Meryt-Neith, taking on the honour of being the wet-nurse to a royal princess.

Akhenaten stood on the pier, proud of his new city, proud of the beauty of his wife, proud of their daughters standing with her.

"I welcome you, Lady of the Two Lands," he said in a loud voice. "Step down from your ship and join me in the new city of the Aten. Here we shall live in adoration of the true god."

"Gladly do I join you, Lord of the Two Lands," Nefertiti said in a strong voice. "Together we shall live here, and give no other god permission to enter."

Stepping onto the pier, she took Akhenaten's arm. She did not take the traditional position of women to the left of their husbands. Akhenaten offered her his right arm, and so she was on the right side of the king – a place of great honour to anyone.

"I welcome you, my noble mother," Akhenaten then said to Tiye., "Step down onto the holy ground of the Aten. This is the place I swear I shall never leave again. I shall remain in this city of the Aten now and forever."

Tiye was just as magnificently dressed and bejewelled as Nefertiti. She wore a golden diadem, heavy jewellery and the sheerest of linen. Her dress had many layers, though, as she no longer needed to show her fertility. Meryt-Neith knew also that she Tiye did use tight linen wrappings to give her body a youthful shape. Her many pregnancies had permanently stolen whatever youth there had been in her figure. Even her breasts were sagging now because of age, despite not having breastfed any of her children. Nonetheless, she still looked formidable and regal in her role as mother of the king.

Tiye descended to the pier to take her place on the left of the king. Akhenaten then walked slowly with his two ladies under the admiring gaze of the people, to the sedan chairs waiting for them. Akhenaten and Nefertiti sat in the first one, Tiye taking her place in her own sedan chair behind them. The royal couple's daughters were not with them – they were to be taken to the palace directly, too young, or too tired after the long journey to attend the inauguration.

Strong, beautiful young men lifted up the sedan chairs and the noise of the cheering people reached another level when the royal couple appeared above the heads of the throng. Thousands of people had already arrived and built their houses in the new city.

Noblemen with ostrich feather fans walked behind the royal sedans. But no canopy bearers shielded the king, his wife or his mother from the sun as they started their journey towards the temple built in the middle of the new city. They wanted their god to see them and touch them with his rays. And they wanted everyone to witness their presence.

Meryt-Neith walked behind the sedan chairs in the scorching sunlight. Her service with Nefertiti had taken her to Gem-Pa-Aten – the temple dedicated to Nefertiti where she worshiped the Aten in Waset. She was used to the sunlight by now, and her skin was tanned, her hair burned almost white by the sun. Her eyes shone like blue jewels in her face. Her exotic beauty drew admiring glances from men and envious looks from the women when they noticed its effect on their husbands.

Ramose walked beside her, and Iahmesu and Seshat right behind them. Their precious beehives would be carried to the garden next to the palace where they were to live, but Mut-Bity was taking no chances and Iahmesu was carrying some of the bees in a little ceramic jar that was closed with a linen stopper. Meryt-Neith had not felt the presence of the Pale Man but it would not be surprising if he tried to reach her now that she had left the protection of Per-Hai. Should that happen, Iahmesu was to open the jar to enable the bees to attack him.

The procession walked to the new temple, and passed inside through the great pylons that were painted with bright pictures of the royal couple worshipping the Aten. The rays of the sun disk ended in small hands that touched Akhenaten and Nefertiti, holding out little ankhs to their nostrils, giving them the breath of life.

In the forecourt a magnificent ox waited. It was white and red and so fat it could barely walk; its hoofs had begun to tip upwards from lack of movement, its belly hung low and its neck was thick, its long horns gilded. The coat of the ox gleamed in the sunlight and around the golden horns a beautiful wreath of flowers had been twined. A fitting gift for the god.

Akhenaten and Nefertiti moved to stand in front of the ox. Four strong men appeared and twisted the ox's head so that it lost its balance. Their role was to make the animal fall to the ground so it could be sacrificed in front of the king.

The ox should have fallen easily in the hands of the men – they had done this for years and knew exactly how to bring an animal down. But now something unexpected happened. After initially losing its balance, the ox regained it and began to put up a good fight. Dust billowed into the air as the animal tried to free itself. The panicked ox bellowed and threw its head up so that one of the men holding it fell to the ground after one of the gilded horns smashed into his side. Thankfully, the tip of the horn did not reach its target and he managed to scramble back onto his feet.

The crowd looked on, muttering quietly. As the struggle continued, they fell silent. That a sacrificial animal would not surrender to the Aten… that was a very bad omen. People also remembered how the sun had turned black in the middle of the day soon after the king had buried his father. Was the Aten showing his displeasure of the new king then? And was this the meaning of this incident too?

The silence grew awkward when the ox stayed on its feet and did not fall to its knees. Then it managed to pull its head free, the rope slipping from the hands of the man who had been leading it, and despite its tame looks it suddenly attacked – charging straight towards the royal couple. Nefertiti let out a scream, and her knees buckled, but the king held her arm so tightly she could not move. Tiye stepped backwards but did not turn away to safety.

People screamed and scattered out of the animal's path. Only the Medjay, the king's guard, moved against the animal without hesitation. Two soldiers jumped forward, catching hold of the ox on its neck and horns in the nick of time, and hanging onto it as it thrashed about. The four men whose job it had been to fell the animal joined in and finally, with a great thump, it collapsed. Its leg kicked the air so that it slashed the thigh of one of the men and his blood sprayed onto the animal's coat. The man fell to the ground and was quickly carried off by priests. The dusty ground thirstily drank up the red trail he left behind him.

The crowd stood still, not knowing whether to cheer. A few hesitant shouts of approval rose from the crowd, and then silence fell again.

Akhenaten had stood still and upright throughout the incident, and Nefertiti also straightened her posture, though those near could see she how much she was shaking. Then the king released her arm and stepped forward, pulling out a long golden dagger from his belt. He moved up to the animal, bent down and looked it in the eye for a short while. And then he lifted his dagger and plunged it into the animal's fat neck.

Blood sprayed high into the air, and onto the king, colouring his garment bright red. He stepped backwards, wiping the blood from his eyes and then turned to the crowd, facing them like a demon who had swum in blood.

"Behold the offering we give to the Aten to inaugurate his temple. An ox, a strong animal that cannot resist the power of the Aten."

Behind him a skilled man slashed the ox's throat properly and its blood pooled on the ground as it finally died.

The royal couple walked past it, through the gore, their sandals leaving bloody footprints as they entered the great courtyard where tables were laden with food and flowers as offerings to the god. The new priests of the Aten gathered in procession behind them and temple musicians began to sing and dance. Behind them, a butcher hacked off the right foreleg of the ox and it was carried away hastily towards the main altar so it could be burned as an offering to the Aten.

The crowd looked quietly at the dead animal and the bloody footprints leading inside the temple. Then the priests ushered them out of the courtyard. They were not allowed any further into the god's sanctuary. Only the King and the Great Royal Wife could address the Aten directly. Everyone else was to worship the royal couple at their own altars at home, so that they would speak on their behalf to the god.

People left at the same time as the carcass of the ox was dragged away towards the kitchens where it would be prepared for further offerings to the god – and to the priests who would eat it after the Aten had enjoyed the meat's essence with his rays.

The court retinue was escorted away towards the palace built for them. Meryt-Neith held Ramose's hand tightly as they walked behind Mutnofret. The boy opened his mouth to say something, but Meryt-Neith shook her head.

"Later," she whispered.

Iahmesu and Seshat walked quietly behind them.

Soon the only ones left in the yard were the amassing flies, attracted by the stench of the blood.

38

UNDER THREAT

Merit expected a reaction from the Pale Man to Meryt-Neith moving out of Per-Hai and so when she began to sense it, she was prepared.

"I can feel his presence," she said to Mut-Bity. "He is observing us. He or one of his servants. But whoever it is, he is strong or I would not be feeling like this."

It was not only that energy was constantly buzzing in her spine. It was angry energy. Whoever was observing them didn't hide their feelings and clearly didn't intend to try.

"He must have noticed that we sent bees with her to Akhetaten," Mut-Bity said.

"Yes, he probably thought his opportunity had come when Meryt-Neith and Ramose left our protection."

"Well, he has no business here either." Mut-Bity rose to her feet.

They had been sitting on the rooftop, watching the last of the ships float downriver. It had been an amazing sight, not only the bigger ships carrying the court and officials, but also the smaller ones that carried more workers, tailing the larger vessels.

The dwellers in the village of the tomb builders, Pa-Demi, were also forced to leave. They had been walking past the palace for many days now, leaving in small groups, carrying their possessions in bundles. The king wanted them to start building his tomb on the eastern mountains surrounding the plain on which Akhetaten was built. Everyone knew that the tomb should have been built to the west, closer to the land of the dead. But the king worshipped the rising sun, and according to him, the dead spent their nights sleeping in their dark tombs and then rose together in the morning with the sun. He would also do the same after his death, and so his tomb was to be made in the east. He would be the first to wake up each morning at dawn with the rising of his god.

A workers' village already waited for the villagers of Pa-Demi in Akhetaten and work on the royal tomb was to commence immediately. Akhenaten's tomb on which they had already started work in the valley west of Waset, where his father and ancestors were buried, was abandoned.

Akhenaten could not have given a clearer signal to the priesthood of Amun that the order of the world had changed. There was no longer a religious role for them in the king's life.

The great temple of Ipet-Isut continued to run as it always had before – it still owned all the lands and riches given to it by previous kings. But no further riches would be donated to it by this ruler. What was more, the king's closest officials no longer had any need to please Amun – they had to be loyal to the king only, and worship him so he would speak in their favour to the Aten. If the king heard his officials had anything to do with Amun, they would lose royal favour; and so the noble families turned their backs on the ancient state god, and their faces towards the Aten.

"When should we leave?" Merit said.

"Soon. But first, I want the river to be empty of all those ships so we can travel to Mi-Wer in peace."

It had been decided that Mut-Bity and Merit would travel to Mi-Wer in advance, and wait for Tiye when she returned from Akhetaten. This might take weeks or months. Tiye had told Mut-Bity that she enjoyed living in Mi-Wer more than in the new city.

"I am not enthusiastic about living in a construction site," she had commented, "but of course I must go there for a while first, to see that the affairs of the court run as they should."

The women knew that she wasn't referring to running the *keneret* and the domestic matters of the king's women. It was Tiye that foreign kings wrote to directly, asking her to influence the new king so that old friendships would not be forgotten. Tiye knew more about the running of the country than Akhenaten did. And she intended to keep her grip on the affairs of the state, using her network of informants and spies.

The Pale Man did not try to reach Merit and Mut-Bity directly – their bees were right next to their house in the emptying palace of Per-Hai. But the day after Nefertiti's ship had sailed, a messenger appeared.

"My lady," he bowed, "I was asked to give you this."

Merit took the carefully folded and tied piece of papyrus.

"Who sent it?"

"I do not know who sent it, but it was given to me outside the palace gates when I had just crossed the River to return to the palace. It was a very tall man, hooded. Very pale."

"My thanks." Merit felt her palms start to sweat.

They waited until the man had left before opening the string that fastened the letter. There were no pleasantries at the beginning, no greetings, no signature. There was no need.

"Do not think you, Meryt-Neith or Ramose are safe from me. I will find an opportune moment and I will take them. I will find Shuet and her family as well. You have kept your secret well, but I will discover them. I have use for Meryt-Neith, as she has proven that she is fruitful, and I will certainly keep Ramose as my heir, but the rest of you are dead."

"Well, he went straight to the point," Mut-Bity said dryly, "not that there is anything in there that we didn't already know."

"I'll write to Meryt-Neith and let her know of this letter," Merit said.

"You do that. Thought he might send a message to her too. It's good to see he has learned his lesson, though. He doesn't approach our bees lightly. Do you feel him now? Watching us?"

Merit concentrated.

"No, not anymore. I must have felt him waiting for someone to bring this letter to us. He has probably switched his attention to Meryt-Neith now."

Merit went to her chest, opened it and took out the colour palette with its ink cakes, a piece of papyrus and the sharp reed she used for writing. She looked at her old notebook at the bottom of the chest, with the Eiffel Tower embossed on it, filled with her notes from the first months in the ancient past, still writing to Elijah even though she knew he would probably never see what she had written or learn of her heartfelt deep sense of loss and loneliness. In thousands of years, anything she wrote would have been destroyed.

But a thought had come to her, when Meryt-Neith had stolen the letter Shuet had written to her father and tried to ridicule Shuet. Meryt-Neith had mocked Shuet by saying that if their father was dead, she would have to find the place where he was buried and leave the letter there, if she ever wanted it to reach him in the afterlife.

This renewed, direct threat from the Pale Man convinced Merit that it was time to start turning her idea into a plan.

Merit took her valuable mirror from the coffer as well. Tiye's face as Hathor, the goddess of love and music, looked back at her from the handle. The disk above her head, between the bovine horns, was made of gold and Merit could see her face in it. On the other side, it was of reddish metal, copper, to remind her of the other side of Hathor – the lion goddess Sekhmet, who almost killed humankind for being disrespectful to the old god Re.

The story was probably an echo of some past catastrophe that had killed most of the inhabitants in the Nile Valley. Still, it showed that people loved, feared and respected the cow goddess.

Sighing, Merit laid the mirror back on top of the notebook and closed the lid of the chest. Then she sat by a low table, moistened her cake of ink with water, dipped her reed in the black ink, and started writing a letter to Meryt-Neith. Ships were leaving daily now from Waset to Akhetaten, and she would be able to send the letter this same day.

39

VIGIL FOR DIANA

Diana didn't wake up for two whole weeks. She lay on her back on the shore of the odd silvery lake, on a thin strip of flat rock where we had made camp. Everywhere else, vegetation had taken root or sheer rock rose straight up out of the water. The palm trees grew in a neat row, as there was no space for two trees side by side. It was hard walking in those places; there was barely space to place your feet.

We took turns keeping vigil by Diana's side. It gave us plenty of time to examine our surroundings, too. It turned out that there was no river or stream running above ground to or from the lake. The water came from below the ground. The lake was at the bottom of a narrow crack in the rocks. The sun barely reached the bottom of the gorge at midday and at any other time, it was in the shade. When we flew up to take an overview of the surroundings, we saw nothing but dry rocky landscape without any paths that might have marked the trails of animals or nomadic people. To see the lake at all you needed to be right next to the crack in the dry ground.

"Bay said there are no Nephilim around here, good or bad. Only a handful of Nephilim know of this place and no one comes here openly. It seems we are somewhere in the Sinai peninsula." Daniel said.

He had been scouting around with Bay and Elijah while Lilith and I took our turn guarding Diana.

I was standing now with Daniel at the edge of the sheer drop. Below us we could see the tops of palm trees that were growing in a row beneath us and to our right.

The sun was scorching, but we were not in any hurry to return. We hadn't had any time alone together for ages, so we were taking the opportunity here. Daniel drew me against him and we melted into a long kiss.

Kissing is an interesting experience when you can breathe through your wings and don't need to catch your breath. Daniel's hands were wandering along my back, pressing me against him. I did the same. Our kiss intensified to such an extent I almost began to tear off his clothes.

"No, no... not like that..." Daniel took a step back so that I almost fell forward when he let go of me.

"Why not? How long do we need to wait?" I was in no mood to stop what I had been planning on doing.

"Long enough to be married," Daniel said, keeping me determinedly at arm's length.

Married. I looked at him.

"So we will get married," I said.

"Yes, we will." Daniel replied.

We looked each other in the eyes for a long time. My desire for him must have been so evident that he took another step backwards.

"We need to get betrothed first. According to Nephilim ways. From our own free will, in front of witnesses," Daniel's voice broke. He was breathing hard, his eyes dark with emotion. "Only after that can we get married."

I pointed down into the gorge.

"We have witnesses right here..."

Daniel breathed in, turned to look at the dry desert and shook his head.

"Not here. I want to get betrothed – and married – properly. Not in a hurry in some desert gorge."

"I don't mind," I said.

"I do. I want to show you the respect you deserve and perform the ceremonies in the proper setting."

"What's that, then?"

"You'll see," he said. "Have you calmed down yet?"

I walked around for a while, trying to concentrate on anything but him. After a while I stopped.

"Okay. But we'd better get back to the others or I will not be able to guarantee my good behaviour any longer."

"Dana, I – "

"It's fine, Daniel. I understand. And I love you even more for it, if that's possible."

We flew back down to the lake. Others glanced in our direction. Bay gave us a wide smile that indicated he knew exactly what we had been up to.

Bay did not leave us during that time. Instead, he concentrated on learning more English, and he learned fast, listening to us talk. He asked where we had come from. We didn't tell him about time travelling, but stuck to our original story that we had come from what in our time would be the Baltic countries in the far north. We told him we had come to meet relatives here – and to bring amber to trade for gold.

"And to see Merit?" Bay asked.

"We didn't know she was here," Daniel said. "That was a wonderful surprise. We thought she had died when..."

"When a great sandstorm separated us years back," Elijah continued the story fluently. "It carried her so far away, I never found her again. And I believed she was dead. None of our searches along the River were successful – for we didn't realise she had ended up in the desert. Had we known there was a village of Nephilim deep in the desert of Kemet, we would have come asking for her."

Bay nodded.

"Yes. Sandstorm. Mut-Bity found Merit in desert. She fall to earth. Was dying. Mut-Bity saved her life. Take her to Mi-Wer."

"Why there? Why not to your hidden village?"

"It was predicted, she tell us. Ancient script say that when the pale winged lady appears, fallen on the desert floor, she was must be taken to Mi-Wer."

"What is this script?" Elijah asked.

"Ancient. Many times made again. Not all allowed to see it."

"Have you seen it?" Daniel asked.

"No, not allowed. Only some women allowed. Mut-Bity is one."

"But how can you tell it was Merit the script was about?" I asked.

"She was where the script say. And when. So Mut-Bity take her to Mi-Wer."

"Could be just be a coincidence…" Elijah said, "but I wish to express my gratitude to this Mut-Bity, once we meet. She saved my wife's life."

"Express gratitude…?" Bay struggled with the words.

"I wish to say thank you to Mut-Bity," Elijah said.

"Ah, yes. When you meet."

Daniel and Elijah sat down beside Diana with Bay. I stood at a little distance, looking at Daniel. I could not have enough of drinking him in. Tall, lean, beautiful. He turned his head to look at me, and his eyes smiled at me, making my heart somersault. How long did he think he would manage to keep me at arm's length…

I shook the thought away. Diana was our main concern now. She just kept breathing deeply, asleep, not waking up.

"She must go to water every day," Bay said, "so the waters heal her."

So we carried Diana to the water every day, and let the silver… somethings cover her until they left on their own. It took a long time every day, but the water was fresh and standing in it felt good in the heat. I did not touch the water with my hands anymore, though, but stood with my arms folded across my chest.

"One time is enough," Bay said. "You started the healing. Water continues."

"Won't she starve?" I asked after two days. "She can't eat or drink while she's unconscious."

"No need when in water," Bay said. "Water feeds her."

We didn't understand, but when Diana's colour returned to its healthy, beautiful shade, and she turned out not to be dehydrated (we did pinch her to see how quickly her skin returned to normal to test it), nor had she lost any more weight, all we could do was wait. We didn't understand the nature of the water. None of us had ever heard of anything like this silver lake so in all likelihood, it was still hidden away in the future – or perhaps it had been destroyed.

Lilith filled me in with what had happened at the Centre, how many and who had died. I cried for those we had lost.

"And you are sure it is Anna who betrayed us?" I asked Lilith.

"Yes. But not willingly, I am sure. They must have got hold of her husband and forced her to work for them," Lilith said, "that would be so in line with the methods of Cain and Angel. Steal someone you love and force you to cooperate or else... No doubt that is what they have in mind regarding you, too."

"Where is Anna now?"

"We don't know. What we suspect is that she is the one who brought Ambrogio here. He can't time-travel on his own. She probably returned to the future after that, but where she is now... I have no idea. She may be in the future – or perhaps even here. I don't want to connect with her, so she can't reel in through the strings to our location and bring Cain's troops here. And Paris knows she needs to be careful too."

"Yes, there was a definite malevolent presence when Anna and Paris connected. Paris knows not to contact her now," I said.

"Good. And sad. Anna was one of our very best weavers."

"Maybe we have not lost her yet. She's just obeying to protect her husband if your theory is correct. If there is a way to free her from that bondage, we'll find it," Elijah said.

"Or at least, we'll try," Daniel added.

On the fourteenth day, Diana suddenly woke up. She just stretched herself and yawned. Then she opened her eyes and sat up. The movement was so sudden I jumped.

"Good morning!" she said. "Gosh, I slept well. And had the most amazing dreams!"

She looked around, not knowing where she was.

"Daniel! Elijah! Lilith! *Dana!* What is this place?"

"A place of healing," Bay said from behind her.

Diana was on her feet so fast it seemed impossible. She stared at Bay's yellow eyes.

"Yes, I am Nephilim. No, not bad."

"Yes… you don't smell like them," Diana said, breathing in deeply, "but where are we?"

"You were bitten by Ambrogio, remember?" I asked. "He almost killed you. And I gave you blood so you would survive."

Diana looked baffled. We could see exactly when her memory returned from the way her expression changed.

"Holy shit…" she said, "it's coming back to me now… I was in a ship with our team… and then something hit me on the head when I had fallen asleep and I went half unconscious and could not resist when someone… that shadow… thing... dragged me through the buffer zone to a… tomb… yes, it was Sithathoriunet's tomb, I can see it in my mind. Ambrogio was waiting for me there and – he attacked me right away. It was… do you have any idea what it is like to be bitten by a vampire?"

Her hand rose to her neck.

"Thankfully, no," Lilith said, "but I have seen people being bitten. It's – not pretty."

"No, it isn't. It is just like an animal attacking your throat… not a trace of humanity left. And the feeling when your blood leaves your body…"

Diana had to walk a few steps to get to grips with the memory. She looked thinner and taller than before. No wonder, not having eaten for weeks.

"Soon the pain subsided, and… OK, not going to go there. Then Dana appeared and gave me a blood transfusion. And then… then Ambrogio drank our combined blood, yes?"

"Yes," I nodded, "having tasted your blood first."

"Oh, but that means… he must have read me like an open book… and he surely caught glimpses of your memories too… he knows of our plan now?" Diana swirled around to look at Daniel.

"You fought him?"

"Hell yes," Diana replied, "I didn't just give in, I was conscious enough to put up a fight."

"Well, then there's a chance that he did not read everything you know," Lilith said, "but we can't trust in that entirely. We need to get back to our team as soon as possible. They of course know of Ambrogio, so he can't attack them unawares. But they don't even know if whether or not Diana and Dana are still alive. Or that we have arrived..."

Somehow, I had managed to avoid that thought completely. No one had told our team we were still alive!

"We need to leave now!" I said.

"First, we eat," Bay said.

Seemingly out of nowhere, he produced a gazelle. He had kept us fed during these two weeks, finding these animals in the empty desert. Out of necessity I had also eaten meat, for the simple reason that there was nothing much to eat if I didn't. Normally I didn't eat any meat and it felt strange and heavy in my stomach.

Bay skinned the animal with ease and we roasted it on an open fire. Where he had found dry wood to burn, we had no idea. It looked like driftwood, so perhaps he had flown to the seashore somewhere for it.

Unsurprisingly, Diana ate as if she had never seen food before.

"I've never been this hungry!" she said. "I could eat a horse!"

"Not eat horse," Bay looked shocked, "horses valuable! Not for eating!"

"Well, it was just a figure of speech," Diana said.

"Figure?"

"Saying. It means that you are so hungry you could eat a big animal," Lilith smiled, "any big animal."

She had also used the healing power of the water – the burned skin on her face was almost clear again.

"Imagine if we could bottle this water and sell it," she said.

"Sell? Why?" Bay asked politely.

"So it would heal many people," Lilith replied.

"Not sell healing water. Healing free," was Bay's response.

"Of course," Lilith said, "a silly thing for me to say."

"Everyone ready?" Daniel asked.

"Yes," Diana stood up.

Her movements were very strong and fast, without a trace of weakness.

"Ok, let's go then," Daniel said. "Bay, can you show us the way?"

"Yes."

I took Daniel's arm, Lilith took Bay's and Diana hooked arms with Elijah.

"Ouch!" Elijah exclaimed and let go of Diana.

"What?" we turned to look at him.

"Diana just gave me an electric shock!" he said.

"Sorry..." Diana looked at her hands, "I don't usually do that. Electric energy..."

"Electric? Energy?" Bay tasted the strange words.

"Well, we'll explain on the way," Elijah said.

And with that, we retreated into the buffer zone and began our journey back to the River Nile.

40

REUNION

Ambrogio and his shadow returned to the Nile Valley and waited at the mouth of what would later be called Wadi Hammamat – the dry riverbed that was the main route to the Red Sea from the Nile Valley. From here, they could see anyone approaching the Nile from the eastern desert. The newly created vampires were running the length and width of the desert for him, following the slightest scents of life, searching for Dana.

After three days, Ambrogio sent his shadow to fetch the vampires back. The shadow had retained its skill in navigating the buffer zone even after inhabiting a physical body. Its very essence was formed from the material of the buffer zone, and it seemed to sense at all the times where the physical world was in relation to the mists surrounding it. With his superior sense of smell, the shadow-man also quickly found anyone whose scent he had known before, so it didn't take him long to return with the vampires.

The vampires arrived using the buffer zone. Ambrogio smelled them and there was no trace of human blood mixed in their scent. Good. They had been obedient.

"You will stay here with these servants," Ambrogio said to his shadow, "while I make my way to where they were headed, Akhetaten.

I gained that information from both Dana's and Diana's blood. If Dana or Daniel come by land, avoiding travelling in the buffer zone, they will probably pass through here. If that happens, you are to hide from them and you will find me immediately and let me know. If they leave the buffer zone, I will smell them as soon as I cross their path."

"Yes, master," the shadow-man bowed.

At nightfall, Ambrogio left. He circled the town of Gebtu near the mouth of Wadi Hammamat. In later times, the town would be known as Koptos, the centre of the worship of the ancient fertility god Min, the maker of gods and men.

Then he moved north. The distance to Akhenaten's capital was about 350 kilometres, so the journey would take two to three days even at his phenomenal speed. He could run a day and a night before having to rest, covering around one hundred kilometres during that time.

He ran the whole night. When the sky began to turn lighter in the east, he moved away from the river so as not to be seen easily by people living there.

This time, he knew the Pale Man was nearby, betrayed by his scent before he could surprise Ambrogio. He stood still and listened with all his senses. It was definitely the faint scent of the Nephilim lord and that meant he was not in the buffer zone. When the air moved, carrying his location with it, Ambrogio turned and walked in the direction he knew he would find him.

"My lord." Ambrogio bowed as soon as he saw the tall form standing in the dusk.

"You disobeyed my orders," the Pale Man said coldly. "I'll give you one chance to convince me why I should spare your life."

"I did not disobey your orders, my lord." Ambrogio's voice was calm.

He did not have to pretend to be calm. What the pale Nephilim lord did not know was that Ambrogio was the assassin chosen by Cain and Angel for over hundreds of years to kill other Nephilim. He knew exactly where to hit, where to cut, how to suffocate and destroy a Nephilim. If this Nephilim lord attempted to attack him, Ambrogio intended to kill him; or at least injure him so severely he would be immobilised.

"Explain."

The Pale Man towered over short Ambrogio, lulled into security by his slight form.

"You asked me to fetch the pale beautiful Nephilim lady from Mi-Wer."

"And you did not do that."

"I prepared to get her, and then it was announced that the King's Mother Tiye was about to leave for the city of Akhetaten. Everyone was running around, and there was no opportunity to take the lady, as she was constantly surrounded by soldiers and servants of Tiye until they boarded ship. Our kind cannot move on water readily so once they were on the river, I wasn't able to reach them."

The Pale Man knew this was the truth.

"So I followed the ships – I had sent my servant in one of them to keep an eye on her."

"Which he clearly didn't do."

"He did. But my servant drew the attention of someone on board; he was not known to anyone and was acting suspiciously, being uncomfortable surrounded by water. They arrested him. When the lady heard of this, she became suspicious too. She knew her own lord wanted her back."

Ambrogio stopped talking and waited. When the pale Nephilim asked him a question, he knew he was in the clear.

"And then?"

"She escaped immediately. By the time I heard the news, she was long gone. I only heard this when the ship finally moored to get provisions and freed my servant when they brought him to land. We had to return towards Mi-Wer, one on each side of the river, to find any trace of her."

"And did you find her?"

"No."

"Well, where were you running to just now?"

There was no point in avoiding the truth – the Pale Man would have guessed it anyway.

"I am heading to Akhetaten. That is where she would have gone in the first place, so that's where I expect to find her."

Ambrogio stood still, waiting for a response.

"Very well. Let's say I believe your explanation. I'll join you again. I've only been able to look for you now as I had other matters to attend to and have finally finished them. I have made a new dark Nephilim to serve me. Beautiful, with golden hair. That's how I like my women to look. There was knowledge I wanted to drink from her, but she fought so hard I'll have to wait until she becomes one of us. It's annoying, but eventually I will get all the details I need from her. Knowledge I have been searching for all my life. I have time in hand now, to see if your pretty lady could be a concubine of mine as well."

"I am pleased you decided to find me," Ambrogio said and bowed with his left hand over his silent heart, "so we may hunt together again. We need to stay here in this world and not enter any mists, even though that will be a slower trail to take. If she has walked the earth, her scent will reveal it. There'll be no scent to follow in the mists."

Also, Ambrogio considered, going on foot he would have time to think how he was going to deal with the Pale Man once he had outgrown his usefulness.

41

WRAPPINGS FOR THE DEAD

Tiye did not return to Mi-Wer for months. Merit and Mut-Bity settled back into their old life in their house. Mut-Bity took care of her bees, and she and Merit wove linen together as did all the women who lived in Mi-Wer. The king had only ever travelled with his favourite wives, and those he was intimate with did not live in Mi-Wer any longer but stayed with him in Akhetaten. Mi-Wer was now a place of servants and older wives who no longer pleased the king's eye, who spent all their days weaving linen. Their production was carefully recorded. There was a never-ending demand for fine linen clothing as well as mummy wrappings, and the weaving business of the king's women brought in a considerable income.

"Who are you weaving those for?" Mut-Bity asked.

Merit looked up at her.

"What do you mean?"

"I have done wrappings for so many years that of course I recognise those for what they are. You are weaving for the dead."

Merit nodded.

"You're right. These cloths I've woven will cover someone who is dead."

Mut-Bity looked at her.

"You are talking about yourself," she said.

"I am," Merit answered.

Mut-Bity nodded.

"You are so certain that you will die here, then."

"Yes. The prophecy was so clear. I am to die here and through my death Shuet will learn a secret that is necessary to keep from our enemies. The ancient secret of the Nephilim."

Mut-Bity continued her weaving, but glanced at Merit occasionally.

"Where the creators are hidden?"

"It seems so. We saved Shuet from the Pale Man as the prophecy gave warning of him in time. If he had caught her or killed her, something in the future would have changed. The secret would have been in danger."

"I have learned that the future changes according to our actions," Mut-Bity said, "so you cannot say for certain that in the end, saving Shuet, and you dying, have anything to do with finding the creators."

"It may not. But I believe it might. Mut-Bity – that text was written by someone who knew me personally. Someone who knows what will happen to me. Someone from the future. Someone from the other end of this story. That's why I am preparing myself."

"Have you felt the Pale Man nearby?"

"No. But I have no doubt that he will appear soon enough. I only hope I have time to finish what I have planned before he comes."

For a few moments, Merit felt as though Mut-Bity wanted to say something. Her hand rose to touch the little leather pouch that hid the small dark fish amulet she had received from an old friend upon her death, the day Seth had brought it from the desert and had become Shuet's husband. Mut-Bity was deep in thought for a while, but then just let her hand fall again.

"I need to go and attend to the bees."

She rose and left Merit to her weaving.

Merit took only short breaks from weaving – and writing. She asked for papyrus to be brought to her and when she was not weaving, she concentrated on writing something in a language Mut-Bity did not understand. It was not a letter, as she sometimes drew lines over what she had already written and rewrote it.

"What are you doing?" Mut-Bity asked one evening when Merit finally put away her writing palette and rubbed her tired eyes.

"Trying to remember."

"Remember what?"

"History."

She would not say anything more and Mut-Bity did not ask.

42

SPELLS ON LINEN

Time passed and despite his threat, the Pale Man did not show himself to either Merit in Mi-Wer or Meryt-Neith in Akhetaten. Merit felt an echo of his presence at times – that telling, prickling sensation in her spine that meant either the Pale Man himself or one of his servants was observing her. The sensation never intensified into a buzz so he was keeping his distance.

Merit corresponded with Meryt-Neith, inquiring about her life, and telling her about their everyday life in Mi-Wer. It was the mundane little things she so wished she could have shared with her daughter and grandson.

Merit sent letters to Shuet as well and received replies. These were passed to her by Mut-Bity, but she had no idea who had sent them on. She read them immediately, savouring every word, imprinting them on her memory, and then burning the letters. She did not want anyone to see them – even if they were written in English – a language that would not even exist for several thousand years. The words written in English in that ancient scroll from the House of Life of Hut-Ka-Ptah in Inbu-Hedj made her cautious. Someone from the future might be nearby, someone who had knowledge of English.

Merit had asked the girls if whether they were interested in learning the language of their father, but only Shuet had said yes. Meryt-Neith had been bitter that he had abandoned them, which was what she believed to be the truth. She had refused, saying there was no use in learning a language no one could speak where they lived. Merit assumed she had forgotten about being asked.

So, for years, when they were alone, Merit and Shuet had talked in English to each other, and Merit had also taught Shuet to write the language after she had returned from the secret valley to Mi-Wer. Shuet learned fast, even though she made lots of spelling mistakes and wrote some words in the language of ancient Egypt when she forgot the English one. Still, her writing was quite legible.

Merit finished weaving her wrappings and instead spent time on painting more words in another strange language on them.

"What is it that you are doing now?" Mut-Bity could not contain her curiosity. "Those words look different from the ones you wrote before."

"I am writing prayers on my wrappings," Merit said, "Words to protect and guide."

"In the afterlife? A Book for Going Forth by Day? Advice so that you find your way in the afterlife?"

"Yes, advice on where to go."

Mut-Bity looked at the text and Merit with curiosity. She stretched the fabric taut and painted the words on the fine linen with the best ink and rolled the wrappings carefully, numbering them. The numbers she wrote with the signs used in Kemet. Some scrolls had numbers in black, the others in red.

"Why are you doing that? Numbering the linen?"

"I am to be wrapped in this order. The highest numbered piece of linen comes closest to my body, and the lowest numbered is the outermost one. First the red, then the black."

Spells for the dead had to recited in a certain order, so this was not odd in itself. What *was* odd, was that Merit had never appeared to be religious – not towards the ancient deities of Kemet, nor to any deity from her own life. Mut-Bity had never seen her pray or show devotion to any god or goddess.

Merit had a wooden chest made for her wrappings and placed the rolls of linen there carefully, using herbs to keep off any ants or termites that might otherwise have found their way inside. She had some blank linen strips also.

In another coffer, she placed the letters she had written. Every time she finished a scroll of linen, she took out the notes she had written before, and from these, she wrote words onto papyrus with her sharpest reed pen, in the strange language she sometimes spoke with Shuet before Shuet had had to flee to the secret valley with her husband, pregnant with their soon to be born baby.

"To whom are those addressed?" Mut-Bity once asked.

"They are for the beekeepers," Merit said.

"The beekeepers?" She could not have surprised Mut-Bity more.

"Yes. For the sisterhood of the bees."

Mut-Bity said nothing.

"Your secret council that knows of the old legend," Merit said, "I need you to help me. I will explain when everything is ready."

"Help you to do what?" Mut-Bity asked.

"I will explain when all is ready," Merit repeated, and returned to her writing.

But that was not all. She wrote another set of letters, using the language of Kemet. She did not let Mut-Bity see what she had written, but even from a distance, Mut-Bity recognised the language as her own. These she also numbered – again the same amount of letters as there were linen rolls with black writing.

Each letter Merit bent carefully and tied with a strong string. All the letters she placed in two leather pouches, according to the language they were written in. She kept the lid of the coffers closed with carefully tied and knotted strings and even used clay seals on the knots to prevent anyone from opening the lid. The servants were curious, but not so curious as to be caught going through their mistress's belongings.

All this writing took Merit many weeks. The day she placed the last linen scrolls and letters into their coffers, a messenger arrived announcing that the Mother of the King, Tiye, life, prosperity and health to her, was returning to her palace in Mi-Wer.

Preparations for her arrival kept everyone busy. Then Tiye arrived and the old routine resumed. Merit spent her days with Tiye, Mut-Bity tended to her bees and came to talk with the Mother of the King in the evenings. The chests with the linen rolls and letters remained unopened under Merit's bed, but still she offered no explanation to Mut-Bity.

43

STEP INTO THE FUTURE

Asule and Khonsu were no longer children, but a young man and woman, and so we moved to a bigger home with two rooms where there were three sleeping niches – one for Seth and I, one for Asule and one for Khonsu.

Khonsu grew tall and strong. Asule remained as short as her parents had been. Her dark skin was healthy and beautiful and when brother and sister stood side by side, the contrast of their height and colouring was striking. Despite not being related by blood, they were more tightly bound to each other than many real siblings. I remembered the distance between me and Meryt-Neith, and felt a longing nothing could ever fulfil. I would never be able to bring back my childhood, never change the coldness Meryt-Neith felt for me.

I taught Asule and Khonsu to read and write as well as I could, and then the job was taken over by a scribe who taught the children of the village. One day I walked with them to the library and the cave that functioned as a classroom. I stood in the doorway, watching them take their places among other students. There were many oil lamps burning as ordinary human eyes could not see as well as Nephilim eyes.

"Today we shall copy the story of Truth and Falsehood," the teacher, a woman of advanced years, said. "Take your seats and writing equipment."

No one paid attention to me standing in the doorway. The children sat down on the mats on the floor, stretched their kilts so they were taut and placed their writing tablets on them. I was lost in my thoughts, and felt like I was falling asleep, which was unusual. I wondered if I could take a nap before the children returned home. My limbs seemed made of stone, they felt so heavy. Was I getting ill? That had never happened before. I'd have to leave now, so food would be ready when the children came back from their lesson.

I looked down and my hands seemed to be glowing. How odd, I observed sleepily. I really did need to go now...

I closed my eyes for just one blink and when I opened them, I was in the misty world and there was no doubt about the silver glow around my hands now. Thin silvery strings extended from my fingers and vanished in midair. They reminded me of the strings that had once come out of my hands when we were dancing, the day mother told Meryt-Neith about who and what she was. What we were...

I was looking into our home through the mist. No one was there. I stepped out of the mist, wondering why I had been there in the first place. I couldn't remember entering it. I knew now that others could also move in the misty world, but it was agreed no one would go there without need. It might draw the attention of the dark ones to us. The mist carried our presence far and wide – our kind could sense each other from a distance in the mists. That is why the knowledge of the mists was taught only to adult Nephilim who could contain their curiosity – children couldn't be trusted with the knowledge. I had found my way in there by accident when I was young, and thought at first I'd thought I had died.

I heard voices from the corridor, and Asule and Khonsu pulled the curtain aside and stepped inside.

"We're starving!" Khonsu announced.

Well, he usually was. It was amazing how much a growing boy could eat.

"You haven't had time to make anything to eat?" Asule looked around. "Can I help you?"

I stared at them. I had blinked my eyes only once and I was certain I had not fallen asleep. I had only felt tired, but I hadn't nodded off. I couldn't have...

"Your lesson is already over?" I asked. "But it's only just begun!"

"Oh no, we went at it for ages..." Khonsu rolled his eyes. "Nothing seemed to satisfy the teacher. I had to write the same piece of text three times. Three! The lesson must have taken twice as long as last time!"

He placed his wax tablet on the table. A wooden tablet, covered with beeswax – the impressions made by Khonsu's reed pen were clearly visible. Beeswax we had in plenty, thanks to the beekeepers. Sisterhood of the Bees, we called them, as most were women.

"Twice as long?" I asked.

"At least," Khonsu said.

I had blinked my eyes once and a long time had passed? Had I travelled into the future during that time? Could moving through time like that even be possible?

I fetched some goat cheese and bread for the children and while they ate, I tried to make sense of what had happened. Was it possible to travel through time in the misty world? Or had I simply fallen asleep for two hours without noticing, and my thoughts had brought me to the place where we prepared food? I had heard of people who sometimes walked at night, still asleep. Could I have been sleepwalking for two whole hours?

I had to test this somehow. I knew the moon would be full in two nights. Seth was away on a scouting mission and was unlikely to return for a few days more. This would be the perfect time...

"I need to work on a scroll intensively for the next two days," I said to the children. "Would you like to stay with your friends for a while?"

"Yes!" They both yelled. "We could go swimming!"

They loved to swim. Children and young ones often went together to one of the underground lakes – one that was not very deep and was lit by sunlight through a crack on the side of the cave wall.

Mothers often arranged some free time for themselves by taking their children to their friends' places for a day or two, and then returning the favour at a later time. So it was not difficult to arrange for Khonsu and Asule to spend time with their friends.

As soon as they were away and the day's work was done, I took a small bowl and a leather flask of water and walked the corridors until I reached one that led upward. It went up to the top of the rocky formation under which our secret village lay. I found a boulder where I often sheltered to watch the stars and the moon, filled the bowl with water and put it into a place where it couldn't be seen easily – next to a rock that was cracked and lined. I placed a thin piece of linen over it, folding the cloth so it went under the bowl.

I went back to the village, walked home and closed the curtain. Then I concentrated on thinking about the full moon – a sight I had seen so many times before, sitting next to the same boulder where I had just left the bowl of water.

I concentrated seeing it as completely as I could. I tried to feel the night wind on my skin, to see how the moon rose silently above the horizon, keeping a part of my mind concentrated on the bowl of water. I strove for a relaxed state of mind, following my breathing with that part of my mind that was thinking about other things than the moon and the bowl.

I felt my hands getting warmer and stole a look down. Yes. They were glowing. Full moon, full moon, full moon... I allowed no other thought to enter my mind.

I felt a slight pop in my ears – like when we closed our wings and fell quickly towards the earth – we used to do that for fun, Seth and I, when we were younger.

A breath of wind touched my cheek and I opened my eyes to see the full moon above me. I barely had the courage to turn my head and look at the bowl next to me. I took it in my hands. The linen was dusty when I lifted it off. The bowl was empty.

The empty bowl and the full moon were my proof that I had travelled two days into the future. I had put the bowl in a place where it was hard for anyone to find it and where I knew the sun would touch it. The piece of linen in its proper place as I'd left it was proof that no animal had emptied the shallow bowl. It had to have been the sun that had dried up the water in the bowl.

I sat in silence for a long while, taking it all in. I could journey into the future using the misty world. As far as I knew, no one had ever done that before.

What would I do with this knowledge? I felt reluctant to tell anyone about my experience. If the word spread, what would be the consequences? Enemy Nephilim would use it to hunt their enemies – it would give them new ways to track and kill us. Maybe the Nephilim council already knew about this – it was a well-kept secret if so. If that was the case, I dare not reveal it to anyone

Listening to the silence of the desert, I decided to keep my secret to myself for now. I would search every scroll in the library for an answer and then decide what to do.

44

LEAVING

Merit observed Mut-Bity and her bees. The sun touched her hair, which still gleamed surprisingly black. So many years had passed, and Mut-Bity stayed the same. She had always had the appearance of being of advanced years but was one of those people whose ageing one didn't really notice. How old could she be? The sun had baked her skin dark brown, she had crow's feet around her eyes, but her posture and step were not those of an old woman, no matter how many jokes she made about her age. Maybe all those herbal drinks she knew how to mix did the trick. That, and good food and the fact she was almost constantly moving about, doing tasks the servants could have done.

"The time has come when I need to leave," Merit said to Mut-Bity when she straightened her back after looking into the beehives.

Mut-Bity turned to look at Merit.

"To leave? Where will you be going?"

"To the Valley. I sense things are about to change. I can't explain it, it's a feeling. I know that danger is approaching, but I don't know where from."

Mut-Bity observed Merit. She knew Merit had strong intuition and flashes of clairvoyance. If she said danger was approaching, Mut-Bity believed her.

"Tiye won't let us leave," she said, "so we need to get away in secrecy so that no one suspects what we are up to."

"We?"

"Well, who else would take you to the Valley? You don't know the way there. How could you – you have never been there."

Merit smiled.

"What of the bees?"

"I'll send word to the Valley for a new beekeeper to come immediately. As soon as she arrives, we'll leave. Remember not to pack anything beforehand – I am sure our servants report us to Tiye if they think we're up to something unusual."

After a month, a sun-baked woman from the Valley appeared on their doorstep. Mut-Bity walked into the garden with her to tell her everything she needed to know about caring for the bees of Mi-Wer. The servants didn't overhear this discussion and the woman left without coming back indoors. They wouldn't see her again; she would return only after they had already left.

Mut-Bity sent the servants on an errand and then carried Merit's chests with the linen wrappings and letters to the back of the garden where the beehives were. A little shed right next to the clay beehives offered a safe place to keep them, as people avoided the bees.

That evening, they sat with Tiye as usual and talked of the great jubilee that was to be held in Akhetaten the following year.

"The king wishes to show the beauty and might of the city of the Aten to the whole world," Tiye said, sipping spiced wine.

She pressed her hand to her stomach in a way that made Merit suspect she was in pain. Her dark skin looked slightly ashen in bright light. Also the tang of herbs in her wine prickled Merit's nostrils. They probably wouldn't be noticeable to anyone else, but with her Nephilim sense of smell, she recognised plants that eased pain, and also blue waterlilies that had a slight narcotic effect. Tiye had been drinking this infused wine a lot lately.

Merit exchanged a glance with Mut-Bity when Tiye placed her hand on her stomach. Mut-Bity nodded slightly. She had noticed it too.

"Invitations have been sent to the kings of the surrounding countries," Tiye said, "and when they arrive they will see that my son is the greatest king, greater than any of them."

No doubt, the glorious show was also meant for the people of Kemet. The king's lack of interest in protecting the borders of the land and abandonment of the old deities had not made him popular. In the background, the priesthood of Amun spoke out against the king. It was high treason, but they were careful not to be caught. No one could be named; it was as if the desert winds were whispering stories of the king's incompetence into people's ears, and they spread just as fast as the wind.

Tiye was furious, trying to find the culprits through her network of spies. The nobility living in Akhetaten did not want to hear the whispers against the king, as their wellbeing was tied to the king's favour. But not every noble family lived in Akhetaten. The farmers didn't care – they stayed close to their plots of land as always and worked to grow enough food to pay their taxes. If echoes of the discontent towards the king reached their ears, they had no power or desire to do anything about it. No one considered them a threat, least of all Tiye.

Meryt-Neith had also written to them, telling them about the new buildings and the magnificent temples. She had settled into her life in the royal *keneret* as one of Nefertiti's ladies, and was now a temple dancer, training others in Nefertiti's retinue. Ramose had grown into a handsome young man and girls were already showing interest in him, which amused Meryt-Neith. Hearing all this news made Merit's heart happy.

"I shall also travel to Akhetaten when the time for the celebrations comes nearer," Tiye said, "but for now, I prefer to stay here. I am not getting any younger and can get more rest here."

Tiye had returned from her latest trip to Akhetaten not long ago, and had been very tired after the journey. The king had ordered her to be present in at the temple rituals every day at sunrise while she had been in the new capital.

"Resting is wise," Mut-Bity said.

"We are both getting old, my friend," Tiye smiled sadly. "I can already feel my life drawing towards its end. No, no… I know this to be a fact. I have lived longer than many, seen my children grow, and my son has become a king after his father. All is as it should be. Soon, I shall join my husband in the fields of Iaru and this thought brings me great comfort. But my concern about my son will never cease, not until the day I die. These are not easy times, and the priesthood of Amun is certainly looking for any opportunity to rise back to power."

The moment of weakness had gone and the sharp look had returned to Tiye's eyes.

"We should leave you to rest now," Mut-Bity said.

"Yes, it is already late. We'll talk more tomorrow," Tiye said and rose from her chair, her hand instinctively pressing her stomach.

Mut-Bity and Merit bowed to her respectfully and waited for Tiye to leave the room.

That night Merit wrote one more letter, to Meryt-Neith.

"I am sending word to her about how she can contact me after I am gone," Merit said.

"What will you say?" Mut-Bity asked.

"I'll ask her to write to the beekeeper here. That won't reveal anything, as the Pale Man already knows the beekeepers are from the Valley."

"True," Mut-Bity said, "but ask her only to write if there is a grave emergency. It's always risky when the beekeepers change post. We have to take detours and approach the opening of the way to the Valley from many different directions in order, to avoid leading anyone there."

"I will write that. Maybe one day, we'll be able to correspond more."

Merit folded the little letter into a neat square, and tied it with a string. She would leave it in the little shed in the garden so that the next beekeeper could forward it to a ship heading to Akhetaten.

By the time the sun rose the next morning, their own tiny fishing boat was already far away from Mi-Wer, heading towards the west on the great lake.

45

A SECRET SHARED

I found nothing in any of the scripts about moving through time using the misty world, despite searching for weeks in the library of scrolls. There were writings about our past, but they were mostly genealogy lists. There were also some stories of our war heroes from battles with the dangerous Nephilim, but those were from ancient times, long before we hid in the Valley. After that, we had managed to stay hidden away. I read through all these scripts under the pretence that I was checking to see if they were too worn and needed to be copied, but there was no hint in any of them about time travel. And most of the scripts were copies of writings from the river valley of Kemet, where the existence of the Nephilim was unknown.

I suspected many of the winged deities were related to us – echoes of the great war when humankind hunted and killed the evil Nephilim when they finally had had enough of them. This war was the reason our kind had to hide as well. And we had remained hidden even after the memory of the battle had faded.

Finally, I decided to tell Seth what had happened. I had to discuss it with someone, and I trusted Seth completely to keep my secret.

"I have never heard of anything like it..." he said. "You're certain this happened?"

He looked me straight in the eye, honestly, with no ridicule in his expression.

"Yes. Suddenly I was there under the full moon and all the water had dried up in the bowl without anyone touching it. Also, one of the scribes had been trying to find me on both days but no one knew where I was."

We were floating on our backs in the silver lake again, hand in hand. The little silver specks caressed our skin, causing a pleasant shiver.

"That is incredible," Seth said. "Could you travel back in time as well?"

"I don't know... what would happen if I did? If I went back to a time when I had already lived, would I vanish from there? Or would I kill myself? Or would there be two of me from then on?"

I had thought about this and decided I would not try to go to my own past.

"But what if you tried to travel to a past before you were born?"

"I have no idea how to do that..." The thought made me nervous and I let go of his hand, and turned to swim away.

He followed me and we swam to the flat rock in the middle of the lake and climbed up.

"It seems your skills are tied to your ability to concentrate. You do it all with your mind," Seth said. "Entering the misty world, and now going to the future through the same misty world. So your mind, and the misty world and these skills... they are all tied together somehow."

We sat on the stone and a deliciously cool draught dried our skins.

"But I need something to concentrate on. Something I know well," I said. "At least I think I do. I concentrated on the full moon that was coming in two days. I know the way the moon looks very well, so it was easy to think of it. But how can I concentrate on something I have never seen?"

Seth's warm hand stroked my arm.

"Maybe you could use the scripts in the library?"

"They are words... formal words... I can't make them into a vivid picture in my mind. Not to the extent I believe would be needed."

"But would you be willing to try?"

"I... I don't think so. What if I got lost there? And then never found my way back? What if I continued living there until I reached the date I was

born? What would happen to me? Could I exist twice? I don't think so... I fear I might die then and we would have lost each other for good."

The thought of losing our children and Seth was too much to even contemplate. I would never risk it.

"Well, maybe you could practise travelling to the future then? That way you wouldn't cross paths with yourself. We could plan exactly where and when you would appear and I would first make sure you have really gone, and then go and wait for you in the destination you choose."

I looked at him.

"We could try that, yes."

Seth smiled and moved closer. He kissed me on the cheek and then bit me gently on the ear.

"But not right away..." he whispered, "as far as I know we are in no hurry to go anywhere, are we?"

His breath tickled my neck and his strong arm wrapped around my shoulders.

"No... Not in any particular hurry..." I smiled. "Did you have something in mind?"

" I do. In fact, my mind is concentrating on only one thought at the moment."

He pulled me towards him and I turned to kiss him. Gently he lowered me on my back on the stone and for a while, we completely forgot about travelling through time.

46

THE HORSES

Ramose was looking at the horses when the strange sensation came over him. Just a few seconds before, he had been feeling healthy and well. For a moment, he wondered whether he had the feverish illness that came and went through the land.

"They are beautiful, aren't they?" a pleasant male voice asked from behind him.

He turned to look. A tall man was standing there, wrapped up in cloth with a covering round his head. His arms were hidden under the fabric, but his face, his hands and feet were visible and were so pale that Ramose thought he'd never seen anyone so colourless. He did not look sickly, though. His skin had an odd golden hue despite his paleness.

But it was the eyes that fascinated him the most. They were a colour he had never seen before, not in anyone's eyes. Oily, bright yellow; and they were observing him keenly, full of interest.

"Yes, they are," he answered and the man nodded, turning his gaze back to the pair of the king's chariot horses that were in training. Ramose felt as if he had been half asleep and suddenly woken up when the pale stranger turned his eyes away.

For a while, they observed the beautiful animals trotting around the dusty ground near the royal stables. The dust rose into the air, almost obscuring the mountains that encircled the plane where Akhetaten was built. It was still early in the morning, before the worst heat of the day.

"You are Meryt-Neith's son, aren't you?" the man asked suddenly, not turning his eyes away from the horses.

"Yes, I am. You know my mother?"

A slight smile made the corner of the man's mouth twitch.

"Yes. Yes, we were… close once. Tell me… does your mother still like bees?"

"Bees?" Ramose looked at the man, surprised.

"Well I remember there seemed to be bees around her all the time years back when we met."

"Oh, I see. I don't know. She never mentions whether she likes the bees or not, but we do have beehives where we live. Iahmesu and Seshat take care of them."

"Iahmesu and Seshat? Who are they? I don't recall them… But then again it was so long ago I may have forgotten about them."

"Oh you wouldn't forget them! They are dwarfs! They were my grandmother's friends. Or her friend's friends… I'm not quite sure. But they were with my mother's family already when they lived in Mi-Wer. They are with the Great Royal Wife Nefertiti's sister Mutnofret these days."

"That must have happened before you were born then… Where were you born?"

The question took Ramose by surprise. Why would a stranger be interested in where exactly he was born?

"I don't know, really. I never asked mother. But I think it was a city by the sea. I remember there were many houses. And ships in the harbour."

"You must have been very small then."

"Yes. I remember nothing else."

"Did you travel with your mother? I understood that she did travel for a while before settling in the service of the Great Royal Wife. Do you know where your travels took you?"

"I don't know anything about any travelling. Mother has never mentioned that we travelled. I don't remember any, either."

"And now you live here."

"Yes. Now we live here."

"Do you have any siblings? A little younger than you?"

A little younger? Why younger? Why not older? What made this man so curious? All the questioning began to make Ramose uneasy.

"No, I have no brothers or sisters."

Ramose hoped the man would stop asking questions now, but no.

"Is your mother married now?"

"No."

Ramose did not say anything more and tried to look as if he was only interested in the horses. The driver was teaching them to do a sharp turn and almost managed to make the chariot with its two wheels topple over onto its side.

"Too sharp! That was close!" the man said, amused.

He was quiet after that, but Ramose felt him observing him, as if he was measuring him. The unpleasant feeling in his spine intensified the whole time. Surely he was not getting the shaking fever disease? He had never been ill in his life if you did not count the scrapes and cuts any young boy was bound to get.

"You have grown into a handsome young man!" the pale man then said. "The last time I saw you, you were quite small. You could already run around, but you weren't speaking yet."

Ramose turned, surprised.

"We have met before?"

"Yes. But you wouldn't remember me. You were too little. Do you know where your father is?" the pale stranger asked suddenly.

"Mother said he is dead. I have never seen him."

"It is sad for a boy to grow up without a father," the man said softly. "Did you ever miss him?"

Ramose had had enough.

"How can I miss someone I have never met? No. I don't miss him. And now I need to go."

He turned to leave.

"I see my curiosity has annoyed you. I apologise."

The man's voice was pleasant and he smiled apologetically.

"It's just that I used to be close with your mother many years ago and when I heard you were her son, my desire to find out more about you got the better of me. Please don't tell your mother about me. You see – I intend to surprise her by visiting her. I hope she will be pleased to meet me again after so many years. And to be honest – I think I behaved rather... inappropriately when we last met. I need to apologise for that, even if she still won't forgive me. I can't let the past stand between us, and would like us to be friends again."

Ramose looked at the man, trying to make up his mind whether to dislike him or not.

"Watch out!" the man yelled suddenly and plunged straight at him.

They fell to the ground just as the two horses ran past them, dragging a fallen chariot behind them. The horses had bolted and thrown their driver off the vehicle. If the pale man had not acted so quickly, the horses would have run right over Ramose.

"Thank you!" Ramose got back onto to his feet. "You move very fast!"

"I am glad I did. You could have died, crushed under those horses!" the man dusted the cloth that he had wrapped round him like a cloak.

"I am in your debt," Ramose said, concentrating on not showing how shocked he was.

While he dusted off his own clothes, the wind dispersed a smell of overripe fruit that was coming from somewhere.

"No, you are not... but you might help me to meet your mother again. Would you? Do you think you could come walking with your mother and encounter me? I am afraid she is still angry with me, and if she hears I am here, she might refuse to meet me. And I really do need to say how sorry I am. I have acted against Ma'at, and will not have any rest until I have made amends."

Ramose looked at the man who looked genuinely friendly now. He made up his mind. This man had saved him from death, or at least severe injury, after all.

"Very well. Tell me where you'll be and I'll bring my mother to meet you."

47

TO THE NILE

We kept away from Wadi Hammamat as we made our way towards the Nile.

"The blood-drinker can be there," Bay said. "We fly other way. We go north."

"That sounds best," Daniel said. "We can't be sure he's there but it would be a logical place to wait for us – or to put others to keep watch for us."

"What others?" I asked, looking down at the dry rocky desert below us – the memory of Ambrogio and his shadow-man running under me at impossible speed still made me nervous.

"Ambrogio is a vampire. If he wants servants, he creates them," Diana said dryly.

"Yes. Of course." I understood.

"It may not be the wisest thing to do but if he is desperate enough to find you..." Lilith said.

"What do you mean? Why would it not be wise of him to create new vampires?" I asked.

"Because they are so voracious in their need to feed at the start of their new existence," Elijah explained, "that usually their creator uses extreme measures to make them understand the nature of obedience. Sometimes, right at the start, their creator breaks their limbs to stop them from running off to hunt. They heal quickly, it's true, but it takes days for them to find whatever human nature they have left in them, so that they will listen to orders. And they wouldn't find it at all if their sire didn't force them to listen. It doesn't always work, either, and some vampires remain completely bestial. They are the most dangerous ones, as they don't care who sees them hunting, and the true vampires hunt them down and kill them. They don't want knowledge about their existence spreading any further. If they do manage to calm down and start to listen to their human side, from then on, their existence is marked by the effort to keep a balance between their hunger and their analytical mind."

"Well, if Ambrogio needs a few days to do this, we've already been away for long enough for him to achieve it..." I said.

"Which is exactly why we need to take care no one catches us taking any road or track that is a logical route to Amarna. If they were waiting for us anywhere, it would most likely be in the south, near the mouth of Wadi Hammamat. That's the shortest way to the river and from there on to Akhetaten " Lilith said.

"How will we ever find our team again?" I asked.

"With this." Diana lifted up her left hand.

Three colourful cords had been twisted into an armband. It looked like a friendship bracelet and I had thought it was a memento of some long-gone friend she was carrying, perhaps a dead Time Walker she had known.

"Paris made this from strings of her pullover after we arrived. That night in Deir el-Medina, before we left for Thebes, before we took on Egyptian clothing," Diana said. "Once we dare use the buffer zone again, you can find her, and through her the team, as you use this to weave our way to her."

Bay looked at the strings and then at me.

"This is interesting. What you call weaving. Can you teach me how?"

"I'm afraid not… it's not something that can be taught. It seems that I was born with the skill."

"I have never heard of anyone do this. To have… strings in hands," Bay glanced at my hands before turning his gaze towards the western horizon again.

"It's a secret," Daniel quickly told him, "one that we would like you to keep. If our enemies hear of this skill, they will come after Dana for sure. She may even be forced to lead them to your secret valley, now that she knows the way there. It seems she can move wherever she wants once she has visited a place."

Bay considered this.

"I understand. I will not tell."

"Thank you," I said.

"Time to go down," Bay changed the subject.

We had been flying near the ground, first towards the north and then to the west, and now we landed in the rocky desert.

"The river is near," Bay said, "some hours more."

"You think we should spend the night here in the desert?" Lilith asked.

"Perhaps that's wise," Elijah said, "after all our body heat would be visible to any enemy Nephilim in the river valley if we flew there by night."

"Well, won't we be spotted even more easily here in the middle of nowhere at night?" I asked.

"The dangerous ones stay in western desert. They don't come often to east a lot. They don't think we are here," Bay said. "I trust they are not here."

"Why would that be?" Diana asked.

"Nothing interesting here. They know we are in west. They try to find us in west."

And so we stayed the night. I wasn't sleepy, so I sat beside Diana who fidgeted and twitched as if she was being bitten by insects.

"How are you feeling now?" I asked.

"Strange. Like I can hear my blood running in my veins. My ears are ringing and my eyes are behaving very strangely too... I can see lots of little shiny dots around me in the air."

"Well, it's no wonder is it? After all, you were unconscious for two weeks," I said. "The strange and wonderful thing is that you are still alive! Maybe it's about blood pressure. Or perhaps the shiny dots have something to do with the silver... somethings in the lake."

"Yes, it could be. I've never heard of water like that before..." Diana lifted her hands as if checking to see if there were silver specks on them. "Healing waters."

"Maybe it's the water connected with the Nephilim prophecy... *She of the silver waters*," Elijah said. Bay turned his head with a look of curiosity on his face but said nothing.

"Yes, but who is the *she*? I mean Dana would be the obvious choice, especially since the prophecy says something about you *knowing her from what she weaves*. I don't weave. Dana does," Diana said.

"We're still clueless about what that strange lake is," I said. "Silver waters or weaving – they don't explain how the water could keep Diana alive. No one should be able to survive two weeks without eating or drinking, without a drip anyway."

"Have you known about the silver waters for long, Bay?" Lilith asked.

"Yes, be there always," his deep voice came from a little distance away. He was walking around, checking the surroundings and had heard Lilith's question easily even though she had said it quietly.

"How did you find the lake in the first place?" Daniel asked.

"Not sure. There always. Our secret," Bay said.

"Are there any more waters like that?" Daniel asked.

"No, we don't know more healing waters."

Daniel nodded. I could see he was thinking hard but he didn't share his thoughts with us.

"I'm going to try to get some sleep," Diana said. "Maybe the specks will go away after a rest. And I hope my muscles will stop aching as well."

"Come over here, beside me. The night is cold," Lilith said and

Diana crossed over to her so they could lie on the ground back to back, covered by my large scarf. It was the same one Ambrogio had given to Daniel to prove he had me captive. I didn't want it back – I had seen him pressing it against his face and breathing in my scent. The look in his cold eyes had been... it was beyond description, but had left me feeling like an animal facing a predator it could not escape. Death was in those eyes. Death, and some strange sort of hunger...

"You sure are warm..." Lilith said, sighing as Diana settled on the ground with her back against Lilith.

"And you feel cool – don't catch cold!" Diana answered.

"No fear of that with you warming me up," Lilith mumbled.

Soon their breathing revealed they were fast asleep.

I couldn't sleep and shortly, Daniel walked over to me and sat down too. Elijah and Bay were also sitting on the ground now. All three were sitting with their backs towards each other, with Lilith and Diana in the middle, so that they could scan our surroundings in three different directions. I sat facing towards the two sleeping figures, and Daniel sat by my side, looking the other way.

"How will this all end?" I asked quietly.

"We have no way of knowing," Daniel said, "but I find it amazing that we were led to the silver waters of the prophecy. That seems to prove that there is truth in it."

"I hope we reach Amarna and can find... whatever we are looking for," I said, remembering at the last moment not to mention the dwarfs and the beginning to the path leading to the Watchers in Bay's hearing. "But even if all goes well, we still don't know what will happen then. Where will the path take us? How long do we have to follow it?"

"Who knows," Daniel said, pulling me closer, against his side, "but we have to take the path and follow it, however long it takes."

I saw Bay turning his head slightly, but not looking directly at us, no doubt curious about the "path", but again, he said nothing. I closed my eyes and breathed in Daniel's scent, my forehead against his shoulder.

When we set off in the morning, it was two hours flight before the Nile Valley suddenly opened beneath us – a fresh green ribbon in the middle of a vast desert.

"Now there's a sight for dusty eyes..." Lilith said as we landed, "do you think we could get any fresh food before we continue our journey?"

"I get," Bay smiled and began to walk away. "I have friends near. You stay here."

Here was at the desert's edge, behind a row of small acacia trees, in a depression on the ground. The morning was young, but already we could see people moving among the mud brick buildings of a small village behind the fields. Sitting behind the trees, we weren't visible. Only Elijah placed himself so that he could look out for anyone approaching.

"I wouldn't mind a dip in the river," Lilith said, "it seems like a long time since I felt fresh and not grungy."

None of us was presentable after days of flying under the hot sun. We were dusty and sweaty and in need of a good clean-up.

"We'd draw too much attention to ourselves if we just walked over to the water," Elijah said, "and the word would spread. Let's wait for Bay to get back."

We didn't have to wait for long. Bay came back, walking along the dusty path between the fields, carrying a bundle. He wasn't trying to hide, but then again he looked like a local. He was tall, but otherwise he could have been Nubian; and there were lots of people of Nubian origin in ancient Egypt. He was preceded by the delicious smell of freshly baked bread. He brought some boiled eggs as well, and a big jug of beer.

It took an embarrassingly short time for us to eat the food and gulp down the beer Bay poured into a clay cup through a piece of cloth that functioned as a sieve. Beer was very different from the beverages of our times – thick, like broth.

"God, I am hungry..." Diana said for what must have been the fourth time.

She tore at big chunks of bread with her teeth and swallowed them almost without chewing, which was probably a wise thing to do. The sand got into everything here, including the food, and that was one of the reasons the ancient Egyptians had such bad teeth, because the sand and grit ground them down right from an early age.

"I don't think anything ever tasted this good..." Diana patted her stomach after she'd filled herself up on a quantity of bread that amounted to a small bakery's daily production. "A little snooze would be in order?"

"No time for that, we need to get on and find the others." There was no way Elijah was going to let us rest.

Daniel turned to Bay.

"Maybe it's time you got back to the Valley."

"Yes, I must send message to Merit about Elijah," Bay was looking thoughtful.

"You haven't done that yet?" Daniel asked.

"No, no time. But Mi-Wer is near here," Bay pointed.

"We are close to Mi-Wer?"

"Yes. A day on river," Bay said.

"Elijah – maybe you should go on to Mi-Wer and find Merit?" I asked.

"I can't leave you now," Elijah said, looking in the direction Bay had pointed, "I'll return after we have found our team. If Merit is in Mi-Wer, she should be safe."

"We'd understand if you want to go there," Daniel said, "after all Merit has knowledge of... what we are looking for."

"No. I don't want to risk leading Ambrogio to her, if he doesn't already know she's here. And first we need to make sure our team is safe from Ambrogio as well. Jason, Layla and Aemilius are mighty warriors, but Ambrogio is a lethal opponent and we don't know all the weapons or followers he might have at his command here. Paris knows how to fight, but she is a weaver who has self-defence skills, not a warrior. Reggie... well, I wouldn't rely on his fighting skills, and Mr. Donnelly has probably never hit anyone in his whole life," Elijah said.

"And Thomas has arthritis," I commented, "the only thing he could do is try to whack someone with his cane."

"Which he wouldn't even have time to lift if Ambrogio attacked them," Lilith said dryly, "so even though I would love to see Elijah reunited with Merit again, he has a point. Keeping our team safe and secure, that's the first priority of our mission."

"What is your mission?" Bay asked. "Not security of... team only?"

"No... there is someone we need to meet in Akhetaten. We need to receive a message from them, and then we can go."

"Where you go?"

"That we don't know," Daniel replied, "because it depends on the message."

Bay nodded.

"I come with you," he decided. "Merit is safe in Mi-Wer. I come and see your people are safe. Then I go to Merit and tell her you are here."

"Thank you, Bay, it may be that we'll need your help," Daniel said.

"Shall we go into the buffer zone now?" I asked.

"The...?" Bay had not heard the term before.

"The misty world," Daniel explained. "Is it safe?" He turned to Bay.

"Akhetaten is far. Takes long time in misty world to go there. Not yet safe."

We looked at Bay.

"Don't tell me... *how* long is this going to take? Will we *ever* get to Akhetaten?" I pressed. "Can't we just risk it?"

After considering it, Daniel replied: "If Bay thinks it's not safe, we'd better not. So now what?"

"We go with ship," Bay said. "The bad ones don't like water."

"A ship. Good idea – but where are we going to find one?" Daniel asked.

"My friend take us," Bay said. "Come."

It felt to me as if a circle was closing as we walked towards the river, keeping our distance from the village so as not to be seen. The place where Ambrogio had kidnapped Diana and lured me to him using the singing device had to be nearby. It seemed so long ago since I had healed Tiye's illness and slept on the floor of her cabin.

Once more, we would be travelling by ship. Long slow days onboard – and without any certainty our team was still in this time anyway. For all we knew, they could have decided we were dead – after all, we had been away for over two weeks. They might have left, and returned to the future.

"As soon as we are on the boat, I might try to connect with Paris," Lilith said, "that much we can risk. I'm a weaver and I'll be able to sense if someone is trying to eavesdrop on the connection."

Bay led us to the riverbank and soon a boat approached from the direction of the village.

"We can't all fit in there," Diana said, looking at the reed boat.

"Take us to a big boat," Bay said.

"Oh, I see..." Diana looked along the river. "Where is it?"

Bay pointed upriver, towards the south. We saw nothing.

"That boat takes only two passengers," Daniel said. "Elijah, you go with Lilith. Bay can go with Diana. Dana and I will follow."

The man in the reed boat looked at us with curiosity and exchanged words with Bay. They seemed to know each other well.

"Go now," Bay gestured.

The shore here wasn't steep. The river curved away from us at this point and the slower current had gathered silt and reeds along the shore. Elijah and Lilith walked into the water. Suddenly Lilith sat down in the water and vanished under the surface.

"Ahh..." she said when stood up again, "I really needed that... a bit longer and my stink would have killed off any pigs in the vicinity..."

I couldn't help laughing.

"Now there's something I haven't heard in a while," Daniel smiled, "laughter."

Lilith and Elijah climbed into the reed boat and the man gave Elijah a paddle. We watched them paddle the boat made of reed bundles upriver until they disappeared behind a bend of the river.

The boat didn't return for a while. Diana and I had already immersed ourselves in the river as Lilith had done and were drying our hair, using our fingers as combs.

"A brush, a brush, my kingdom for a brush..." Diana mumbled as she tried to untangle her curly black hair.

"OK. Diana – you go with Bay," Daniel said.

"No, you first," Bay said. "I come last. If someone comes."

So Daniel and I waded through the water to the boat. Daniel got in first with the agility of a swimmer, almost lifting me into the boat after him. I sat in the middle, behind the man, and Daniel sat behind me.

The boat moved fast even though we were going upriver – the man was an experienced paddler and Daniel was strong. I could concentrate on looking at the green shoreline. There were no buildings in sight here but I was still nervous we could be seen.

The ship was anchored at some distance from the shoreline. It was not nearly as big as Tiye's had been, but large enough to carry us all. We steered towards the ship, and the man in front of me had a discussion with the men on deck. Then Elijah reached over the side and helped us up onto the deck.

"You made it safely. Now we're just waiting for Bay and Diana," Lilith said, with relief.

The boat left and we sat down. The men were even less surprised than the reed boat's owner had been at our foreign looks.

"They must have an idea of who we are... or what we are," Lilith said.

"If they know Bay... we should ask him."

Then the boat appeared again.

"Something's wrong," Daniel said.

Indeed, the boat was approaching very fast.

"We leave fast," Bay said when he climbed on deck, out of breath, "evil ones see us."

"Where?" Daniel looked around.

"There!" Bay did not point but turned his eyes.

"Lilith and Dana – cover your hair and stay seated," Daniel whispered, "Do not speak English. They may hear."

Lilith threw my old scarf over our heads and we sat together, hoping to look like two women sheltering from the sun. Diana's black hair did not look out of place here, and Elijah's hair was black too. Daniel sat down behind us – I could only hope his blonde hair would be hidden behind us.

Bay remained standing. I turned my head ever so slightly to see the shore. I didn't require the evidence of my eyes to know what I would see, though – my spine was buzzing slightly.

Two enemy Nephilim men were standing in full view on the shore, staring at us.

48

ANGEL'S FOLLOWER

No one paid any attention to Anna walking behind Angel through the tent city where the foreign dignitaries had been lodged. The guards standing in front of their masters' tents stared at Angel's beauty with open mouths. A lowly servant in coarse clothing was so overshadowed by such loveliness that she might as well have been invisible.

The hot wind blew the long, blond hair that reached below Angel's waist so that it rippled around her tall, curvy form. Her linen garment was the finest anyone had ever seen – but then again none knew that the secret to its faultless weaving was that it was machine-made three thousand and three hundred years in the future. It caressed her beautiful body, showing off her shapeliness.

Angel had chosen the Greek motif of "running dog" to decorate the hemline of her dress, woven in contrasting dark green and decorated with small turquoise beads. A heavy golden necklace with big polished turquoise beads gleamed around her neck, and her earrings brushed her shoulders. Broad golden arm rings and finger rings with glistening jewels shot colourful beams of light as her hands moved. A sash the colour of lapis lazuli, stitched with tiny golden beads, moved in front of her as she gracefully stepped forward in her fine sandals, her head held high. She was the living image of self-confidence. Her movement, her expression, her whole being expressed to the watchers that they were not worthy to even address her. Yet she clearly enjoyed the attention.

Anna kept on walking behind her mistress, carrying a sack so full of Angel's clothing and jewellery that it forced her to stoop forwards. She felt the unpleasant tug of her shadow in her solar plexus. That meant it was close by. She almost expected to see its part human, part animal form jogging alongside her. Anna's shadow was a twisted version of her own features, moulded from the dark energy of the lower buffer zone. But the shadow could not be too close to her now – they did not like full daylight, and their orders were to stay hidden from human eyes unless told otherwise. Still, she felt nauseous, not yet used to the darkness attached to her.

Angel and Anna had studied the layout of the city of Akhetaten before leaving. Angel had been pleasantly surprised to note the tent city of the foreign dignitaries grouped around the desert altars, stretching along the road to the northern tomb and the main city.

"Now we can approach the city coming from the right direction. That will make them more likely to believe I am royalty from another country," Angel said to Anna.

"How will they know you have come from the tent city, my lady?" Anna's question had earned her an amused look from Angel.

"They will remember me, rest assured."

Now Anna understood what she had meant. No one would forget the goddess-like blonde beauty of Angel once they had seen her.

Angel had an excellent memory and she walked into the city and towards Nefertiti's North Riverside Palace as if she had been living there all her life. There was a broader way from the tent city to the great road – the Royal Road running through the centre of Akhenaten's new capital – that led from the North Riverside Palace to the centre of the city. It led to the administrative buildings and the two Aten temples, and then towards to the south again where the Maru-Aten was, the palace of the king's wife Kiya, which was at some point given to the king's daughter Meritaten.

Anna had no idea what Angel was going to do when they reached the palace. How would she make her intentions known without speaking the language? What was she planning to do?

Women and children gawked at them from the doorways of the little houses as they walked into the city proper. The outlying town had grown organically outside the officially planned area, but the way that led to the Royal Road was wider.

The northern part of the city was divided into two by a wadi – the effect of flash floods coming down from the higher desert were clearly visible. Anna saw staircases leading to the wadi floor from the houses on the south side of it. On the northern side, there were no stairs, at least none that she could see. Probably, the wadi floor was used as a route to somewhere, perhaps to the Nile, Anna suspected.

The northern part of the city was split into sections by roads, all running north-south. They were real roads, not just footpaths as could be found in the poorer parts of the city. New houses were being built in the eastern part because the west was completely built-up and the houses were very close to each other there.

The houses were big here and some had their own grain silos – a sure sign of the large number of dependents the house had to feed.

Angel walked without haste, looking fresh and poised. Her higher body temperature meant she didn't sweat during the hottest part of the day. She enjoyed the heat like a snake, soaking up its warmth.

Anna walked behind her, bent over, sweat running down her back and sides as well as from her armpits as she tried to keep pace with Angel's long, leisurely strides.

How had she ended up in this situation? How had Angel found out about her husband, enabling her to kidnap him and turn him into a vampire? Anna loved her husband with all her heart, and he was the only reason she would ever have betrayed the people of the Centre.

Only the Centre was no more… she had seen the smoking ruins, had been to the hospital where the survivors had been taken. She had seen Lilith's burned face and sunken eyes, seen the grief that had hunched her posture.

Anna, depressed and afraid, couldn't take in all that she was seeing.

The beautiful monster walking in front of her, who had forced her into this trap, would one day make Anna's existence even worse. She would turn Anna into a vampire so that she could be united with her husband. Anna had some idea of what that existence would be like, but she had to believe there would also be love. She was willing to accept every other aspect of being a vampire if only she and her husband could be together again.

Anna knew about Ambrogio's protracted life now, not lengthened by hundreds but by thousands of years, because he had been metamorphosed by a dark Nephilim, rather than by a human vampire. She would have that same chance, she and her husband, transformed to vampirism by an evil Nephilim. She found solace in that thought, since the worst thing she could imagine was losing her husband. Obeying Angel's orders would make it all worthwhile – *if* she survived the transformation. But that was a risk she was willing to take.

Having been orphaned as a teenager, Anna could not cope with being alone and unloved. The memories of the street gang she had joined after running away from the orphanage were filled with the sights and sounds of violence, isolation and sadness. No. She would never be alone again.

All her muscles were aching when they finally reached the gateway to the palace, where Angel stopped and Anna peered upwards under her burden. Two pylons reached skyward in front of them; between them was the way into the palace and above it a window of appearances. The royal couple, Akhenaten and Nefertiti, could show themselves to their people from here.

Anna hadn't realised there would be one of these windows here, believing the only one was in the centre of the city. Curiously, she looked up at the painted pylons. The bright palette of colours surprised her. Akhenaten and Nefertiti were depicted there, receiving the blessing rays of the Aten. And everything was painted in pigments so vivid, they dazzled the eye.

A tall figure looked down from the window of appearances, staying in the shadows, a woman.

"You stink," Angel said to Anna without turning her head. "Back away from me."

"Yes, my lady," Anna whispered, lowering her gaze as she took a few steps back. She did not dare drop her sack onto the ground even though her arms were shaking with fatigue.

Two authoritative black-skinned guards stood in front of them. Anna remembered that Akhenaten surrounded the royal family with soldiers, led by the chief of police, Mahu. Wherever Akhenaten and Nefertiti went, the soldiers followed. He did not feel secure even in his own city. Whatever the priesthood of Amun had done before Akhenaten's fifth year as king, it had made him fear for his life.

Angel stood, regal and beautiful. Anna waited for something to happen. And it did – but not the way Anna had expected. No one approached them, no one drove them away. No one spoke to them first. No. It was Angel who spoke to the guards. Fluently, in the language of ancient Egypt.

49

MEETING

"Where are we going?" Meryt-Neith asked.

"It's a surprise," Ramose replied.

Meryt-Neith had been pleased when Ramose had asked her to go for a walk in the evening. He was quickly becoming a handsome young man, and she knew he would soon prefer the company of beautiful young women to that of his mother.

Nefertiti had left the Northern Palace shortly before them. They stood by the window of appearances, watching the horse-drawn chariots thundering towards the city centre.

Akhenaten and Nefertiti each had their own chariot. The king's horses were both white. Nefertiti's horses were bays of a deep red colour with gleaming black manes and tails.

The royal couple appeared often to their loyal citizens in the mornings, galloping with their horses like the northern wind. Even when she was heavily pregnant, Nefertiti steered her chariot alongside that of the king to show the people her fertility.

Nefertiti had grown to be a skilled horsewoman who drove her own horses and needed no charioteer. The older daughters accompanied them often, screaming with joy, poking the horses with long sticks to make them run faster.

When Nefertiti went to the temples with the king to worship the Aten, Meryt-Neith went with her and danced and sang under the rays of the sun, as a leader of the temple dancers. They praised the bounty of the Aten, and the thousand mudbrick offering tables were the visible signs of the wealth of the king.

Meryt-Neith left earlier than the Great Royal Wife to be ready at the temple when they arrived. She had to get up long before the sunrise to reach the temples in time, but she still loved dancing. The moment the sun's red edge silently rose above the horizon from the direction of the wadi where the royal tombs were being built, was a moment of peace for her – followed by a joyful hymn by the temple singers, praising the light of all creation. The young girls and women would dance and shout to invigorate the god Aten to a new day, to the rhythm of ivory clappers in the shape of hands.

Meryt-Neith would do it later today, too – go dancing with young girls whose skins were deeply tanned from exposure to the sun, but not yet aged by it. Meryt-Neith, who should have looked like a mature woman by now, rather than showing signs of ageing looked almost as young as the girls she led in the singing and dancing.

"You have inherited your mother's looks. And you never age. This is so with your mother as well," Nefertiti had said a few days earlier.

Meryt-Neith had detected a note of envy. No wonder. Nefertiti's beautiful face had begun to show signs of ageing from constant exposure to the sun, and her body was rounded now. She had six living daughters – Meritaten, Meketaten, Ankhesenpaaten, Neferneferuaten Tasherit, Neferneferure and Setepenre. Setepenre was the youngest, now two years old. Meritaten would be reaching womanhood soon and was her father's favourite.

And finally, the king had a living son as well. Tutankhaten had been born at the same time as Setepenre. When Nefertiti had not been able to produce a male heir, the king had married his youngest full sister Baketaten. She had become pregnant almost immediately and given birth to the long-awaited heir. The king had been beside himself with joy and Baketaten now lived in great luxury in Nefertiti's palace.

Nefertiti had found it hard to share in his joy. She had wanted to be the mother of the future king. Still, she had a few fruitful years left, Aten willing, and did her best to please the king, to get him into her bed so she could become pregnant again. She showed all due respect to Baketaten, who was the Daughter of the King, Wife of the King and Sister of the King – and possibly the future Mother of the King. Nefertiti's title as the Great Royal Wife was higher than any of Baketaten's, but Baketaten was of nobler birth.

But the more childbirth had transformed Nefertiti's body to that of a mature woman, the more the king had shown his affections to a younger wife, Kiya, who had given birth to a daughter, also named Meritaten. Already the daughter's name had been carved in stone in Pa-Maru-En-Pa-Aten, a temple south of the city centre:. *"The King's bodily daughter, his beloved Meritaten-Tasherit, to the King of Upper and Lower Egypt, who lives in Ma'at, the Lord of the Two Lands Neferkheperure-Waenre, born to the wife and great beloved Kiya."*

Nefertiti disliked Kiya, and wouldn't allow her to live in the Northern Palace with her and her daughters when it became clear that she was the king's new favourite. But Kiya still received recognition through having a palace of her own, a great sign of favour. All the other women of the king's household, the secondary wives, sisters, aunts and others who were dependent on him, lived together without the luxury of privacy.

Nefertiti ignored Kiya, indicating to the world that she considered her to be just another woman of the *keneret* the king took his pleasure with. However, she could not erase the fact that a whole sun temple had been built in her name – the king had created a role for Kiya in worshipping the Aten, just as he had for Nefertiti.

Kiya was very beautiful, but in a different way to Nefertiti. She was taller and still had the svelte form of youth. Also, her teeth were still beautiful, while eating sweet wines and bread had already started to cause problems for Nefertiti's teeth. She smiled less often in order to hide this.

Kiya was always happy and laughing and the king often talked of her as his beloved. He had given her the title *'The Wife and Greatly*

Beloved of the King of Upper and Lower Egypt, Living in Ma'at, Lord of the Two Lands, Neferkheperure-Waenre, the Goodly Child of the Living Aten, who shall be living for ever and ever'. In short, she was called *hemet mereryt aat* – Great Beloved Wife.

The more Kiya rose in favour, the more Nefertiti felt her own hold over the king was slipping. Meryt-Neith had often seen the look in her eyes change when Kiya was mentioned. The eyes became piercing and cold. Nefertiti's ladies never mentioned Kiya to Nefertiti if they could avoid it, just as they knew it was wise to avoid the king's eye. Anyone he showed interested in or took to his bed would be sent away from Nefertiti's palace immediately.

Nefertiti turned more and more to the use of outward signs of power to prove that her status was still above all other women. She often wore her blue flat-topped crown and heavy golden necklaces. She and her daughters always wore red sashes over their dresses of the finest linen, something only the closest members of the king's family were allowed to do. Meryt-Neith was one of Nefertiti's most trusted ladies and had been there when she had ordered a stone portrait of herself to be covered with gesso and shaped to give it a more youthful appearance. It was clear that Nefertiti was afraid of getting old and losing the king's favour in bed.

She tried to keep her power over him, going everywhere with Akhenaten and sitting next to him while he managed the affairs of state. She discussed the Aten's will with him, and through the years, had managed to acquire a position no other wife had with him. She was to Akhenaten what Tiye had been to Amenhotep, a co-ruler, even though she didn't hold that as an official title – yet. But no one could deny that in front of the Aten, she represented all the women of Kemet, and through her they could make their wishes known to the god.

It was easy for Nefertiti to follow the king everywhere as he had kept his word and never left Akhetaten. No longer did he follow the age-old habit of kings in journeying the length of the Great River to show himself to his people throughout the land

Next year, there would be a great jubilee of all nations. The king intended to show off his new city to the rulers of neighbouring lands, and invitations had been sent to all their kings so that they could see for themselves the might of their overlord. This was the wish of the Aten, said Akhenaten, and as he was the only one who could speak directly to the god and hear his answer, no one was to doubt this.

It was whispered that Nefertiti was so irreplaceable now, that the king was planning to make her his official co-ruler. Meritaten would then become the Great Royal Wife, as a co-ruler could no longer bear that title. The Great Royal Wife needed to be someone from the king's immediate family and Nefertiti was certainly not going to let Kiya have that honour, on that pretext or for any other reason. She didn't want Baketaten to gain that title either.

Nefertiti assured the king that their own daughter would be the perfect choice. She reminded Akhenaten how his own father had elevated Tiye to divinity and then married his daughter Sitamun so there would be a new Great Royal Wife from the immediate family. Akhenaten, who venerated his father, agreed with her that as his father had done this, it was a sign that he should do the same.

Meryt-Neith knew the rumour to be true, she had heard enough discussions between the royal couple. Meritaten's behaviour had also changed recently; she behaved in a much more dignified way and began to stress her budding feminine beauty. Her side-lock of youth was shaved off and she wore beautiful wigs on her bald head every day now. Her parents must have made it clear to her what was to come.

Plans for the jubilee were made with grandiose new ideas added to them almost daily. That was why on this day, Meryt-Neith and her ladies would dance for the Aten later on, not at sunrise; the royal couple were going to have a discussion with the officials this morning regarding the jubilee and let the high priest perform this morning's greetings to the Aten. The king didn't always perform the morning prayers at the great temple any more. Frequently, he and Nefertiti showed their reverence to the god privately in their palace.

It would be some hours before the royal couple returned and so Meryt-Neith had plenty of time to walk with her son.

Ramose led her towards the royal stables. The boy loved horses and wanted to own some himself.

“I can’t afford the price of a pair of horses, let alone feed them,” Meryt-Neith had said when Ramose had asked for a pair. "Only the very wealthy can afford to keep horses."

“Can’t you ask the king to give me a team of horses?” Ramose asked.

“I can’t request horses from the king! And even if I could, why would he give you horses? Have you done a special favour to earn such a royal gift? Maybe you should train to be a charioteer. You could build yourself a career in the military and rise high in the ranks. If you are skilled enough in battle, you might even capture some enemy horses for yourself,” Meryt-Neith said.

Ramose stopped to look at a pair of especially beautiful, well-muscled horses being led towards the stables by a strong-looking charioteer. The horses held their heads high and flattened their ears against their polls as they passed by, baring their teeth. They were real war horses with slit nostrils. The slits helped them to breathe more easily when the tight nose band was in place, and were supposed to help prevent them from neighing and revealing their presence to the enemy. Not that it was likely a battle would ever be fought on the plains of Akhetaten.

"So, is that why we came here? Did you bring me to see the horses, then?" Meryt-Neith asked, amused. “Don’t think that will encourage me to acquire some for you, however impressive they are.”

"No, Mother, that’s not why we’re here. There’s someone who wanted to meet you. He knew who I was and said he needed to talk to you."

Meryt-Neith stopped abruptly.

"Who?"

"A stranger. A pale man who... Wait!"

Meryt-Neith turned and ran. Ramose ran after her.

She hadn't got far before a tall figure stepped into view from behind one of the stable walls. Meryt-Neith almost hit him in her urgency to get away.

"Meryt-Neith," the man took a step backwards, placed his hand over his heart and bowed deeply. "My lady."

"Go away!" Meryt-Neith hissed just as Ramose caught up with her.

"I apologise for the secrecy. But I knew you wouldn't come to meet me if you knew it was me," the man said, bowing again. "I only wish to have a few words with you."

"I have nothing to say to you. I will have the king's soldiers sent after you!" Meryt-Neith's voice was trembling with shock.

Ramose looked at them both, alarmed at his mother's reaction.

"Who *are* you?" he demanded of the pale stranger.

"As I told you, I was once close to your respected mother," the Pale Man said, "and I have regretted my bad behaviour all these years. I needed to come and apologise and I'm sorry to have used you as the intermediary. Meryt-Neith, you must believe me when I say that I have no ill intentions towards you or your son."

He extended his hand and Meryt-Neith stepped backwards to avoid it. Ramose moved between her and the stranger.

"Yes, I deserve that," the Pale Man said, looking sad.

Meryt-Neith looked at the man she hated with all her heart. He stood there, calmly, with an apologetic look on his face. Meryt-Neith's heart beat erratically, bile rose into her mouth and her limbs started to tremble from sheer terror. Her whole being screamed at the memory of what he had done.

"I do not trust you, no matter what you say." She had to fight to regain control of her voice. "You are to leave now and never come back."

"I will leave, but I hope you will give me a chance to have a few words with you in private," he said. "I am sure you would also wish these words to stay between us alone."

His eyes turned to Ramose. Meryt-Neith felt the cold fist of fear grab her heart. She could not have him reveal to Ramose that he was the boy's father. She would not let Ramose hear what he had done to her.

"Very well," Meryt-Neith straightened her back, gathering all the courage she had inside her. "Ramose, stay close by. Shout for help if it seems necessary."

Ramose's eyes grew angry. He did not move aside but remained between his mother and the man.

"What has he done to you in the past, Mother?" he asked, and his voice was cold.

"I insulted your mother badly," the man said, "but that is between us. You stay there and call for help if you think it necessary, but I assure you I have no ill intentions towards your mother."

Ramose stood still for a while, but then Meryt-Neith touched his hand.

"I will listen to what he has to say. You wait here."

She walked past him. Ramose had to step back when a chariot trotted between them on its way to the training grounds. When it had passed by, he could see that the man was talking quietly right into his mother's ear. She stood like a statue, hands clenched into fists.

"Nothing you say will ever convince me of your good intentions," Meryt-Neith said quietly, not trying to hide the hatred in her voice, "you are not capable of feeling any compassion towards another living thing."

"And I don't blame you for feeling like that. All I can do is to try to convince you I have changed. What I was when I saw you last... I deeply regret what I did," the Pale Man said quietly.

Meryt-Neith turned to look into his eyes. They were calm, tired.

"I have studied the ways of Ma'at and understood that I had no right to force myself on you no matter what our past was... Not even when you gave birth to... we were never married in the eyes of others."

"Are you saying what you did would have been acceptable if we had been married?" Meryt-Neith's voice oozed with contempt. "Beating me, raping me, hurting me? Threatening the lives of those who gave me shelter?"

"No. I am not saying that. Meryt-Neith... I have changed. What I did is against Ma'at and if my heart was weighed against the feather of truth now, it would be found wanting."

"You can never undo what you have done to me and no doubt there were others before me! Why do you think I would for a moment believe that the High Lord of the dark Nephilim would feel the need to apologise to anyone?" Merit spat.

"Why indeed..." the Pale Man looked down, "but I tell you I am no longer the High Lord of the Nephilim."

"The evil Nephilim, you mean. You were never our lord!" Merit said. "And I don't believe a word you say!"

"I don't expect you to, either. Not immediately. But I had to come and tell you this. I'll leave now. I may come and visit in the future..."

"Don't. I forbid it. I refuse to see you!" Meryt-Neith said the words slowly, intentionally.

"That is your right. If I do come, I will send you word and wait for you. If you don't come to me, I shall leave, I swear. Until next time. I can only hope that one day you will come and talk with me from of your own free will."

"Never!"

"If that is so, I will respect your decision. But I feel great pain for my past actions. I need you to accept my apology."

"You may *need* as much as you like. But I don't need to take your wishes into account. When did you ever respect my needs? Your kind can never change!" Meryt-Neith hissed. "Never!"

"How do you know that to be true?" the Pale Man looked earnestly into her eyes. "You know that a bite from what you insist on calling dark or evil Nephilim will transform your kind too. What if it is possible to reverse it? To return to what my kind were before changing? Have you ever considered that?"

Meryt-Neith hadn't. But she was too filled with fear and hatred to think of anything but getting away from this, her worst nightmare standing in front of her. All her instincts screamed for escape.

"I'm leaving now." the Pale Man turned away from her.

"Stay away from my son..." Meryt-Neith whispered to his back.

"Our son," the Pale Man said so quietly Meryt-Neith barely heard him. He turned to look at Ramose who was trying to overhear their discussion.

The look in his eyes shocked Meryt-Neith. She had never seen such longing in the Pale Man's eyes.

"If you don't believe me, ask our son how I saved his life the first time we met. If I had wished him harm, would I have done so? But I will respect your wishes. I will not approach your son nor tell him who I am. But you do understand he will soon learn he is not ordinary. Have you told him yet what he is?"

Meryt-Neith said nothing. When he received no answer, the Pale Man bowed to her, nodded to Ramose and turned to walk away.

Meryt-Neith had but a moment to gather herself before Ramose was by her side.

"It is all right, Ramose," she patted his hand, "I was taken by surprise. I thought I had made it clear to him I did not want to see him ever again. After all these years, I never thought he would show himself to me again."

"Your hands are all cold!" Ramose took them into his.

"It was a... shock," Meryt-Neith said, pulling her hands free, "but he said what he came to say and apologised for his behaviour. We won't meet again. We're going back to the palace now. I need to leave for the temple soon with the dancers of the Aten."

She turned to walk away, looking calm and composed again. Inside, she was in turmoil. Had the Pale Man really saved his son's life? How could he possibly have changed? How could she make her son forget ever seeing him? She never wanted to hear a question about him from Ramose. She wouldn't be able to stay calm if he started questioning her. But she had to put up the pretence, starting now, that all was well.

She forced herself to walk normally, paying attention to her shoulders and arms, so that her steps looked relaxed. Years of dancing helped her – she was used to being in control of her body.

But if she thought she could fool Ramose, she was wrong. The boy looked hard at the back of the pale stranger as he walked away. What had he done to mother? It had to be something terrible or she would not have reacted the way she did.

"You'd better not try to approach us ever again, or else..." he mumbled out loud.

As if he had heard the boy, the stranger turned, saw him looking and lifted his hand in greeting. Ramose did not return the gesture. Then the man disappeared behind the stable block.

50

THE BEAUTY

"You see him there," the Pale Man indicated, "looking at the horses?"

They were standing on top of a building, sheltered by the wind catchers and woven screens so that the neighbours couldn't see them. A canopy of cloth shaded them from direct sunlight. From here, the entrance to the North Palace could be seen clearly.

The girl's gaze followed the direction of his pointing finger. Her sharp eyes fixed on the form of a tall, lanky young man, even though he was so far off that ordinary people would not have been able to make him out.

"Yes, my lord," she said. "Do you want me to kill him?"

"No! On the contrary!" the Pale Man said. "I want you to seduce him. I want you to make him fall in love with you."

The girl tilted her head so that her heavy black hair swung against her thighs and observed the youngster for a while longer.

"I am to bed him, my lord?" She turned to look at the Pale Man.

Her eyes were a deep yellow colour.

"Indeed you are. I want you to learn through him all you can about his mother. Meryt-Neith is her name. I want you to discover where his mother's sister is hiding. I need to find her soon. I am trying to convince Meryt-Neith that I am no longer a threat to her, but that will take time, if I ever can. The boy may have access to the letters Meryt-Neith receives from her mother and that cursed Mother of Bees. They know where to find the sister. It is important that both Meryt-Neith and Ramose suspect nothing, so do not ask too eagerly. Do you understand?"

The girl turned away and the northern breeze wafted her hair forward from her back to cover her nakedness.

"I will bed him then. I know Meryt-Neith. I arrived in Akhetaten with the same convoy of ships as she did. I will find out all there is to know about Meryt-Neith's sister for you. What is her name?"

The Pale Man pulled the girl towards him.

"Her name is Shuet. And before you bed anyone else, I think we shall have our own moment of pleasure."

The girl did not resist. She accepted his dominion over her, even though he was her own father in the sense that he had made her into blood-drinker. He had created her some years back to be his eyes and ears in Akhetaten after transforming her.

The Pale Man had controlled other concubines in the royal court for hundreds of years. Most he simply kept as his mistresses without changing them, killing them once they began to show signs of ageing and no longer excited him. That way, he avoided any unpleasant scenes of jealousy after he had chosen another girl to satisfy his needs. The girls were selected for their looks and lowly status. Servants could move about unnoticed, and when they went missing, no one bothered to go about looking for them for very long. Also, they were easily bought and ridiculously willing to spy for him – little trinkets, linen and oils went a long way in acquiring the young women's services.

This one, however, he had decided to turn into a blood-drinker because of her youth and extraordinary beauty. She had beautiful, warm-coloured skin that spoke of Nubian ancestors, slightly almond-shaped eyes and an unbelievable cascade of shiny black hair. Turning her into a vampire had enhanced her beauty, so much so that she couldn't continue as a servant in the household of Nefertiti any more.

The Great Royal Wife was well known for throwing out any girl that was beautiful enough to catch the eye of the king, just the kind of thing a jealous woman would do, and the reason the Pale Man had rid himself of all his previous women. This one he intended to keep for a while and turning her into a blood-drinker meant she would stay beautiful for much longer than any ordinary human would.

He had had this house built for her, given her servants and the status of a married woman whose husband travelled up and down the River as a trader. Noble families gave merchants orders of the items they needed, and the merchants then travelled about acquiring what was wanted. In exchange, they were given surplus goods by the nobles as payment. Linen cloth, wine, even furniture.

The servants had learned to stay away whenever the master of the house appeared. He always sent a note before his visit so the lady of the house could make sure her servants were absent. His visits only lasted a few hours. Sometimes they went hunting together to satisfy their hunger with blood. He only permitted the girl to drink animal blood of course, since only Nephilim sated their hunger with the blood of humans.

"You need to see the lad secretly, so that his mother doesn't find out. She might recognise you for what you are, my lovely," he said to her as they were lying side by side, letting the wind cool their skin. "Your skin colour would certainly remind her of me."

The girl's skin had a definite golden hue that made her stand out in a crowd of ordinary people.

"I shall send word when I learn their secrets," the girl said. She rose from the pillows. "Do you wish to eat now, my lord?"

"Well, I might."

The Pale Man enjoyed the total feminine submission of this girl. If only Meryt-Neith had been the same! If she had not escaped, pregnant with his heir, he might have forgiven her. But she had disobeyed him, and he had punished her. He would do that again, but at first he needed to lure her into accepting the lie that he had changed. She would have to follow him willingly, out of reach of those cursed bees. And she must bring Ramose with her.

He heard the sounds of a struggle from the staircase and rose expectantly. Yes, he was indeed hungry. Enjoying the cool breeze, he did not bother covering himself as he waited for his food to be brought to him.

When he glanced towards the stables again, the boy was gone. Ramose. His heir. He would get him and would turn him into his own when the moment was right. But first, he needed to get rid of the many who were standing in his way. Shuet and her offspring first, as they were a threat to all his kind. Then Merit and Mut-Bity. Meryt-Neith he would keep as long as she could breed. But eventually he would either kill her or transform her. He hadn't decided which it would be, and it was likely to be a spur of the moment decision. Much would depend on whether Meryt-Neith became submissive to him or not.

"Here you are, my lord," the girl was standing behind him, naked. She was holding a young servant, a boy this time. The boy tried to pull free, but the girl controlled him easily in her grip with ease.

"Thank you, my lovely," the Pale Man said. "Come here," he ordered the boy.

The boy was perhaps twelve years old. He looked at the Pale Man suspiciously.

"Come now," the Pale Man said without raising his voice, and hesitantly the boy did as he asked.

The Pale Man took his hand lazily, pushed him on his back on the pillows with one quick movement and covered his mouth with his hand. The boy kicked and flailed his hands and tried to scream.

The Pale Man lifted his free hand, hitting the boy with his fist so hard on the side of the head that he lost consciousness. Then he bent down, bit him in the neck and drank until the boy was dead.

51

PLEASE BE ALIVE

"It appears she didn't travel to Akhetaten this way," the Pale Man said.

"That seems to be so," Ambrogio agreed, "at least not by the eastern shore of the river."

They were surveying the scene from the top of the mountains that surrounded Akhetaten. Arriving on the southern edge of the city just as the sun went down, they watched as lights appeared on the rooftops. Outside the larger houses, lamps were lit in the gardens too, where the families were ready to enjoy the pleasant surroundings following the labour of their servants, who had refreshed the plants with jar after jar of water. Ambrogio noticed the tall forms of shadufs, now unmoving in the darkening evening. During the day, the shadufs would constantly be swinging up and down for the endless queues of servants carrying huge water jars. Leather bags hung from the long end of the pole, which was lifted, full of water, by the counterweight at the other end when working. Most of Akhetaten's gardens were not close to any waterway and had to be watered by hand.

"I'll circulate in the city, to see if I can catch her scent there, my lord," Ambrogio said.

"And if she isn't there?"

"Then I'll keep travelling north. Whichever way she is going, I am sure she is heading to Akhetaten. If I cannot smell her, I'll ask for her. With her striking looks, people are bound to pay attention to her."

"Do so. I know her scent now, too, so if she comes to the city directly from the eastern desert, I'll know," the Pale Man said, "Also, news travels fast in a city, and I have informants here who will advise me as soon as a tall, blonde, beautiful young woman appears."

"You are not going to follow me northwards?" Ambrogio asked, showing only mild curiosity.

"No. I have things to do here. I need to find my new servant. You remember her?"

Yes, the girl he had turned into a vampire the last time they were here. Ambrogio had brought two calves for her to feed on throughout her change and they had left her in a cave in the surrounding mountains.

"She's presentable enough after her change to please me again, and it is time I gave this one a place to live where I can visit her. I had to get rid of the last one not long ago. Luckily the new one is pretty enough for me not to kill her. I'll find a house for her – I'm sure my new servant's family will be more than eager to get rid of her."

Any vampire who remained with their families after they had been transformed was soon thrown out. They rejected normal food and animals began to die mysteriously around the house. Sometimes, the animals were found dead in the house if the newborn vampire found the call of blood irresistible. And they could seldom resist. As the girl had been changed only recently, she was ferocious, and her behaviour must be causing her family to think she had lost her mind. Her skin would appear strange to them. They might even catch her feeding. Fearing the new monster among them, they would shove her outside, never to include her in the family circle again, not knowing that it was fortunate the vampires of this period only drank the blood of animals. Ambrogio had been the first to create vampires who drank human blood.

The Pale Man clearly didn't concern himself much about whether or not the knowledge of blood-drinkers spread, having left the girl to her own devices. In the future, that would change, and vampires would exert themselves to keep their presence hidden, not least out of fear of other vampires.

Ambrogio had killed hundreds of rogue vampires himself without the need to ask permission of any council of vampires – he had created the system and he was the overlord of them all. No one would dare judge him for killing a vampire if he so chose.

He knew that vampires could not keep their existence secret completely – there were records in human history of their activity, though science never admitted the truth of any of these stories. The fact that vampire bodies disintegrated on their death so that nothing remained for scientists to examine was fortunate. It was only the skeletons of ordinary humans who had been thought to be vampires that were ever found. The state of these human skeletons showed the fear their own communities had felt, and the lengths they went to in order to keep the apparent vampires in their graves after death. The dead had been stabbed through the heart, or had a tile placed in their open mouths, between their teeth. And the fact that their ordinary human remains survived revealed how wrong their accusers had been.

"I will return as soon I can," Ambrogio said, "and I must ask you not to touch the lady should you find her. She is important to my master, and he will certainly not be forgiving if any harm should come to her."

"Harm? That depends on what you mean by harm…" the Pale Man looked amused. "I may take a little taste of her… or perhaps just bed her if she is beautiful enough."

"She is not to be bitten and you are not to touch her in any way," Ambrogio said as calmly as possible. "Those are my master's explicit instructions. And I have to advise you that should you ignore them, his revenge will be beyond anything you can imagine."

"Really, now? Let's not forget I am the High Lord over all my kind here. You think he has power over me?" The Pale Man's voice was icy. "This is not his kingdom. It is mine."

"I am sorry to say this – but you would lose. He has soldiers and weapons you have never heard of, ones you cannot even begin to imagine. He will overpower you, my Lord."

Ambrogio knew that they could bring in an army of vampires he had trained himself to kill Nephilim. And then there was the battery of modern weaponry of which the Pale Man had no concept.

There was no pretence of politeness between them any longer. The Pale Man stared at Ambrogio and Ambrogio looked back at him directly in the eye without flinching.

"I see you are not as submissive to a Nephilim lord's command as you should be," the Pale Man said.

"I am submissive to the orders of my own lord, which is as it should be," Ambrogio said. He forced himself to lower his gaze and bowed slightly. "I do not wish to be impolite, but I need to state the truth of things as they are. My lord Cain will have his revenge if the girl is harmed in any way. If you find her, you are to keep your distance, not reveal yourself to her in any way that would enable her to recognise what... who you are."

The Pale Man had clearly never been told that he was subordinate to a lord stronger in power than he was. Ambrogio felt his anger like little electric snaps on his skin.

"I am quite eager to meet this lord of yours," the Pale Man finally said with gritted teeth, "to see if he really matches me in power."

Ambrogio said nothing, just bowed slightly again. This was the first time the pale Nephilim lord had lost his temper in front of him.

"I am leaving now," Ambrogio said. "My advice would be to make the wise choice not to touch the girl if she appears here. My lord may be potent when angry, but he also rewards his allies abundantly. You would gain more if you chose to be an ally of his."

"You are not to give me advice, servant!" The Pale Man snapped.

"I am only worried about your wellbeing and survival," Ambrogio replied, "which is the only reason I would dare to speak in this way. That, and the fact no one else is hearing this who could question your position as High Lord."

The word *survival* hung in the air between them. That was a direct threat against the Pale Man. If he was ever going to attack Ambrogio, that moment was now.

In a way, Ambrogio was waiting for him to attack and would even welcome it. He could destroy the Pale Man – this so-called lord had no idea how many Nephilim Ambrogio had killed in the past. In his arrogance, the Pale Man could not even conceive of this short blood-drinker having the skill to overcome a Nephilim.

But he might still need the Pale Man, whose knowledge of the lie of the land far surpassed that of Ambrogio. He had learned to keep his own emotions in check – something the Pale Man obviously had never had to do. That gave Ambrogio the upper hand. He was so used to not showing his emotions around Cain and Angel that he did it effortlessly.

"I apologise if my way of expressing my concern was impolite and hope you will understand my motives. I should take my leave now." Ambrogio kept his eyes on the ground.

After a long pause, the Pale Man spoke.

"Go. Return as soon as possible. I will not touch the girl if she appears. For now."

"Thank you, my lord," Ambrogio bowed deeply, turned his back and walked away.

He circled the city in the darkness, breathing in the intoxicating scent of the blood of living pulses. But Dana's scent was not among the heady odours of Akhetaten. Nor could he find a trace of any other member of her team. After several hours, Ambrogio turned towards the desert, running back to the mountains and avoiding the tomb workers' village to the east of the city. He intended to keep away from the northern part of Akhetaten – Nefertiti's palace was heavily guarded and he would have to get past it if he wanted to search the riverbank. In his need to avoid being seen, he climbed the hills, turned north and only dropped back to the river when Akhetaten lay behind him.

He ran with determination, intent on finding Dana, if she had survived.

What he would do if Dana was dead? He pushed the thought away.

"Selene?" he sent a message to the deepest part of his being. "Are you there?"

A sensation – like the touch of a gentle hand, or a kiss as light as a butterfly's wing. But no words. The blood of Diana and that of the two sailors was too strong. Whispers of their consciousness masked Selene's presence. He had not thought of that – he had been so happy to feel Selene, to hear her voice after thousands of years, and yet had been stupid enough to return to drinking human blood. A mistake. All the blood he drank carried the memories of the people he had killed or turned to vampires. And with the memories came endless muttering voices. In the end, it was like standing in an echo chamber full of whispers so that no individual voice could be distinguished. They had covered Selene's voice completely, so that eventually, he had stopped drinking human blood and gone back to animals for nourishment. Animal blood carried memories of the animal's life too, but those memories were fleeting, without words, and soon gone. Now he had three whispering voices covering Selene's presence again – he would have to wait, perhaps for a long time, before these new whispers vanished.

He cursed out loud – how had he not thought of this!

But if he could find Dana… surely her silver blood was so strong it would wipe away any trace of disturbance and he could be one with Selene again? They would be united, forever, and disappear into the vastness of the continent that was Africa. They would never find her, never force him to be their servant again… and if they tried… well, he now had the knowledge that gave shadows an individual existence and could build a shadow army loyal only to him.

For a while, Ambrogio closed his eyes and ran using his other senses. His extended existence had let him develop a degree of precision that meant he could hear and be aware of trees and plants if the air was moving even a little. Rough terrain too; it was as if the wind that caressed the ground whispered its shape into his ears, forming a map in his mind.

Ambrogio searched for the memory of Selene – what she had looked like when she had smiled at him shyly in Delphi, on her way from the town to the temple to serve as a priestess. How the first wrinkles had appeared on her youthful skin. What she had looked like under the silent moon right before he killed her. He could almost see her, almost... but somehow his inner eye was not as sharp as his physical senses and recreating Selene's image was getting more and more difficult as time passed.

Was he losing her for good? Her whispers no longer formed words in his mind. Her appearance no longer came to him with the clarity of the early years. She had always been his anchor, his only reason to keep on living in the darkness that was a vampire's existence. He had only wished to find a way to bring her back. He had tried to mix their blood – his and Selene's, who was the first human victim of a vampire – into new female bodies. And he had failed, managing only to push Selene further back into the depths of his mind.

"No!" Ambrogio shouted, not caring who heard.

No. He would not lose his love, his twin soul. Dana *had* to be alive! The Nephilim were strong, she must have survived... she must have!

But what if water caused her the same kind of pain as it did vampires? What if the water of the Red Sea had killed her after Ambrogio had deliberately weakened her?

"No!" he whispered.

In his desperation, the only thing he could do was to run faster, to breathe more deeply, in an effort to trace her scent. To find the only one who could ever give Selene back to him.

Be alive. Please be alive.

52

LOVELIER THAN NEFERTITI

Ramose had never seen a more beautiful woman. Not even the Great Royal Wife Nefertiti was as lovely.

He first saw her at dusk, on his way back from the stables again.

Mother had said it was time he chose a profession. He could read and write but was not good enough, or interested enough, to become a scribe. Horses were the thing he loved the most. He had asked if Mother would put in a good word for him so he could begin training as a charioteer.

"You do realise you don't just jump into a chariot and start driving?" mother had asked. "You'll be going through training with weapons, and probably begin by cleaning the stables before you're allowed even to touch the horses. You wouldn't have any say when or where you were sent on duty. In time, you might have a chance to rise up the ranks, but to begin with, you would be nothing but a common soldier. That is not an easy life."

"I don't mind. I want to learn to handle horses and maybe own a pair and my own chariot one day."

"Horses are very expensive animals to keep – you'll need to be rich to be able to own them."

"I'll find a way!" Ramose said with the certainty of youth.

He really did not know of anything better than horses – until the evening when the mysterious beauty walked towards him.

He couldn't help but stare. Her huge almond eyes were a mesmerising golden colour, made even more stunning by the skilled application of the bright green eye paint she used. Her warm-coloured skin had a golden tint too and her heavy black hair was oiled and curled and decorated with beads. It was plainly her own hair, not a wig and she was equally clearly proud of her curls. Her lips were red, her eyebrows defined and painted in black. Her hips swayed softly as she walked, and the movement of her thighs made the sash hanging from her hips swing from side to side. Her tiny feet were protected by beaded leather sandals and the setting sun seemed to turn the dust rising from her steps into gold.

She was escorted by two male servants and a servant girl who was pretty but looked plain beside her mistress. They seemed a little nervous for some reason, but Ramose did not waste time wondering why. He only had eyes for the beauty approaching him.

She stopped when she saw him, nodded her head slightly and one of her male servants approached Ramose.

"My lady wishes to know where she may find the overseer of all the horses," the man said. "Would you know?"

"I... I don't think he is at the stables... you are talking about Ay?" Ramose stammered.

The lady was asking for the highest official in the court after the king, his advisor Ay, who had the honorary title Father of the King. He was also the father of the Great Royal Wife Nefertiti.

"Yes. If he is not here, is there some other official my lady could meet?" the servant asked.

"I am sorry... what is this about?" Ramose blurted out.

The beautiful young woman stepped up close to him. Ramose desperately concentrated on looking at her face rather than the fine dress pressed against her beautiful form.

"My husband has received a pair of chariot horses and sent me a letter asking me to go and see the horses are well and getting the best of care," she said in a pleasant voice that seemed to resonate in

Ramose's spine. "Perhaps you know the way around here and can help us find someone who knows where the horses might be?"

Ramose knew that the king's horses were kept in their own stable. But there was another stable nearby for the horses of the highest officials – not all had space to keep their horses next to their houses in the city, especially those who had not started building their houses early on, so they had missed the opportunity to claim a large plot for their grain silos, gardens and other buildings.

"I would be honoured to help you, my lady," Ramose bowed slightly. "This way."

She was wearing a heavy perfume that enveloped Ramose when she came even closer. Ramose did not know whether he liked it or not, but it proved to him that this lady was wealthy – perfumes were very expensive. And her husband owned a pair of chariot horses... they had to be very rich indeed.

He stole a quick look at the woman and caught her looking at him. She lowered her gaze and smiled shyly. Ramose swallowed. Gathering his courage, he spoke.

"May I ask what your husband does for a living to be able to have fine horses?"

"You may," she said, walking beside him with small, dignified steps. "He is a merchant – he trades horses among other things. And he bought this pair for himself from Naharin at the same time he was acquiring horses for the king. They have been trained the way Kikkuli, the horse master of the king Suppililiuma, has advised. My husband told me Kikkuli found a way to train the best war horses so that they can endure much more hardship than any other horses. They are much in demand."

Ramose had heard of Kikkuli. Anyone who had anything to do with horses, had. The stallions trained with his method were the best horses in the world. In his eagerness to see the horses, he lengthened his stride.

"Please, I cannot keep up with you," the lady said, with laughter in her voice.

"I am so sorry," Ramose said, slowing down. "I am not used to walking with fine ladies."

"Surely you have ladies in your own family. Your clothing tells me you are from a noble family."

"Well, yes... my mother is one of the ladies of the Great Royal Wife," Ramose said with pride in his voice.

"Indeed? I am in very fine company then!"

Her pretty smile made Ramose's heart beat faster.

"Here we are." Ramose had to turn away so she would not see the effect she was having on him.

The lady looked at the stable building.

"Oh, the smell is too much..." She did not go any closer but turned to her servant. "Go and ask someone to bring my husband's horses out for me to see."

The servant went into the stables without fear. Ramose had not dared to go in there because officially, he had nothing to do with the horses and the stable masters were a mean lot. Every boy in the city would have been in the stables if they were allowed, so none were. Those in military training were the only ones permitted to enter.

Ramose tried to look as if he belonged here. They drew many glances, but it that was no wonder, considering the lady's looks.

Then a thundering neigh came from the stable building and a man appeared, leading a beautiful stallion outside.

It was not very tall, but well-muscled and almost pitch-black. With pricked ears, it danced out of the darkness into the red light of the setting sun, its coat shining.

Ramose sighed at the sight. Never had he seen a more beautiful horse.

"You like horses, I see," the lady said.

"Yes, I do."

Another horse was led out of the stables. A stallion, again, and of the same colour as the previous one. Their only difference was that this horse had a white sock on its near hind leg.

"They are very beautiful, my lady," Ramose said. "You are so lucky to have such magnificent animals."

"Well, I wouldn't know much about horses. I can see they are beautiful, but I am too scared to touch them."

"Oh, but do, you'll love the smooth feeling of their coats," Ramose said, moving up close to her in his eagerness.

The lady looked at the lively horses with a worried expression. The horses were dancing in circles around the men who did their best to show off the beautiful animals, their hoofs kicking up dust and stones, their tails in a shiny arch in the air. Clearly, the lady's husband was someone of importance.

"Very well, I will touch a horse but only if you stand next to me and they keep still. Otherwise I will never find the courage," the lady said, looking very young and scared.

"As you wish," Ramose straightened up with pride at the lady's words. Too often, the grooms and masters had marched past him as if he was a nobody. Now, here he was with an important noble lady, who owned a pair of the finest horses Ramose had ever seen.

"You go first," she smiled nervously.

Ramose approached the nearest stallion, the one with the white sock, and lifted his hand. The horse turned its head towards him curiously, its ears going back and forth. Ramose let his fingertips slide gently along its shoulder. The horse stood still, letting out a long breath from its nostrils. They hadn't been slit to prevent the horse from neighing and revealing its chariot to the enemy, Ramose noticed.

How wonderful the animal felt to his touch… strong, warm, alive… he spread his fingers and let his hand run the length of the stallion's back.

The lady approached and lifted her hand.

Suddenly the horse threw its head up, and its eyes rolled so that the whites showed. Neighing, it stepped backwards as if it was afraid of the slight woman, staring at her with ears now flat against its head.

Ramose turned and for the briefest moment, the woman's golden eyes struck him as odd. They stared at the horse intensely, eagerly, not afraid. The lady's mouth was open so that her pretty white teeth showed, and for a while she looked like a golden-eyed lioness almost ready to jump.

But he must have misinterpreted what he saw. The next moment, the lady had stepped back, shaking.

"No, I cannot touch it – I fear it will bite me, kick me!"

Ramose felt protective towards her.

"Maybe it's best you keep your distance from this one. But you can see that the horses are well cared for and healthy," Ramose said.

Both horses were both staring at them now, backing away, ears still flat.

"Now they are both nervous. Horses are like that – one gets scared, and all the others want to escape too," he said. "You may take the horses back inside," he then ordered the men as if he had authority in the matter.

"Yes, do take them back. I will let my husband know all is well with them. Thank you," the beauty said in a nervous voice.

The horses were led away.

"Could I ask you to walk with me back to my house?" the woman said. "I feel a bit shaky still and it would give me comfort to know I have a strong young man to look after me."

Ramose felt protective of her, and a little guilty. After all, he had tried to force her to do something she did not want to do.

"Of course. I feel I am to blame… I should have understood horses are not for women," he said. "The least I can do is see you safely home."

He found nothing odd in the fact the lady did not consider two adult male servants to be enough protection. They were only servants, after all. He was a free man, the son of Nefertiti's lady-in-waiting who was a famous dancer before the god.

He shortened his step so that they could walk side by side to the northern part of the city. Night had already fallen as they approached the house. It was a big house with three storeys and a garden, too.

"This is where I live," the lady said. "Thank you for all your help."

Another servant carrying an oil lamp came out to greet them. Its beams made the lady's face look almost inhumanly beautiful. Her eyes seemed almost to swirl in the light. Her heavy perfume was making Ramose's head spin.

"Perhaps you might like to share a cup of wine with me?" she suddenly asked. "I couldn't just leave you outside after all you have done for me. My husband would never allow such impoliteness."

"I think my mother is expecting me back..." Ramose stammered.

"Please, just one cup. She doesn't need to know about it. We will have servants around us all the time, so my request is not improper in any way. And I am sure your mother would accept my offer as a thank you if she were here."

She looked so young and beautiful...

"Very well, I can't refuse you," Ramose said, smiling.

She smiled back.

"That makes me so glad. Follow me!"

She turned to walk inside and Ramose followed her, his eyes glued to the sensual sway of her hips, and the perfumed hair that hung down to her thighs.

53

SUBTERFUGE

The way the two Nephilim were following our ship, it was clear they knew there were other Nephilim on board.

"Who can they be?" Diana looked at them as they appeared on the eastern shore again. They just stood there, watching our ship approaching as we headed south, and staying put until we had almost vanished from sight. "They must be using the buffer zone to follow the ship – no one could have that much energy to keep up with us on foot."

"I've no idea who they are… but because they haven't attempted to cross the water or come to this ship, I conclude they are enemy Nephilim." Elijah said.

"We need to find the rest of our team," Lilith said, "but with these two on our tail, we can't go ashore. And I don't want to try to connect to Paris now, just in case they have someone in the buffer zone close by us."

"If we use the buffer zone, I have no doubt we'll be attacked," Daniel said. "We need a way to get rid of them to give us the chance to weave our way to the rest of our team. Ideas, anyone?"

I looked at the water.

"I have an idea," I said. "I could go and find our team on my own. All I need is the bracelet Paris gave to Diana."

Daniel raised his hands in a gesture of denial.

"Not a chance. Not with Ambrogio about and not with those two following us. How could you get away without them following you?" Daniel asked.

"Remember what happened to me under water?" I asked. "When I escaped Ambrogio in the Red Sea?"

Lilith looked at me.

"You turned into... the pure Nephilim can breathe under water for a while, using the wings as gills... but you turned into some kind of a..."

"Mermaid?" I smiled.

"Well, for lack of a better word, let's say mermaid. With a sort of fin and tail and everything, if I understood you correctly? I've never come across that before. How about you?"

Lilith was looking at Daniel and Elijah.

"Well, some stories relate that the purest Nephilim lived in the seas in the past. Living in them, not just able to breathe to survive for a while in extreme conditions. And Dana's bloodline has surprised us in the past, with healing and electric sparks, not to mention vapourising a whole lake. And now this ability to not only breathe underwater but also to transform into a... mythical creature. I believe her," Elijah said, adding, "I see no reason *not* to believe her."

"Well, that's why I made the suggestion. We can't just sail for days and let those two follow us everywhere. If I slip into the water unnoticed from the western side of the ship..."

"That would be the starboard," Diana commented tartly.

"Most kind, thank you... so if I slip into the water on the starboard side of the ship unnoticed, and swim away from them underwater until I am far enough away to enter the buffer zone without them sensing it... I might find the team and warn them about Ambrogio and the dark Nephilim."

"And then get right back here," Daniel looked at me, grabbing my arm to emphasise his words. "I don't want you alone out there."

"Yes, and then return here right away," I squeezed his fingers, hoping he would not realise how nervous I was.

The others looked at each other.

"Very well then," Lilith said. "Let's try it. The next time those two disappear from sight, over the side you go, into the water."

We didn't have to wait long for the next disappearance of the two Nephilim. No doubt they would be waiting for the ship nearby upriver. Their disappearances and appearances happened so frequently, it was clear they didn't want to leave the ship unobserved along any stretch of the river where the ship could put anyone ashore. That was the confirmation we needed that they were hunting us, waiting for us to leave the boat.

"Now is the time," Daniel said, "they are nowhere to be seen and I don't sense them around either. How about you, Elijah?"

He wasn't leaving anything to chance.

"I agree. I don't sense them anywhere near right now," Elijah said.

"Here," Diana gave me the bracelet, "and here," she gave me the hairpin Elijah had carried with him as an anchor to this time. "Just in case, so you can find your way back to us more easily. It worked well enough the last time."

I pinned the hairpin on the neckline of my dress and put the bracelet on my wrist, trying not to think about it so I would not inadvertently weave myself to Paris right there.

Bay said a few words to the ship's crew.

"I say to them you go under water. But not worry, you not drowned, you good swimmer," he said. "Look around good when under water. Crocodiles."

Daniel looked as if he was going to stop the whole plan right there.

"No crocodiles here, not now," Bay touched his arm.

"Better not rely on that information. Be quick," Lilith said.

I approached the side of the ship, throwing one final look backwards to be sure the two Nephilim were nowhere to be seen. The crew of the ship were staring at me as if I had lost my mind.

"Here goes!" I took a deep breath and jumped into the water.

The cool water felt different here. Softer. Calmer. I let myself fall away from the sunlight again. I looked around but saw only fish, no crocodiles. Below me a large fish with whiskers swam away from me. Had to be a catfish – I had heard they could give an electric shock so I kicked my feet in the water to gain distance from it.

I wasn't going to waste any time. I concentrated on my wings and opened them underwater. The shockwave pushed a school of fish away from me and then the wings curved around me just as they had done in the sea. I looked down and sure enough, the dolphin-like see-through tail fin was there.

I tried to remember what it had felt like when my wings began to function as gills in the sea and drew in a breath with my whole body. The sensation of pure oxygen flowing in was soothing.

I looked up, expecting everyone to be looking down from the ship, but it was no longer there – the current was floating me downstream.

The bubble my wings formed around my torso filled with water again. I wondered if I could push the water away somehow but this was not the time to experiment.

I took off the bracelet and squeezed it in my left hand, thinking of Paris. My right hand inside the bubble began to become misty and soon enough the strings began to form from my fingertips.

At the last moment, I hoped I was far enough from the two Nephilim so they would not detect me in the buffer zone.

Then the strings shot out with full force and yanked me with them.

For a brief moment, there was mist, but almost immediately, I fell onto a dry surface.

Again, I couldn't breathe. I was literally a fish out of water.

Someone shouted. A familiar voice. I writhed on the dry ground, inside my bubble of water.

Someone touched me. Strong hands were lifting me up.

The bubble burst as soon as the hands touched me, shooting water everywhere, and my wings took in a deep breath of air. I gasped air through my mouth too. My transformation from mermaid to Nephilim was not quite smooth yet.

"Dana! It's Dana!" Paris shouted.

For it was Paris. She ran to me, kneeling down to hug me. Her dress got all wet but she didn't mind.

"You're alive! Thank God, you're alive!" Grandma's arms were also around me, "Thank God!"

My head was spinning still and I felt nauseous.

"Give her some space," Reggie said.

After a while the world stopped swirling and I could look around.

They were all there. Grandma, Reggie, Mr. Donnelly, Paris, Jason, Aemilius, Thomas. Only the scribe Ahmose was missing. We were in a house. I could see a garden outside. Beautiful wall paintings covered the walls of the room – reeds, ducks, flowers. The floor was decorated with a painting of a pool with fish in it. Rows of garden flowers were painted symmetrically around the pool. It reminded me of the floor paintings of Amarna that local farmers would destroy in the future, in the early 20th century, angry at the tourists trampling their fields on their way to see the sights. Could these have been the very paintings? I didn't remember ever checking what they had looked like.

"Where is this place?" I asked when I felt I could open my mouth without throwing up.

"This place is in the northern district of Akhetaten," Reggie said, "Tiye's ships sailed straight here after you disappeared. We thought it best to come along. If we had stopped somewhere along the journey, you might never have found us. But as this was our original destination, it was only logical to carry on here. And probably we wouldn't have been allowed to leave anyway."

"But what was that you just did?" Paris asked. "For a while you looked like a fish!"

Thomas had still not said anything, he was staring at me with his mouth open. A normal reaction to seeing a winged mermaid appear out of thin air, I figured.

"What happened to you? And where is Diana? The last thing we saw was your wings opening, scaring the living daylights out of everyone on the ship. And then you were gone. Tiye was afraid of us after that, but you had somehow convinced her that you were to be trusted, so thankfully, no harm was done to us," Jason explained.

His skin was tanned and he looked like a professional wrestler now, wearing only a kilt.

"Give the girl some space," Mr. Donnelly said.

"I'm not sure anyone should see Dana at the moment. Not until we know what has happened," Reggie said.

"Ah yes, the guards..." Mr. Donnelly rubbed the bridge of his nose.

"What guards?" I got up from the floor and squeezed water out of my hair.

"Well, after Tiye was convinced you were a goddess of some sort, she put us all under heavy guard so that no one could approach us again without her leave. She does not want word of us spreading – this is the city of the Aten where other deities are not allowed. Which means we have guards at the gate, guards in the garden, and even guards on the rooftop, ready to barge in at the first sign of any unexpected activity," Jason spread his arms to take in the whole house.

"Quite. It might be best if we try to convince them that all is as it should be right now. That was quite a splash you made there," Mr. Donnelly said to me.

Realising I was still sitting in a pool of Nile water, I got to my feet.

"Everyone – go out in the garden or somewhere else, try to look like everything's normal. Layla and I will stay indoors and talk to Dana. Then we'll decide what we're going to do next," Reggie said.

"I'm off to the garden," Jason said.

"I think I'll go there too," Paris decided and walked out of the room.

"I'm going up to the roof. I'll get the servants to bring me something to eat and drink to keep them busy, so they stay away from you. I never tire of looking at the scenery," Mr. Donnelly said, patting my hand. "I am ever so happy to see you safe and well. We thought you were dead when you did not return and were making plans about how we might approach Nefertiti's sister without you. Thomas – would you stay outside the door in case someone tries to enter? You speak the language fluently. Just in case you need to divert anyone."

"I'll join you," Aemilius said.

They left the room, drawing the curtains on both doorways. Mr.

Donnelly went inside the house, to the steps leading up to the roof, and Thomas and Aemilius waited outside the door leading to the garden. Thomas cast a long, disbelieving look in my direction as he passed by me and clearly still couldn't say a thing.

"Lucky there were no servants here when I arrived," I said.

"Lucky indeed," Reggie said, "otherwise Tiye would probably know of your arrival already. But sit down and tell us everything."

I did, trying to be brief. It was a tall order, trying to condense everything. Reggie did not interrupt me, only nodded his head from time to time, and seemed to be making some kind of mental notes as I spoke.

"Right," he then said, "so to summarise, we all survived. Ambrogio is after you for some other reason than we originally thought. Anna is in Angel's grasp. And there are dangerous Nephilim about that we should avoid. Daniel and Elijah have arrived with Lilith. I am very glad to hear that! And Merit is now in Mi-Wer?"

"Yes, that's about it," I said.

"And you turn into a mermaid when immersed in water? It can't be just being in the water or it would have happened every time you took a bath… must be something to do with the breathing process that ignites the change. How interesting. It would be wonderful if we could do some secret genetic tests on your kind… but I'm afraid that kind of knowledge would leak out and every Nephilim would be in danger."

He pulled his fingers through his hair in that familiar way, indicating he was about to start some kind of scientific discussion. I interrupted him before he could continue.

"We need to decide what to do now. We need to work out how to get the others here from the ship without those Nephilim following us."

"But that should be easy, my dear," Reggie smiled.

"What? How?"

"Well, they can't cross water. Or at least they avoid it as much as they can. And when you weave, you don't need to use the buffer zone much, it appears. The fact that they have not attacked you using the buffer zone seems to confirm they don't want to use it over water. Why else would they be following you on the shore? So, you go back there, and bring them in one by one. Your transitions are almost instant, it seems. Do this when those two on the shore don't have good visibility to the ship, and only take one person with you at a time to make it as fast as possible."

"You think that might work?" I asked.

"Yes, I think so."

Jason's voice came from the garden. He was speaking loudly but in a conversational tone.

"Oh yes., I think it may be a good idea to leave soon, so others don't see you."

Paris laughed.

"Indeed. The guards are coming in."

They spoke in English, which the guards of course did not understand.

"The guards are coming into the house to do a check, which they do often," Reggie said. "Go quickly. And return as soon as you can – I'll ask Paris to come into the room and we'll keep the curtains closed so when you get back, you can avoid being spotted right away."

Now we heard Thomas speaking in Egyptian to someone approaching.

I took Diana's hairpin and concentrated. Almost instantly orange strings shot out of my hand. In a flash, I was gone. The last thing I saw was Reggie toppling over a jar of beer – probably to hide the water I had splashed all around the room.

I almost bumped into Diana on my return.

"Whoops, sorry!" I said.

"Did you find them?" Lilith hurried to ask.

"Yes. They were in Amarna. Tiye had put guards around the house they are in. But they are all well. Reggie said that I could just weave my way to them with you, as it seems I don't spend much time in the buffer zone."

"Well, sometimes it takes a while..." Elijah said, "it isn't always instant."

"Yes, it seems you can zap your way instantly to a place when you are alone. But when you have others with you, it slows you down a bit… remember when we found our way to Diana last time?" Daniel said.

"True… but if I take only one of you with me at a time, that should make the transition faster. I think…"

"Well, our two friends are on the shoreline again, so we'll have to wait a little longer to test the theory…" Diana tilted her head slightly towards the two figures without actually looking at them.

We waited, deliberately avoiding staring at the two Nephilim, though they had to know we were aware of their presence.

"Let's go into the cabin while they are looking. When we start disappearing one by one, they won't see it."

"I think Lilith and Diana should be the first to go," Elijah said, "then us. They'll probably notice it when Nephilim leave, so we'll need to move pretty fast then."

"Here, take this…" Daniel opened the thin silver chain that hung from his neck and gave it to me. "If you take Diana first, you won't be able to use her hairpin as an anchor for you to return to us anymore."

I couldn't hold the chain in my hand so I put it around my own neck.

"We take ship more west," Bay said, "Water makes it difficult to sense for them. Soon, the river is wider."

We wasted no time. One by one, we walked into the little cabin. Only Bay stayed on deck. There, I took Diana's hand first of all.

"Let's hope this works… and remember to be quiet when we arrive."

We did enter the buffer zone but only for a short moment. Then we arrived in the room where Reggie, Paris and Grandma were already waiting.

"Diana!" Paris whispered and hugged her.

I did not take Daniel's chain off, just grabbed it with my hand, Bright blue strings pulled me back to the ship in a heartbeat so I could carry on with my task.

Paris wiped away tears when she saw Lilith.

"We were so afraid you had all died!" she whispered. "I am so happy to see you!"

“Lilith…” was all Grandma said before she hugged her.

I left them hugging each other and returned to the ship.

"They should vanish soon enough…" Daniel said, looking through the woven wall of the cabin. "And… there they go!"

Bay spoke to the ship's crew and they started rowing the ship towards the eastern shore.

"Leave quickly," Bay said, “I stay in sight. I need to keep the enemy following me. But after you all gone, I cannot go to Mi-Wer, to Merit. Has to wait or they will find her.”

"Elijah…" I offered him my hand, and in a flash we were gone.

"Elijah, my boy!" Reggie patted him on the back the way men do when they are emotional. "This is indeed a day of joy!"

Daniel was not inside the cabin when I arrived. I stepped out and found him talking to Bay.

"Daniel, we should go," I said.

He turned towards me and then his eyes focussed on something on the shore. His expression froze.

"What is it?" I asked.

"Who is that?" Bay asked simultaneously

I turned to look.

There was a figure on the eastern shore again. He was far off now that our ship was closer to the western shoreline. But with my enhanced vision, I could see him plainly and clearly, standing there, south of our ship. The northern wind must have already confirmed our presence on the ship to him.

Ambrogio.

54

CURIOSITY

"How big is your family?" Nefertiry asked. Her eyes were closed and her hands behind her head. "Is it only you and your mother? I mean... you have not mentioned anyone else."

Ramose lay on his side, looking at her naked beauty.

"We have family elsewhere, but I haven't seen them in ages..." he said.

She turned her head towards him and opened her compelling golden eyes.

"How sad... Family is so important. I miss my own family..." she said solemnly.

"Where are they?"

Nefertiry rose and walked to the low table where a bowl of dates and a jar of wine waited. She took some of the dates in her hand, took a cup of fine wine into another and returned to the bed. Ramose could not take his eyes off the golden-brown body that had given him such pleasure for weeks now.

"Here, have some dates," she said and bent over Ramose to give the fruit to him.

Ramose had something other than eating in mind, but Nefertiry pushed the cup into his hand. Careful not to spill any wine, Ramose sat up.

"My family is dead," Nefertiry said, touching his arm with her cool hand.

Ramose could not believe how cool she was – her skin felt delightful in the heat of the day, and she never seemed to sweat.

"I am sorry. What killed them?"

"A disease brought by a ship when we lived in Inbu-Hedj," Nefertiry sighed, her eyes downcast. "Everyone died but me. A friend of my father's took me into his care after his wife died, and married me when I came of age so he could give me a respectable position. But he is never here, and I suspect he has women elsewhere. I am of no interest to him… Even though he has no heir, he still isn't interested in me."

"He must be mad…" Ramose dropped the dates and reached out and pulled her to him, eager to satisfy his needs again. He could not get enough of her.

"Not now… the servants may return at any moment," she said, pushing his arm away from her waist. "And I don't want to create trouble. But I could not help myself, I have been so lonely because my husband shows no interest in me. My heart began to sing as soon as I saw you for the first time… and then you saved me from that horse… Next time, I will send you to the stables if he asks about the animals. I don't like them, they are too fierce for me."

She shivered. "But tell me about your family? Why have you not seen them? Where do they live? Are there many of them? Wouldn't you like to see them?" she asked.

Ramose chewed on a date and drank the sweetened wine. It rose to his head, making him feel confident about himself.

"Here, take some," he offered a date to her.

"No, I only eat in the evening. I can't grow fat and ugly, or you will not find me attractive anymore," she laughed.

"I could never pass the whole day without eating something!" Ramose smiled. "You women are stronger than us men in that respect."

She smiled back.

"I love to see a man with a healthy appetite. But tell me about your family!" she insisted. "I haven't had one for so long, I'd love to hear about yours. Please. It would help to make me feel less lonely."

She got up again and began to dress herself. Ramose sighed at the clear sign that their intimacy was over for now.

"Well, my grandmother lives in Mi-Wer. And she has a trusted servant with her; one that even the Mother of the King asks for advice."

"Really? Do they ever visit here?"

"No, they haven't visited here ever, I think."

"How sad, why not?"

"I suppose their duties keep them occupied at Mi-Wer… but they do write letters – my mother and grandmother."

"They do? How wonderful it would be to receive a letter from someone… not that I could read it, but I could have it read for me!" Nefertiry combed her perfumed hair with her fingers, the heavy locks rising and falling behind her back. "I don't think I have ever seen a letter in my life!"

"Really? Not ever?"

She took his tunic from the floor where he had thrown it in his haste to get her into bed, and gave it to him.

He got up.

"No, not ever. I can't read. But I would love to see a real letter…"

She bit her lip and looked at him with that shy look that made his heart beat erratically.

"Do you think… Would it be possible for me to see a letter your mother has received? Just for a few moments? I would love to hold a real letter for a while. Just hold it. You could return it immediately after that so she wouldn't even notice."

"What a strange request," Ramose smiled.

"Now you think I am silly!" She looked sad.

"Well, not silly. A bit strange… but I'll see what I can do," Ramose said gallantly.

"Oh, thank you!" Her smile was radiant. "Just don't let anyone see... I mean... if word got out, they would really think me silly..."

"I won't," Ramose laughed.

"And that is all the family you have? Your mother and grandmother? No cousins? No aunts or uncles?" she was back on the subject as she escorted him out the garden gate at the hottest time of the day. Not many were in the alleys at that time.

"Yes, my mother has a sister, but she left many, many years ago to live with her husband in another country. She has never visited. I don't know if she has children. Probably."

She placed a cool kiss on his lips.

"Go now, my handsome. The servants have been told to come back at noon. I don't want them to see you. They might tell my husband."

Ramose kissed her back, and then turned to go.

Letters... A woman who could not read wanted to see letters... Well, if that made her happy, he could bring her some letters to touch.

55

LETTER FROM MERIT

The letter was waiting for Meryt-Neith when she returned to her rooms. It had been placed on the low table in her reception area. Mother had written again.

A servant brought her a bowl of water and folded a cloth next to it. Meryt-Neith dipped the cloth into the water and washed the dust from her skin.

Nefertiti had been tired today after they had returned from the Aten temple. She had a pounding headache and Meryt-Neith suspected it was because her eyesight was worsening. The king's certainly was, even though he was good at hiding the fact. He insisted on looking directly towards the sun when worshipping the Aten. Nefertiti often closed her eyes behind her husband's back when he wouldn't notice it. But as it was, Akhenaten no longer read any documents himself, and needed bright light just to make out his surroundings. As a result, the rooms of the palaces – both the North Palace and the palace in the city centre – were lit with hundreds of oil lamps at all times. The side-effect of this was that the warm light showed off the brightly painted walls and pillars in their full glory, all the plants, animals, scenes of the royal couple and their daughters.

The king had gone to Kiya's palace and with the Great Royal Wife resting, Meryt-Neith had some time for herself now.

After cleaning up, she took the little letter from the table. The string was different this time. Usually Merit used a coarse linen string to close her letters, but this was more of a ribbon than a string. Still, the knots were tight.

Meryt-Neith wondered why the letter had been left on the table – usually Merit's letters were given to her directly by a messenger who waited for her if she was not there.

While Meryt-Neith was opening the strings, Seshat walked in. Two bees were travelling in her hair.

"You've been to the bees, I see," Meryt-Neith smiled.

"Yes, how could you tell?" Seshat smiled. "Ah, my little pets revealed the secret, I see. Is that a letter from your mother?"

"I think so, who else would send me a letter..." Meryt-Neith took a little obsidian blade she kept in a ceramic jar and cut the ribbon so she could open the letter.

She dropped the ribbon on the table while Seshat bent her short legs and sat on a mat on the floor next to the table.

"What's the matter with the bees?" Seshat asked as Meryt-Neith opened the folds of the papyrus letter. Mother always folded her letters into a tight square, small enough to fit the palm of a messenger's hand.

"How so?" Meryt-Neith raised her eyes.

"Just look at them."

The two bees had flown off Seshat's hair and were now hovering over the cut ribbon, moving quickly from side to side, landing on it and then rising into the air again.

"It's as if they don't like the ribbon. Strange."

Seshat looked at the bees.

"How about the letter? Put it down there, a little to the side."

Meryt-Neith did. The bees paid no attention to it and she took it up again.

"Now that is strange... I wonder what's on that ribbon..." Seshat said.

"Well, they are bees. You can't tell what they are thinking."

Meryt-Neith opened the letter and began to read.

"Oh... They are leaving Mi-Wer. Mother and Mut-Bity. Or rather they have already left."

"Why?"

"Mother writes here that she has a sense of danger closing in. She asks me to be careful and warns me that... *he* has not forgotten us, even if he hasn't shown himself."

Something in Meryt-Neith's voice made Seshat suspicious. She sounded nervous.

"Has he? Shown himself, that is?" Seshat shot an arrow in the dark and from the way Meryt-Neith paled, she saw that it had hit home.

"Where?" she asked quietly.

"By the stables. He met with Ramose there and asked him to bring me to meet him. The boy of course did not know what... who he is. He tried to convince me that he has changed."

Seshat snorted.

"Exactly. I didn't believe it either. A thing like that can't happen."

"Did you tell Merit?"

"No. I did not want to worry her. It is no surprise that he knows where I am. And as nothing happened – I did not want to worry anyone. Also, I have our bees with me all the time."

At that Seshat tapped the little clay tube she had with her at all times, attached to a sash on her waist. Meryt-Neith carried bees too, when she ventured away from the beehives. She had a leather pouch hanging from her neck. It was punctured in a decorative pattern so that the bees could breathe. A little drop of honey kept them nourished. She took the bees to their hives in the garden as soon as she returned to the palace every day and replaced them with new ones. They did not mind her picking them up with her fingers, and never stung her, or Ramose for that matter.

"What else does your mother say?" asked Seshat.

"She says I can get a message to her by sending a letter to the beekeeper of Mi-Wer. They will forward the message on to her. But she requests I don't do that apart from in an emergency. Forwarding the message to her will put the beekeeper and the messengers in danger, as they are surely observed by the dark Nephilim."

"She is wise, your mother. What else?"

"She says she will write to me sometimes, and I can give my response to the messenger who brings it to me. But the letters are always to be given to me directly, and I must answer immediately, so the messenger can leave without drawing any attention to themselves. And the last thing she writes is that I must burn all her letters."

"But where is the messenger who brought you this letter, so you could give them him your answer?" Seshat asked.

"There was no one," Meryt-Neith said. "The letter was waiting there on the table."

"Against your mother's specific instructions?"

"What instructions?" Ramose walked in.

The boy looked happy. He had changed these last few weeks – become more certain of himself. He was not so shy among women anymore.

"Ramose," Meryt-Neith hugged her son, "Do you know anything about this letter? It was here when I came back."

"Oh that, yes..." Ramose smiled. "I was here when the messenger came with the letter. You were still away, so I took the letter and let him go."

"Him? Who was he?"

"Just a servant who had received it from someone."

Seshat looked at the boy.

"How odd. These letters always come directly to your mother and are never left with someone else," she said.

"The servant must have misunderstood, then," Ramose said, "But there was no harm done, was there? After all, I took the letter from the servant and put it on the table to wait for you. No one else has touched it."

"But anyone could have," Meryt-Neith said, "after all, I wasn't here."

"I am sure no one has," Ramose said. "Don't worry about it, mother. It is not as if many people here can read."

That was true. Most of the women could not read, and none of the lowly servants. And higher officials couldn't enter the private rooms of the Great Royal Wife's ladies. Even Ramose's presence was frowned upon after he had become a young man. But Meryt-Neith's rooms were a little apart from the king's own family and women, so technically speaking Ramose was not in the women's quarters.

"Well, I'll make one more trip to the stables before they are sealed for the night," Ramose said.

He had told Meryt-Neith that a rich merchant's family had asked him to check on their chariot horses every now and then. He had been so proud of this and was at the stables every day now, looking at the fine stallions.

"Have you eaten anything?" Meryt-Neith asked.

"Yes, a servant brought me food earlier."

Ramose turned and walked away.

Meryt-Neith read the letter one more time, went over to an oil lamp lit in the bedroom and touched the letter to the flame. When it began to burn, she let it fall into a ceramic bowl and returned to discuss the matter with Seshat.

56

CHANCE MEETING

Ambrogio closed his eyes and allowed himself the luxury of a long, deep breath. Her scent coming from the ship was strong and tempting. For a while he remembered the metallic tang of her blood, mixed with a slightly rosy perfume that had touched his palate. He thought of how delicious her blood would be when he tasted it again.

He had found her. Now to make sure she would never escape again. He was not going to let her out of his sight.

He opened his eyes, not caring if they saw him. After all, they knew he was after them. Just as he suspected, they were staring at him from the ship – Dana and Daniel, side by side. There was a third Nephilim there too, dark-skinned, one he had never seen before. He breathed in to catch his scent also, to memorise it for future use.

Satisfied, he started heading back south along the riverbank, in the same direction as the ship, waiting for it to pass him before he started running. He covered his head, as there were villages nearby and he did not want any of their inhabitants to see his skin.

The ship caught up and then passed him. They were still on deck, looking at him.

Ambrogio began to run without ever losing sight of the ship. It was closer to the western bank of the river, and he hoped they weren't planning to go ashore there. They could of course leave the ship any time using the buffer zone, and it was unfortunate that he did not have his shadow with him so he couldn't follow them there. But should that happen, he knew where they were headed. Dana was alive and it was certain that she would go to Akhetaten. That's where he would find her, eventually. He only hoped they weren't planning on leaving through the buffer zone – he would need to run at full speed after that, to be sure he caught up with them before they completed their quest. And Ambrogio knew he would need to feed soon if he was to run such a distance without stopping.

His attention was so completely on the ship and its passengers that the two dark Nephilim took him by surprise.

He felt the heat of their bodies an instant before they grabbed him from behind, and that was all the time he needed to react.

Maybe they were planning on killing him, to drink his blood. But they didn't get the chance – and didn't seem to notice that they had caught another blood-drinker, not a warm-blooded person.

Ambrogio went straight into action instinctively. Over two thousand years of hunting, killing and fighting had embedded self-defence and attack so deeply in his system that he had already bent over and thrown the attacker face down onto the ground before his thoughts became coherent. He had his knee on the attacker's back in a flash, yanking the assailant's arms behind his back, ready to dislocate his shoulders if necessary.

Now he had the attacker in a position where he could reach the root of the wings. Even though they were not opened, injuring the spot where the wings unfurled from a Nephilim's back forced them to open. After that, it was just a matter of slashing the veins and holding the Nephilim still until their blood drained out. Usually they were unconscious before this happened, as attacking the wings seriously affected their ability even to breathe normally.

Had this been a trained fighter, Ambrogio would probably have had more of a struggle. It seemed these ancient Nephilim felt so sure of their supremacy that they weren't getting proper military training.

He noticed that this Nephilim was plump and his muscles were weak.

Ambrogio's mind was as sharp as ever. Had the Nephilim been alone, he would have killed him. But when he saw his companion, he quickly decided on a more effective approach.

"I bring greetings from your high lord," he said, straightening up and pulling Cain's golden pendant out so it hung in front of his robe.

The Nephilim on the ground got to his feet immediately. Ambrogio sensed his anger, but his eyes were fixed on the pendant. It was clearly the mark of a Nephilim lord and made from gold, indicating that Ambrogio was high in the rank of servants. No dark Nephilim would want to face the wrath of a Nephilim lord – and killing a servant who wore the badge of gold was a sure way to anger one.

"Your lord is the Pale Man," Ambrogio said without showing any fear.

Their posture changed from aggressive to cautious.

"Who are you? How do you know our lord?" the plump Nephilim asked, rubbing his shoulders.

"And what are you?" the other one, who looked more athletic, asked.

"He is a blood-drinker..." said the plump one. "I should have smelled it, but we were upwind of him..."

"I am. I am the highest servant of my lord Cain. I am here on his mission. See that ship?" Ambrogio pointed.

"Yes, there are the other kind of Nephilim there," the plump one said.

"There are. And you see those two on deck? The pale ones?"

Dana and Daniel were looking back – the ship was already way past them.

"Yes. We have been following them. Them and Bay," the fit one said.

"Bay?" Ambrogio asked.

"He is the leader of the other kind. We don't see him often. We are to follow him if he shows himself. These are our orders."

"Orders of your high lord?" Ambrogio asked.

"Yes."

"We are to follow him to discover where they hide," the plump one opened his mouth again, earning an angry look from his companion.

Clearly, he had said more than he should have done, but Ambrogio pretended not to notice.

"And I am to follow that lady where ever she goes, to bring her back to my lord Cain. She left her clan without permission. Your high lord himself has been helping me to track her down. He is waiting for us to return to Akhetaten to meet him there," Ambrogio said. "I would be honoured if we could join paths. We are after the same ship, after all."

The two Nephilim looked at each other.

"Very well. But we're not planning on following them on foot," the fit one said.

"Of course. And that's all the better for me – if you will allow me to travel with you in the misty world, you will make my work easier. And you will earn the gratitude of my lord. And your own lord too."

"Is your lord rich?" the athletic one asked.

After gold, Ambrogio understood. The evil Nephilim were always greedy.

"Extremely. You cannot begin to imagine his riches. And he is generous to those who help him."

"I can imagine a lot," the fit one said.

"Yes, we can," the plump Nephilim hurried to add himself into the picture.

"My lord lives far away, but as soon as I get word to him of your help, he will reward you."

"He has gold?"

"Gold. Horses. Servants. Wives. Palaces. Ships," Ambrogio said. He turned to look at the vessel as it grew smaller in the distance. "Should we be going?"

"Take his hand," the first one said.

The plump one grabbed Ambrogio's hand and pulled him into the buffer zone.

57

ESCAPE THROUGH WATER

"What shall we do now?" I asked. "We can't go through the buffer zone with them lying in wait for us."

We had just watched the two Nephilim appear out of the buffer zone behind Ambrogio and attack him. The First Vampire's reflexes were so fast I only saw a blur of movement as his attacker fell face-down on the ground.

It hadn't come to a full-blown fight. We'd seen them talk for a while and then they vanished into the buffer zone.

"They could be waiting for us anywhere," Daniel said, "and I am sure Ambrogio will convince them not to let the ship out of their sights now. I fear his shadow is not far off either. He's probably waiting in the buffer zone near our ship."

That meant I couldn't make even a very quick transition through the buffer zone.

"I might manage to escape them if I was alone, but even one person with me will slow me down..."

"You could go alone – but you're not going to. There is a small risk, and I won't let you take it."

Daniel pulled me closer and kissed the top of my head.

"So it looks like we have to carry on travelling on board this ship and stay out in the middle of the river," he said.

"Unless..."

The thought hit me.

"Unless what?" Daniel asked.

"We both go through the water!" I said. "You can breathe underwater too, surely? Have you ever tried it?"

"I have," Daniel said, "Once. Soon after my wings had opened. I could breathe there for a few minutes, but after that, it became uncomfortable."

"And...?"

"It felt odd, but I did manage to breathe there for a while. No bubble formed around me, though; and definitely no dolphin tail!"

"Maybe that is a female thing? Maybe they are called mer*maids* for a reason?"

It was a weak joke, but it eased the tension.

"A few minutes may be all we need," I said. "We could just let the water carry us downriver, coming up to breathe if necessary, and when we are far enough away, I'll weave us to Akhetaten."

"It's worth a try," Daniel agreed. "Even if Ambrogio's shadow is in the buffer zone, I don't think it can follow us through water."

"I stay on top of ship so they see me," Bay said, "I pretend to talk to you in cabin. Give time."

"We need to go immediately," Daniels said, "It's only been minutes, and I am sure Ambrogio is persuading them to keep the ship in their sight even now."

"Go," Bay said, "use the cabin. I lead them away."

The walls of the cabin were not solid – this ship had panels that could be lifted away to create more deck space. We went to the cabin, loosened a panel and one after the other slid into the water – I went first, then Daniel.

"Hand in hand," I said quietly.

Out of habit we took a deep breath before diving. With kicking movements we went downriver fast. When I felt the need to breathe, I shook my hands free and let myself fall downwards.

Daniel had stronger lungs than I, and so he remained underwater, to see what would happen.

Each time in the water seemed to be easier for me. I opened my wings and took a deep breath through them. They extended around me and downwards too and I felt the tail shoot out, down from my feet. Once more I was inside my own bubble, breathing effortlessly.

Daniel now swam to the surface, took a breath and came back down. He gestured at me to stay put and concentrated on breathing. Soon I saw tiny bubbles forming on the surface of his wings. He gave me the ok-sign and we floated downriver with me using my dolphin tail to stay with him – my hands were inside the bubble so I could not hold his hand. The bubble moved when my hands did, stretching, but I had not yet tried to grab anything in my mermaid form and was afraid I'd burst the bubble. Now I just wanted to get us as far away as possible, as fast as we could.

With my tail, my movements were almost lazy – each kick shot me forward with such speed Daniel had trouble keeping up.

Finally, I headed up. Daniel gave me a sign to wait and went first. He looked around, and returned to me, gesturing upwards with a nod.

I followed, swimming near to the western shore, into a thicket of reeds. I got up on my feet, still inside my bubble and now I needed the bubble to burst. I pushed with my hands and breathed in through my wings.

With a splash, my wings opened again, throwing the water around as if I were a water fountain.

"Now that was a sight!" Daniel said. "You really did look like a mermaid. Or perhaps a maiden swallowed by a dolphin. You were inside the bubble of your wings – which were not black, by the way, but transparent – and your hair was floating around you inside the bubble."

I had not paid attention to the fact that my wings really had been colourless underwater. I looked at them and they were black again. How beautiful they had been when they first opened – bright white. And here, in the ancient past, they had turned black with silver veins.

"Well, can we see the ship anywhere?" I asked.

"No. The ship's a long way off, I am sure," Daniel said.

"Ok. Let's go then. Hold my arm," I said, "and close your wings, so they won't give off a buzz that the enemy Nephilim can hear."

I took Paris's bracelet and squeezed it into my hand, closing my own wings too. The strings shot out, dragging us off to the buffer zone. We were in the mist only for a few minutes, and then it grew lighter.

We tumbled out into the middle of the rest of our Time Walker group.

The welcomes were so loud and cheerful they were bound to draw some attention, but we didn't care. We had arrived, and no one had seen our wings.

A servant pulled the curtain from the door leading inside the house and looked at us, surprised. Then he turned and walked away.

"He will now go and let Tiye know you have arrived," Reggie said, "so try to invent a good story about how you managed to avoid the guards. And also about who you are," he nodded at Daniel, Elijah, Diana and Lilith.

"I suppose you'll have to play the goddess card..." Reggie said.

"In the meanwhile, let's get you some dry and proper clothes. You can't be seen in jeans and T-shirts," Paris said to Lilith and the brothers, "and something for Diana too, that dress is too short."

We followed her inside the house to a bedroom where there were several chests. Paris opened one to pull out linen shirts and kilts. Diana, Lilith and I stayed there as we changed into traditional Egyptian dresses. The brothers went elsewhere and soon returned wearing sleeveless shirts and kilts.

We had only just made ourselves presentable when Tiye's soldiers arrived.

58

ACCOMPLICES

"He didn't suspect anything?" the Pale Man asked.

"No, my lord," Nefertiry smiled. "He believed me when I said I just wanted to hold a letter in my hands, to see the writing. He thought my behaviour was funny, and endearing. That's what he said."

She had held the letter Ramose had brought, turning it upside down and sideways.

"Which way am I supposed to hold this?" she had asked.

Ramose had laughed and turned the letter round.

"Like this."

Nefertiry had read the whole text, of course, but Ramose had no idea she could read. She had pointed to various parts of the letter, asking what the words meant. She had been careful not to ask Ramose to translate the letter for her.

"I need to get the letter back now, Mother will return soon," he had said finally.

"Of course. Thank you so much for showing it to me." Nefertiry had kissed the tip of his nose.

Nefertiry had taken a ribbon and tied the letter back into its original shape. Ramose left and returned the letter before Meryt-Neith had returned.

"And Merit wrote that Meryt-Neith can send her a message in case of an emergency?" the Pale Man was standing on the roof of the building, his eyes fixed on the North Palace. It was dusk, and he could see the flickering lights of oil lamps through the Window of Appearances above the main gate. The royal couple appeared there in their full glory when it was time to reward someone, throwing gold down to the bowing official or military officer. *Rekhyt* birds were carved on the sides of the opening leading to the palace – lapwings with human hands raised in adoration towards the royal couple, symbolising the ordinary people of Kemet.

Nefertiry turned onto her stomach and closed her eyes, content after their lovemaking. Two dogs were waiting, fastened down ready for her to drink their blood. They were staring at the humans, their tails between their legs, shaking. Humans didn't recognise what the Pale Man and Nefertiry were, but animals always knew they were predators.

"Yes. She is to write to the beekeeper in Mi-Wer, and the message will be forwarded to Merit."

"Well then, we'll arrange it so that Meryt-Neith has an emergency to write about."

He pulled his long-sleeved shirt on over his head, covering his nakedness, running his fingers through his colourless hair. "But we can still wait, there is no hurry yet. I want to see if I can get Meryt-Neith to believe that I have changed. It would save me so much trouble if I can get her to find her sister for me without having to turn her into one of us first. The change can take weeks and it's not always successful. She may die. Women will do anything you ask, if you manage to make them fall in love with you, so I'll try that once again."

"If you did turn her, and she didn't die, would you then take her as your wife?" Nefertiry asked.

The Pale Man detected a hint of jealousy in her voice. All the better –jealous women were even more willing to please a man, to assure him they were his best choice.

"I might. But that does not mean I couldn't keep you as well. As long as you please me."

She turned to look at him over her naked shoulder, smiled, and then swung her body round, extending her arms towards him. She really was beautiful.

"Always, my lord, always."

He turned his back on the view of the palace and walked across to her, pulling off the shirt he had just put on again.

59

KHONSU COMES OF AGE

Khonsu's wings opened earlier than most other Nephilim, but he was not as young as I had been. He was already fourteen, whereas I had been but a child. Remembering the shock I had felt, I had prepared him in advance for the paralysis and the pain.

While he lay there unmoving, eyes huge with the fear he had thought he could control, we stayed with him. Asule did not let go of his hand the whole time – she fell asleep by his bedside, sitting on the floor. Seth and I didn't need much sleep, but after two days, even our heads began to nod.

I woke up with a start, hearing Asule's deep breathing, and Seth's quiet snore. I had fallen asleep. But it wasn't the sound of my family sleeping that woke me up. It was someone speaking.

"Don't worry. Once this is over, you will never feel pain like this again."

It took me a moment to understand what I was seeing and hearing.

"Mother!" I whispered.

For it was my mother, bending over Khonsu, stroking his hair. The boy's eyes were the only thing he was able to move and they were fixed on his grandmother's face. You could almost hear the silent scream behind his eyes. Why the transformation was so painful was part of our past that no one understood. It had always been like that and we had all gone through the same ordeal. It was as if we had to give birth to ourselves so we would be reborn from human to Nephilim.

"Shuet!" she smiled.

I almost cried with joy – how I had missed her during these years! Seth woke up too, but Asule was too exhausted and kept on sleeping.

"Seth!" Mother hugged him.

I could not find words. Mother smiled. And then Mut-Bity walked into the room.

"Mut-Bity!"

Asule woke up at those words.

"Asule, this is your grandmother, Merit," I said to her.

Asule nodded her head, but still didn't release Khonsu's hand.

"I've already introduced myself to Khonsu," Mother said, smiling. "What a handsome young man he has grown into! And Asule, you are truly as beautiful as a butterfly."

Asule smiled, pleased with the compliment. She was indeed; small, slender and growing into a beautiful young woman with a dewy, dark skin, luminous eyes, high cheekbones and a sensuous body.

"How long has Khonsu been in this state?" Mut-Bity asked.

"Two... almost three days," Seth said.

"Should be over soon, then," Mut-Bity said.

And it was. After half a day Khonsu suddenly breathed in deeply and moved his hand.

"He can move again!" Asule said.

We all rushed to his side.

"Water..." Khonsu whispered, his lips barely moving.

Asule was already pouring water into the cup she had been using to moisten Khonsu's lips.

Within the hour, Khonsu was back to his normal self. He stood up. He devoured the food we had prepared for him and then finally sighed, content.

"Now you should try to open your wings," Seth said, "but not in here. We need to find somewhere with more space."

We followed them of course – and many others appeared as if from nowhere. It was a matter of great interest to everyone in the secret valley when a Nephilim grew their wings.

We walked to a crossroads of many tunnels which opened up into a wide space.

"Go right to the centre," Seth said, pointing, "and then concentrate on the sensation on your back."

Khonsu closed his eyes.

"It feels odd. As if someone was drumming on my spine very fast."

"Good. Concentrate on that," Seth said. "Try to make it more intense. It won't hurt. And concentrate on the spot between your shoulder blades."

Khonsu stood still, his fists clenched with the effort.

"Look! They are opening!" Asule whispered.

Usually when a young Nephilim opened their wings for the first time, it happened at uncontrollable speed that could send anyone nearby spinning away. Not so with Khonsu. His wings appeared first as two shiny dots between his shoulder blades and then gradually and beautifully reached first up and then down like the wings of a butterfly. First in a tight furl, and then slowly, slowly opening to their full size.

And they were beautiful. They were golden in colour – a pale, shiny yellow.

"He is certainly your son," Mut-Bity smiled, as proud as if she was the grandmother.

Sighs of admiration went up on all sides.

Khonsu looked up, to see the tips of his wings. Slowly the veins began to become more solid, flowing up and down to the tips of the wings.

Asule moved up to him, being careful not to make contact with his wings. She knew how sensitive to the touch they were.

"How beautiful they are!" she whispered, unable to look away from them.

Seth and I looked at each other, proud of our son.

"He is certainly your son." Mother repeated Mut-Bity's words and hugged me round the shoulders, smiling.

"As if there ever was any doubt..." Seth smiled too.

I could only stare at the golden wings with their beautiful silver veins.

60

EXPOSURE

"My lady..."

Meryt-Neith raised her eyes from the sash she was embroidering. It was late, but as she did not need much sleep and had very sharp eyes, she often sat embroidering in the evenings. She chose to do this in her own rooms now, as it seemed to annoy the Great Royal Wife that Meryt-Neith could see so well with very little light.

A servant was standing in the doorway.

"Yes, what is it?"

"I was asked to bring you this, my lady."

The servant gave her a beautiful little jar made of alabaster. The lid was tied securely with a long string that circled the jar several times, always returning to the knob on top. Looking at it from above, the string formed a decorative effect that resembled the rays of the sun.

"Thank you, you may go," Meryt-Neith said to the servant, who seemed to be eager to see what was in the jar.

She opened the cord carefully – it had three colours in it – a white, green and red string were twisted together. She might have use for it later.

Inside was a bundle of the finest linen, again tied with a similar cord. Curious, Meryt-Neith opened the bundle.

A beautiful necklace made of golden nefer-amulets glistened in the dim light of the oil lamp. A little piece of papyrus with writing underneath... Meryt-Neith took it and read the words.

"Once I placed this around the neck of a beautiful young girl but I took it away. Now I send it to her in the hope that she will wear it even though her own beauty outshines even gold."

Meryt-Neith threw the necklace away as if it had burned her hand. It hit the wall with a clink and fell onto the floor.

"No, someone might see it..." she said to herself, picking it up again as if it were a coiled snake.

She ended up wrapping the necklace into its original bundle which she fastened tightly again. She put the lid of the jar in place and rewound the string as it had been. Then she took the jar to her private chest, placed it under everything else that was in it, and wound rope around the knobs of the chest to close it. The servants knew they had no right to open this chest.

She well remembered the day when the Pale Man had approached her for the first time, pretending to be bringing a similar nefer-necklace to the Great Royal Wife Tiye. He had allowed Meryt-Neith to try the beautiful piece on.

Oh, how delighted she had been. She had decided that one day she would wear a similar necklace. Now she didn't want to touch it even with a long stick, go anywhere near it.

She tried to keep watch on the servants for many days after this, but never saw the woman who had brought the jar to her again. She wanted to send the jar back to the sender, but only that servant would know where it needed to go.

Then came the day that Seshat and Iahmesu came to see her.

"We are very worried," Iahmesu said.

"What is it?"

"It is Ramose," Seshat said.

"What of him? Has something happened to him? Has... has *he* done something to him?"

Iahmesu did not look surprised, so Seshat had clearly told him that the Pale Man had approached Meryt-Neith.

"Not yet. But we need you to come with us to witness something with your own eyes... quickly now."

Meryt-Neith followed them out of the palace and into the city. Near the palace, the dwarfs were a familiar sight to people, so not much attention was paid to them. Seshat led them to a woman selling vegetables. She was sitting in front of a three-storey house not far from the North Palace, but not quite bordering the great road leading south to the centre of the city.

"Welcome, my friend," the woman said to Seshat. "My eyes are pleased to see you healthy and well."

"My heart rejoices to see you successful and well," the dwarf woman replied. "I asked you earlier if we might use your roof for private meetings," Seshat continued. "Would it be convenient for you if we did it now?"

"Oh yes, please be my guests," the woman said.

Meryt-Neith realised how little she knew about the life of the dwarfs outside the palace.

They climbed the steps to the second storey of the narrow house, and from there to the roof.

"Stay behind the screens, and only peek through them," Iahmesu said.

"What am I supposed to be looking at?" Meryt-Neith had to bend down, being so tall. Otherwise her head would have been above the woven screens.

"Look at the rooftop behind the next house," Seshat whispered.

It took a while for Meryt-Neith to see the naked figures on the roof as they could only be seen through a narrow gap between their own screens – people used them to gain some privacy in this tightly built city. Then the young man turned his head and she saw his profile.

"But... that's Ramose!" she whispered.

"Yes, that is Ramose. What they are doing is not something to worry about as he is a young man already and it's to be expected. It is the one he is with..." Seshat said.

The other naked figure was a ravishingly beautiful young woman with long black hair. She got up from the pillows and walked to fetch something. As she did so, she moved into the sunlight for the briefest moment. Her dark skin gave off a strange golden glow, an almost metallic flash.

Meryt-Neith breathed in.

"Is she...?"

"No, she is not Nephilim. But she is a blood-drinker," Iahmesu said. "Ramose does not know about it of course. He has never heard of blood-drinkers."

Meryt-Neith remembered hearing the rumours about small animals disappearing in a strange manner - and then their carcasses being found outside the city.

"Is she the one who kills all the animals?" Meryt-Neith asked.

"Yes. But that is not the worst thing. She is the Pale Man's concubine." Iahmesu was unable to keep the anxiety from his voice. "We have spent lots of hours here on the roof, after Seshat began to suspect something and we had Ramose followed to see where he goes every day. He spent so many hours away – well, however much he loves horses, we didn't believe he was at the stables all that time. Yesterday we saw him there on the roof with her. Doing... what they are doing now. It cannot be a coincidence that she has seduced the boy."

Meryt-Neith felt her blood turn cold.

"We have to get him out of there now!" she said.

"No, we have to wait until he comes back on his own," Iahmesu said, "and then you'll have to tell him what she is. And who the Pale Man is. And why the woman made Ramose's acquaintance in the first place. That is the only way to keep him away from her."

"Do you think he will believe me?" Meryt-Neith said. "The story is too unbelievable!"

"You'll have to convince him."

"How?"

Meryt-Neith could not tear her eyes away from the rooftop.

"We have a plan..." Seshat said.

When Ramose returned, it was the hardest thing for Meryt-Neith not to let him see how worried she was. Seshat smiled at the boy.

"Ramose. Would you be kind enough to help me carry these clothes?"

She pointed at a pile of freshly washed clothes they had hurriedly gathered from Meryt-Neith's chests.

"Of course," Ramose said, "Where to?"

"To a friend's house not far from here. They need mending and she has promised to help. My legs and hands are so short it is difficult for me to carry them myself."

They left, Ramose's arms full of his mother's clothes.

Meryt-Neith followed them from a distance to the house they had been in earlier that day. She walked slowly and only entered the house when she was certain they were already upstairs.

"Up here?" she heard Ramose asking.

"Yes, my friend asked us to bring them here. She wishes to enjoy the fresh breeze while working. You know how hot it is."

Meryt-Neith listened to their conversation on the second floor, near the stairs.

"Oh, look! " Seshat said, "There. Two roofs away!"

Ramose said nothing.

"Is that a dog?"

Meryt-Neith climbed a few steps so she could see Ramose and Seshat.

The boy was looking towards the woman's house. Meryt-Neith took the last steps quietly. She saw what was happening on the rooftop. The screens were still in place there, but a short figure was crouching behind them, on the outside.

Iahmesu. How had he managed to get to the rooftop without being detected?

Meryt-Neith saw how Iahmesu pulled the screen aside carefully so the gap grew wider and the scene was revealed to them. Behind the screen was a woven cage with a dog in it. Iahmesu took a stick that was lying on the roof beside him and poked at the animal through the cage.

The dog let out a yelp of protest. Iahmesu quickly retreated behind a wind catcher.

"What is he doing there?" Ramose sounded baffled. "Does he know the... owner of the house?"

"Just look," Seshat said and her voice was harder now.

And suddenly, the beautiful woman was there on the rooftop. She arrived so fast that her movement was a blur. She looked around and saw the dog cage.

What happened next was not an attractive sight. Opening the cage, she reached in. Her movements were fast and specific as she lifted the dog out, bent her head and bit the animal's throat, ripping into its flesh so that blood spurted high. The dog screamed.

Ramose opened his mouth but no sound came out. The woman was so concentrating on her meal she did not realise the screens were open wider than usual to reveal what she was doing.

Suddenly, there was movement on the roof next to theirs and a man appeared. Meryt-Neith pulled Ramose back.

"Stay silent!" she whispered.

They hid behind the screen when the man noticed what was happening on his neighbour's roof.

As the beauty lifted her head, blood smeared across her jaw, she saw the onlooker and froze. The man yelled, and she turned and disappeared from the roof.

"Come. We need to talk," Meryt-Neith said to Ramose and, like a sleepwalker, the boy followed.

61

RETRIBUTION

The Pale Man showed no mercy. He ripped her apart, limb by limb, and she was still alive when he twisted her neck and pulled her head from her limbless torso.

She had known what was coming when he had come for her and led her to the river.

"Please, my lord, let me still serve you!" she had begged.

"You were exposed. The whole town is full of stories about you – a beautiful woman who eats animals alive. You have to disappear. And that's not the worst of what you did. I have been seen entering your house, and people talk of me as your husband. Now I can't show myself in my own house any longer and have to find another one. You have ruined my plans!"

She had understood then that there was no hope. She tried to run, but he was too fast and too strong for her. In a few strides, he had reached her, pulled her by the arm and holding her torso with his free hand had ripped the arm off.

She had screamed, but he did not care. He tossed the arm into the river. There were crocodiles about, so there would be nothing left for anyone to find. If any part of her wasn't detected by the animals, it would vanish quickly enough anyway. The blood-drinkers' bodies crumbled into dust in a surprisingly short time.

Her blood had been thick and almost black, oozing from her veins like dark honey.

He threw the head in the river as well, by its long, black hair, and finally the torso.

Pity. He had almost liked her. She had given him great pleasure. But he had others and would create yet more to serve his needs.

Without wasting time, the Pale Man turned and vanished into the mists. Meryt-Neith should have received the letter by now.

62

THE QUARREL

The letter arrived after sunset that same day.

"This was left by a scribe in town," the servant girl said. "He delivered it to the palace and asked for it to be brought on to you, my lady."

Meryt-Neith's hands shook as she read the letter aloud. Seshat, Iahmesu and Ramose listened.

"I shall have our son, and you cannot stop me. You will not be able to hide from me in Akhetaten. I am gathering my servants to keep an eye on your every move. I wanted you to come back to me from your own free will, to give me children. But I see now that you have decided otherwise. We'll only ever have one son, and once I have him, I have no need for you anymore. Be prepared to die."

Ramose was pale with shock and fury. He had learned the truth about the Pale Man only moments before and was in emotional turmoil.

"Why did you not tell me who he was?" he hissed. "I had the right to know!"

"This letter should prove to you why I didn't tell you," Meryt-Neith said. "He is dangerous. And he is an evil Nephilim who only wants an heir. And that means he wishes to make you like himself. My life is of no value to him any more as I refused his advances."

"But when he wanted to meet you – you should have told me then!" Ramose's voice broke from emotion.

"It's too late to regret it now," Iahmesu said. "Your mother did what any mother would have done – she tried to make sure he would never return and to keep her child, you, safe."

"With the help of bees? How ridiculous is that! Do you really think I believe any of this?"

"You should. And you can't go anywhere without the protection of the bees any longer. If he decides to abduct you by force, they will be your only protection. He won't come alone if he does want to take you. He did so once before, to kill me and my family. He only let me live because I was pregnant with you. He would have killed your grandmother, me, my sister and her husband, without mercy. It was only the bees that protected us. They killed his men and chased him away so that my sister and I could escape."

"You mean we are stuck here forever? In these rooms, in this city, never far from beehives? I won't have it!"

"You have to accept it. You don't want to turn into a blood-drinker yourself!" Seshat said. "You've seen how they behave! Your own father's mistress had no trouble in taking you to her bed as well. That's not normal! And you saw how she fed herself? If your father gets you and turns you into one of his own kind, that is what you will be doing too. Only you will be drinking human blood! Can you create that scene in your mind?"

Ramose was too agitated to give in.

"And wings! You say these... *Nephilim* have wings! If that is so, show me yours!" he turned to face Meryt-Neith.

"I never got my wings..." she said.

"So why should I believe you are a winged creature? Or that any such creatures exist? I don't believe any of it! The... she... she was simply insane, and not a creature you call a blood-drinker. And he... my father – he did not try to abduct me earlier, instead he saved my life! I won't believe you! I will go about wherever I please. You can't stop me!"

Ramose stormed over to the doorway but Iahmesu blocked his way. Meryt-Neith had never seen Iahmesu move so fast.

"Ramose. It is night. There is nowhere for you to go. If you wish to go out, do so in the morning. We do understand your anger, but we also need you to calm down and consider what you have seen and what we have told you. Think about the words in that letter especially – he stated in no uncertain terms that he will come for you, and that he will kill your mother. Also, if you go about in the state you're in now, the soldiers will most likely arrest you."

That was true. The palaces were heavily guarded – had been so ever since the city was first built. The king did not forget how the priesthood of Amun had threatened his life all those years ago. And even now, when their power had been stripped away from them, there were still too many of them alive and carrying a grudge against the king. So, no one was allowed to move about in the palaces at night when the king was present. And this evening, he was here in the North Palace, together with his Great Royal Wife.

Ramose turned around.

"And your sister! You never told me stories about my aunt! Why has she never visited, never let us hear anything about herself?"

"Because of me. Because of my relationship with your father. He only used me to get his hands on my sister. Only I was too vain and foolish to understand that," Meryt-Neith said.

Meryt-Neith's answer seemed to throw Ramose off balance.

"Why? Was he in love with her then?"

"No. He wanted to kill her. And he couldn't get to her because the bees protected her."

"To kill her? Why?"

"Because she is a silver Nephilim, and the evil ones believe a silver Nephilim will kill them all," Iahmesu said.

"Silver? What does it mean?"

"It means she is special. Her wings are silver. And she is dangerous to the evil Nephilim," Seshat said.

"Where is she, then?" Ramose asked.

"In hiding. She will never come to see us, because she knows the Pale Man is around. He will kill her as soon as he sees her, I am certain of that. He will never give up the chase."

Meryt-Neith did not say anything about Shuet's pregnancy at the time of the attack.

"You're not going to tell me where she's hidden?" Ramose insisted.

"No. And the reason is not only for her safety. I don't know where she is. They have kept the information from me because of the Pale Man's interest in me. Should he attack me, I wouldn't be able to tell him my sister's whereabouts for the simple reason that I don't know where she is. The last time I saw her was before you were born. The night *he* attacked us."

Ramose could not find anything to say in response.

"We had been following the blood-drinker for a while. It's not the first time we have encountered her kind," Seshat said, "or rather, we did not follow her ourselves. We managed to get the sister of a young boy who went missing some time ago into her house, as a lowly servant. She was more than eager to help, as the last time her brother was seen alive, he was going into the lady's house. His bloodless body was found on the riverbank. His sister suspected she had killed him, and someone we knew heard her talking about it," Seshat continued.

"You followed me too, then," Ramose stated the obvious.

"Of course. We wanted to be certain that you were... having a relationship with her," Iahmesu said. "We wondered why she had chosen you, but then, one night, *he* appeared. He didn't leave for an entire day. And so she did not send word to you to come and visit. By then, we had received word about him from the servant girl and came to see for ourselves whether the tall, colourless man was indeed – your father."

"That was a dangerous thing to do..." Meryt-Neith said.

"Had to be done. After that, we were wondering how to make you understand what she was," Seshat turned to Ramose. "In the end we realised that you would only believe it if you saw her feed. The sister of the boy that was killed said that she had seen dogs on the roof, in a cage. They all disappeared, one after the other. She must have been paying someone to bring her the animals. We thought she wouldn't wonder, then, if yet another dog appeared on the roof. So, while the blood-drinker was away, the girl let Iahmesu in with the dog. And the rest – well, you all witnessed what happened."

Ramose fell silent.

"Maybe it is best we all try to sleep now," Iahmesu said. "There is nothing to be ashamed of, Ramose. You were not to know. But now you know the truth. Think about all of this, and let tomorrow bring its wisdom."

Ramose rose and went to his own little room – it was only big enough to fit a narrow bed. He pulled the curtain across the doorway.

"Ramose..." Iahmesu said, "you need to keep some bees with you."

He took with him his own little clay tube containing a few bees and pulled back the curtain a little so he could give it to him.

"Keep it open. The bees will stay in the room near you. We'll bring you new ones in the morning."

Meryt-Neith sat down on the low chair she had received from the Great Royal Wife. Its legs were shaped like those of a bull, and it was made of good, hard, dark wood.

"I need to write to her," she said, "to my mother."

"Yes, that would be wise. Let her know what has happened here," Seshat said.

"But whom can we trust to take the letter to Mi-Wer?" asked Meryt-Neith.

"I shall send word to someone we know and trust," Iahmesu said, "someone who can travel and take your letter to Merit."

"First thing in the morning, then," Meryt-Neith said.

"First thing," the dwarfs answered, "but we're going to bring you more bees before we lie down for the night."

When they returned with more bees, Meryt-Neith was already writing her letter.

63

A FEW MORE WORDS

"You got the letter?"

"I did, my lord."

The Nephilim he had sent on the errand bowed and handed the Pale Man the tightly bound papyrus folded into a tight square.

"And the messenger?"

"Dead. They did not know we were following the dwarf when he took the letter to their messenger. I kept my distance as you requested and only attacked the messenger after they separated and he went to search for a boat that would take him downriver."

"Good. You've done well."

With a sharp knife, the Pale Man cut the cord and opened the letter. He was sitting inside the house in which he had installed his dead blood-drinker woman. He had entered it through the misty world and no one had seen him coming. The servants had all scattered when the rumour of their mistress's behaviour had spread. No one wanted to stay in a house that belonged to a demon. She had disappeared, but no one knew she was dead, and none of them wanted to be present should she return. This suited the Pale Man perfectly.

"I hope my letter finds you all well. I am only writing because he has

returned. He has threatened my life and said he will abduct Ramose. Could you take Ramose to live with you, to hide him? Please answer as soon as you can. We are living in fear, our safety now dependent completely on the bees.

Meryt-Neith"

"Perfect." The Pale Man's smile was cold. "Now, let's revise this letter a little. Bring the scribe."

Another Nephilim outside the door pushed a scared man inside.

"You need not fear me." The Pale Man looked at him. "I am only asking you to add a line to this letter. You need to write it in the same hand as this one and you will be richly rewarded. Do you think you can do this?"

The man looked at the letter.

"Yes. The writing is somewhat crude, but I can imitate it."

"Very well. Here's what I want you to write: *I beseech you, come yourself to fetch your grandson – I trust no one else and we live in daily fear. I will send him to Mi-Wer with a beehive to protect him.*"

The scribe sat down on the floor cross-legged, pulling his kilt taut over his thighs. He placed a board on his lap, spread out the letter on it and dipped his reed pen in a moistened cake of black ink. Very carefully he wrote the extra line, fitting it between the last line and Meryt-Neith's signature.

"I don't think anyone will see the difference, even if I say so myself," the scribe said.

"Good. Now. If you ever tell anyone about this, you will die. If you keep your mouth shut, I might have further uses for you."

The scribe swallowed.

"I would never tell anyone!" He fought to keep his voice calm.

"Indeed, you will not. Give him his payment," the Pale Man said, turning his back, "and make sure he leaves unnoticed."

The scribe's expression brightened greatly when he saw the golden ring in his palm.

"Thank you, my lord! I shall be faithful in your service!"

The Pale Man gave no answer and the scribe was pushed out of the room and out through the back door in the garden wall.

"And we have someone to take this letter to Mi-Wer, I trust?" he asked when his Nephilim servant returned.

"We do. A merchant is headed downriver today."

"Good. Give him the letter and pay him well so we can be sure he will deliver it."

"Yes, my lord."

His job done, the Pale Man vanished back into the misty world.

64

THE FIRST GATE

"Where are you taking me?" Merit asked.

"Just follow me. There is something you need to see."

Mut-Bity marched on through the corridors leading from cave to cave in the Hidden Valley. She led Merit out of the living quarters, through the storage caves and to an unused part of the cave network.

Merit looked around in awe at the structures of the secret Nephilim village. Mut-Bity had told her about it, of course, but words couldn't do justice to reality. The smooth walls, the steps and corridors, the caves. The walls were decorated with carvings showing winged Nephilim, hunting scenes, wildlife – in a realistic way, resembling the art of Akhetaten, not tied to strict conventional rules.

"How long has this place been here?" she asked.

"For so long, we have lost count of the years. Enough for even Nephilim generations to have died," Mut-Bity said. "We came here first when we escaped the dark Nephilim; when they started to drink human blood. They wanted our secrets, to find out who knew about the hidden creators. When they drink blood, they can read their victim's mind."

"Yes, that is true..."

Merit remembered the first time she had learned of her own

heritage. She had been told that the evil Nephilim could read the memories of the ones whose blood they drank. She had found it hard to believe and still did. How could blood carry consciousness, or memory? Still, she had learned that the enemy Nephilim often chose to kill their opponents' leaders by drinking their blood instead of infecting them, and having to wait for them to tell their secrets voluntarily. It could take weeks for the infection to take hold, and during that time, the bitten Nephilim leaders most often chose to kill themselves to keep their loved ones from harm. In order to avoid their victims destroying themselves before they could pass on their knowledge, their enemies chose to drink their blood instead, which meant they gained everything they wanted to know from the blood.

When finally Merit and Mut-Bity arrived at a small cave with an uneven floor that was not used for storage, Mut-Bity stopped.

"You asked me to find the White City of the desert. The one in the scroll from the House of Life of Hut-Ka-Ptah in Inbu-Hedj?"

"Yes. The place I am to be buried in," Merit said.

"You believe this to be true, then?" Mut-Bity asked.

"I do. I have made preparations for it. I will show you soon."

Mut-Bity turned towards the wall of the little cave and began to climb. Despite her age, she was strong and agile, and Merit had to hurry to keep up with her. To her surprise, there was an opening high up on the wall, hidden from view of anyone standing on the floor of the cave.

Mut-Bity turned into a tunnel and Merit followed. They felt their way forward with their hands until light began to seep in, showing the floor and walls. That is when Merit saw the ancient paintings of the walls. Animals of all kinds – she could see giraffes, and bulls, birds, and elephants. Even fish. And then human forms that looked like they were swimming. Merit remembered the pictures she had seen of the ancient Cave of Swimmers in Gilf Kebir – these were quite similar.

The tunnel rose and fell and then, after the last turn, it opened out onto a lake. Merit had never seen anything like it.

The sun shone into the water through a crack in the stone. Where the light hit the water, it was as if the water was alive, a swirling, moving silver water.

Merit stood, with her mouth open.

"What is this place?"

"This," Mut-Bity said, "is the first gate on the way to the abode of the gods. The Creators. I believe the abode is the White City you are searching for."

"Gate? To the White City?"

"Remember the old legend. Only one of us at a time in the Hidden Valley knows how to reach the abode of the Watchers, as you call them."

Merit understood.

"You. It is you."

"I am the guardian now. I was the apprentice of the last guardian of the gates and when she died, she sent me the object that makes the stories come true. The one that will lead me to the abode of the gods."

Merit remembered.

"It was the stone that Seth brought to you so many years ago... After you brought Shuet back to me."

"Yes. That little stone is needed to go through the gates of the underworld."

"The underworld? What do you mean? How?"

Mut-Bity looked at the water, deep in her thoughts. She held the smooth black stone openly on her palm, and Merit could now see its fish-like shape and how the light reflected on small markings on its surface.

"The absolute decree has always been that only one person is to know how to travel through the gates. But then you came, just as the legend said you would. You came from the future for a reason. The scroll from Hut-Ka-Ptah says that you are connected to the Scroll of Thoth, the scroll that reveals all the secrets of creation. The secrets of the Watchers. And my stone leads to the Watchers. We are united in this. And so, I am going to tell you what I know. You shall be my apprentice, but one who shares the same knowledge as I do."

"And if I die, as the scroll said?"

"If you are indeed the Golden Goddess, and if Shuet is to learn important knowledge when she buries you, I can only think that this knowledge is what I am going to teach you. How you will convey it to her, I don't know. This knowledge is not to be told to outsiders. That is our precaution."

"Precaution?"

"You can't be sure you will die. And so, you can't pass the knowledge to Shuet just in case. You have to find another way to do so after your death, should it happen. The more people who know any secret, the greater the danger of the knowledge spreading."

"After my death? Can't you just take Shuet as your apprentice after me? Or right away? Instead of me?"

"I may be dead by the time you die. I am not young, Merit. And you may still live long years after I am gone. Death is the mystery over which we have no control. And the scroll made it clear the secret is hidden where the Golden Goddess is buried. If it is as you believe, that you will die, and you are the Golden Goddess, then it is you who will somehow convey the knowledge to her. There is a reason that it has to be you who tells her, not me. That is why I am not choosing her as my apprentice. There is something more in all of this, something that has to do with you and Shuet. Something important between you two that has a some meaning and must happen. Something that would not happen if I told everything to Shuet now..."

"But if I am to die, and you die of old age before taking a new apprentice – isn't there danger then that the knowledge will disappear from the face of the earth completely?"

"There is. But the scroll was quite clear about Shuet's role in all this. If she learns something of importance when she buries the Golden Goddess, and if that goddess is you, it means that you need to convey the message to her in a way that she understands and can carry it forward into the future."

Merit looked at the walls of the cave surrounding the silver lake. There was a big flat rock in the middle of the lake, almost like a small island. And there was something odd about the walls behind the lake. It was as if there was writing there... Markings that did not resemble any writing signs she had ever heard of. Geometric forms, shapes that repeated like the letters of the alphabet. She didn't concentrate on them for long, though. She turned to look at Mut-Bity.

"I have already prepared for my death," Merit said, "and I think I know how I can pass on this knowledge so that only she will understand it, if she is the one who will bury me."

"Indeed. If. I only hope this doesn't come to pass. But it seems that sometimes, our lives are meant to go along a certain path as a part of something bigger. Something we don't understand as yet, but those after us may make sense of it all one day."

Mut-Bity took Merit's hand between hers and squeezed them. Her eyes were moist.

Emotion choked Merit. To hide it, she bent down to run her fingers through the water. The silver specks began to follow her fingers. She stopped moving and the specks covered her fingers.

"They tickle," Merit smiled, "what are they?"

"That is part of the knowledge you are to discover. So I am going to pass on to you all the knowledge I have. Firstly, I am going to tell you about the twelve gates of the underworld. And what this fish stone is about. Here. Let's sit down."

They sat down, facing the shimmering lake, and Mut-Bity began her story.

65

STEPPING OUT OF THE PAST

"Where is Shuet?" Merit asked Khonsu and Asule.

They had just returned from their lessons and placed their writing boards in a niche in the wall. Merit had prepared food for them – during the months Merit had been with them, their life had settled into a routine that everyone appreciated. Shuet and Seth had more time together, Khonsu and Asule loved being with their grandmother.

"Mother said she will be away for a day and then return," Khonsu said.

"Away for a whole day? Where did she go?"

"She didn't tell us. But she will be back tomorrow," Asule said.

Seth found them talking about writing when he arrived.

"I am glad to see you here, Merit," he said, "grandchildren should get to know their grandmother. And Mut-Bity too, of course."

"Why did you not come to see us earlier, Grandmother?" Khonsu asked.

"Your grandmother was in the service of the Great Royal Wife of Kemet," Seth said before Merit had time to answer. "No one can leave the royal court without permission."

"You asked the Great Royal Wife to let you come and see us?" asked Asule.

"Of course she did," Seth said and ruffled Asule's hair, making his daughter giggle.

Merit thanked Seth with her eyes. She didn't want to worry the children by telling them about the Pale Man. She would have to, eventually, but not so soon after meeting her grandchildren for the first time.

Later, when Khonsu and Asule had left to meet their friends, Seth turned to Merit.

"I think there is something you should know. About Shuet. She does not want to talk about it, but..."

"What is it? Is something wrong?" Merit tried to keep the fear from her voice.

"No, nothing is wrong. But something is... well, strange. I'll explain it to you later when we are alone. It involves the moon – perhaps we should go and see the full moon tonight?"

"The moon? Very well. If it requires the full moon for you to tell me what I need to know, then by all means."

"And don't mention this to Mut-Bity either. Not unless Shuet says we can."

"I won't," Merit promised.

What could be such a secret she could not even mention it to the person she trusted the most?

When Khonsu and Asule were asleep, Seth gestured for Merit to follow. He placed his finger on his lips and silently, they left.

Seth led Merit upwards along a narrow corridor. All the routes out of the cave system were very narrow for a reason – they would be easier to guard should anyone try to attack using them.

The path led near to one of the peaks of the rocky hills that hid the underground village. The wind was so strong it tore at their clothing. Merit looked at the horizon, trying to see if a sandstorm was coming. The stars shone brightly all the way to the horizon. No sandstorm, then.

"Now what?" Merit asked.

"Now, we wait," Seth said. "As a precaution, we'll wait by that rock there. The enemy Nephilim haven't found us yet, but we try to limit the amount of time we're out here in the open, just in case they fly past. This is where Shuet learned to go to the misty world on her own many years back. No one had told us about it before and we thought it was great magic."

"In a way, it is..." Merit said, "and a skill not everyone has. I, for one, can't enter the misty world without help."

"Nor I," Seth said. "I have no trouble in moving once I am there, though."

Merit said nothing about how the buffer zone had spat her out when she had tried to escape Mi-Wer heavily pregnant. She had almost killed herself and her unborn daughters. Since then, she had never dared try again.

They stood next to the high rock, watching the vast desert and the rising moon. Somewhere under it, in the east, were Meryt-Neith and Ramose. How Merit longed to see them as well. She cursed the Pale Man in her mind, and the Nephilim prophecy that made him want to kill Shuet and her family. What if none of the prophecy was true and they were forced into hiding because of a stupid superstition?

She thought of Elijah and looked at the sheer drop to the desert floor. She would never see him again, would she? Wouldn't it be easier just to take one step and not open her wings? The thought tempted her for a short while, just as it had done many times during her years here in the ancient past, but as before, she shook it off. No. She had children and grandchildren now. Her heart was broken because she had lost Elijah, but she would live for her family. She had experienced the love of a twin soul, even if only briefly, and that memory would have to carry her through what remained of her life, however long – or brief – it might be.

The moon rose higher and nothing happened.

"What are we waiting for?" Merit whispered.

"Any moment now..." Seth did not answer her question.

And then she appeared in front of them as if someone had snapped their fingers. Where there had been nothing but empty space all the way to the orb of the moon, stood a female figure, framed in the cold moonlight.

"Shuet!" Merit almost jumped from fright. "Where did you come from?"

Shuet had appeared so abruptly, it did not look as though she had stepped from the mists. There was usually a moment when the one moving back to the physical world looked misty, before solidifying quickly. But Shuet just appeared, suddenly, sharp and clear, without that hazy transition. Just as if someone had clicked a switch.

Shuet looked at Seth.

"You told her. I asked you not to tell anyone!"

"Tell me what?" Merit asked. "What are we talking about?"

Seth looked at Shuet.

"My love... I think this is something your mother should know, and so I made the decision to bring her here."

Shuet said nothing. Seth sighed.

"The reason I wanted to bring you here and see Shuet's appearance is that she came from the past."

"The past?"

"Yes. Shuet can travel through time."

Sudden hope rose up in Merit's mind. Elijah had spoken of time travellers, but they had all been ordinary people. No Nephilim could travel through time on their own. And now her own daughter, a Nephilim, travelled through time?

"Is Seth speaking the truth?" she asked Shuet.

Shuet sighed, her already pale form blanched by the moonlight.

"Seth always speaks the truth."

"How do you do it? Can you travel both ways? Forward and backward?"

In her excitement, Merit took Shuet's hands and pulled her closer.

"I can only travel forward," Shuet answered.

"How far into the future can you travel?"

Merit's hands gripped Shuet's with such force that she stepped back.

"You are hurting my hands, Mother."

Merit let go of her hands.

"I am sorry, I didn't realise... but there is a reason I'm asking you. How far into the future can you go?"

"Not very far... at least, I don't have the courage to try travelling far. I am afraid I won't find my way back. I need to go to a place I know, and use something as my guide. An image in my mind."

"What do you use? How do you do it?"

Merit lifted her hands, but then folded them in front of her before having to grab Shuet's hands again.

"I use the full moon. I need to have seen it somewhere and then I think of the full moon in that place when it is not the full moon's time. It seems I am pulled to the next full moon in that location when I do that."

"So you need the same place. And only travel as far as the next full moon?"

"Yes. I have now tried it many times and always end up at the chosen spot at the next full moon. Never further than that in time. When I leave, I appear in the future almost as if I took just one step. There is never a longer period of waiting to arrive."

"So, no time passes for you?"

"I don't know. I don't think so. I tried it by taking a flower with me once. To see if it had wilted before I arrived. But no, it was just as fresh as before. If I had been somehow unconscious in the mists for a longer period before arriving, surely even a desert flower would have died without water?"

Seth moved over to Shuet and wrapped his arm around her shoulders.

"The beautiful Moon Daughter travels into the future by moonlight..."

He kissed her on the cheek and Shuet smiled.

How lucky those two were to have each other... Merit felt an involuntary tear escape her eye. How her heart ached to see Elijah again...

"Can you... can you take anyone with you when you travel?"

"I don't know. I have never tried."

"Would you be willing to try? With me?"

Shuet considered this.

"If you wish, mother," she then said, "but I can't guarantee this would be without danger."

Merit nodded.

"I understand. And I am willing to take the risk. Could we try at the next full moon?"

"Yes, two days before the full moon," Shuet said, "no more. I don't want people wondering where I keep vanishing every full moon."

"Of course," Merit's heart was beating so fast she thought she would faint.

She would have to wait for a month to see if she had finally found a way to travel into the future, with the help of Shuet. And if she had, could she ever use her daughter's skills? It would mean Merit could reach her beloved, and Shuet would have to leave hers. If indeed she could not travel backwards in time...

Could she ever even consider such a price?

Tears welled up in Merit's eyes and she turned towards the wind so it could dry them without Shuet and Seth noticing. The conflict was too great.

She took a few deep breaths to calm herself down. No. Even if the experiment was successful, she could never ask her daughter to leave her family. She would continue with her original plan.

66

ANOTHER DEMON

Meryt-Neith was returning from temple duty, feeling elated as always by the rhythm of the music and the entrancing movements of the dance. Her route home took her past the Window of Appearances. As she approached it, automatically she glanced along the royal road leading to the temples of the Aten in the distance.

The tall blonde woman and her servant caught her eye immediately. They were approaching the North Palace, walking right in the middle of the road. Heads turned to watch them pass. And it was no wonder: the woman was a ravishing beauty. Her long, blonde hair moved behind her in the wind, and her dress pressed against her beautiful body in a way that left nothing to imagination. Her gold jewellery flashed blindingly in the sun.

But it wasn't only her looks that caught Meryt-Neith's attention. A familiar sensation began in her spine. She felt it faintly at first, then with greater urgency. Meryt-Neith touched the leather pouch hanging from her neck and the bees responded noisily. They sensed it too; the approach of an enemy Nephilim. The woman was still far off, but her height and appearance marked her out as Nephilim. She must be one...

Meryt-Neith stayed in the shadows, standing as close to the

opening of the Window of Appearances as she dared, until she was sure. Then she stopped a servant who was hurrying past her carrying a beer jar.

"Go to the gate, now. Tell the guards the tall blonde woman and her serving woman are not to be allowed inside the palace."

"My lady?" The servant seemed unsure.

"You know who I am?" Meryt-Neith straightened to her full height and looked down at him. "I am a royal wet-nurse, and the leader of the dancers of the Aten. I am in the Great Royal Wife's direct service. If I say you are to do this, you will do it. Or you will face the consequences. Leave whatever task you've been set and run to the gate. She is *not* to enter! Tell the guards that this order comes from the Great Royal Wife."

The servant bowed, placed the beer jar on the floor and hurried off.

Meryt-Neith retreated even further into the shadows. As she did, the tall blonde woman looked up and for a short moment, the sun shone into her eyes. Yellow eyes. She wasn't looking at Meryt-Neith, though. Meryt-Neith kept as calm as she could so the Nephilim woman wouldn't sense her presence, and opened the pouch hanging from her neck. She heard the woman speak to the guards blocking her way, demanding entrance.

Three bees climbed out and took to the air. They circled around for a while, and then flew out through the Window of Appearances and down like tiny birds of prey.

Meryt-Neith heard a scream. She peeked out.

The beautiful blonde Nephilim woman was waving her hands, shooing away the bees that were circling her angrily. She screamed at her servant, who had dropped the bundle she was carrying and was trying to help her mistress, waving her hands around her in the air too.

The bees turned to attack her as well. Why was this? She looked like an ordinary human and she didn't have the skin of a blood-drinker. What did the bees sense in her?

The commotion was such that people began to take notice. Palace personnel hurried to the Window of Appearances to look down, and people who had been walking nearby began to gather closer. The soldiers guarding the gate did not move a muscle, though. Meryt-Neith saw the servant she had sent to stop the Nephilim lady from entering appear through the gate. He tapped the shoulder of one of the soldiers and spoke to him.

Then one of the bees managed to sting the Nephilim woman, who let out a howling sound and slapped her neck. Her beautiful skin turned grey where the sting entered. Even at this distance, the change was obvious. The patch spread fast; soon the whole side of her neck was an ashen grey. The beauty looked as if she was turning into a mud woman. The people nearby gasped and made gestures to protect themselves from evil.

The woman yelled something at her servant and grabbed her by the hand. And then they simply vanished, as if they had sunk under water. For a while, their blurry forms were visible, and then they were gone.

People started screaming.

"Another demon!" someone said. "She had the same kind of skin as the one who ripped animals apart with her teeth!"

Meryt-Neith stared at the place where the woman had been standing with her servant. She alone knew what had happened. The woman had escaped the bees by going into the misty world – a place Meryt-Neith could not enter. The buzzing feeling had gone, so it was clear the Nephilim woman was far away now.

So the Pale Man had sent someone to get into the North Palace. A beautiful woman – so that she could catch the king's eye no doubt. And get close to Nefertiti's ladies, near Meryt-Neith and Ramose.

Well, the bees had driven her off, making it clear she should stay away from this place. Meryt-Neith hoped the Pale Man wasn't planning to send any other Nephilim to Akhetaten. Or ordinary people who were after Meryt-Neith, not before Ramose had been sent to safety. The bees might keep them safe from Nephilim, but not from humans. That thought made Meryt-Neith uncomfortable.

With fear in her heart, she turned back towards the palace, trying to work out what had made this incident so strange. Something familiar, yet unexpected…could it have been the language the Nephilim lady had used with her servant, when she was screaming at her to help?

Yes, that was probably it. It resembled words she had heard before, words her mother had spoken sometimes with Shuet. The language of their parents…

Could it be the same language? Was the dangerous Nephilim lady from the northern countries as well? If so, why had she travelled all this distance to come to Akhetaten? Surely there was no sense in that. She must have been the Pale Man's servant.

Merit shook her head. She prayed she would never see this Nephilim woman again, and that the bees had ensured that she would never come back.

67

LETTER FROM MERYT-NEITH

"What is she doing?" Seth asked Mut-Bity quietly.

Merit was sitting on the floor, next to a basket with long strips of linen in it. One after the other, she stretched them tightly over the writing board on her lap and wrote on each strip with black ink and a brush. No one knew the language she was using. The symbols were odd and didn't look like any writing Seth had ever seen.

"Spells for her wrappings. She believes everyone should have their wrappings ready before they die," Mut-Bity answered lightly, not lifting her eyes from the piece of clothing she was repairing. "I thought she had already finished doing those, but it seems she has remembered some more spells."

"Surely she isn't planning for her death yet?" Seth said.

Mut-Bity concentrated on her needlework and did not answer.

Seth didn't question her further, but there were times when he returned to their home to find Merit there alone, sitting by the table, carefully writing words in the same strange language onto a long papyrus scroll. Seth recognised it as a Book of Going Forth by Day, the scroll that showed the dead the way through the dangers of the Afterworld and into eternal life in the blessed fields of Iaru.

For months, they had stayed with Shuet's family, and settled well into the happy routines of everyday life. But then Merit began to use all her free time for finishing her wrappings and did very little else during the hours Khonsu and Asule were studying. When they came back, she always put her work aside and concentrated on the children for the rest of the day.

Two nights before the next full moon arrived, Shuet spoke to Asule and Khonsu as they were having their evening meal.

"Grandmother and I are going on a little trip to the desert," said Shuet.

"Can we come too?" Asule asked eagerly.

"No, dear," Shuet kissed her cheek, "not this time, because we have an errand to do. I promise we'll go to the desert together later."

Asule accepted the answer easily. She never complained, but took things as they were. Shuet looked at her tenderly. How she resembled her real mother now. Time would never erase Ibah's face from Shuet's memory, because she had returned in Asule's smile, and the comparison was even greater now that the girl was becoming a young woman.

They walked along the path to the top of the hill again, Seth following them.

The moon was already in the sky, close to full.

"What do we do now?" Merit asked.

"Hold my hand," Shuet said, "I need to concentrate."

She closed her eyes, and Merit took her hand. It began to feel odd after a while. It was almost as if the touch of Shuet's hand was making Merit's skin tingle. She looked down and to her surprise saw that the colour of Shuet's hands had changed. They were glowing, a pale silvery glow that grew stronger every second.

And then, suddenly, they were in the mist. There was no feeling of movement, though. Shuet kept her eyes closed, and then took a step forward, pulling Merit with her.

Instantly the mist turned into glue that started to enclose Merit. Shuet's hand simply disappeared from Merit's, and as before, the mists rejected her.

She turned to see Seth still there.

"It didn't work, then," Seth said.

"No. This isn't the first time that's happened. For some reason, I can't enter the misty world anymore. I used to, with Shuet's father, but not when... after I became pregnant with the girls."

"Not everyone can move in the mists," Seth said.

"We'd better go back," Merit sighed.

"Perhaps we should wait for a while, so the children don't wonder why your errand took such a short time," Seth said. "We can tell them that Shuet has taken on guard duty for herself. She's done that a few times during the night, now that the children are big enough to be left alone."

"Ah, yes, you are right," Merit admitted.

They sat on the rock surface and observed the almost full moon in silence.

"Why are you preparing for your death?" Seth asked suddenly.

Merit sat still for a long while.

"I have knowledge that indicates that... I may die here."

"Here? In the Valley?" Seth was surprised.

"I mean that my death is predestined – I can't avoid it," Merit corrected her words.

"You have seen this?" Seth asked.

"Yes," Merit thought it best not to contradict his assumption that she was a seer of the future.

"Does Shuet know?"

"No. I haven't told her. I have only told Mut-Bity. Visions can be erratic and not always true – the future changes constantly because of the decisions we make. But this... vision is persistent. So I am preparing for my death."

Seth carried on looking at the moon. "Death – if so, the thought of losing you soon, now that we are a family again... it wrenches my heart. And sets me wondering why our kind exists at all, when we are so pursued and hated by those who are like us. To live estranged from one another – you, parted from your daughters, knowing that you will die before your time. Why should this be?"

"Is it any easier for Asule, who doesn't bear the same burden that we do, but has her own burden to bear?"

"No, that's true." Seth expelled his breath in a sigh. "The responsibility I feel for her is only made bearable by her own courage and determination to live her life to the full. Her parents – victims of a conflict that wasn't even their own..."

"Perhaps that's what gives us our reasons to exist, to live. For those who've died, and those who are yet to come. For those who gave their lives for us in a conflict that wasn't of their making."

"There's wisdom in what you say and I find it comforting." Seth's voice sounded more cheerful.

The moon floated serenely above them and the sounds of the desert occasionally punctuated the silence of the night.

"What are you writing on your shrouds? It's an odd language," Seth said.

"Yes, it is. It's from where I come from," Merit said.

"Why?"

"It is the tradition where I... come from."

"Oh, so it is like the Going Forth by Day – the scroll that tells the dead where they need to go in the afterworld?"

"Yes, a bit like that. But in my own language. And I think I have now finished writing them. That gives me some peace of mind."

Seth did not pry any further.

"Do you wish me to keep this knowledge to myself?" he asked.

"If you would, yes. I may tell Shuet one day, but not now. Not when I have only just met my grandchildren. I want this to be a happy time for all of us for as long as possible."

"Then I'll say nothing," Seth said, standing up. "I think we can return now to the children now."

They spent the evening with Asule and Khonsu until they went to sleep. This took some hours as the youngsters never tired of hearing stories about life by the great River that they had never seen.

Merit then wrapped the linen strips into rolls, reading through what she had written on them. Her lips moved and she nodded occasionally. Carefully, she placed each roll inside a wooden chest. Seth noticed she had numbered the rolls. The number was the first thing you saw on each roll. Half of them had been numbered in black, half in red.

"They are to be used in a certain order?" Seth asked.

"Yes," Merit said, and did not elaborate.

"Tomorrow we'll go to meet Shuet when she returns," Seth said.

But in the morning, after the children had left for their lessons, Mut-Bity hurried in, carrying a folded and tied piece of papyrus.

"A letter. From Meryt-Neith. Come from Mi-Wer."

Merit was on her feet instantly.

"She was only to write if there was an emergency," Merit said.

"Open it," Mut-Bity said, but Merit was already cutting the strings around the letter.

Merit took in the text in the letter and she paled.

"What is it?" Mut-Bity asked.

Merit swallowed and then read aloud the contents of the letter aloud.

"I hope my letter finds you all well. I am only writing because he has returned. He has threatened my life and said he will abduct Ramose. Could you take Ramose to live with you, to hide him? Please answer as soon as you can. We are living in fear, our safety now dependent completely on the bees. I beseech you, come yourself to fetch your grandson – I trust no one else and we live in daily fear. I will send him to Mi-Wer with a beehive to protect him.
"

Meryt-Neith"

"I must go!" Merit said, "I will not have the Pale Man take my grandson. I'm leaving immediately. How long has this letter been on the way?"

"It was sent at the last full moon. A ship brought it to the beekeeper in Mi-Wer and she forwarded it immediately, as instructed," Mut-Bity said.

"A whole month? Anything could have happened in a month!" Merit's voice was thin with fear.

"If Meryt-Neith has been wise enough to send the boy to Mi-Wer on a ship with a beehive, he should be safe. The water will protect him, and the bees do the rest. But we need to fetch him here," Mut-Bity said. "I will come with you."

"No. I need to fly there immediately," Merit said, "that will the quickest way."

"I could come with you," Seth said, "and carry Mut-Bity."

"No. You need to stay here so that Shuet knows what has happened when she returns. And Mut-Bity... I feel you have to follow, and... bring my linen chest. It is too heavy for me if I wish to fly fast."

Both Mut-Bity and Seth looked at Merit, shocked.

"You believe..." Mut-Bity began.

"Yes, I do," Merit said, "if it is ever going to happen, I think it will be now. He will follow Ramose, I am sure of it. I will have to defend him, and in doing so it's likely I will die. So, find a donkey, and bring my linen chest after me. I will write a letter to Shuet."

Merit took a piece of papyrus and began to write in haste. Seth saw she was using that odd language of hers.

"Give this to her when she returns," Merit said, folding the letter quickly. There was no need to tie it with a string – no one but Shuet would understand what she'd written. "I'll leave now."

"But the enemy Nephilim may see you!" Mut-Bity said.

"I can fly fast. And it is not likely they are around here anyway, especially not in the middle of the day if they can avoid it. They have no reason to suspect anything in this area, so I am confident I won't be seen."

"Please, don't be hasty. Wait for a while," Seth said. "We have our own soldiers returning soon, they could escort you. Bay and his men should be returning in a day or two from their guard duty."

"Who is Bay?" Merit asked.

"The leader of our council. He has been away for months, following the movement of our enemy, and has sent word he is coming to visit the Hidden Valley soon," Seth said, "He is a strong warrior. He could protect you even from the Pale Man."

"But I can't afford wait for a day or two! Every moment counts. What if the boy doesn't know who the Pale Man is and allows himself to be lured away from the beehives? No, I have to leave now."

Merit filled a flask with water, put some bread and dried meat in a bundle and together with Seth and Mut-Bity walked up to the top of the hills hiding the secret valley. The hills wrapped the length of the Valley in a crescent shape, containing all that they had ever known of peace and joy.

"The gods be with you," Mut-Bity said. "I'm leaving immediately after you, as soon as I'm ready. I'll be out of the Valley within the hour."

"And I will tell Bay where you have gone," Seth said.

"No. Tell no one. We'll send word if Bay is needed. Shuet will send word. If I am already dead, there is nothing Bay or Nephilim warriors can do. If you don't hear from us, no Nephilim warrior is to show themselves in Mi-Wer. The Pale Man may try to ambush them. This whole thing may be a trap to lure our warriors into a fight with Pale Man's forces. I don't want anyone in danger because of me. If we get Ramose out of Mi-Wer, we will appear here in the Valley as soon as we can. If we need Bay's help to get him out, we will send word. And give my letter to Shuet," Merit said, opening her grey wings.

"I will," Seth said – but Merit was already flying towards the East.

68

TO MI-WER

I came out of the misty world under the full moon immediately after stepping into the mist. Mother's hand was no longer in mine. The moon was not only full but in a different part of the sky, so I knew the two days had passed.

I turned to see whether mother and Seth were there waiting for me, but saw only Seth, his red hair looking almost black in the moonlight. Something in his expression alerted me.

"Where's mother?" I asked, worried. "She let go of my hand. Did she find her way back?"

"She couldn't enter the mists for some reason and so she didn't leave in the first place. She should have been here waiting to welcome you back, but something happened and she had to leave in haste," Seth said.

He couldn't hide the concern in his voice and so my own anxiety increased.

"What happened?"

"She received a letter right after you left. A letter from Meryt-Neith. The Pale Man threatened her and Ramose, and Meryt-Neith sent Ramose to safety in Mi-Wer. She asked your mother to come and fetch him from Mi-Wer. The letter had been on its way for a month already, and your mother

was very worried about what might have happened over such a long period of time. So she decided to leave immediately."

The world turned silent around me. Something opened in my mind and I saw mother wrapped in a terrible black shadow that was eating her. She was reaching for me – her arms desperately tried to reach me from the midst of the swirling darkness that was attempting to absorb her. No matter how I tried, I could not see her eyes. There was darkness where her eyes should have been.

Fear squeezed my stomach with cold hands, and shock made my ears ring.

"No! No! It is a trap!" My throat constricted with fear so that I could barely speak. "He will be waiting for her there, the Pale Man! How long ago did she leave?"

"She left almost two days ago. She flew alone and wrote a letter for me to give to you. Mut-Bity left soon after her, with a donkey, carrying her linen chests."

"My mother's chests? Why?"

I knew full well what was in those chests – the linen my mother wanted to be wrapped in after death. I could see Seth was choosing his words carefully.

"I think she explains everything in her letter to you. Come, so you can read it right away."

I started off at a run, down the narrow corridor leading to the village. Seth ran right behind me until we reached a corridor lit with oil lamps. I turned towards our home, hurrying with long steps.

"Stop, stop!" Seth said. "I have the letter with me! Read it here so you don't scare the children. There's enough light here."

I came back to the nearest little ledge where a small oil lamp was burning, creating more shadow than illumination. Still, it gave enough light for me to read.

The letter Seth was handing to me was not tied with strings.

"Have you read it? What did it say?"

"No, I did not. She wrote it in a language only you and she understand – I saw her writing it so I know. That's why she didn't seal it with strings, I am

sure. And it was a letter to you, not me, so I wouldn't read it even if I did understand the language."

I opened the letter and began to read. It was long, on three separate pieces of papyrus, written in the language mother called English, the language of her past. A language she had taught me. And I could not believe what I was reading.

"What is it?" Seth asked when I just stood there as if I had taken root, reading and re-reading the letter as if it would make more sense that way.

"I... I can't tell you," I whispered, "she asks me not to tell you until it is certain that she is..."

I could not say the word.

"Dead?" Seth asked.

I turned to look at him and his next words confirmed my worst fear.

"The chests Mut-Bity is to take to Mi-Wer through the desert contain the shrouds your mother made for herself. And if she asks for her shrouds to follow her... I fear she is now certain she will die. But as Mut-Bity agreed to deliver them to her, how could I object to either one of them leaving? Merit has written spells on them in that language, " Seth pointed at the letter. "You saw her do that yourself. Two nights ago, when you left, she told me she had foreseen her death. And that's the odd thing – she used the word here. That she will die here. But she wasn't talking about the Hidden Valley."

Having read the letter, I understood what mother had meant. But I could not tell Seth.

"I need to go to her, right away," I said.

"No! If the Pale Man is waiting for Merit, then he must at least suspect that you might follow her. Then he will have both of you. And maybe Ramose too. I will not let you leave alone. If you must go after her, I'm coming with you."

He tried to wrap his arm around my shoulder but I pushed him away.

"No! I will not have our children orphaned. You have to stay here with them, Seth. If I am in danger, then so are they. The Pale Man will want to kill Khonsu because he is our child and he is a silver Nephilim too. And of course he would kill you as well. I have to do my mother's bidding, in this letter she makes me promise I will. I must go to her alone. She asks that I keep the rest of my family safe."

"Not alone!" Seth said. "Never!"

"What are you two arguing about?" a deep voice asked.

We had not noticed Bay approaching. He must have just returned from his long absence.

"Nothing serious," I said, sending Seth a warning look not to say a word. "I came back from the desert and found my mother had left for Mi-Wer while I was gone. Family matters."

"Ah, I see. I heard Merit had arrived in the Valley some months ago. And you weren't expecting her to leave so soon?"

"No, I needed to talk with her about something. I must go to her. Seth doesn't want me to leave alone. He is worried about the dark Nephilim seeing me."

"Well, I am sure there is no danger in you flying over the desert," Bay said. "I don't know what's happening, but it's as if the enemy Nephilim have suddenly vanished – not the faintest trace of them anywhere, not even in the mists. Still, don't use that way if you don't need to. Nearer to the River, they probably keep a stronger guard, in the misty world as well."

"Thank you. I won't go there."

How I wished later that I had not followed his advice and had hurried through the mists where travelling was faster. How I wished I had disobeyed Mother's desire to keep this whole thing a secret from Bay and the Nephilim Council.

Bay walked away.

"You should have told Bay what was happening. He could have sent an escort with you, soldiers who could have defended you and your mother against the enemy!" Seth said. "Even if Merit did not want him to know."

"No! She told you not to do so and told me in her letter that I am not to reveal the true cause of her journey to anyone. No one! That whatever happens is... meant to happen and if someone intervenes, we may change the future in ways that we can't comprehend, ways that will result in chaos."

"Future? Chaos?"

"Yes. Mother has seen the future and has warned me of this. And... I am to come to her with Mut-Bity."

Seth lifted his hands in a helpless gesture.

"I can't convince you to wait? What was in that letter?"

I shook my head. I had not taken it in myself yet. The unbelievable things my mother had written. I was desperate to find her, to talk to her. I just could not believe what I had read.

It took all the effort I could muster to act calmly in front of the children and say lightly that I was intending to visit Mi-Wer.

"Oh, do take us with you!" Khonsu said eagerly, excited by the idea that I was simply going on some sort of visit. Like all young people coming into adulthood, he wanted to see the world and felt his familiar surroundings were too small for the great plans he had for himself.

"Not this time. But I promise you will see it one day," I said. "I have things to attend to that can only be handled alone."

"Oh come on, father! Tell mother we can go with her!" Asule turned to plead with Seth.

"Not this time, Asule. Later," Seth said.

I could see he was very worried, though he tried to act as if nothing was wrong. He didn't quite convince Khonsu, though, for I saw him looking at Seth curiously.

"I'm leaving at first light," I said, "so I can be back with my family soon."

If I had left in the middle of the night, right after returning from my trip to the desert, Asule and Khonsu would surely have suspected something was wrong. I knew our headstrong son – he might get it into his head to follow me. And if there was the slightest chance Mother could be safe and return to us, I was not about to tell them what was going on.

So, as soon as the sun rose, I opened my wings and headed east. A long veil hid my face, and my sleeves reached below the tips of my fingers. On my feet, I had sandals and socks to prevent the sun from touching my skin. Tears ran from my eyes, and I was not sure if it was because of the bright light or the turmoil in my mind.

Two days' flying would take me to the great lake west of the River. After hours of travelling as fast as I could, the sun was high above me. Then, I saw a small figure in the middle of the vastness of the desert – Mut-Bity, leading a donkey that was carrying chests on both flanks.

I headed down and landed right next to her. I had arrived silently, but the donkey alerted her to my approach so I saw her turn to observe me. When her posture relaxed, I knew she had recognised me.

"Shuet. So you got her letter, then?"

"I did. And I can't bring myself to believe what she said! About herself, where she comes from, why she thinks it is necessary for her to face the Pale Man alone!"

Mut-Bity kept on walking, apparently not surprised at all.

"Believe it, for it is true." Her words confirmed what I had suspected.

"You knew? You've known all along?"

"Yes. She told me. Where she came from, years ago. When you were still infants."

"And you never thought to tell us?"

"I did think about it. But it was not my story to tell."

"She told you about the... scroll... the one that relates to the place of the Neteru? Where our ancestors are hidden?"

"She did. I have seen it myself. But you need to hurry on now. Ask me more later. I'm coming along behind you just as fast as I can."

Without saying another word, I rose up into the air and continued on my journey. Only when I was already far ahead did I begin to wonder about Mut-Bity's words. What had she seen for herself? The scroll? Or the place of the Neteru? If I saw her again, that would be my first question.

I saw no Nephilim on my journey. Not my own kind, and no evil ones either. If the desert people saw me, they were well hidden, for I did not see them.

And then, at dusk on the second day, the great lake came into view. I knew where the fishermen's village was and decided to stop for a short while. I had drunk all my water, and was thirsty, hungry and exhausted.

So many years had passed. I no longer saw Mut-Bity's old friend among the people who came to greet me. I was given a warm welcome nevertheless. The children stared at my wings with their mouths open, but the adults were calmer. They had been friends of the secret Hidden Valley for a long time, and the people of the Valley sent them provisions and goods as a thank you. It was a poor village, but no one starved, and all had clothes on their backs.

"Please, come and rest for the night," a young pregnant woman gestured towards one of the mud huts.

"I am sorry, I have no time. But if I could have something to drink?" I asked.

I was given a cup of beer. I thanked them and drank hastily.

"Have you seen my mother?"

"We know your mother," an older woman said, "she is a friend of Mut-Bity and has visited us. And we remember you too when you were here before, as a child. We considered you beautiful. You may be colourless but no one has eyes like yours..."

I forced a smile onto my face.

"But my mother has been here?"

"She came here two days ago – just to have a drink, like you. She was in a hurry to get to Mi-Wer," the woman continued. "She did say you would probably follow her and asked us to tell you to be very careful when you approach the city. She warns you might be in danger if you show yourself openly."

"Thank you, I'll be careful."

"Can we help you with whatever it is you are about to do?" one of the fishermen asked.

"I wish you could help... but no. Someone is threatening my family, and my sister's family. My mother suspects he will be in Mi-Wer to catch my sister's son and has gone to protect the boy. I only hope she is wrong... but I know she is in danger. She should not have gone alone!"

"Then you must leave and find her. But take care – don't put yourself in danger too," the man said.

"I will be careful."

I took to the air again, but did not go very high – I intended to fly following the shoreline of the lake, not over open water. And there were people about, so I planned to keep from view if I could.

Night fell and I flew on under the stars, observing my surroundings constantly. Enemy Nephilim would spot my body heat if I flew too high. But then again, I would see them, too.

No Nephilim were anywhere, though, only night animals scurrying about. They showed like reddish blobs of light to my eyes. If I had been calm, I could have heard the starsong reflected from them. But I was too afraid, too worried, to hear the music of the sky.

The next morning I arrived near Mi-Wer and landed at a distance, observing the buildings. Should I go to the palace on foot?

No. I would draw attention to myself because of my looks. I would use the mists to approach. I knew the house mother would be in, it was our old home, and so I would enter directly unless I felt the presence of the dark ones nearby. But I still felt nothing. If the Pale Man had followed Ramose to Mi-Wer, then surely he or his servants would be here? Why were they absent? Unless Meryt-Neith had managed to get Ramose safely away somewhere and the dark ones hadn't noticed it.

Or...

Unless they already had what they wanted.

I stepped into the misty world without a second thought and hurried to mother's house. I came out of the mists on the roof and listened intently to hear if anyone was inside.

Nothing.

I walked down the same stairs the Pale Man had used when he came to attack us all those years ago. Then I saw the form lying on the low bed of the bedroom. The same bed Seth and I had shared before we left.

"Mother!"

For it was my mother. She wasn't moving. She was facing the wall, her back turned to the doorway, totally unresponsive. I felt the greatest pain I had ever known. The Pale Man had sprung his trap and killed her!

I ran to her and turned her onto her back. Then her hand moved slightly and I saw she was holding the mirror Tiye had given her many years back. The one with the faces of Hathor and Sekhmet. A sharp knife was on the bed and I saw she had scratched the handle of the mirror.

She was breathing. I could barely see her face underneath her hair.

"Mother! Are you well?" I whispered.

I pushed the thick, wheat-coloured hair from her face so that I could see her. I stared at the blood on my fingers. And then Mother opened her eyes.

I had arrived too late.

69

IN THE HOUSE OF THE DEMON

"We need to stick to the story as planned," I said. "I don't want us to be imprisoned here."

We were standing in the reception room of the house. The guards had been given strict orders not to let us out and now we were waiting for the Mother of the King, Tiye, to arrive.

"Of course," Grandma said.

I was standing together with Daniel and Elijah, near the dais on which a royal chair had been placed. The arm rests were in the form of winged cobras and its legs were those of a lion. On the back of the chair was a magnificent image depicting blue lotuses touched by the arms of the sun disk Aten. The part of the backrest where the Aten shone was gilded.

"Imagine if that had survived to our days..." Reggie said to Mr. Donnelly.

"Indeed... it would be considered a marvel!"

"It reminds me of Tutankhamun's throne," Diana said quietly from the other side of the room.

Thomas looked at her curiously.

"So the little prince will survive to adulthood?" he asked.

"He will," Paris said.

"Will he become king?" Thomas asked.

We looked at each other, and no one answered. We had told Thomas about the events of more modern history, but not about the time of Akhenaten, the idea being that this way, the knowledge would not slip out so no one could change the course of history inadvertently.

"Very well. I understand – you can't tell me, so as not to interfere with the future. But if he has a chair like that, I suspect he will be king. And his name is not Tutankhaten anymore? It seems then that he won't be worshipping the Aten like his father, when he becomes king. But don't worry – I will keep this knowledge to myself."

One little word, and Thomas could draw all these conclusions from it. Diana looked embarrassed at having let slip Tutankhamun's name. She looked a bit feverish still, and thin. And she still had a voracious appetite.

The house we were in had a large garden and three storeys. Thomas told us that a merchant's wife had lived there in the recent past, but there had been some strange happening involving the slaughter of animals. After that, she had disappeared completely.

"The neighbours here say that she was a demon," Thomas said.

"How did you hear about that?" Diana wanted to know. "I mean, if no one is allowed to leave the house, how did you meet any neighbours?"

"Well, the next-door neighbour's wall is only one narrow alleyway away. I went to the roof and was sitting there when the master of the neighbouring house appeared. We had a good chat. He seemed relieved that I was an ordinary person. And then he told me that a strange lady lived here before. Her skin was golden brown, and she ate animals. As in ate them alive."

"Sounds like a vampire," Diana said.

"Could be. When she was witnessed doing that, she escaped and never came back. And the house has been vacant ever since. The owner of the house, her husband, hasn't shown his face either. The neighbour had never seen him, but he had heard stories that he looked odd too. When the King's Mother arrived and heard the story, she ordered the house to be taken for her own use and we were escorted here. This way, we are close to the palace should she need to meet us," Reggie said.

Ancient Egypt became him – he was tanned and looked years younger. He and Mr. Donnelly were probably having a blast, seeing all the ancient people and manners up close. Mr. Donnelly's only constant complaint was about not being able to use his glasses when anyone other than the team was around.

"Should we be worried about the owner of the house returning? He is most likely a vampire as well, if the woman living here was one."

"We should be worried, yes, but not about the master of the house being a vampire," Elijah said. "Remember that vampires only drank animal blood at this stage in history. If you were a vampire, you were made into one by a dark Nephilim. And if the story going around here is that her husband looked strange somehow, that may explain it."

"Great... we are sitting ducks in a house that belongs to an enemy Nephilim?" Jason sighed. "That means we have to take turns on guard duty and stick together. No more walking alone in the garden. And we all need to sleep in the same room."

The scribe Ahmose didn't live with us and we hadn't seen him much. But then, one day, he appeared to announce that the King's Mother was finally going to visit us that evening. He looked across at Elijah and Daniel and bowed.

"I see that you are of a similar... kind as Dana. Welcome," he said.

Daniel looked at me, raising an eyebrow.

"He knows. He's Merit's friend. Merit taught him English too," I said.

"We need to go and find Merit soon," Daniel said.

"We will. But first, we need to locate the dwarfs," Elijah said, "now that we are here."

"Dwarfs?" Ahmose asked. "What are their names?"

He did not seem surprised at our request – dwarfs were much respected in ancient Egypt, and so it was no surprise to find them at the royal court.

"Well, they are a bit odd..." Reggie scratched his head, "they are *King's Wives Live Forever* and *His Mother is Re*."

Ahmose smiled.

"Well rather strange names they are indeed... I don't remember hearing names like those before."

"But there are dwarfs here?"

"Yes, there are."

"Are any in the service of Nefertiti's sister Mutnofret?"

Ahmose opened his mouth but did not have time to answer.

"Shush, I think I can hear her arriving," Grandma said. "Please find out if there are any dwarfs in Mutnofret's company and let us know."

Grandma's hair had grown and she looked so much younger than her official seventy years. All those years in the buffer zone, away from the touch of time, had a lot to do with it. That and her strict exercise regime and healthy eating. I heard she and Jason had been wrestling to keep in shape.

"But only where servants or soldiers can't watch, of course," Jason had said. "I mean, it would have been a bit embarrassing for me to lose to an old woman at wrestling in front of all those guards."

"Old woman..." Grandma had snorted, "I'll make you eat those words yet."

Aemilius laughed silently, which made the scar on his face more visible – a reminder of an ancient battle he had fought in as a soldier of Rome. Paris shook her head. Jason and Grandma grinned at each other.

A familiar figure appeared in the doorway. An official that we had already seen in Mi-Wer. He announced all Tiye's titles and soon after that, Tiye herself appeared in the doorway, followed by a servant carrying an ostrich feather fan on a stick.

Everyone bowed respectfully as Tiye walked through the room and seated herself on the chair. She looked at me and spoke. The elderly scribe Ahmose interpreted her words.

"My heart rejoices to see you alive and well. Tell me what happened."

"I will, but I must ask your people to leave the room so they will not see us," I said.

Upon hearing Ahmose's translation, Tiye's servants looked at me as if they couldn't believe their ears. Tiye, however, said one word and they all left quickly.

"Draw the curtain to the room," I said. "Aemilius, go outside and make sure no one is eavesdropping. Or trying to see us."

Aemilius nodded briefly, stepped outside and closed the curtain.

I waited until it was quiet. Tiye did not divert her eyes from me. They were very tired eyes. She looked so sad I thought something bad must have happened.

"Please translate this," I said to Ahmose, "I left to save my servant who was taken by demons."

Ahmose hesitated only a moment, and then interpreted my words. Tiye's eyebrows rose. She said something, and her voice was not as commanding as it had been in Mi-Wer. It must have been because of my wings – they had opened spontaneously when Ambrogio had called for me, so many people had seen them. Or perhaps it was the fact I had healed the pain in her stomach.

"Why did the demons take your servant?"

"Because she is my servant. These demons wish to harm me, and so they attack those who are close to me," I said, "and we have heard there was a demon living in this very house before we came here. We are worried about the safety of my people if we stay in this house."

Tiye considered this. Then she spoke and Ahmose translated.

"The demon has left. And soldiers will be in this house constantly. They will protect you. I do not wish you to be in danger – inside the palace many people come and go. Here you can be amongst yourselves, with my guards to guarantee your safety. You will stay here."

I turned to look at the others. Silently, they nodded.

"Very well. Are we to be prisoners in this house?"

"Not prisoners, valued guests."

"Can we go outside?"

"No," Tiye said, "I wish you to be safe. You especially," she nodded at me.

She pressed her hand instinctively to her stomach. So, she did not want me to leave, in case she needed healing.

"Who are these new people?" she then asked.

"Here is Lilith," I said, "who is a trusted servant of mine."

Lilith bowed, her eyes downcast.

"And these are Daniel and Elijah. They are... of my kind."

Tiye's eyes moved nervously to the two tall figures by my side.

"Now," I said.

Together we all opened our wings. They crackled with electricity and reached to the ceiling.

To Tiye's credit, it has to be said that she did not show fear. She rose to her feet and bowed in a dignified manner.

"I am honoured to be in the presence of gods," she whispered, "and I am honoured to have the attention of a healing goddess."

"Now that you have seen who we are, you do understand you are not to restrict our moving about," I said, as we had planned.

"Indeed. I will not restrict your movements. But your servants are to stay here in the house, guarded at all times by my soldiers."

"Do not translate what I am about to say," I said to Ahmose and turned to Daniel. "Can we accept this or should I demand we all can all move about freely?"

"I think it may even be wisest that everyone else stays in the house," Daniel said, "after all, we can sense if a dark Nephilim is nearby, but they can't. Also, Ambrogio is bound to appear at some point. He won't come in here with so many soldiers about, but he could quite easily attack on a crowded street."

"I agree. And I think one of we three should stay here at all times, so we'll have pre-warning of a Nephilim approach," Elijah said.

I nodded to Ahmose as a sign that he should now translate my words.

"Very well. You have spoken wisely, Mother of the King," I said. "Now we request you not to tell anyone what you have seen here."

"You have my promise," Tiye said and we closed our wings.

If I was not mistaken, I saw a flash of disappointment in her expression as our wings disappeared from view.

"If I may say so, I think Dana should stay indoors," Tiye said. "Many on my ship witnessed her wings, and you have arrived here unnoticed. My guards are not to speak of you to anyone, under pain of death, and it is best no one else knows the winged goddess is here. After the... demon incident in this house, I think it wise. And if I also may suggest... that you keep your true nature a secret as well?"

Tiye was certainly courageous to speak like that to what she thought were deities. We glanced at each other. She looked at us and continued speaking.

"There is a certain... intolerance in this city towards... gods and goddesses," she said, "I am afraid the king would not look favourably upon you... if you..."

Of course. The king's intolerance towards other deities than the Aten. It was common knowledge that ordinary people worshipped their house gods as before, but what would they do if they really believed we were gods in the city where only the Aten was accepted... The king would not do anything if he believed we really were gods, but our presence could make his kingdom of the Aten crumble before its time. That would really change history.

"We will be discreet," Daniel answered on our behalf. "To any outsider, it will seem like we've been invited to take part in the great jubilee of all nations, to honour the king's beautiful city and show his rule over lesser kings."

He bowed slightly towards Tiye, who looked relieved. I thought she was not so worried about Elijah and Daniel; her concern was for me. Her eyes caught mine for a while and I smiled at her reassuringly.

"Have you been well, Mother of the King? Is there something you wish to discuss with me?"

We had already agreed this between ourselves, to keep Tiye on favourable terms with us. If she had any ailments, I would try to use my healing skills to make her feel well.

"Now that you mention it..." Tiye said and looked around.

"I understand. Please everyone, leave us. Only Ahmose can stay and translate," I waved my hand at the others royally.

They walked out of the room as if I had every right to order them about. I turned towards Tiye. Ahmose stood next to her, slightly bent at the waist, ready to translate.

"How may I help you feel better?" I asked.

"I have just received a message that a beloved friend has died, so if you can mend the ache in my heart..." Tiye said.

Her voice faltered and she cast a strange look at me.

"I am afraid I can't do that," I said, "though I am very sorry you have lost a friend."

"As am I... but I know, I have to bear the pain in my heart. And no one can help me there. I have more physical ailments, though, as is common in old people. Perhaps you could help me with my aching joints?"

I nodded.

"I think I can help you with those."

I took her hands into mine and the now familiar tingling feeling told me that my healing energies were responding to the imbalances in her body.

She smiled gratefully, and closed her eyes. A tear fell down her cheek. The friend must have been special to her. When she opened her eyes again, she looked directly at me.

"Who are those two gods to you? Are you brothers and sisters?"

"The one with blond hair is my... husband," I said, as there probably was no such word as fiancé in ancient Egypt., "The other one is his brother. Merit's husband."

"Her husband? The one she lost before her girls were born?"

"Yes – he finally heard of Merit being here and hurried to meet her," I said.

At that, Tiye slumped in her chair, and covered her eyes with her hand.

"Please, scribe, call him in. I need to speak with him."

Suddenly I knew exactly what she had to tell Elijah.

70

THE PLAN FOR THE FUTURE

Mother's eyes were no longer bright blue. Their colour had dulled to a dirty green. She looked at me. There were bite marks and bruises on her neck as if someone had been trying to strangle her. I saw the damage to her skin and the cuts on her arms and upper torso where the fabric had been torn.

"I was right," Mother whispered. "He was waiting for me here. The King's Mother had left the day before and not many guards remained. That meant he could come into this house and wait for me here without anyone noticing. He could do that as there are no bees in the house now."

The horror was too much for me to speak. I stared at her bitten skin, her eyes that would be turning yellow in the coming weeks.

"Shuet," she whispered, "it is all right. For some reason, this was meant to happen."

"Meant to happen? That you would be injured so badly, changed forever, by those who want to destroy us? How could that ever be meant to happen? How could it ever be... all right?"

Mother did not move and I saw that she was in pain.

"Did you read my letter?" she asked.

"I did. And I can't believe it!"

Now she moved, trying to push herself into a sitting position. Instinc-

tively, I helped her. She whimpered with pain and the cuts on her skin ruptured and bled. The blood was bright-coloured but trickled slowly.

"It's the truth. I was born three thousand and three hundred years in the future before I entered Kemet. I was newly married, and I was in the desert with your father, in a place where there is a small circle of stones. That is where I fell through time and found myself here. I was planning on killing myself when I understood what had happened. And then I found out I was pregnant. Without you two, I would have killed myself, I am certain of it."

She sat with her eyes closed, her clothes and bed tainted with blood.

"The Pale Man is a part of an old legend that says that a silver Nephilim will be the ruin of the evil ones. You know about this."

I could not speak.

"With the help of the scribe Ahmose, we came into possession of an old text that spoke of finding our creators. Our forefathers. It told of the secrets of creation that were still there to be found, if one could find the abode of the Neteru, the gods. Our creators, who in my time were called the Watchers. Our holy scrolls mention them, winged creatures that took human wives. The word we used... will be using for them is angel."

"What did the scroll have to do with you?" I whispered.

"Not me. You. It warned me that the Pale Man was after you, and said that the Mother of the Bees should take you to safety when he arrived. It also spoke of you burying the Golden Goddess whose name was Beloved."

"Merit?"

"Yes, that is how my name translates."

Mother winced, a shadow crossing her face.

"The pain...I can't begin to explain how much this... change... hurts," she said, "it is like a boiling of the blood ..."

With a shaking hand, she pulled her hair from the matted blood on her neck.

"I will always love you, whatever you become," I said.

"No, you will not. After turning into a creature like the Pale Man I would no longer be the person you knew. I would no longer be capable of feeling love for you. But don't worry. I don't intend to let that happen. I intend to die before I change. And – I need you to kill me."

I was on my feet before I could think.

"No! How can you ask that of me? I will never kill you!"

"Oh, but you must," Mother grabbed my hand, "you see... I know the secret now. I know where the Watchers are hidden. And if I transform, I will willingly tell the Pale Man all he wishes to know. That means that he will find the knowledge that should stay hidden, and with it, he will gain power over all creation. That is why I fought him so hard – to prevent him from drinking my blood so he couldn't gain the knowledge immediately. And eventually he gave up. He is certain I will change soon – and why shouldn't he be? You can see how deep the bites are and his saliva entered my body. That is how they change us into one of them. Soon, I won't want to kill myself anymore. I'll start to welcome the change in me, to enjoy it. I need to act quickly, long before that moment comes. If you do not kill me, I will do it myself. Please Shuet, help me."

She sat still for a long while, listening to her body.

"You see, Shuet – the scroll we found with the scribe Ahmose not only said that you should bury the Golden Goddess, it said you would learn something while you did so. Something important that is connected to the Watchers – and I have done my best to make it possible for you to have the knowledge the scroll spoke of. The scroll was ancient, and Ahmose was about to copy it so its message would not be lost. And that part of the scroll that spoke of you, me and Mut-Bity was written in English."

"English?"

"Yes, the language I spoke with your father. A language that won't even exist for many thousands of years. The only ones who speak it here are you and I. And Ahmose, of course. I taught him the language after we returned from Inbu-Hedj with the scroll."

"And Bay..." I said, "I taught it to Bay too. He found it... amusing to learn. And Seth's mother..." I was babbling nervously.

"I am sure it doesn't matter, as they cannot read it," Mother said.

"Matter? Why should it matter?"

She breathed in deeply and rose to her feet.

"It is important that no one but you understand what I have written on the wrappings I created for myself. Seth thought I was writing spells, advice on how my soul could reach the fields of Iaru. But that is not what I have written. Is Mut-Bity on her way with my coffers?"

"Yes, I saw her..." I said.

"Good. Listen. I will now explain what I want you to do. The coffers will contain my shrouds, two kinds of them. And my two scrolls of Going Forth by Day – or the Book of the Dead as people will call it in my time. The one I have finished is in a wooden tube and this is to be placed on my chest. But there are only pictures in the other one. You are to write the texts under each picture according to the instructions I have written. Those instructions will be in the coffers as well. I would have written them myself, but I thought I still had time and so I did not do it yet. You must do it for me. Are you ready to listen to what I need you to do?"

"Let me wash you first..." I had to do something physical to keep control over my thoughts.

"Listen, then, because I will be speaking while you do that," mother said, "for I do not know how fast my change will go. I may have weeks, days, or only hours. So listen carefully. Promise?"

"I promise..."

And there, that day, my mother told me about her plan. An amazing plan to let my father know, in the future, how to find the place where my mother would be buried. The place where the secrets of creation were. And how I should deliver this message to him through time.

71

THE END

We walked to the garden of Mi-Wer, together for the last time, mother's hand gripping mine. Her step was slow and I could tell from her breathing how afraid she was. She tried not to let it show, and I pretended not to notice. So we kept up the pretence, each for the sake of the other. I could not rob her of her dignity, not during these last moments.

We stopped when the beehives came into view.

"You are... certain..." my voice broke.

"It has to be so," mother said, squeezing my hand in hers.

She lifted my hand to her heart and I felt it beating. Slowly, heavily. I would remember my mother's heartbeat. The first thing I had ever heard when I had been in her womb, the sound that had told me I was safe as long as she was my mother. And now I felt my mother's heart for the last time.

"Take me to my bees," she said, "so I may escape the life of darkness."

I did as she asked.

The bees, our protectors. For the last time with mother, I thought of their own existence so closely entwined with ours. Their lives, the secrets of the hive and the sisterhood who tended to them. All too brief thoughts, contending with the anguish in my heart.

The bees recognised us and flew out to greet us as they always did, circling us in their familiar harmonious way. Then, their movements changed. The round peaceful sweeping curves around us turned into sharper darting movements aimed in our direction. I felt mother's hand shaking in mine and wrapped my arm around her shoulders.

It was too late to retreat now. The buzzing was becoming louder, angrier.

Mother knelt in front of the beehives stacked in neat formation.

"Hold me," she whispered.

I knelt next to her, and despite my resolution to stay strong, began to cry.

Mother lifted her arm and pushed her hand through the opening of the biggest hive. I closed my streaming eyes, but nothing could shut out the sound of the bees. That would stay with me forever.

72

TREACHERY

Mut-Bity stood still, mute with grief.

"My dear friend..." she whispered finally. "Why did you have to fulfil this prophecy?"

Mut-Bity had arrived too late to see her alive.

Merit was lying on her bed with her arms over her chest, hands together. Shuet had placed them in the position used when the people of Merit's time prayed to their God. Merit's eyes were closed, her expression peaceful. Her right hand was almost grey, its skin dark and scaly. The cuts on her neck and hands were clearly visible. Her hair was freshly washed and Shuet had pulled it over her chest, under her hands, in an effort to hide the wounds on the upper torso. It gleamed golden in the light of the oil lamps. She had been dead long enough for her skin to lose all its colour, but, marking her as different from ordinary people, her body had not begun to decompose.

"She killed herself because I could not do it..." Shuet whispered.

Her eyes were almost swollen shut but she no longer had any tears.

"How... how did she..." Mut-Bity tried to finish the sentence.

"The bees. She walked to the beehives and sat down in front of them. She put her hand inside the hive."

"Oh Shuet, my dear..."

"The whole hive attacked her. I pulled the veil that shielded me over her head to save her face. Her eyes had begun to change, Mut-Bity, but love was still shining from them despite their oily green colour."

Shuet heard Mut-Bity sob.

"She did not die immediately – she hadn't transformed completely, and her body resisted longer than I would have wished. Each sting was like a stab in my own heart. But I did not turn away, I looked into her eyes all through her death and I know she saw the love I felt for her – would always feel for her. I hope my love made her death easier for her, less painful."

"Shuet... you brave, kind..." Mut-Bity's voice was breaking so badly that she couldn't finish.

After a while, Shuet continued. "When I saw she was finally going to leave her body, I kissed her on the forehead and cradled her in my arms, pressing her against my bosom. She had done so when she gave me life, and now it was my turn to be the mother escorting her to the life hereafter."

"Have you left her alone since... since..."

"No. I promised to stay with her. I had held her while they stung her. I held her when her soul left her body, Merit, my mother, true of voice. Then I carried her here, so you could see her before she is prepared for death. They have asked for her body so many times now, but I said they could only take her after you arrived. There are already rumours that she was a goddess because her body has not begun to decay."

Mut-Bity knelt next to Merit and gently stroked her hair, tears streaming.

"We will now do what you asked of us..." she said. "We shall bury you as you said we should."

"And we will send your message to the future." Shuet's voice was firm.

"To Elijah, your father," Mut-Bity said, not turning her eyes from Merit's beautiful ashen face.

"I've already written to Tiye," Shuet said. "The letter is on its way to

Akhetaten. I thought she should know. I wrote that mother will be buried in our family tomb."

"Good. Here are Merit's coffers."

Mut-Bity opened the lids.

"You know what these are?"

"Yes. Mother explained what I have to do."

Shuet lifted out some of the neat linen rolls and looked at them.

"You know what they say?" asked Mut-Bity.

"Not yet. But I am to be there when she is wrapped in these, to read them. To understand what will happen and how to send the message to my father so that the enemy Nephilim won't discover the secret of the Creators. She wants him to find them."

"The Watchers," Mut-Bity said.

"Yes."

"Did she tell you about the Pale Man? How did he manage to catch her?"

Shuet's face hardened.

"Yes. She said he was waiting for her here in this house. Ramose never left Akhetaten. *He* brought greetings from Meryt-Neith. He said they were back together again."

"No!" Mut-Bity looked horrified. "But that would mean Meryt-Neith betrayed your mother!"

"Yes. I curse my sister. I would not be surprised if she came here to gloat over her success. She has always hated me, and accused Mother for not loving her enough."

"She can't come here, not now," Mut-Bity said. "The jubilee of all nations is about to start, and she cannot leave her duties as the leader of the temple dancers."

"Her duties? How is she going to dance under the sun if he has changed her!" Shuet spat.

"She may not yet have turned. Remember why the Pale Man wants her – because she is fertile. Because she can carry his children. So she can dance all she likes and the sun won't hurt her. But she would never admit to knowing of his plan – if she admitted that, she would lose everything. As seer, Merit was Tiye's confidant and considered great in magic. And if Tiye learned about Meryt-Neith's role in this, she would fall from grace immediately. Tiye might even go so far as to have her killed. So no, she will never admit to being back with the Pale Man again; and never admit collaborating with him to get Merit."

Mut-Bity rose to her feet.

"The Pale Man may come back for you any moment now."

"No. Mother said to him that she had come without telling anyone where she was going. So he had no reason to expect my arrival."

"I don't trust that. I'm going to fetch the bees."

Mut-Bity walked out of the room with tired steps.

Shuet looked into the other casket and pulled out the strange thing her mother had called her '"notebook'". It had pages, sewn together at one side and hidden under flat pieces of wood covered with leather. A strange structure was pictured on the cover – it looked a little like a djed-pillar, but Shuet had no idea what it was. Mother had never let them play with it, and had kept it hidden. She opened the cover and began to read.

Mut-Bity returned with a tube made of clay with bees in it.

Shortly afterwards, Merit was taken from her house. She was carried on a stretcher to the place of washing, and the women of the *keneret* lined the way, howling their grief and throwing ashes on their hair, beating their naked breasts.

Shuet and Mut-Bity walked behind the stretcher until it reached the tent erected for the washing of the dead. They did not go inside.

"Shuet..." someone whispered.

Shuet turned to see her old friend the slitter. They had sat together for many nights when Shuet was learning about how the dead were prepared for eternal life. That had been when she could see the dead. After giving birth to Khonsu, she had not been able to do that anymore.

"I am very sorry to hear of the death of your beautiful mother," he said, "and if you request it, I will be there for her all through the seventy days of beautifying her for the afterlife."

Shuet looked at him. He was already old, stooped and white-haired. But he was one of the people who had been her true friends in the past.

"I would be honoured if you would be her slitter," she said, "and if you would watch over her for as long as it takes for her body to dry in salt. I will be there for the wrapping. And I need a tent for myself right next to the place of death. Tent, oil lamps, a bed and writing equipment."

"It shall be arranged, as you are Merit's daughter," the slitter said. "I am certain the Mother of the King will arrange for a fine tomb for your mother."

"No, she will be buried in my family's tomb," Shuet said.

"I have already sent for our people so they can come and carry her when she is ready," Mut-Bity said.

The slitter bowed and walked into the tent of washing.

A tent was erected for Shuet next to the place of embalming. She and Mut-Bity carried Merit's chests there by themselves. Mut-Bity arranged for beehives to be erected next to the tent.

For the forty days it took for Merit's body to dry, Shuet stayed inside in the tent that had been raised next to *wabt-net-wet*, the place of embalming, writing the texts under the pictures of the Book of the Dead according to her mother's instructions.

73

A DEATH KEPT SECRET

"How is he?" Lilith asked Daniel.

"He doesn't speak. He doesn't eat. He's still staring at the wall. He doesn't even seem to be aware of me, or anyone else..." Daniel said.

He had just left the room Elijah was in.

"When did Merit die?" Grandma asked me.

"Tiye told me she received a letter from Mi-Wer, from Merit's daughter Shuet. It said that Merit had arrived there the day after Tiye's ships had sailed. She was attacked by an unknown assailant and was wounded so badly she died a few days later."

"Unknown assailant?" Aemilius rubbed the scar on his face, as was his habit when he was deep in thought. "Why would anyone unknown want to attack her? Just because she was on her own?"

"We know there are enemy Nephilim here," Daniel said, "maybe they discovered she was alone and took advantage of it. Note that they did not kill her immediately – she died from her wounds later. Sounds to me as though someone was trying to infect her."

"Could we retrieve her body?" Paris asked, "so that Elijah could have... closure?"

"Tiye told me that she has already been prepared for the afterlife by now – and taken to her family tomb," I said.

"Her *what?*" Daniel asked.

"That is what she said. She told me that she had sent for provisions so that Merit could be mummified in the best possible way. And that Shuet had said in her letter that she would escort Merit's body to their family tomb. I don't know where it is."

"But... Merit had two daughters... Shuet and Meryt-Neith. And as far as we know, Meryt-Neith is right here, in Akhetaten. Surely she needs to be told her father is here!" Lilith said.

"I did ask about that..." I said, "after Tiye had told Elijah."

"Well? Where is she? Meryt-Neith?"

"There is something strange about that... Tiye told me that we are not to tell anyone about Merit's death. Or that Elijah is here. I assume that includes Meryt-Neith. I have a feeling there was something in that letter she received from Shuet..."

"We need to talk to Tiye," Grandma said. "Is Ahmose around?"

"No," I shook my head. "It seems he had not heard of Merit's death either, and was so shocked he almost fainted at the news."

"Why is this such a secret, then?" Daniel asked. "There really is something deeper in all of this." His voice betrayed his own sadness, along with a hint of anger that at such a difficult time we should find ourselves even more constrained from taking action.

"We *will* find out what it is," Lilith said, "but Elijah must be our main concern for now. The last time he thought Merit had died, he almost killed himself. He had been given the wild hope of finding her again, only to hear now that she really is dead after all. I am afraid Elijah will follow her..." Her voice trailed away but we knew what she was thinking.

"I will stay with him as long as needed," Daniel said.

"Thanks, Daniel," Lilith said, squeezing his hand.

He went back to Elijah's room.

And so none of us left the house. Elijah mourned his dead wife and Daniel watched over Elijah, I wasn't to leave the house as there might be people about who had seen my wings. The others were in danger of being attacked by Ambrogio – or the owner of this house who we now knew was most likely an enemy Nephilim.

We were trapped and all we could do was to wait for a chance to speak to Tiye, and to Ahmose if he could find the dwarfs.

But days went by, the great jubilee of all nations started, and still no one came to meet us.

74

SHUET'S WORDS

"The Mother of the King wishes to see you," Nefertiti said to Meryt-Neith as she arrived carrying yet another little glass jar of heavily scented oil on Nefertiti's instructions. She had fetched it from the room where the cosmetics were kept, the queen trusting Meryt-Neith more than her other women, who might return with the wrong item.

"Me?" Meryt-Neith was surprised. "I will see the Mother of the King as soon as you dismiss me."

The Mother of the King had arrived on her ship some weeks ago, but so far she had not paid any attention to Meryt-Neith. It was like being a child again, when Shuet was Tiye's favourite and Tiye had barely looked at Meryt-Neith.

There were wild rumours of something extraordinary happening on her ship, but Tiye spoke of it to no one. Her retinue was placed in houses around the city, and she brought only her most trusted servants into the North Palace. Meryt-Neith had heard that the house of the blood-drinker who had seduced her son had also been commandeered for this purpose. Foreign dignitaries had arrived from the north and had travelled with Tiye on her ships to Akhetaten to take part in the great celebration of all nations.

Nefertiti sat on a chair, and servant girls began to smooth the oil Meryt-Neith had brought into her skin.

The jubilee of all nations was to start the next day, and the Great Royal Wife and the eldest daughter Meritaten had been preparing for the event days. Meritaten would take on her role as the Great Royal Wife, and Nefertiti was to be presented to the foreign dignitaries as equal to her husband. In her new role, she could no longer carry the title Great Royal Wife. Nefertiti's hair had been shaved off carefully – she would be wearing her tall flat-topped blue crown during the event and no hair was to be seen underneath. Meryt-Neith had even seen Nefertiti fit the blue *khepresh*-crown on her head. It was the crown of the kings, and only the ruler of the country was supposed to wear it.

"You may go now," Nefertiti said. "I don't need you at this moment, but come back after your meeting."

Meryt-Neith bowed and headed for Tiye's rooms. The Mother of the King was also being beautified, but in her own rooms. Meryt-Neith was allowed access immediately.

She had expected to see Tiye receiving similar treatments as Nefertiti, but instead she found the Mother of the King sitting alone without a servant in sight.

"You asked to see me, Mother of the King. I am honoured and wish you life, prosperity and health!" Meryt-Neith bowed.

Tiye extended her hand, holding out a letter.

"Read this letter. Out loud. And then we need to talk."

Hesitantly, Meryt-Neith took the offered letter. It was written in an unknown hand.

"I am writing to you, greatly respected Mother of the King, to let you know of my mother's death," Meryt-Neith read the first part and looked at Tiye curiously.

"Continue." The old queen's voice was harsh.

"My beautiful mother Merit is now being prepared for everlasting life, to become True of Voice in front of the gods..."

Meryt-Neith's stared at the letter, horrified.

"Read on."

Meryt-Neith could not. She let out a scream that was like a howl, pressing her hand over her mouth and then fell to her knees, in the middle of a painted pond with ducks and papyrus plants.

"Mother! My mother!" she wailed, bending down so that her head touched the floor. "My mother!"

Tiye stood up, and picked up the letter from the floor.

"She was killed by a tall man, colourless like me. Taller than me. He is the father of Meryt-Neith's son Ramose. I was there when mother died and she told me he had said that Meryt-Neith knew what he was about to do."

"No!" Meryt-Neith lifted her head. Her face was streaked with the green malachite she had used to define her eyes, "No! I did not! But I do know the man my sister writes about. For the letter is from her. *Colourless like me.* I have not seen my sister since that very same man attacked us in Mi-Wer and forced us all to flee."

"Your mother said she never knew who the attackers were," Tiye said.

"She knew. That man... he seduced me. And I, foolishly, gave myself to him willingly. I did not see what he was. But he is Ramose's father and he has threatened me on several occasions after I left. Me, my mother, and my sister."

"What do you mean by not seeing what he was? What was he then? A demon?" Tiye asked.

At the last moment, Meryt-Neith understood she couldn't say yes. Because if she were to say the Pale Man was a demon, that would make Ramose a demon's son. She would do nothing that would endanger the life of her son.

"No. He is no demon. He is just a man, but not ordinary, no! He is cruel. He only wants power, and riches, and he will kill for them. I did not see that. Not until he came to our house to kill us all."

"Why would he want to kill you all?" Tiye asked.

"Mother had something he wanted. When he did not get it, he decided to take it by force. It was some old writing. A scroll. I don't know what was in it. But he was willing to kill for it!"

"And how did you all kill his three accomplices, then? I remember Mut-Bity requesting three large woven baskets and two soldiers to carry them away. Each of which held the body of a dead man. For if he is the same one who attacked and killed your mother, he didn't die all those years ago in Mi-Wer."

"Mut-Bity saved us," Meryt-Neith said, "she had seen him with me, and as a precaution had brought her bees inside. She... she ordered the bees to attack him."

"Mut-Bity... yes, the bees would do as she asks..." Tiye did not seem at all surprised by this. She took a step back. "Now, read the rest of the letter."

Meryt-Neith took the letter and read it out loud in a broken voice.

"When Mother is ready, we will take her to be buried in a tomb of her choosing. Mut-Bity and I will go with her, and never return to Kemet again. Now I must do my best to let our father know where she is buried so he may come to her, and speak her name again so that she will live for all eternity in the realm of the dead. I ask of you to let my sister know of what has happened. I do not wish to speak to her ever again. I wish the Mother of the King life, prosperity and health. Shuet."

She placed the letter on the floor and covered her face with her hands, leaning over and crying.

"My mother! He has killed my mother!"

"Are you saying you had nothing to do with this?" Tiye asked.

Meryt-Neith looked up.

"Nothing! How could I ever want to kill my own mother! *He* of course said that to turn my mother's heart away from me in her final moments. And my sister's, too. He has his revenge now for my not accepting his advances. He has now taken my family away from me, all but Ramose."

Tiye was quiet for a long time, and Meryt-Neith tried to stop her sobbing.

"Do you have wings?" she asked suddenly.

Meryt-Neith looked at her, mouth open in surprise. How could Tiye know of Nephilim wings? Had mother told her? Or Mut-Bity?

"No, I have no wings," Meryt-Neith answered. "Why would I have wings?"

"I met a relative of your mother's. She travelled with me on my ship from Mi-Wer. And she had wings."

Meryt-Neith did not understand.

"A relative? Who? With wings?"

"Yes. She arrived from a faraway country with... with her servants and officials. And she said Merit was a relative. If she had wings, then surely Merit had them too. And you."

"No... I have no wings..." Meryt-Neith did not know what to believe. "What did she look like? What was her name?"

"She looked a lot like you. Her hair is shorter but of the same colour. Her name is Dana."

"Dana... I have never heard of a relative called Dana..." Meryt-Neith said, "but then again, Mother told us she came from afar and lost her way, and got separated from our father... it was a big storm that made her... lose her way."

"Yes, your father. What do you know of him?"

"I... nothing, really. All I know is that they had only just been married and then they were separated. When I was a child, I thought he had abandoned us."

"No, he did not abandon you..." Tiye said.

Meryt-Neith looked at her. *What did she know?*

Tiye turned and walked back to her chair.

"I shall have to consider what to do with you. I need to make sure these accusations are not true. You know how important your mother was to me. For now, you are not to leave your rooms. You may go."

Meryt-Neith got to her feet, her ears still ringing with shock, wiping her face dry with her hands. She left the room and ran to her own rooms, drawing curious glances.

No one was there. She sat down on her bed heavily, trying to take in what had happened. The Pale Man had killed Mother – and accused her of conspiring with him to get it done! Poisoned her mother's mind against her in her final moments. That was beyond evil, beyond all his actions so far. And now, she had lost not only her mother, but also her sister – and Mut-Bity. Would Seshat and Iahmesu also leave her when they heard of this?

She got up, not being able to sit still in her agony. She noticed a figure standing outside the doorway. Tiye had sent a soldier – and Meryt-Neith could only think it was because the Mother of the King did not trust her and suspected Meryt-Neith might run away.

Did she really think Meryt-Neith was capable of murdering her own mother?

75

AN OLD FRIEND

Ambrogio observed the house from a distance. Almost immediately upon arriving in Akhetaten, he had become aware of the stories about the beautiful demon woman who ate animals alive. The house she had been living in had been empty until recently, and no one had seen her husband since she disappeared. Out of curiosity, Ambrogio had gone to see the house, guessing who had owned it.

The house was situated at the edge of the Northern suburb where bureaucrats lived, along with merchants and fishermen. It was close by the North Palace of Nefertiti.

And when he arrived, he smelled the team almost instantly. A stroke of luck, perhaps, but he would have found them soon enough by his own efforts.

Akhetaten was packed with people from all over Egypt as well as the surrounding countries, the crowds milling about on the streets providing the perfect cover for him to walk past the house numerous times a day. He walked along the broad road leading to the North Palace, and also surveyed the narrow lane separating the team's house from the next one. He circled the garden wall too. Every time he passed, he paid attention to the guards – who they were, how often they changed, and where they were stationed. His acute sense of hearing and smell told him the precise location of the team members as well as the guards.

There were so many exotic-looking people around that his golden skin did not draw much attention, especially when he kept his head covered all the time. He even saw a few Asian people and was probably taken for one himself.

The team did not budge from the house and the soldiers standing guard at the gate and on the roof made him cautious about entering. He would bide his time. If he possessed any quality, it was patience.

He didn't look for lodgings in the city but spent his nights in the desert where it was easy to catch animals to feed on. There were plenty of dogs about too, and the inhabitants of the workers' village, now occupied by the former tomb builders of Deir el-Medina, raised pigs. He stole two piglets, but stopped there. He needed to let his hunger grow again to sharpen his senses.

He was missing his shadow, but trusted the man would arrive before long. They had fallen into an established pattern for hunting, the shadow standing guard at a location, waiting; if the prey did not appear within a reasonable time, the shadow-man entered the buffer zone and spooled himself back to Ambrogio. Now that the physical connection had been severed, it could take his shadow longer to find him. Once the shadow-man arrived, it would be far easier to observe the activity of the house and make plans.

The tent area housing the foreign dignitaries near the North Palace had become a city of its own. Huge tents sheltered the kings and nobility of neighbouring countries, all heavily guarded by soldiers. Everyone was trying to impress everyone else, and so bright colours and gold glittered everywhere. Steady queues of people were trying to get an audience with the king, who now resided in the central palace, and crowds of city people gathered right along the roads leading to the palaces to watch them pass. Ships sailed in every day, bringing provisions and grass for the horses to feed on. Every available scrap of free space was rented to the foreigners in return for luxury goods and cloth.

Seven days after arriving in Akhetaten, Ambrogio was walking among the buildings of the southern part of the city, about half an hour's walk from the city centre.

He made his way along a big road running parallel to the Royal Road to see the house of the vizier Nakht. Arriving at a junction with a narrow lane, he saw a familiar-looking man appearing from the gateway to the next big house. Ambrogio stopped, recalling him the instant he saw him.

Thutmose, the sculptor whom everyone would know in the future as the creator of the beautiful head of Nefertiti – in modern times it would be the main attraction of the *Neues Museum* in Berlin and pictures of it would spread around the world. Ambrogio had seen many of Thutmose's works in museums – he was the official court sculptor of the king. *"The King's Favourite and Master of Works, the Sculptor Thutmose; The Praised One of the Perfect God, the Chief of Works, the Sculptor Thutmose."*

He and Ambrogio had sat together many a time, drinking wine in the buffer zone in ancient Greece. Ambrogio's skin had been burned from the spit of a Nephilim lord, but he had not yet become a vampire at that point. It was the legacy of the poison in the Nephilim spit that made his skin burn badly in the sun. He had been saved by a being whom he had taken to be Hades, the master of the realm of the dead, who had carried him off, away from the daylight world to the City of Immortals in the buffer zone. There was light there, but it seeped from everywhere and did not burn his skin.

Of course, the powerful and evil Nephilim lord who had saved him had not been a Greek god at all. He was Cain, who by that time had already spent centuries collecting mortal people for the city he had established in the buffer zone. How Thutmose had made his way there, Ambrogio didn't know. But the reason had no doubt been for his skills in sculpting – these were used to create the shadows that were attached to all the servants of the dark Nephilim. Ambrogio had learned that he had created Ambrogio's shadow as well.

Ambrogio walked among the hurrying crowds along the road, returning several times to look at the house complex behind its mudbrick wall. He left in the early evening, returning later when the street was empty, and climbed over the wall onto the sculptor's plot of land.

The sculptor was nearing the end of his career now – his face lined with age, his belly rounded with good living, his skin tanned by frequent trips to the quarries. Soon, he was expected to die. Out of curiosity, Ambrogio had read about his tomb. But he knew for a fact that the sculptor would never be buried there.

On one side of the gate, there was a house that was separate from that of the sculptor. There, Ambrogio found a place to hide himself up on the roof. The row of trees that had been planted as a screen hid him from view. On the other side of the gate was the house of Thutmose's family, a sizeable building two storeys high, with a raised and canopied doorway. Behind it would be the narrow house where his workshop was located. Perhaps he was working on the bust of Nefertiti there even now.

At the end of the house, secured inside the compound through its own protective wall, was the granary with four silos – a sign of the great number of dependents the sculptor fed. His family, his servants, his apprentices. And beyond that a stable – containing the horses that revealed how wealthy and successful a life the sculptor had created for himself. He had been very proud of his horses, telling Ambrogio many times how he, as a favourite of the king, had been given the horses as a gift. Sometimes, he had ridden in his chariot along with the nobles and their teams as they thundered along behind the chariots of the royal couple.

Behind the trees growing in the pits that had been dug for them, lay the courtyard where the largest stone statues were made. The Central City was filled with statues of the royal family, most of which were made here. Images of the royal family only, with not a single statue of a god or goddess among them. People were expected to worship the statues of the royal family as their gods in shrines and chapels, and the major temples, such as the Great Aten Temple, had several statues of Akhenaten and Nefertiti with offering tables in front of them.

Water was supplied to the house from a well, with a spiral staircase leading down to the water. It was securely sited inside the garden since water was a precious resource. The sculptor did not yet seem to have acquired one of the new water-lifting devices, a shaduf, so his servants must still be having to carry the water for the house and garden in jars all the way up the well steps. The workers had access to their own well close by their quarters at the other end of the yard.

The house on which Ambrogio had hidden himself belonged to Thutmose's son and family, Ambrogio presumed. Thutmose had talked about them often in the City of Immortals. To meet Thutmose, he was going to have to get over onto the roof of the main building.

People were still walking about, so moving like a shadow, Ambrogio slid from the roof he was on, hiding in the shadows of the trees that were deepening in the dusk. When the yard was finally empty, he sprinted across it to the stables, climbed easily onto its roof and from there jumped the distance onto the rooftop of the wedge-shaped workshop.

His movements were so fast that a young boy who was leaving the house of the workers saw the blur of movement from the corner of his eye and turned his head, but made nothing of it. He probably thought Ambrogio was just a large bird.

Windows gave light and air to Thutmose's house, high up in the ceiling of the main room. Ambrogio peered inside.

A feast was being prepared. The low tables were covered with delicate foods, and servants were hurrying about bringing more. Wine jars were placed next to all the tables. Oil lamps burned in niches in the wall as well as on the tabletops.

The lady of the house appeared, dressed in her finest and adorned with jewellery. Plenty of gold chains hung from her neck. She glanced around to make sure everything was in order. She appeared to be much younger than her husband, which wasn't unusual in times when women often died in childbirth and the widower soon took a new wife to take care of his household. This one was pregnant, too. Ambrogio could hear the pulse in her slightly rounded belly; it sounded like a horse galloping. Barely audible, but there. He observed the wife with mild curiosity, wondering whether she was the wife of Thutmose or perhaps his son. Thutmose had been very much in love with his wife, he had said as much to Ambrogio. He had mentioned a double coffin that he'd designed for them so they could be buried together. Whether he had done that or not, Ambrogio didn't know. But he understood the sculptor's desire to share eternity with his beloved wife. It was what Ambrogio wanted as well, with Selene.

The pregnant lady waved all but two of the servants from the room. Then, the sculptor appeared in the doorway, carrying something wrapped in linen. This. he placed on its own table next to the wall decorated with painted flowers and plants.

Ambrogio noticed two doorways – the smell of food was coming from one of them. He remembered that he'd read about one of these rooms being the one where Nefertiti's famous bust had been found.

Voices rose from the gate, audible inside the house. Ambrogio kept still – he would see who was coming soon enough. The lady of the house moved some oil lamps closer to a stone stela set at one end of the room. It revealed Akhenaten and Nefertiti worshipping the Aten. The household in turn worshipped them so they would speak on their behalf to the Aten. Two little statuettes were standing in front of the stela, the dwarf god Bes, protector of homes, and Taweret, the hippo goddess of childbirth. The sculptor's wife only spotted them when she moved the lamps to give better light to the stela. She quickly snatched them up and gave them to a servant who hurried out of the room just as the guests arrived.

The first person to enter the room was a soldier, his hand on his dagger. He scanned the room and then stepped aside from the doorway. Thutmose's wife bowed low.

For it was the Great Royal Wife Nefertiti who stepped into the room. She resembled her sculpted and painted image enough for Ambrogio to recognise her, even if she was much older-looking. Next to her was a girl in her teens. That would be one of her daughters, judging by the way she behaved. She walked one pace behind her mother, but her posture indicated to the room that she was a member of the royal household.

The sculptor Thutmose bowed his way into the room behind them and went over to the linen-covered item he had placed on the table.

"I am honoured that you visit my humble abode, oh Great Royal Wife – life, prosperity, health. And the eldest Daughter of the King, Meritaten, welcome."

Nefertiti nodded her head briefly to acknowledge she had heard him.

Thutmose's wife did not say a word, merely bowed and swept her hand in the direction of the chairs. Nefertiti and Meritaten sat down.

The sculptor walked to the table and lifted up the linen cloth. It was not the famous bust of Nefertiti, but one just as beautiful. Nefertiti looked at it for a while and then smiled.

"You have captured the likeness admirably," she said, turning to Meritaten, "hasn't he?"

Meritaten clapped her hands excitedly.

"Just like me!" she said. "Well done!"

Ambrogio saw the square stone extensions that revealed the head was to be attached to a body of stone later. Meritaten would have a full statue of herself, no doubt to celebrate her rising status as the new Great Royal Wife of her father.

The sculptor smiled and bowed again, confident of the success of his work. The lady of the house clapped her hands and servant girls approached with cups of wine.

Ambrogio observed the banquet from the window. Nefertiti and Meritaten had not brought many people with them, just a few guards and two young women who were probably the daughters of nobles, honoured to be put in the service of the Great Royal Wife.

The scent of perfume was too strong for Ambrogio's delicate senses and soon he withdrew from the window, returning to the garden and leaving the sculptor's house by climbing over the back wall.

He turned to walk away and froze at a familiar scent. No, two scents that he recognised, mingling into one. He pressed himself into the shadows and waited, listening. Thankfully he was downwind, so his scent was not being carried to one he wanted to avoid.

He couldn't see them, but kept completely still until he was certain he was alone. He then backed slowly off until the scent was faint enough for him to trust he had not been detected or followed. He turned and started running, away from the city, into the night.

He ran all the way to the worker's village where he had stolen the piglets. There, near the pigsty, he stopped. The smell of pigs would erase his own scent should someone start searching for him.

He cursed quietly. He needed his shadow, and he needed it now, to take him away from Akhetaten.

Angel had arrived.

76

ON THE ROOFTOP

The first morning of the celebrations came and we were still stuck inside the house. Elijah had not improved. He barely noticed our presence, spending most of the time sitting on the floor, leaning against the wall, his eyes dull. When he did walk about, it was as if he didn't see us, and he barely ate a thing. Daniel did not leave his side, forcing him to eat and drink when he could, and so we all just spent our time in the house.

The days passed slowly. Aemilius and Jason wrestled to keep in shape. The guards seemed to appreciate this show of force and watched them with interest. Lilith and Grandma exercised together, which was clearly an even more interesting sight to the guards in the garden. Mr. Donnelly and Reggie sat inside the house, their noses buried in scrolls. I had sent word to Tiye – Thomas had written it down for me – that Reggie had asked for scrolls with stories to be sent to us, so that we could spend our time translating and discussing them. I wasn't quite certain it was the proper thing to do, but clearly my message had got through and a scribe arrived at the gate with a servant carrying a large basket filled with papyri. He looked at us with round eyes and we had no doubt that rumours about the strange visitors to the demon lady's house would be circulating soon. Thankfully, we did look sort of normal, at least our skin did not have the odd golden hue of the other Nephilim and vampires.

"Those two would probably be happy if we were stuck here forever..." Diana shook her head. Through the open doorway that led into the garden, Reggie and Mr. Donnelly could be seen in deep debate over translating something, their heads almost touching. We were sitting on a bench by the wall, watching Jason and Aemilius trying to throw one another to the ground. Grandma and Lilith were taking a break and walking around the garden, deep in discussion.

“Do you know what those two got up to soon after we arrived?” Paris asked.

“Reggie and Mr. Donnelly? No, I don't," said Diana. "Go on, tell us."

“They couldn't bear the thought of being in one of the most famous cities of the ancient world without actually experiencing it for themselves. So they slipped out. It seems they had been watching the guards change, and noted that there were always a few moments while the old guards were talking to the new ones in the garden before they changed shift. For a short time, the gate to the street was left relatively unguarded. So out they went.”

“Really? Our scientists? Must have been Reggie’s idea,” Diana laughed.

“Actually, no. It was Mr. Donnelly’s.”

“He kept his rebellious streak quiet then!”

“No one noticed they'd gone until they were escorted back at spear point.”

“No! What had they done?” Diana asked.

“It appears they tried their language skills on a scribe, the street vendor kind, who writes letters for a fee. A sort of ancient free-lancer. They asked him what he was writing and he showed them.”

“Well that's not very threatening. Why the spears?” I asked.

“Our Mr. Donnelly forgot where he was – as much as that was possible – and to see better, put his spectacles on.”

“Oh no...” Diana rolled her eyes.

"The scribe looked up, saw the spectacles and screamed. I think it may have been something about a four-eyed demon. As there are soldiers everywhere, it wasn't long before his shouts caught their attention, and before our intrepid adventurers knew it, they were arrested. Mr. Donnelly had managed to slip his glasses into Reggie's hand, and Reggie hid them in the sash he used as a belt. Luckily, it was a broad piece of cloth and the spectacles are quite small, and so they did not find the glasses because they were hidden horizontally on his waist, under the sash."

"They did manage to speak enough Egyptian to say they were under the protection of Tiye. The soldiers escorted them all the way back and our guards confirmed they lived in this house."

"I take it Tiye did not take that too well?" I asked.

"Probably not. I'm not sure the guards ever told her what happened – might have been a bad career move for them. But from that day onwards, the guards have been watching us like hawks all the time, especially if we venture anywhere near the walls of the garden," Paris said.

Diana smiled and shivered.

"Are you feeling any better?" Paris asked Diana. "Has the fever gone down?"

"No, but I don't feel like I have a bug or something. I'm just feverish," Diana said.

Paris placed her hand on her forehead.

"True... are you sure you don't have some parasite or something like that? I've heard they can cause a persistent fever. Many parasites live in water, waiting for a host and you were in that silver lake for a long time."

"Perhaps, but oddly, if so, I don't feel any the worse for it. Besides, that was a place of healing. I don't think the water had parasites. Unless those silvery things could be described as such," Diana wrapped her hands around her knees. Paris and I glanced at each other, but said nothing.

Even before the sun was up, the scribe Ahmose arrived. He didn't wake us, though. He didn't need to. Daniel and I required very little sleep, Elijah had sat staring at the wall the whole night, and the others had rested enough during the long days of inactivity. There's only so much sleeping a person can use as a way of passing time.

"I can only spare a few moments," Ahmose hurried to say, "for we are all to go to witness the moment when the King and the Great Royal Wife greet the Aten as he rises. But I managed to get away to let you know – I think I have found your dwarfs!"

The atmosphere grew almost electric. Finally – finally a clue as to how we could finish our mission, to find the first clue to the path leading to the Creators.

"Tell us," Lilith hurried Ahmose who was still catching his breath – he'd hurried to get to us and was not used to running. Like all scribes, Ahmose didn't get much exercise, as his round belly and laboured breathing revealed.

"I am sorry I could not come to you sooner, but I was not permitted to leave the palace. The Mother of the King had given orders – I was Merit's friend, and she is afraid that anyone who was close to her is in danger. She seems to think that whoever killed Merit..."

Ahmose had to take a breath and close his eyes. Merit's death had been a blow to him as well.

"...that whoever killed Merit could be after her family and friends as well. Why this is, I do not know. But that is why you too, as her relatives, are kept here under guard."

"Yes, we understand," Diana said.

"We are all very sad at her death. But please, go on," Grandma was impatiently waiting to hear his news, "tell us about the dwarfs."

"Well, Nefertiti's sister Mutnofret has two dwarfs. Iahmesu and Seshat. And actually, they were Merit's friends too. When Mutnofret does not require their company, they are free to move around. And guess with whom they usually are?"

"No time for guessing, do tell us," Lilith said.

"Meryt-Neith."

We stared at him.

"As in... Merit's daughter Meryt-Neith?" Daniel asked.

"Yes. She is Nefertiti's servant. She was the wet-nurse of Meritaten and has stayed with the Great Royal Wife after that. She and her son Ramose."

"Elijah has a grandson?" Diana asked the obvious – after all if Meryt-Neith had been a wet-nurse, she must have had a child of her own first.

"Yes. His father is unknown to me. But Ramose is a handsome young man, tall and dark," Ahmose said.

"We need to tell Elijah... maybe this is just what he needs to give him the will to live again," Grandma said.

"I asked the dwarfs if they knew any other dwarfs with the strange names you gave... *King's Wives Life Forever* and *His Mother is Re*. They laughed and said that I was in the presence of the very same persons. Mutnofret had given them those names when she had arrived in the court as a child, around the time Nefertiti gave birth for the first time. No one remembered the names anymore, only the dwarfs themselves. And maybe Mutnofret herself."

"Thank you! How, then, can we approach them?" Reggie asked.

"You cannot leave the house, the Mother of the King has forbidden it for anyone else but Daniel and Elijah. And it seems even you are not leaving now," Ahmose looked at Daniel, "and even if you did, you could not get near them for days, not as long as the festivities continue. But I will try to find a way to get them to visit you," Ahmose went on, "and now, I must go. You might want to watch from the roof when the king and the Great Royal Wife leave the palace."

"That sounds like a good idea," Diana said. "I am bored stiff!"

She stretched to emphasise her words. She still looked thinner than before. The fever must be draining her energies. She would need to see a doctor as soon as we had returned to the future, which, we all hoped now, would be happening soon enough.

"I am going to force Elijah out of that room," Daniel said, walking off.

As we went up the steps up to the roof, the two guards there straightened their posture when we appeared. Anxious expressions crossed their faces when we went to the edge of the roof.

"Better take those pillows and sit down so they don't think we're planning on jumping down..." Grandma said.

We did just that, but it didn't cause the guards to relax. They stood slightly in front and to the side of us, staring intently at the rooftops of the other houses that were now full of people. Everyone was gazing at the North Palace looming through the dusk. There was still a steady flow of people walking along the main street towards the plain where the tent city of the foreigners stood.

The sound of steps on the stairs made us turn – Daniel was literally pushing Elijah onto the roof. It pained my heart to see the dull look in his eyes, as if his mind was locked away behind a grey wall, barely registering what was happening.

Our house was high enough and at an angle to the next house, so our line of sight wasn't blocked in any way, giving us an excellent view of the North Palace. But it wasn't the North Palace from which the royal couple came. The sun was rising when we saw the gates of the palace open. Inside, fires and lamps were burning – it was a scene straight from a movie. Then a line of soldiers filed out. They marched some way south from the gate and formed a corridor. Then from our right, the direction of the centre of the city where the Aten temples, the ceremonial Great Palace, the police and army barracks and the offices of the bureaucracy were situated, a big canopied sedan chair appeared. Before it, at its sides and behind it, hundreds of soldiers were marching. Two figures were sitting under the canopy, side by side.

That was when we saw Akhenaten and Nefertiti with our own eyes for the first time. They both wore heavy beaded collars and they were both wearing the blue war crown associated with kingship.

"She is equal to the king... she is indeed shown to be equal to him, a co-ruler. The crown proves it. Oh, to have a camera!" Reggie sighed.

"Or glasses..." Mr. Donnelly gave the two guards an almost hostile look. As long as they were present, he could not use his glasses.

"Or have better eyesight from birth..." Jason said, elbowing Daniel in the ribs.

Daniel, Elijah and I needed no binoculars – we could see clearly for a great distance and I stared at the royal couple as they were carried towards the plains between the city and the mountains that surrounded it. Even from this distance and despite the lack of light, I could make out their features. When they came closer, the others could see them clearly too. Nefertiti looked older than her beautiful bust in Berlin. I found it hard to believe I was actually seeing her with my own eyes. Elijah also took a step forward for a better view – a sign that he was showing interest in something at last.

"They are going to the desert altars," Reggie explained when the procession turned away from the main route leading through the ancient city.

The desert altars were to the southeast of the North Palace. The tent city of the foreign dignitaries was set up around it and they could now admire the king of Kemet performing the offering rites to his great god as the sun rose over the horizon. Festivities would take place there too, next to the altars.

"I wish we could go and take a look..." Reggie said.

"Best not," Grandma advised. "It's not just about keeping safe from our enemies. Remember, the great plague or cholera or whatever it is will start to spread from there."

But as it was, only Daniel could have left the house and he wouldn't move from his brother's side. So we sat on the roof, earning some interested glances from the people who spotted us from their own rooftops. They must have wondered who these people were that were so heavily guarded in a house that had belonged to a demon.

"Somehow I have a feeling I should try to look as ordinary as possible," I whispered to Grandma.

"No point. You couldn't look ordinary here no matter how hard you tried," she snorted. "And besides – it's better that they can see we have ordinary looking skin. We're all just odd foreigners, not demons."

"I wonder when we'll be able to meet the dwarfs... what were their real names again? Iahmesu and Seshat?" Paris said, sitting next to Jason who was holding her round the waist.

They were no longer bothering to hide the fact they were an item.

"Soon, let's hope. And hopefully they have the knowledge we need so we can get back home," Jason said. "I could do with a good hamburger for starters."

"And deodorant," Lilith sighed.

"And good shoes," Grandma said.

We were used to the sandals by now, but they were hard on feet that had habitually worn modern padded trainers. Not to mention the grains of sand and grit that were everywhere, causing abrasions. Inside the house, we soon learned to walk barefoot and only used our sandals when we walked on a sunbaked surface outside.

"Will you be leaving for your own time if you find what you came to find?" Thomas asked.

"Yes, if what we find does not require us to stay here any longer," Grandma said.

Thomas looked sad. No wonder – having fallen through time to ancient Deir el-Medina he had established a family here. He missed his own times, but to get back there, he would have to leave his own family behind. He had not asked, but we knew he was tempted to ask us take him with us.

"It is hard for someone from the past to get used to the future." Aemilius had guessed what Thomas was thinking. "I know from my experience. Everything has changed too much. Not just things – people too, the way they think. Your values may not be accepted anymore. You don't know about many daily things people talk about and may be ridiculed for it by those who don't know you come from the past. How everything works – the society, the technical things. You may end up in dangerous situations when you don't know what is dangerous. It can feel like a nightmare."

Thomas sighed.

"I know. It would be hard for my family to come with me, if I did want to leave. They don't even speak my language."

"You never taught them?" Aemilius asked.

Thomas shook his head.

"You have been here for so long that even if you managed to get back to your own time, you would miss your family," said Lilith.

"Also knowing what you know about life after your departure... it wouldn't be easy to live with the knowledge of future catastrophes," Grandma said, "the wars, the genocides, the illnesses... You might be tempted to try to change the future."

"I know, I know..." Thomas sighed, "so I think I will stay here, with my family, and die here. Maybe I will be able to send you a message through time, so that you can come to my tomb and speak my name so I will live forever in the afterlife."

He accompanied his sentence with a little joyless chuckle.

"Now that's a thought – to send us information about where you are buried in the past," Daniel said.

"How would you go about it?" I asked.

"I'd probably have to hack the information into stone surfaces wherever I could," Thomas said, "in the hope that some of it would make it through the millennia. It's how the Egyptians go about it, isn't it?"

He smiled sadly.

"How would you choose where to write?" Mr. Donnelly asked.

"I could try to remember which places would still be there in my future. And then go there, I suppose." The mournful note left Thomas's voice. "What an intriguing idea."

He, of course, did not know that this was exactly how the Time Walkers sent their emergency messages if they were trapped in time somewhere after losing their weaver. They wrote their name on a monument that still existed in the future – mentioning walking and a hint of the times they were trapped in.

The historians of the Time Walker Centre were constantly on the lookout for books and other information that suggested history had been changed. Mostly, ordinary people didn't notice when some historical detail had suddenly altered, it was as if their memories switched without them realising. Just sometimes, the consciousness of something not matching with an earlier memory sounded a faint alarm. The historians who worked at the Centre were the kind of people who noticed and remembered these changes, subtle though some of them were. It seemed the historians were capable of retaining a memory of how history was written prior to the change, and noted when some detail had altered since they last researched it. An old history book, for instance, sometimes printed decades earlier, suddenly had an extra sentence mentioning a detail that had been placed in time by a Time Walker team.

When our historians noted negative changes, they were frequently the result of the enemy Nephilim travelling into the past to kill and steal. It was the historians of the Magellan Centre's library in the buffer zone who directed the teams to certain times and places to prevent the enemy Nephilim from meddling with history – and to prevent them killing people who were important to the Centre. Our enemies often went hunting for those people, if they could learn their names and from which time they had been brought to work at the Centre. This is why anyone who had been taken from the past into the future kept their history close, only revealing their real name and location and time to those they could trust absolutely.

The enemy Nephilim also spied on Time Walkers to see who they approached in the past, to prevent them from getting new supporters.

"No one's going to let you into a temple if you go around chiselling your name amongst those of the gods, though. You could only really do it safely if the temples were abandoned," said Paris.

"Well, that would will certainly require some thought," Thomas smiled, seemingly cheered at the thought of having a plan.

For a few days now, I had been in a melancholy mood too. I'd been thinking about my parents a lot – and my cat Nugget.

"They probably think we are all dead," I said, voicing my thoughts. "We've been here for weeks already. The police must be looking for us."

"Well, not you at least," Grandma said, "you're accounted for. Before the shadow attack, I wrote about two dozen emails in your name telling your folks about all your studies and the trips you were making to different museums. Our techies added you into photos in front of some well-known museum pieces. And I scheduled the delivery of those emails so they have been going out at the rate of about one a week."

"But if my parents answer those emails?"

"Tinky has the password to an email I set up in your name. She promised to respond to them. The good thing is that she's staying with your parents of course, and hears all their concerns about you, so she knows what to write to lower their suspicions that anything's wrong."

"You really do think of everything..." I said, not knowing whether to feel relieved or slightly shocked.

We sat there, listening to the sounds coming from the plains behind the houses, near the desert altars. Shouting, ululating, chanting, horns blowing. Rows of soldiers marched in tight formation up the main road and onto the plains.

The sun rose higher in the sky. On the plains before the altars, the royal couple would be sitting, receiving the tributes of all the nations. Exotic animals, slaves, riches. The marching soldiers raised dust clouds that billowed over the rooftops.

"Do you think Nefertiti's been announced as co-ruler by now?" Diana asked Reggie.

"It's still a matter for discussion... she certainly had a very high role next to the king, so it is possible. There's the evidence of the crowns too, which we saw with our own eyes. But no one in our times is really certain," Reggie replied.

I put up my hand to shade my eyes from the sunlight, to get a better view of the tantalising glimpses of activity on the plains beyond the houses. Turning my head, I started to take in a panoramic view and then stopped abruptly. I felt like I was choking.

"Daniel..." I barely found the voice to whisper.

He heard me, though the others did not.

I pointed.

It didn't take him long to see what I was pointing at. In the middle of the crowd, a tall blonde figure was standing on the opposite side of the road, looking straight at us.

"Shit!" Diana saw her too.

Angel smiled in our direction. A little distance away stood Anna, her head bent, a heavy sack at her feet. And next to Angel stood a tall hooded man, who, from what we could see, was very pale. His height alone would have told us what he was, and the buzz in my spine confirmed it. Angel had found herself an evil Nephilim lord.

"Shit!" Diana repeated.

The rest of us just stared at them.

77

THE PALE LORD

After the bee sting, Angel had fled into the buffer zone. Her soft, glowing skin would temporarily take on the appearance of something that had been dead for some time. Beneath the grey colouring, the veins were clearly visible, like a black spiderweb under the surface of her skin. The dark patch spread quickly until it covered the side of her neck and cheek. Her left eye was pulsating oily yellow in the middle of what looked like a dark grey hole.

She let go of Anna's hand, fell down on her knees and threw up.

Anna stood there, horrified, unable to do anything. Her shadow stood beside her, showing signs of distraction. Maybe it that had something to do with the fact that it was Angel who had attached it to Anna, and through this connection it fed Angel information about Anna. The connection went both ways so it was now feeling some of the pain Angel was experiencing.

"Help me, you idiot!" Angel gasped.

"How, my lady? What caused this?"

"The bee sting... I am allergic to bees!"

Angel clasped her throat with both hands, pulling at the skin with her fingers until it bled. It seemed to have become so brittle that it couldn't be stretched without bleeding. Dark blood slowly trickled down, looking like black syrup. And all Anna could do was stand there, not daring to touch the dark Nephilim blood.

Suddenly, a figure appeared from the mists. It approached them quickly, revealing itself soon as the strangest looking Nephilim Anna had ever seen.

It was a man, but one without colour. His eyes were piercing oily yellow like Angel's and he was tall and muscular. Angel looked up at him and he looked back at her, tilting his head like a reptile, without showing any emotion. He spoke – a mesmerising sound that seemed to draw Anna towards it. The smell of rotting fruit was overwhelming. A dangerous Nephilim – and a high lord, if the hypnotising effect of his voice was anything to judge by.

He paid no attention to Anna. Instead he stared at Anna's shadow and now his expression was surprised. When he spoke. Anna didn't understand what he said, but Angel clearly did and answered him. Where had she learned to speak the ancient Egyptian language?

The man knelt down next to her, drew Angel's hands away from her neck to see better and asked something. Angel lifted her hand with one finger pointing up and said a word Anna recognized. *Bit*. It meant a bee. The man spoke calmly and helped Angel to her feet.

"Follow us," Angel's voice was hoarse. "I told him I was stung by a bee. He understood. Hopefully he can help me..."

The colourless Nephilim put his arm around Angel's waist and opened his wings.

How strange he looked – those pitch black wings on a totally colourless Nephilim. Even the veins were black, so Anna could not detect the blood pulsing there. They did not reflect light. The effect was that of black velvet in shadow.

They travelled in the buffer zone for what must have been an hour, Anna's shadow gripping her hand and dragging both her and the heavy sack along. At times, it looked over its shoulder and regarded Anna impatiently. She felt a tug in her solar plexus when the shadow did that, as if it was hurrying her along. There was a strange connection between them – Anna felt anger and even at times hate emanating from the shadow, mixed with loyalty and willingness to serve.

The Nephilim lord was too fast for them, and Anna soon lost sight of him and Angel. The shadow, however, seemed to know exactly where it was headed. When they came out of the buffer zone, they were in a cave in the desert.

Angel was sitting, leaning against the wall, her mouth open and saliva dripping onto her chest. Her throat seemed to be so constricted she could scarcely breathe. The pale Nephilim was standing next to her, not offering any help, just observing Angel fighting for her breath with his hands folded across his chest. There was mild curiosity in his eyes.

When Anna and her shadow appeared, the Nephilim lord turned to look at them. With one quick step, he came over to Anna, grabbing her by the arm. His hot touch burned her skin but she was too scared to protest. He looked into Anna's eyes and she froze like a mouse in front of a snake. Then, losing interest, he released her, turned to the shadow and seized it by the arm.

Angel whispered something and the Nephilim lord answered. He turned to Anna again and placed his hand on the back of her neck. Anna felt a strong tug in her solar plexus and the shadow twitched. He then turned to the shadow and with one strong movement pulled it as far from Anna as he could in the limited space of the little cave. The tug was so strong Anna almost fell onto the cave floor.

He laughed and said something again. Anna had studied the ancient Egyptian language along with the rest of the Time Walker team, but she found it hard to follow what was being said. The language was pronounced in a completely different way from what she had expected. But she thought she had taken in a little; as far as she could tell, the man seemed to be asking about the shadow, what it was and why it was created.

Angel answered, slowly. Her skin began to lose the grey colour and return to its pale glow. Her speech became faster. Anna caught a word here and there. The word Dana came up many times.

When the pale Nephilim answered, Angel looked at him sharply.

Anna thought she picked out the word *weba* –"servant" – and he also pointed at Angel. And then Angel clearly said the words "*Ambrogio webai*" – my servant Ambrogio.

Had this dark Nephilim met up with Ambrogio?

Angel was breathing much more easily now. She spoke to Anna.

"He has met with Ambrogio, who was chasing Dana as he was ordered to do. He lost track of her for a while, but two of this Nephilim lord's servants saw Dana on a ship and met with Ambrogio, too. Dana was not alone on the ship. From what I've just heard there are some familiar faces around here. Not just your team, but it seems Daniel and Elijah have made it as well."

Hope began to raise its head in Anna's mind, but she hid it quickly, so the shadow would not notice. It did feel something, though, as it looked at Anna sharply. Anna focussed on trying to understand what was being said, hoping if she concentrated hard enough, it would hide her emotions.

Daniel and Elijah were here. Maybe Lilith too. If they saw her – would they punish her for what she had done? Or was there still hope for her?

The pale Nephilim lord walked out and when he returned, he was carrying a gazelle that was still moving. He pulled the animal's head back and offered its neck to Angel. She smiled and bit deeply into the animal's flesh.

Anna watched colour return to Angel's skin as the animal died. The pale Nephilim was measuring her newly returned beauty with appreciation. Angel was used to being admired, and accepted it. If anything, her posture was now slightly flirtatious.

"Now we're leaving for Akhetaten," Angel said, "for Ambrogio will be there. And I have a few things to discuss with him... He might not be easy to find. He is like a stealth missile, fast and undetectable if he so wishes. But I intend to find him."

Her voice was sweet, but there was an icy undercurrent. Anna knew why. The only way Ambrogio could have been lost to them was if he had somehow cut the strings connecting him to Anna and Angel.

And that meant he was no longer following Angel's orders. Anna didn't have a clue why. Did Angel?

"You'd better eat something first." Angel pointed at the gazelle.

Anna looked at the lifeless animal and shook her head.

"I'm fine. I have a little bread left," she dug into a pouch hanging from her waist and took out a piece of hard bread. She had brought it with her from the future.

"Eat it fast, then, while I discuss the details with our helper," Angel said.

Anna broke off a piece of the bread and put it in her mouth. She forced herself to chew and swallow it, though her mouth was dry. The mesmerising hum of the Nephilim voices lulled her into a strange, thoughtless state.

"Enough rest, we're leaving now," Angel's voice said, forcing Anna back to reality.

Anna got to her feet and they stepped into the buffer zone.

78

SHADOW-MAN

Ambrogio had retreated to the harbour, as that was the least likely place Angel would look for him. They shared a deep dislike of water and neither spent time close by it if they could avoid it. Angel was still unaware that Ambrogio had already sensed her presence and was staying in hiding from her. In hiding from both Angel and Anna, in fact; he had smelled Anna even before Angel, thanks to the fact that apparently Angel didn't let her servant rest or wash. The weaver literally reeked.

Ambrogio suspected this was part of Angel's way of getting enjoyment through dominating Anna, forcing her to stay filthy and go without rest. It was a reflection of Angel's nature, this taking pleasure in the oppression of others, and one that Ambrogio had noticed in other Nephilim. It seemed particularly noticeable in Nephilim who had been transformed when still very young. And Angel had been very young, stolen from her mother by her biological father Cain. Ambrogio had been the one who had brought the girl to her father, and he had witnessed her change after the girl's mother had been torn to pieces for disobeying Cain.

How fierce Angel had been, how strong in her hatred towards those she had trusted to save her from that house of horrors in 18th

century Frankfurt. Cain had used that fierceness, that hate, to bring her up to be his first in command after Dana's father had escaped the destiny Cain had planned for him. His disappointment in his son, Dana's father, had sealed Angel's leading position in Cain's hierarchy for the future, a role she had filled perfectly. Almost. Ambrogio knew of her affection for Daniel, though Angel had no idea that Ambrogio was aware of it. Angel's feelings for Daniel went beyond pure lust and the desire to own and submit. No. Angel's emotions for Daniel had a tender aspect – emotions that should be alien to her as a leader of the Nephilim who opposed Daniel and his like. Emotions Cain would take as a sign of severe weakness; emotional weakness that he considered an offence deserving the death sentence.

The next night, the shadow-man finally returned to Ambrogio, bringing with him the two vampire sailors. The shadow stepped out of thin air in front of Ambrogio as he was sitting in an alley bordered by the mudbrick storage buildings that the merchants and fishermen of the north city used. No one disturbed him there – something about his unmoving presence made people uncomfortable and no one asked him about his business. He was used to it; the subconscious of ordinary people seemed to warn them of danger, steered them clear of his totally still form.

"You took a long time to show up," Ambrogio said to his shadow.

"I am sorry you are displeased," the shadow bowed submissively. "We waited; and when it was clear that the one you wanted was not coming through the passage we were guarding, we began to run to Akhetaten. We did not go to the buffer zone because if she had gone through there, there would not have been any scent to follow. Also, your children would have been seen if anyone was moving through there. They are still wild, and might have acted erratically. While we were running, I taught them to hunt."

Ambrogio looked at the two men. Their skin had lost the usual translucency of people who had recently been turned into a vampire. They seemed to have gained more muscle and looked very strong. His direct children did, mostly. Their children would not be so strong, though – if they produced any. First generation vampires created directly by dark Nephilim were the strongest of all, but after that, the potency of the vampire blood diminished quickly. The further down the family tree a vampire was created, the weaker it would be. Some were not much more than mere mortals who lived a few decades longer than ordinary people.

"My lady Angel has arrived. I caught scent of her yesterday, but she did not sense me," Ambrogio said. "I need to stay downwind of her. She must not find me! Take me to the other side of the river and then return to keep an eye on the house where the Time Walkers are. I will explain to you where it is. You might be able to spy on them from the buffer zone for me. Show Angel to these, my children, and ask them to follow her, find out what she is up to, and report to you. And you, in turn, will report to me."

"As you command, master." The man bowed.

The shadow-man's English skills had improved fast once he'd grown used to the man's body, which Ambrogio had given him. The strong accent had all but gone.

"We need to leave immediately. Tell these two to stay in hiding and not to hunt while you are away. It appears that the pale Nephilim lord's previous woman was not careful enough and was seen feeding on a dog. Now the city is filled with tales of the demon woman who ate animals alive. She disappeared and I have no doubt that she was killed by her Nephilim lord. He has a new girl round here somewhere, and she is not to see any of us either."

The shadow-man spoke to the vampires and they left, vanishing into the dusk, hiding in the long sleeves and head coverings they must have stolen from some village. Ambrogio's shadow then took his hand and they entered the buffer zone. When they came out of it, Akhetaten was far away on the other side of the river.

"Good. I'm going to find a hiding place here, and you keep your connection to me open so I can follow what is happening."

The shadow bowed.

Ambrogio, using the night for cover, walked past the last villages and into the desert. Angel's arrival meant a swift change of plan was needed. She'd be bound to encounter the Pale Man at some point, and that way, the Pale Man would learn about Ambrogio's deception. That meant Ambrogio was going to be dependent on his shadow to know what was happening in the team's house – he couldn't risk it himself. It was fortunate that the Pale Man had never seen Ambrogio's shadow, and Angel probably still believed that Ambrogio had destroyed it on her orders.

Now the pressure was on to seize Dana before Angel attacked her, because that was only a matter of time. He and the shadow who now occupied the body of a man had been together for so long that he could focus and connect to it easily. Not for the first time, he was grateful for his decision not to destroy his servant when Angel had ordered the massacre of all the shadows who had taken part in the attack on the Time Walker Centre.

And Angel had no idea he had managed to put his shadow inside a living human being. She wouldn't be on the lookout for an ordinary-looking peasant.

Ambrogio smiled. A cold, contented smile, knowing that for now, he still had the upper hand.

79

SHROUDS

After forty days in the salt that dried her body, my mother's limbs were still flexible enough for the embalmers to fold her arms across her chest, as I instructed them. That was a position reserved for kings, but they raised no objection to my orders.

I held back tears. My beautiful mother was one of the dead now and everything had been carried out to ensure her afterlife would be blissful. The scent of good oils and perfumes and resin arose from her form. They had not been able to remove the darkness the bees had caused to her skin when they killed her. Her long hair was washed and plaited as if it were the most expensive wig. Her internal organs had been dried and embalmed and were securely placed in their jars.

I still recognised her. She looked so serene. I tried to feel her, tried to see her in the way I had been able to see the dead in my youth, but grief was too close and my senses were blocked. Maybe I would never see the dead again.

The only thing I could be happy about was the fact that she had not been transformed. I had lost my mother, but she had made sure the Pale Man would never get the secret knowledge she had about the Watchers. I had it now. And I knew I would do exactly the same thing as my mother had done. If he ever caught me, I would kill myself. But I would take every precaution to avoid that happening. I had to make sure the secret for which my mother had given her life would be safe, and that my father in the distant future would receive the knowledge he needed to find mother and the secrets she guarded.

There was no writing on the very first layer of linen wrapped around my mother's body. After that, I used the linen she had made for herself. Taking each roll from the basket, one by one I gave them in the right order to the embalmers, beginning with the highest number and ending with the linen that was numbered one. They looked at what they thought were spells for the dead with curiosity. Those who could read, could not understand what any of the writing was about, and I just said they were in my mother's own language. They didn't question that.

When the linen marked with red numbers had all been used, I placed the scroll that my mother, true of voice, had made between her hands where they lay on her breast. The scroll was inside a wooden tube to make sure it wouldn't be crushed in the later layers of linen. This would be the letter she had written to my father, the Book of the Dead as it would be known in the future. There was another copy, with different writing that I had done, to be used in the way she had instructed me.

Then the other linen rolls that had been numbered in black were used – wrapped around her, again starting with the highest number and ending with the number one.

When the last of the linen with writing was in place, I found Mut-Bity waiting for me outside the embalming tent.

"Is all ready?" she asked.

"Nearly. There is one more thing I need to do. I must deliver a letter to Seshat and Iahmesu in Akhetaten."

"Surely you are not going there yourself! And what letter is that?"

"A letter to my father. Mother is sending him a message into the future so he may come and, by following her clues, find her body. And with that discovery he will find the knowledge of the path to the Watchers."

Mut-Bity nodded her head solemnly.

"Yes. Your mother told me something of her plan. But how is your father going to get that letter from Iahmesu and Seshat? He lives in the distant future so how will the message reach him?"

"I am to travel to a time and place my mother told me. And I will leave a

message there. She said my message would be written down for future generations, and that my father will be able to get it and find my letter as a result... I don't know if it's possible unless he should fall through time into the past like mother did. Or maybe he'll find her tomb in the future. But however it is to happen, mother was certain he would receive the message. And so I will do this. It was her dying wish."

"You said you will travel to a time and place... what do you mean?" Mut-Bity asked. "Do you mean as in... travelling through time somehow?"

"Yes. I have already done that. I will explain everything when we have time. Now I need to deliver my letter to Akhetaten and we have to leave after that."

"I will have someone take it there for you. The Pale Man will certainly attack you if you go there."

I considered this.

"That may be wise. I am surprised he has not come back yet to see Mother turn into one of his kind. After all, he has no reason to believe that won't happen."

"That surprises me too... maybe he doesn't know she is dead and is so certain of his victory, he's not going to bother," Mut-Bity said. "It's stupid of him, but the arrogance of the enemy Nephilim can make them behave like that. He may also be... occupied with your sister. Let's take the opportunity to leave this place right away, before he learns of Merit's death. Do you have your letter with you?"

"Yes."

I gave her the letter to my father that I had written in my tent.

"I'll have it delivered to Iahmesu and Seshat. Don't worry, it will arrive safely," Mut-Bity turned and left.

I do not know to whom she gave the letter. I was in a hurry to finish the preparations for the burial of my mother.

Her wrapped body was placed in a simple wooden coffin, and carried to the harbour at the sun's last light. The women who had known her and loved her in Mi-Wer followed us, wailing and beating their breasts, throwing dust and ashes on their hair.

A boat was waiting for us – not a fisherman's boat but a bigger one.

Mother's coffin was placed on it and covered with a heavy cloth embroidered with red and green – a gift from the Mother of the King.

We stepped onto the deck of the boat as well, and Mut-Bity spoke to the crew. They turned the ship onto the river and then towards the great lake. Slowly, Mi-Wer sunk from our sight in the diminishing daylight as we began our journey. When the city was no longer visible, I turned my back on it and faced the west. The crew of the little ship sailed using the stars as their guide, unafraid of the night.

I would never return to Mi-Wer again.

80

NOT AS PLANNED

Meryt-Neith walked to the store where the perfumes and cosmetics of the royal women were kept in niches. Beside her, the wall paintings of waterfowl and plants looked so real that the marsh seemed to move with life. Under her feet, the rippling lines on the painted floor represented the river teeming with fish and birds. White birds in flight decorated the yellow walls, with papyrus and lotus and horizontal friezes of water beautifying the scene further.

Everyone else was at the festivities, but Tiye had given orders that Meryt-Neith was to stay inside the palace, even if she was no longer required to stay in her own rooms. With nothing else to do, she had come here, to make an inventory, to see what needed to be restocked. So much of the cosmetics stored had been used in preparation of the great jubilee. She didn't have her bees with her, as they didn't like the strong scent of perfumes.

She was alone in the room when he appeared. The strong buzz in her spine alerted her so that she had just enough time to step outside into the garden where gardeners were working.

He wasn't alone. He had with him the most beautiful Nephilim woman. Tall, with blonde hair rippling to below her waist. Meryt-Neith recognised her immediately as the one who had been standing outside the gate and been chased away by the bees. The combined scent of rotting fruit given off by the two of them was almost too much to bear. They remained standing inside the room, looking out.

"Greetings," the Pale Man said, amused, "are you alone?"

"No. There are others about," Meryt-Neith replied, as calmly as she could.

"I brought someone to see you. Someone who knew your father."

Nothing could have surprised Meryt-Neith more.

"My... father?"

"Yes," the beautiful Nephilim woman said. "You see, I am to marry his brother. I heard that your mother... disappeared in the past, and gave birth to you here. I never saw her, so I can't say if you look like her, but you certainly have a resemblance to your father."

"Where... where did you meet him?" Meryt-Neith asked.

She did not dare to step any closer. How could this dangerous Nephilim beauty be marrying her father's brother? Was the brother transformed? Had her own father also become evil?

"I met him in northern lands. Far away," the woman was measuring her with her eyes, "but he is closer now. And I believe I shall take you with me to meet him."

Meryt-Neith stepped backwards. She was not going anywhere with any malevolent Nephilim.

"I will not come with you."

"Oh, but you will. We have your son, you see. And you wouldn't wish him to come to any harm, now would you?" she said.

Ramose? They had Ramose? Meryt-Neith realised she had not seen Ramose for many hours.

They were clearly on excellent terms with each other, the Pale Man and this beauty. Perhaps they were lovers?

"I don't believe you," Meryt-Neith said.

It was the Pale Man who replied. "You should. Shall we show him to you? He was easy enough to approach – being drunk makes young men rather susceptible to beauty. So I ordered my servant, a lovely young woman, to approach him. Despite him being suspicious of pretty young ladies with golden skin now, she did manage to lure him to an alley where my two Nephilim servants waited. They captured him and took him to my new house where he is now my prisoner. Your mother will join us there soon too. It will be quite a family reunion..."

"What do you mean? She can't join you!" Meryt-Neith spat.

"Didn't I tell you?" the Pale Man smiled. "I went to meet her. I intercepted your letter to her, added a few words and lured her out of hiding. She came to Mi-Wer, where I was waiting for her. Oh, she fought me bravely enough, but I lost count of the times I bit her. She'll be one of us in a few weeks. And if only you – "

To his surprise, Meryt-Neith started laughing and crying at the same time.

"So you don't know?" she said

"Know what?" The Pale Man, confused by her reaction, stepped out of the room and into the garden without caring who saw him.

"She killed herself after you left. Shuet wrote to the King's Mother. And now I understand why she suspected I had something to do with it. It was those words you added to my letter!"

"Killed herself?" he yelled.

The gardeners stopped working and turned to look at them.

"Yes. Did you expect her just to wait until she became one of you? And by now, she has been prepared for death and – is already buried, if I have calculated the time of her death, and the time needed to prepare her body correctly," Meryt-Neith said. "So you see – whatever you wished to learn from her is now forever out of your reach. I never saw the scroll you wanted me to steal so badly, so I have no idea what's written in it. And my mother has now taken the secret with her beyond this life, so you'll never know what it was."

The Pale Man stepped closer, his face twisted with rage.

"You are going to regret this!" he hissed.

"Me? Why should I regret your sloppy work? If you intended to turn her to the ways of darkness, you shouldn't have left her alone to kill herself. Shuet was there when she died, she helped her to die! And now Shuet is the one who has buried her. Having done so, she is now my mother's true heir, the owner of whatever mother left behind."

He moved so fast Meryt-Neith barely had time to twitch before he had her by the arm. His mouth opened twice as wide as normal and Meryt-Neith knew with certainty he would bite her now.

Then his beautiful companion was there too, pushing him and Meryt-Neith apart.

"No! Not yet. We need her. We need her to be unharmed for now, so that we may force her father and my husband-to-be to do as we want. After that, she is all yours."

From the corner of her eye, Meryt-Neith saw two servants who had walked into the garden freezing at the sight of the mighty Nephilim lord attacking the Great Royal Wife's lady.

But before they could call the guards, all three vanished into thin air.

81

BACK TO AKHETATEN

"You are certain of this?" Ambrogio asked.

"Yes, my lord. Your lady Angel is now together with the Pale Man," the shadow-man confirmed. "I waited for them near the house and they walked right up to it and showed themselves to the ones you are hunting."

"This means they have something planned... something that does not require them to attack without warning..."

Ambrogio sat still for a while. Events were moving even faster than he'd thought they would.

"Did you hear them speak?"

"I went as close as I could in the throng. I stood near them. They spoke the ancient language..."

"Angel did? She knew how to speak Egyptian?"

"Yes, my lord. And the weaver, Anna, was there too."

"What did they talk about?"

"Angel seemed be talking about their plan. *Now that we have her, we will get them out of the house*. That is what she said. Then she seemed to sense something and turned to look back, but I was standing among townspeople and looked the other way, so she would not pay attention to me."

"Good. She has no idea you are my shadow. But it seems now that I must come back to Akhetaten. I need to hide as closely as I can get to them – and you must be ready to take me inside the house using the buffer zone when I tell you."

The shadow extended his arm and Ambrogio took it. When they came out of the buffer zone, they were in an alley. Ambrogio had walked here so many times, he knew they were only a few houses away from the house in which the team were lodged.

"Take me to a roof where I can see their dwelling. And then, go back to the buffer zone and observe the room that Dana is in. Make sure you aren't seen. Stay far enough away so they can't sense your presence. And if you feel Angel and the Pale Man approaching, make yourself scarce until you are sure they have passed. After they step out of the buffer zone, they won't be expecting anyone to be there. Angel has no idea a shadow is about and she won't be expecting any in this time and place. The team's weaver and the Nephilim will be in the physical, in that house. They won't be trying to sense anyone in the buffer zone. That is when you are to go closer and listen carefully to what is being said."

They retreated to the buffer zone and from there, found an empty rooftop from which Ambrogio could watch. There were big baskets behind which he could hide if anyone came up to enjoy the cooling breeze.

He didn't need to wait long.

"Already?" Ambrogio asked.

"Yes, my lord. They are approaching. They are not alone. They have a Nephilim woman with them. And she is not one of their kind."

"So it begins…" Ambrogio said. "Take me to the buffer zone so I may observe. And then bring my two children to me."

Ambrogio knew they were close because he could smell them. First, unmistakeably, Anna. And then Angel and the Pale Man. And another scent which had to be the Nephilim woman – the cinnamon undertone was clearly there. Unchanged, then. He knew Angel's sense of smell to be acute, but trusted that Anna's sweat was too pungent for her to pick up Ambrogio's own almost non-existent scent.

He didn't catch a glimpse of them, his shadow was too experienced to let them to be seen. Then the feeling in the buffer zone changed, the sense of electricity vanished and the scent of the three began to fade.

They had stepped out of the buffer zone into the house of the team.

82

FATHER AND DAUGHTER

They stepped out of the buffer zone straight into our midst.

"Greetings," Angel said sweetly as we jumped to our feet.

Daniel was in front of me in a second. His wings shot open to form a wall between me and Angel. Even Elijah moved now, stepping closer, but beside the arrivals, not facing them.

Another form was standing next to Angel. A tall, colourless man, who was clearly a Nephilim lord. He stared at me and said something in ancient Egyptian.

"My lord here says that you are indeed as beautiful as he expected. Meet your future husband, Dana dear. He is going to take you as his wife," Angel said briskly to me as if Daniel was not even there, "which, I am sure, is the best outcome for all parties with an interest in the matter."

"That's not going to happen," Daniel's voice was cracking with anger.

"Oh, but he will have what he desires, Daniel. You see, we have someone Elijah will certainly want to meet. And if you don't do as I say, well..."

She pointed at the hooded figure standing with them, whose hands were tied, and whose features couldn't be seen because of the fabric pulled over her face.

I guessed it almost right away.

"May I introduce your daughter Meryt-Neith to you, Elijah?" said Angel in the same sweet tone.

Elijah's whole body started into life. He looked with disbelief when Angel pulled the cloth away to reveal the face of the Nephilim woman.

She was lovely. Her long blonde hair was darker than Angel's, her eyes were piercingly blue in her tanned face. She didn't look at Elijah, though, not until Angel said something in ancient Egyptian. Then her expression changed and she turned to look at Elijah, eyes round.

Elijah blinked, and moved towards her.

"She resembles Merit, does she not?" Angel asked.

Elijah stopped.

"Good. Not a step closer. We will exchange her for Dana."

"You can forget that, Angel," Lilith said.

Angel turned to look at her, her eyes measuring Lilith from head to toe with contempt.

"You will do this. Because you see – we also have her son. Elijah's grandson, Ramose. You wouldn't want anything to happen to them, now would you?"

Someone moved at the back of the room. Anna. And next to her stood… a shadow. A real shadow attached to Anna. It was looking at us without fear. Its features resembled those of Anna, but it had a canine snout and hind legs. It turned its head, regarding all of us, its dark eyes angry and alert.

Anna was looking at Grandma and tears were streaming down her cheeks. She looked exhausted, depressed, and scared.

Grandma reached out and touched her hand, whispering something. I noticed Anna's hands were covered in red blotches.

"Take your hands off my servant," Angel said, "she is my property now."

"How did you convince her to serve you?" Jason asked.

"That was so easy. You mortals should never fall in love. Once you do, it's only a question of kidnapping the significant other and you will do anything we want," Angel said. "That's just what we did. Then we turned Anna's husband into a vampire. Anna serves us without hesitation now, because I have promised to make her one as well, so they can be together again for all eternity... or however long they happen to survive. Sweet, isn't it? So Anna, don't be showing your former colleagues any empathy or I may have to reconsider our agreement."

Anna bent her head and stepped away from Grandma. She didn't raise her eyes again, just stood there like a beaten dog. Her shadow seemed to gain power as she slumped, until it was standing as upright on its hind legs as it could.

"Now. I don't expect you,to be able to make a decision right away. So I'll give you until tomorrow. We'll come back then to make the exchange."

The Pale Man had not turned his eyes away from me all this time – his arrogance made it clear he didn't consider Daniel a threat. His eyes under their heavy lids travelled up and down my body and a cold smile spread across his face. Suddenly, I felt very afraid. I had not seen such evil in anyone's eyes ever before.

I remembered the bees and wondered where they were. Surely they should have attacked Angel and the Pale Man by now? We had been carrying a beehive with us on board ship, the kind of bees that were supposed to attack the dark Nephilim. The hive was in the garden, much to the annoyance of our guards.

Then Angel, the Nephilim lord, Meryt-Neith and Anna, with her shadow, were gone. Lilith lifted her hand to quiet anyone who was planning to speak, because it was clear that's what we all wanted to do at once.

"We have just one day to plan. We need to use every second of it. Daniel, go and check that they really have gone."

Daniel stepped into the buffer zone and returned.

"No sign of them."

"Jason, connect to Paris – Daniel, take Jason to the buffer zone. Jason will alert us if anyone is trying to eavesdrop."

Paris crossed over to Jason and concentrated. She wove strings from the palms of her hands and though her fingers. She then tied them round Jason's wrist. Daniel took Jason's hand and the two of them disappeared into the buffer zone. The strings extending from Paris's hands vanished from sight in midair, but remained taut, telling us Jason was still nearby. Soon Daniel returned, alone.

"Now, if anyone has any ideas..."

A voice from the street gate interrupted us. The guard there was talking to someone and a familiar voice answered him.

Ahmose the scribe was back.

"Go and say they can be let in," Lilith said to Thomas who still seemed shocked at the sight of all those Nephilim and the shadow.

"Yes, yes..." Thomas hurried away as fast as he could, leaning on his cane.

"I'd better hide, so they don't see the strings," Paris said, moving into the next room, out of sight. The strings followed her hands, passed through the wall and vanished from sight along with her.

Thomas returned quickly, with Ahmose and two short figures.

"Here are Seshat and Iahmesu," Ahmose introduced his companions.

The dwarfs, a man and a woman who had already passed their youth, bowed low on their bent legs. Their sunbaked faces looked at us curiously.

"Life, prosperity, health," the man said and this time Thomas translated, "I am Iahmesu. Or *His Mother is Re*, as Mutnofret named me when she was still a child."

"And I am Seshat – or *King's Wives Live Forever,*" the woman said.

"We are very happy to see you. We have been told you carry a message from Merit for us," Lilith said.

The dwarfs looked at each other.

"You are Merit's relatives?" Iahmesu asked.

"We are," Daniel said.

"Are you aware that... that she has died?" Iahmesu asked.

"We are. This is Merit's husband Elijah," I said. "He is heartbroken. And he received a message saying that you have a letter from Merit to him."

The dwarfs looked at each other and then at Ahmose who nodded his head reassuringly.

"They are... of similar kind as Merit," he said and Thomas kept on translating their discussion.

"We need you to prove it," Seshat said suddenly, "for there are those who wish harm to Merit's family and friends. We are not to trust anyone without proof."

"We understand," Daniel said.

The curtain to the garden was closed again, and we stood side by side, Daniel, Elijah and myself, and opened our wings.

The dwarfs showed no fear. They merely observed our wings and then Iahmesu lifted his hand.

"That is enough, we believe you. Also you do not have the smell or the eyes of the evil Nephilim."

We closed our wings.

"Do you know Merit's daughter lives here, too?" Seshat asked.

"We have just seen her. Two enemy Nephilim came here with her," Grandma said.

"What?" Iahmesu looked utterly surprised when he heard Thomas's translation. "Who? Don't tell us it was a tall, colourless Nephilim lord!"

"It was," Daniel said, "the very same. And a Nephilim lady who wishes to kill Lady Dana."

He pointed at me.

"Yes, of course. You have silver in your wings. The Pale man wants all silver Nephilim dead. Shuet, her husband, their son, you..." Iahmesu said.

"Shuet? She is a silver Nephilim?" I asked.

"She is."

"And she has a son who is a silver Nephilim too?"

"Yes, Khonsu," Iahmesu said.

"So you or Merit – or both – carried the silver gene!" Lilith said to Elijah. "Dana is not the only one!"

Elijah finally said something.

"Is... Meryt-Neith a silver Nephilim too?"

“Not that we know of… her wings never opened. Not after she…” Seshat began and then closed her mouth.

“What is it?” Elijah demanded. “Tell us! She is my daughter, I have a right to know.”

He looked at both Seshat and Thomas. Seshat took a deep breath.

“She suspected she was damaged somehow, hence why her wings would not open. Not after she…”

She hesitated and then continued.

“You see, the Pale Man, the one you just saw, is the father of her son Ramose. She was very young and did not know what he was, and he seduced her and she became pregnant.”

The following silence lasted for several minutes.

“My grandson’s father is a lord of the dark Nephilim?” Elijah asked. “How... no, he can't be!”

“Yes. But your grandson is not evil. Nor is Meryt-Neith. But you're saying they brought her with them to meet you?”

“Yes, to exchange her for Dana. And they're threatening Ramose too, unless we agree to their demands. They'll be back tomorrow, they said,” Daniel said.

“I need to sit down,” Seshat said. “How did he get her? Did the bees not protect her?”

“And where were our bees?” I asked. “They should have attacked the Pale Man and Angel as soon as they appeared here!”

“You have bees here?” Iahmesu asked.

“Yes, the kind that should attack dark Nephilim. We brought them with us from Mi-Wer on our ship,” Lilith said.

“Yes, I took care of the bees on the journey,” the scribe Ahmose said. “I learned how it is done while we lived in Mi-Wer.”

“I’ll go check on the bees,” Aemilius said.

“I'll come with you,” Iahmesu said. “I know how to handle them.”

They went into the garden together only to return a few moments later.

“Dead,” Aemilius said. “Someone had poured some kind of foul-smelling oil into the beehives and the bees are dead.”

“But who?” Reggie asked.

"Anna. She had red blotches all over her hands. She is not a vampire – yet – and so the bees don't see her as a threat. Or, rather they are not sure what she is. She was the only one who could approach the beehives and be stung without being killed. At least, she could have done if she was fast enough, before the bees reacted to the shadow attached to her."

"They must have done the same in the palace as well," Iahmesu said, "or else they couldn't have reached Meryt-Neith. How were her eyes? Were they still blue?"

"They were," Grandma said. "She has not been changed yet."

"And they will return tomorrow… Seshat, did Ramose tell you where he was going?" asked Iahmesu.

"No, he just said he would probably not be home tonight. He went out with some other young men, celebrating."

"We need to find him – maybe the Pale Man lied about having him. We need to be sure, and find him if he is still free. I have short legs, and don't move fast. But Ahmose, could you go with either one of them," – a nod towards Daniel and Elijah – "and search the places where people are eating and drinking tonight. Ask if anyone has seen Ramose and take him to safety if he is there."

"Of course," Ahmose said, "but before we leave, did you not have a letter for Elijah?"

"Yes, we do," Seshat reached for the pouch on her hip. "It arrived this morning, after we had already left for the jubilee of all nations. The messenger caught us just before we were about to leave with Mutnofret. We're still on that same journey, so we have not been to the palace yet. That's why we had not heard of Meryt-Neith's disappearance either."

Indeed, the clothes of the dwarfs were magnificently embroidered and they had gold jewellery around their necks and arms.

The folded papyrus appeared in the light of the oil lamps.

"There is writing in Merit's own language here," Seshat said.

Elijah moved closer and gently took the letter from her hands. He opened it and began to read. We watched him in silence.

After all the dangers, we had finally reached our destination, and received the letter that was to tell us where the path to the Watchers would start.

When Elijah finished reading he closed his eyes and finally his tears began to fall. He began to sob, pressing his hands over his eyes. Daniel wrapped his arms around his brother and held him.

"This came with the letter," Seshat said and offered yet another piece of papyrus, this time a small scroll, "for Elijah."

"May I have a look at it?" Lilith asked when Elijah showed no signs of taking the scroll.

"Yes," Elijah said. His voice was choking.

We stood still while Lilith opened the scroll that contained the first clue on how to reach the Watchers.

83

OUR ENEMY'S ENEMY

We sat up all night planning.

"We've now achieved the original purpose of our mission," Jason said. "The safest thing to do would be to get back to the future now, before they come back. We have the clue; and we have the anchors to the future we brought with us when we left too soon. Modern things."

I looked at the small piece of papyrus Elijah was holding together with the letter. Merit hadn't written what was on the smaller piece – that was from their daughter Shuet. The first clue to the path of Watchers was written on that separate piece of papyrus according to Merit's instructions, but just as I had been reaching for it, Grandma had stopped me.

"I am sorry to say this, dear, but if the worst comes to the worst, it's best you don't have the knowledge about where the path starts," she said.

If the worst came to the worst... she meant that my blood would reveal what I knew to the enemy Nephilim. But Grandmother was right. That was how it had to be. I had just caught a glimpse of a picture painted in ancient Egyptian style, and text that appeared to be in English.

"And I brought things from the Magellan Centre with me," Lilith said, "things I had picked out of the rubble. So we have items that should take us directly to the Centre."

"But if we leave, what about Elijah's daughter and grandson?" Grandma said.

"I'm sure that is exactly why Angel followed us here in the first place," Daniel said. "She must have heard from Anna that Merit had given birth to Elijah's child or children, and known immediately how to get the upper hand, if only she could get to them before we did."

"Of course. But now we need to plan how to save their lives, and Dana's too," Aemilius said, adding in typical warrior style, "I say we ambush them. Attack them with weapons when they're off-guard."

"Come on Aemilius, I know you're a fighter, but how would you ever ambush a high Nephilim lord, not to mention Angel? With unimaginable luck, you might succeed in surprising one, but not the two together," Jason said. "Besides, we don't know where they are located here in the city, or even whether they're still here at all. So the only place we could ambush them is in the buffer zone, when they come back. And they would sense us from a long way off. To ambush them, we need to find them here, in the physical world. Any suggestions on how to do that? We haven't left the house, we don't know the lie of the city, and there are tens of thousands of people here. There's no clear street structure in residential areas, just houses crammed in wherever there's space. Not to mention the tent city and all those foreigners..."

"Perhaps I might be of assistance."

The voice coming from the garden froze my blood.

Daniel shot out of the room, followed by Grandma, Jason and Aemilius.

Ambrogio was standing under a tree. How he had arrived unnoticed, nobody knew. And how long he had been standing there was anyone's guess.

He raised his hands in the air in a gesture of surrender.

"Before you attack, I have to tell you I am not alone," he said quietly. “Also if you attack me, I will be forced to leave and you may never have your chance to ambush your enemies.”

Grandma grabbed Daniel’s arm.

“Wait.”

Daniel wanted to attack Ambrogio – hundreds of years of hostility electrified the air between them. He had killed so many of Daniel’s Time Walkers. He had stolen me, with the intention of killing me.

“Why on earth would you help us? When all you want is to get Dana?” Grandma asked, not letting go of Daniel’s arm.

Ambrogio tilted his head in agreement.

“That is so. But I have no desire for Angel to get Dana, just so she can kill her. For that is all that Angel wants. Nor do I want the Pale Lord to force Dana to become his wife, which might make it impossible for me to reach her anymore. No. For the time being – I suggest we join forces to stop this from happening. From then on – you'd be wise not to trust me. But for now, I may be your only chance.”

“Forces? What forces do you have?”

“His shadow, no doubt,” I said, “ready to drag him away to the buffer zone if we try to attack him.”

Ambrogio turned his eyes on to me and acknowledged my words with a nod. Again, the cold emptiness of death looked straight into my soul. But now I was certain I felt something else… that same elusive something I had sensed in him earlier. Before I could analyse the sensation any further, though, he looked back at Daniel.

“Indeed, I have my shadow-man. But now there are two others as well, servants neither the Pale Man nor Angel know about. Step out, so we can see you,” he said quietly.

The shadow-man stepped out of the buffer zone, and with him were two muscular men.

“Vampires!” Aemilius hissed. “Give me my sword so I can destroy those abominations.”

“That they are. Vampires. Maybe even abominations. But they are my creations. I created them so I could find Dana,” Ambrogio said. “I am their sire, and they are my offspring, and they do as I order them. They move quietly and unseen. And they have spent time learning the layout of this city. If anyone can find Angel, they can, together with my shadow."

The shadow-man showed no emotions, just observed us with his strange smoky eyes. I wondered whether there was anything left of the original owner of the body, imprisoned by the shadow's essence and Ambrogio's blood.

"How have you managed to put a shadow inside a man?" Lilith asked. "I can see he is not attached to you. That's never been known – until now."

"He is not attached to my body. And if you believe I would give away any of my hard-won knowledge or skill – think again."

Seshat and Iahmesu had not left us and they stepped forward now. They looked at Ambrogio and it was plain that they knew what he was.

"Now, are you ready to hear my plan? If you do not agree with it, then say so and I'll leave and will hunt for Dana on my own after they have taken her. It will be difficult and I may not be there in time before the Pale Man does what he wishes with her... he will make sure they are surrounded by his own forces and I can't destroy them all. So once they have her, he *will* do as he pleases. I know this. I have walked this ancient ground with him for weeks. If he wants something... or someone, he doesn't ask for permission."

I stole a quick glance at Daniel who reached back to take my hand and squeezed it. Daniel would never let that happen.

"Speak," Daniel said. "We'll listen."

"Thank you. Shall we go indoors? Not the shadow and my children, they can go back to the buffer zone before the guards start paying us any attention."

We made way for Ambrogio to walk past us into the house. When he passed Mr. Donnelly, he nodded his head.

"Mr. Donnelly," he said, acknowledging his presence.

Somehow, that sign of Victorian civility was creepier than anything he had said before.

. . .

Angel arrived the next evening, stepping out of the buffer zone and into our midst.

"Charming, you are burning incense," she smiled, seeing us, "a rather strong smell, but delightful in its own way. How nice to see you're settling in as locals. Now, have you finished your considerations?"

"We have," Lilith said, "and we'll agree to the exchange – with one condition."

"You are in no position to state terms," Angel said.

"But we are. You see, we can go back home whenever we wish, and leave Meryt-Neith and her son here. Nothing forces us to save them. Elijah doesn't have the same emotional attachment to them as he had to their mother."

Angel sensed something was not quite as she had planned. She observed us through narrowed eyes. She didn't know we had found what we had come for, but I could almost hear her mind puzzling over why the team would be so willing to give me away. Her eyes moved around the room until they came to me. Yes, she had to suspect that I was no longer needed for our task. Her eyes flicked ever so slightly to my throat. She was already planning on drinking my blood and learning from it what we knew.

I couldn't help it: I swallowed, nervously. Angel's eyebrow rose slightly and the corner of her mouth lifted in amusement.

"Our condition is that the exchange takes place in an open space, in full daylight. And we must all be present," Lilith continued.

"Oh no. Dana's going with me now."

"Take her with you now and leave us with no certainty of ever seeing Meryt-Neith or Ramose? You must take us for fools," Daniel said.

"Daniel, darling... none of this would be necessary if you would just admit we are betrothed. I would have no need to take Dana from you if that was the case, now would I?" Angel purred at him.

Daniel looked at her and for a while their eyes locked. I felt my heart thump when I saw the longing in Angel's eyes, and her angelic beauty. It seemed to me that they looked into each others' eyes for too long without speaking, without noticing the rest of us.

Then Daniel spoke, still looking into Angel's eyes.

"Do you mean that you are willing to betray Cain, not bring him what he ordered you to fetch? Didn't he command you to bring Dana to him, unharmed – his creation, his grandchild, the only Nephilim Weaver who can move through time?" Daniel asked. Then, after a slight pause, "Are you disobeying him?"

Angel did not say anything, just raised her head without turning her eyes from Daniel. I wanted to step between them to stop that look, to hide that longing, that wanting… that lust.

"Just as I suspected, then," Daniel said. "Does Cain know he has a rebel in his family?"

"Cain need never know," Angel said sweetly. "I can convince him that Dana met with an accident that forced her to stay here in the past. And if you give Dana to me now, at least she will live. As long as the Pale Man finds pleasure in her, that is. If he doesn't, her time may be short. But if she comes with me now, she will live as one of his concubines – as long as she remains obedient to him."

She was looking straight at me now, certain of her victory. She had Elijah's daughter and grandson hostage, after all. I saw Daniel's hands squeeze into fists. Elijah stood behind him, and his eyes had come back to life, no longer dulled with despair. He observed Angel with keen attention.

"No. You go and tell your new lord that these are *our* conditions. Everyone concerned will meet in an open space where there are other people around. And the exchange will happen only if we see Meryt-Neith and Ramose, unharmed. And go and tell your lord this," Daniel continued, "if they are not there when we get to the meeting place, we'll leave instantly and go back to the future. It's not the first time we have had to sacrifice our own people for the greater good. We don't do it lightly – but believe me, we will."

Angel's pupils changed – suddenly her eyes had become snake-like, all the adoration gone. Clearly the shot about her being subordinate to a new lord had hit home.

"If you don't do as we say, you'll find us gone in no time," Lilith said calmly. "We have strong weavers among us. You only have Anna, who is ill and exhausted and can never follow us as fast as you'd need to travel to catch us. Your choice."

Angel stood like a statue for a while and then she quickly sank into the buffer zone and was gone.

No one said anything for a long time. Then Ambrogio stepped out of the next room.

"Did it work?" Grandma asked.

"Yes. She did not smell me because of the incense. And my shadow is following her now to their abode and to learn all he can about it. He will return shortly, so be ready to leave. And be ready for a fight. You do know how to kill Nephilim as powerful as this, yes?"

"Of course," Daniel said.

"Good. You may need to do just that. And now, we wait."

We stood still, waiting for the shadow's return.

84

UNAFRAID

"Well, I didn't believe they'd simply hand her over to me without any resistance," the Pale Man said.

He was sitting in a chair, with his long legs stretched out before him. They were in a room of the house he had bought, using as an intermediary the same scribe who had forged Meryt-Neith's letter. No one had seen them entering.

"It was worth a try, my lord," Angel said.

"I will have her, though. She will make a fine wife for me, if she is submissive enough. If not – well, I can still use her for a while and then make her into one of us. Maybe I'll even manage to make my seed take root in her – " Angel saw his look of pleasurable amusement " – and if that were to happened, I'd probably keep her as she is, even if she isn't obedient. I need another wife capable of giving me children."

"There might be a slight problem there. Turning her into one of us, that is," Angel said.

The Pale Man looked at her, curiously. His eyes travelled up and down Angel's body and to her surprise, his cold expression made her anxious. What was this? She was used to Nephilim and mortals lusting after her and had used such men for her own pleasure many times. But when she thought about the Pale Man touching her... something felt wrong. What is was, she didn't know, but her senses warned her and she suppressed a shiver.

"Explain," he said.

"I'm afraid she can't be turned into one of us. She carries silver blood in her body, and can't be transformed. Only killed."

"What?" the Pale Man rose so quickly Angel's eyes barely realised he had moved. "Why didn't you tell me about this before?"

He stood in front of her, towering over her.

"There was no time, and I didn't think it would be essential for our plan. I am telling you now, so you will know what to do with her once you have had your pleasure," Angel said calmly.

Thankfully, years of experience with Cain's ways had taught her to show no fear and so she was able to keep her composure now.

"Do you not know of the legend that a silver Nephilim will be the doom of our kind?" the Pale Man yelled.

"I am aware of this, which is why I think it's best that you get her and make sure there's no danger of her harming us. This is why my lord Cain also wanted her back. She left without his permission, and Cain will not tolerate having her running around free. I am Cain's second-in-command, and in a position to give orders about her fate, and for our own safety, I say it is wisest to keep her here, as your prisoner - as long as you don't wish to kill her, that is." Angel coolly turned her back on the Pale Man. "Now, we need to let them know whether we agree to this exchange on their terms – or not."

She walked away from the Pale Man who, unaccustomed to such behaviour from any woman, stared after her in fury.

"Well?" Angel asked, not showing even a hint of fear.

The Pale Man had to admit he admired her strength and her great beauty. Perhaps he would take them both as his wives... yes, the thought entertained him. If this woman thought she was free to do as she pleased, she would soon learn her lesson.

"Very well. Let them know we agree to this exchange. We will meet for the exchange near the desert altars, among the festivities. Tell them to go there and we will find them."

"I shall let them know," Angel said.

A slight movement caught her attention but when she turned her head, there was nothing.

"Just a moment," she said and quickly entered the buffer zone.

No one. She must have imagined it.

85

THE FIGHT

I thought I had lost Kitty for good, as I had not seen her since our escape from the cave. But this night, while I waited for the sun to rise, I couldn't even try to sleep. I sat on the roof of our house, afraid of watching the horizon grow light. And then I felt someone beside me.

I turned my head and Kitty was there, her translucent form floating in the air next to me.

"Kitty! Where have you been? Do you know what's happened?"

"I got lost in the dream world of the people of this city. I have trouble moving around the buffer zone here. It's as if I don't belong here in the past."

Her voice was faint, but I heard her words.

"None of us do…" I said, "but do you know what's been happening here?"

"You'd better tell me," Kitty said, "and after that, I will stay very close to you so I don't get lost again. Did you know that even though dead people should be able to move easily in the afterlife, here it's like the buffer zone is… sticky? It grabs me and tries to push me away from the world of the living. Maybe it is trying to tell me it is no longer my business to meddle with the physical world."

"I hope not," I looked at Kitty. "I would miss you terribly if you left for good."

"Perhaps my time to leave is coming soon, but I will stay with you as long as I can," she said. "Now, tell me everything that's happened since you dived into the sea."

I did. Kitty came so close to me I could feel her slight, feather-like touch against my skin.

"And so they are giving you away to your worst enemy tomorrow? I can't believe it!" Kitty said.

"Well, we're planning to make sure it never happens, of course. And we have the surprise element of Ambrogio and his... allies," I said. "Still, it could all go wrong. They may get me after all, despite all our plans."

We both sat in silence. My imagination was galloping like a bolting horse, thinking about what would be in store for me if the Pale Man managed to kidnap me.

In the depth of the night, most people in this city were sleeping. I looked at the rooftops, at the temples towering over the city, the thousands of little houses. I knew that death had already arrived in Akhetaten with one or more of the foreign delegations. Many people would die, including some in the king's immediate family. The King's Mother Tiye would be among them.

But this death, be it cholera or plague, would also play a part in saving ancient Egypt from its weakened state. When Egyptian dominion began to crumble in the adjoining lands because of Akhenaten's disinterest in military rule, many of the Egyptian soldiers would be taken as prisoners to the Hittite kingdom. And the soldiers would carry with them the very illness that was about to cripple Akhetaten. As a result, the Hittite kingdom would begin to crumble as well, and it would no longer pose a threat to Egypt.

I felt the disease in me – not as an illness I had myself, but as a buzzing in my blood. My hands were tingling the way they had before I had laid them on the King's Mother's belly to heal her. My body could sense the illness spreading through the houses I was looking at and it wanted to use its healing powers.

What if I was forced to stay here – would the plight of the great number of ill people around have an effect on my body? Would it drain all my energies while healing others?

I shook the thought away. I could not heal the whole city.

Steps. I turned my head to see Daniel approaching.

"Kitty," he said.

"Daniel," Kitty's whisper greeted him.

"May I sit with you?" Daniel asked.

I took his hand and pulled him down next to me. He wrapped his arm around my shoulders.

"You do know I will never allow anything bad to happen to you, not as long as I have life in my body to stop it?"

His free hand stroked my cheek, his dark blue eyes made me promises of safety.

"If it becomes inevitable that you can't prevent me being taken, I don't want you to put yourself into danger," I said. "Leave. And maybe come back later and try to release me."

"He will not... have his will with you," Daniel said, looking at me deeply in the eyes, "never."

"Never say never," I said, "it may yet happen. I only wish he wasn't... he wouldn't be... my first..."

Daniel wrapped both hands around me and kissed me fiercely, possessively.

"And he won't be. I will kill him first. I swear."

"Don't swear things you can't be sure about," I said.

"No matter how strong he is, he's no match for me and Elijah," Daniel said.

"Is Elijah in any condition to fight?"

"I am," Elijah's voice came from behind us, "and he's going to pay for what he did to Merit. This, I swear."

There was rage in his voice. His twin soul was now truly dead. It could be that revenge was the only thing that kept him going now. That, and the hope of saving his daughter and grandson.

We sat in silence throughout the rest of the night. At sunrise, chanting and music began to rise from the temples and from the direction of the desert altars.

"Time to leave," Daniel said.

We got up.

"I won't be visible to you," Kitty said, "but I am not letting go of Dana. If you need to leave for the future in an instant, I don't want to be left behind. The way I get lost in the buffer zone here... I don't know where I'd end up."

I felt her touch on my arm after that but could not see her.

"Everyone, eat!" Grandma said when we came down to the first floor.

"I couldn't eat a thing," I said.

"You must! We need to be strong, and a hungry body is an obstacle during a fight. But don't eat too much. Just enough to give yourselves energy."

"Here," Diana offered me a piece of bread and I forced myself to chew it.

Diana took her position as a guardian by my side when we all marched to the garden and then to the gate leading to the royal road.

"I feel I have to say my goodbyes to you now," Thomas said. "I can't walk fast and I'll be of no use to you in a fight."

"We will miss you," Grandma said, hugging him in what I knew was her bear-like embrace.

"And I will miss you," Thomas said. "I'll take my leave of you and head straight to the harbour. I'm going to try to get to a ship out of here. I'm going back to my family. If you should stay here, send me word. If not... I will try to send you a message through time. Goodbye, dear friends! I wish you every success in what you are about to do."

Paris, Diana, Lilith and I hugged him too. Aemilius, Jason, Reggie and Mr. Donnelly shook his hand and patted his back the way men always do. Elijah and Daniel nodded at him solemnly, their thoughts already focussed on what was to come.

The guard standing at the gate tried to stop us, but Daniel simply shoved him aside and opened the gate.

"Tell him we are going to the Mother of the King, and that all is well," he said to Thomas.

Thomas did, but the guard seemed unconvinced.

We hurried along the road in a group. I stole just one glance behind us, only to see Thomas leaning on his cane, with a raised hand.

I raised my hand too. He lowered his with a nod and began to walk the other way slowly, towards the harbour. He would disappear into the past now and we would never see him again.

"I hope Seshat and Iahmesu are doing their part," Diana said.

"They are. They are mourning for Merit, and wish to have her death avenged."

Despite the great number of foreigners in the city, we couldn't help drawing attention to ourselves, Daniel, Elijah and myself being so tall, and Reggie almost as tall as we were. Grandma and Diana were now ready to defend me and their steps reflected their mood and betrayed their training as fighters. Jason, Lilith and Mr. Donnelly also stood out as foreign-looking, despite the mixture of nations around us. Aemilius was probably the only one who didn't look out of place, with his Mediterranean appearance. But even he drew interested looks, most likely because of the deep scar on his face.

"To the desert altars, then," Elijah said, turning towards the tent city.

The celebrations had lasted for days, maybe even weeks. Everywhere we went was overflowing with people.

We walked where the throng was not quite so dense and then stopped.

"Let's wait here," Lilith said.

We did not have to wait long. I felt Kitty's hand squeeze my arm and almost instantly, Angel and the Pale Man appeared.

"Where are Meryt-Neith and Ramose?" Daniel asked.

"In a house nearby. We couldn't be certain you wouldn't renege on your side of the deal and try to free them. It made sense that you'd try that – trusting that we'd behave ourselves because we wouldn't want to draw the attention of all these crowds," Angel said, her eyes caressing Daniel's form. "You can come with us to meet them and we'll make the exchange there."

We looked at one another. This was not as we'd planned it, but there was no going back now. Of course we could have left right there and then – Paris was holding one of Lilith's objects in her hands, a piece of wood from the ceiling, and I had one too – one of the key cards to an office. Lilith was holding a brass door number from one of the resident wings of the Magellan Centre.

"We're not using the buffer zone. We'll walk," Daniel said. "And any foul play and we are off, permanently."

I saw a flash of disappointment in Angel's eyes. They had been planning on going through the buffer zone. Of course, they would...

"They must have their own soldiers ready in the buffer zone," Grandma muttered quietly.

Daniel nodded, he had heard.

"OK, let's get this done," he said. "Walk ahead, and we'll be right behind you."

The Pale Man's eyes narrowed under his head covering. But he turned and began walking, Angel beside him. Daniel walked right behind the Pale Man and Elijah was breathing down Angel's neck.

Grandma and Aemilius walked in front of me, Jason and Diana behind me. I was inside a square formed by four lethal fighters.

Reggie, Lilith and Mr. Donnelly were our rear guard.

We didn't hurry, and the Pale Man and Angel turned to glance back on many occasions. Angel always looked over her shoulder the longest, gazing only at Daniel. But we reached the outskirts of the city soon enough, and entered one of the alleyways. This forced us to squeeze closer to one another, but we didn't lose our formation.

"Here," the Pale Man finally stopped and pointed at one of the bigger houses. It had a garden and two storeys, but was much smaller than the house we had occupied.

He opened the gate and entered the yard, followed closely by Daniel. Angel went next, shadowed by Elijah. The rest of us hurried through the narrow gate as quickly as we could.

No one attacked us.

"This way," Angel said sweetly, "they are waiting for you, Elijah."

Ambrogio's shadow had already told us the layout of the room. And Ambrogio's latest children had checked the surroundings of the house – ordinary people in ordinary houses. When the attack would come, it would come from within the house.

We followed them into a reception room with a column at its centre. Meryt-Neith stood there, tied to the column so she could not move. She appeared unharmed and looked at us with round, desperate eyes. She was gagged, her long hair falling over her face.

"Meryt-Neith..." Elijah said.

This was the moment they had been waiting for. They must have planned on our guard going down at the sight of her. As soon as Elijah had said her name, two Nephilim soldiers with opened wings appeared from the buffer zone behind him.

But how wrong they had been. We had learned the layout of the house from Ambrogio's shadow. Elijah was a soldier to the core, and he was raging. Daniel was too experienced at fighting to let anything distract him. And as they had been expecting an ambush, Daniel was facing in the opposite direction to Elijah. We had already agreed beforehand that everyone without wings would try to get out of the way, and they did – pressing themselves against the wall so there would be plenty of room for the fight.

The brothers jumped on the two Nephilim as soon as they sensed them. Their wings shot open, and they clashed together with the enemy so that the air was screaming with electricity.

Elijah got to his soldier first and lunged at him with the tips of his wings pointing forward. He literally pierced the soldier with the points of his wings and the evil one fell to the ground, bleeding.

Daniel and the other Nephilim soldier were circling each other.

Angel moved almost at the same instant as Elijah and Daniel had. She jumped towards me and opened her dark wings, threatening me now that my protectors were occupied with their own fight.

I backed up, my foot caught on something and I fell onto my back. I just had time to open my wings and wrap them around me fast, so that Angel's wings didn't get the chance to touch me.

The Pale Man stepped forward the same moment that I fell, but Elijah attacked him so quickly the soldier he had killed hadn't fully fallen to the floor.

The Pale Man opened his wings – and they were opaque, pitch black. Even the veins. He looked like a pale angel straight out of hell.

He hadn't expected to meet anyone of his own strength and when Elijah threw him through the air against the wall so that the whole house jolted, I saw genuine surprise in his expression.

And then Angel was upon me again. She was screaming now, her mouth wide open like a lizard's, spit falling from her lips, her eyes filled with yellow madness. Her wings beat mine so that pain shot through my whole being.

Daniel was now in full fight with the other Nephilim warrior.

And then three things happened.

Just as Angel's fury was at its worst and she was hurting my wings so badly that I almost lost consciousness, Diana came to the rescue. Despite orders to stay out of the way, she moved up behind Angel. Something very strange was happening to her. She crouched down, doubling over like she had a pain in her belly. And then she straightened herself and the unimaginable happened. Two orange coloured wings opened from her back and she lunged at Angel.

Angel was not expecting it and looked over her shoulder, not believing what she was seeing. But she quickly recovered, turned towards Diana and began to defend herself.

And then, two small figures appeared in the doorway. They shouted and pointed and armed soldiers stepped into the room. The sight of so many winged Nephilim made them stop in their tracks. Iahmesu pointed at the Pale Man who had managed to get back on his feet despite Elijah's attack.

The Pale Man looked at the soldiers, at Diana and me, and disappeared so fast into the buffer zone that it was as if someone had thrown a switch.

And then another figure appeared out of the buffer zone. Ambrogio had arrived, just as he had promised. He appeared right in front of Mr. Donnelly and Reggie who tried to stand against the wall, away from the fight.

He attacked Angel before she had time to react, kicking her in the knees from behind so that she lost her balance and fell to the floor face down right next to me. Without emotion he lifted his hand and chopped Angel on the neck, and on the back, just above the wings.

She let out a gasp and then a horrible rasping sound. Her hands flew to her throat as she tried to breathe in vain. Her eyes rolled back in her head and then she was unconscious.

"Where is the boy?" Grandma shouted.

"In the back, in another room!" Ambrogio said. "My shadow guards him."

The soldiers still hadn't entered the room, but the surprise effect was enough for now.

Seshat and Iahmesu had gone to Tiye at sunrise, to tell her they had found the man who had killed Merit and kidnapped Meryt-Neith and Ramose. Tiye had immediately sent soldiers with them to arrest the Pale Man and they had followed us to the field of celebrations. When we left the field and walked to the house, it was a surprise; but we had done so slowly, so that they could follow us. They had been given orders to arrest the Pale Man only when Meryt-Neith and Ramose had been found.

"Get the boy!" Grandma shouted to Aemilius who ran out of the room with Jason.

And then everything went wrong.

Meryt-Neith screamed through the cloth that had been stuffed into her mouth. We turned to look and caught a glimpse of the Pale Man by her side. He disappeared immediately, but he had managed to do his worst. There was a deep gash in Meryt-Neith's throat and blood was welling onto her shoulder.

Almost immediately, we heard another muffled shout from the back room. A young man's voice.

"Ramose!" Seshat shouted.

"Tie her," Ambrogio said and ran to the back of the house where the voice had come from.

Diana quickly grabbed her sash and tied Angel's hands tightly behind her back. I got to my feet and gave Diana my sash so she could tie her feet as well.

That was when the mud brick house started to collapse. It hadn't been very sturdy to start with, and the fighting Nephilim had beaten the walls with their wings.

Seshat and Iahmesu ran outside with the soldiers.

"Quickly, we need to get out now!" Lilith shouted. "Dana, you have to do this, we don't have time to weave strings! Everyone, grab Dana! Aemilius, Jason! Come back!"

They all ran to me, Jason and Aemilius coming into the room as I fumbled through the pouch hanging from my waist. There, there it was! The flat plastic key card, its edge curled by heat.

A big chunk of the ceiling fell down next to us, bringing a chest with it. It split into pieces at the impact. Something hurtled from the chest towards me and Diana caught it in midair. Everyone grabbed me and I directed all my energies into my hands. The greyish and blue strings shot out of my fingers almost instantly and just as another piece of the ceiling came down where we stood, the strings yanked us into the buffer zone.

The last thing visible before the vortex of the future opened up to us was Meryt-Neith. She was still alive, tied to the pillar, her shoulder and chest red with her blood. She looked at me, horrified, crying, her face distorted with fear and pain.

And then the house disappeared into a cloud of rubble and dust, the mists closed around us and the past disappeared.

86

FAMILIAR FACES

Ambrogio ran to the back of the house just as it started to collapse.

"Where are you?" he shouted.

"Here, master!" his shadow's voice came from a room behind the stairs. "He is here!"

He ran into the room at the same moment the Pale Man appeared there, his wings now closed. Good.

"Well, well," – he did not seem to be disturbed by the fact the house was collapsing around them – "we meet again."

Ambrogio did not answer. A crash and shouts came from the other room. A cloud of dust billowed along the corridor and into the room they were in.

"Say goodbye to daylight or the night or whatever is your realm of existence," the Pale Man said, moving towards Ambrogio, "for now, you are going to die. You stopped me from killing the silver girl. You deserve to die; and this time, death will be final."

Ambrogio prepared for the fight, bending his knees slightly, ready to jump whichever way he needed.

The Pale Man attacked first, only to grasp thin air where

Ambrogio had been. He turned to see where he was and saw him by the tied and gagged Ramose. The boy's head was hanging down and a broad strip of cloth was wrapped around his head, securing and silencing him completely. Ambrogio saw blood running from the side of his neck.

The Pale Man attacked again, to the same effect. At his third try, he met with the unexpected. Suddenly there were three other figures by Ambrogio's side: a man with cloudy eyes, and two blood-drinkers. Together, they all turned on the Pale Man.

Ambrogio did not hear anyone approaching, but suddenly Meryt-Neith, coated in blood, was at the door. She was wiping dust from her eyes, trying to see into the room. Her other arm hung uselessly by her side, with a deep wound from shoulder to wrist. The falling roof must have cut the ropes that had tied her.

Ambrogio could not pay attention to her. Along with his servants, he was doing his best to kill the Pale Man. He managed to get behind him just as Meryt-Neith knelt by Ramose and began to tear free the ropes around his ankles with her one good hand.

Ambrogio hit the Pale Man at the spot where the wings would open and he fell onto his knees, his wings half opening. But it was not enough to make him give up. He rolled onto his back, sat up, breathing in with great difficulty, and reached for Ambrogio.

The shadow appeared, wrapping its arms around the Pale Man's neck. The two vampires attacked his arms and neck, strong teeth tearing into him. The Pale Man roared in fury but the lack of oxygen began to have its effect.

Meryt-Neith had managed to get Ramose's legs free and they stumbled to the doorway. The house was swaying now, its outer walls were falling down and sunlight was streaming in through the dust.

Ambrogio should have killed the Pale Man, but something happened that threw him off guard completely. It was enough to allow the Pale Man to drag himself free and disappear into the buffer zone, bleeding from the vampire bites.

It was the boy, Ramose. Meryt-Neith had used her good hand to pull the gag off, over the boy's head. As she did so, he turned his head to look into the room and for a while his face was lit up clearly by sunlight through the collapsing wall. And it was a face Ambrogio knew.

For the first time in his existence, Ambrogio froze, unable to move, enabling the escape of his enemy. He looked into the boy's eyes for a brief moment before Ramose found his feet and ran out of the house, followed by Meryt-Neith. She turned to look at Ambrogio too, to be sure he was not following. Their eyes locked for a short moment. Her features looked oddly familiar as well, but she was so covered with dust he did not recognise her at first. And then they were gone.

Ambrogio's mouth formed the name connected with the features of the boy he knew so well, right from the days in Delphi where it had all begun.

"Cain?"

And then it came to him where he had seen Meryt-Neith before. Despite the rumbling noises and falling tiles and beams, his hand reached into a pocket sewn into his long kilt. It was still there – the singing device he had used to kill the silver Nephilim. The same device given to him by Cain so he would win the trust of what Ambrogio had thought to be a goddess. The beautiful golden-haired goddess who had given him his kithara so he could take part in the singing competition in Delphi. Take part and win. Meet Selene, fall in love, and be cursed into the darkness by a dark Nephilim who lusted after her.

Cain had wanted him to steal her silver bow that could cut the very fabric of creation, create openings to the buffer zone for anyone to walk through. The silver bow of the goddess who had turned him into a vampire. The same Nephilim woman who had just escaped the collapsing house with her son.

"Artemis..."

Ambrogio formed her name with his lips only, the dust had stolen his voice. His lips distorted into a snarl. But Artemis was already gone.

Then the house collapsed, and his reactions carried him towards safety, with the walls trying to bury him without success as he ran through the reception room, towards the garden. Noticing a figure under the rubble, without thinking, he bent down, lifted Angel up into his arms and ran out.

87

THE CHANGE

Meryt-Neith sat in her room. She had been washed and her wounds had been attended to.

She felt a strange sensation in her blood and knew without having to look that her eyes were changing colour.

She still had some time as herself, and she intended to use it.

He would come for her and Ramose, soon. She knew that. The Pale Man's body hadn't been found in the collapsed house. And already, Meryt-Neith felt a new passion rising inside her. The desire to own, to order others, to dive into the deep darkness that felt so familiar it must have always been there. Maybe it was the very thing that had lured her into the Pale Man's arms in the first place.

The part of her that still carried the light of her previous existence fought the darkness. She felt it getting weaker by the moment. She didn't have much time left.

She took her writing equipment and wrote a short letter.

"When I gave him into your care, you promised me that if I ever sent you word telling you to hide, you would take him to the ends of the earth if necessary. The time has now come. I have been bitten, and am transforming. Take him, take my son, and leave. Hide him from me for all eternity. If I ever send you another letter asking to see my son, know that it is evil writing that

letter, not me. Do not trust any communication from me from now on. I will now say goodbye to life as I knew it and enter darkness. I do not have the courage to kill myself. My last wish is that you will make sure my son has a safe life, away from me."

She didn't even sign the letter for fear it would fall into the wrong hands and reveal her as the writer. She read the letter through once, and then tied it into a tight square with several strings. She wrote the recipient's name and location on top.

"It is written?" Seshat asked.

She had been sitting silently in the room.

"It is. I cannot trust anyone but you to make sure this reaches her."

"We'll leave it with Iahmesu today to take it to someone who will be trusted to deliver it. After that, we are returning to the desert and will never come back again."

"That's good. And it's good that you never told me where the secret village is," Meryt-Neith said, "for I would have revealed it all to him before long. For he will surely arrive for me soon – and for Ramose."

"I so wish we could have stopped this from happening," Seshat said, her voice choking.

"But you couldn't. No one could. He bit me and he bit Ramose even before that. I can't kill myself – I only hope I will still have some of my mother's love left afterwards. That's the only reason I'm choosing to remain alive. To be with Ramose, to try to guarantee his safety however I can."

Meryt-Neith hugged Seshat.

"Goodbye, my friend. I am sorry this is how it all ended."

"Not as sorry as we are…" Seshat's voice broke.

She took the letter and walked out, her shoulders shaking from her sobs. Meryt-Neith never saw her or Iahmesu again.

Some weeks later, Meryt-Neith walked up onto the roof of the North Palace. Meritaten lived here now as the Great Royal Wife, and Nefertiti had moved to the centre palace to rule the land as the King's equal.

No one paid much attention to her as she sat there under the stars.

The change was near now. Its dark song sang in her veins, caressing her mind like intoxicating wine. Earlier today, when she looked in a mirror, she had seen that her eyes had turned yellow. She had spent some time admiring the slow oily pulse. So beautiful. So powerful. So strong.

As she breathed in, she felt a crack in her back. She looked behind her and saw something rising from her shoulders. She smiled. Her wings had finally appeared. No pain, no paralysis, just two beautiful, dark wings unfurling in the darkness of night. There was no moon. That was good. The moon was too bright. But her dark wings seemed to shimmer with a light of their own. She was more powerful than the night – she could light her own steps with her wings from now on.

And behind the beauty of her wings stood the Pale Man, smiling.

She rose to her feet.

"I am so happy to see you as who you were always meant to be," he said.

And she smiled back at him, pressing her body against him, feeling his satisfying reaction.

"As am I. This should have already happened, a long time ago."

"You were not convinced that easily. But now that I finally have you, you shall have all eternity to enjoy your power with me," the Pale Man said.

"Shall we go now and fetch our son and leave this miserable place of mortal men?" Meryt-Neith smiled at him and he caressed her cheek with his hand, letting his finger rest a while on the side of her mouth that was drooping slightly. It had never really healed after he had beaten and raped her in the past. But in a way, it added interest to her expression.

"Yes. Let's do that," he replied.

Meryt-Neith gave him a deep kiss and took his hand. Together, they fell into the mists around the world.

At the harbour of Amnisos near the royal palace of Kunusa in the land of the Keftiu, a Nephilim woman opened the letter a ship had brought to her.

She wiped away a tear after reading it. Meryt-Neith had been a good friend during the months she had stayed here before the birth of her baby.

Meryt-Neith had told the woman what had happened to her, and given her baby boy into her care, for she had no children of her own.

"I cannot take him with me. *He* will surely come after him if he hears of his birth. I will return with Ramose, but one day, I am sure, he will transform me into a creature like himself. I hope that day is far in the future. When it happens, I will write to you, and you must promise to leave this land, and hide my son."

"I promise you this," the Nephilim woman had answered Meryt-Neith, "but give your son a name before you go."

"I will not. I must not know his name. It might lead me to him, if I come here, asking about him. You name him after I have left. And when you go, change your own name as well. And never try to reach me after I have sent word that you must escape."

Meryt-Neith had left with Ramose soon after that, on a ship heading for Kemet.

And now the woman from Keftiu was boarding another ship, along with the blond young Nephilim man who was eager for adventure, to fulfil her promise to his mother. The ship left the harbour, opened its sails and disappeared into the Great Green.

PROLOGUE TO NEPHILIM QUEST 4

He watched her from the window as long as she was visible, walking away down the street. He could see from the position of her shoulders how shocked she was. He could tell from the way her steps slowed down before she turned the corner how much she wanted to look back. But he had told her not to...

He had warned her, explained what she was, and then told her to leave and never come back. It was the hardest thing he had ever done, harder even than escaping Cain.

She was his twin soul. He had known it the moment he had seen her for the first time in the park – the delicate-featured young woman who seemed to be ashamed of how tall she was.

He had thought she knew what she was, but she didn't. And eventually he had to tell her, as they were lying side by side in his bed.

He closed his eyes, forcing back the tears. No time for that. He had sensed *them* near him yesterday. That painful buzz in his spine that always told him when Cain's Nephilim were near. He had seen them from a distance, walking in the park, searching for him, and drawing curious glances from people because of their height. He had escaped, it seemed, before they had come close enough to sense his presence. But if they knew where to look for him, his beloved was in danger too. And so he had pushed her away, promising he would search for her when it was safe again.

After she had left, he waited until morning, not showing himself at the window. Fortunately, they did not find their way to the little boarding house where he had rented a room under a false name.

When the sun rose, ending the darkness Cain's soldiers preferred, he slipped out of the house. All his senses sharpened to detect any followers, he walked towards the Thames. He knew where the steps leading to the water were. Looking around, he made sure no one was watching – then he quickly descended the stairs, stepped into the water and dived under.

The water was filthy, disgusting. He could scarcely see anything. But that was good, it meant that no one could see him, either.

When he was deep in the water, he waited until the necessity to breathe became so strong he had to draw in a breath. As before, his wings responded and opened underwater with such force that the water around him created a small tsunami that rose up and travelled towards the banks of the river.

It was his mother who had told him how to hide underwater.

"He can't follow you there. None of his servants can," she had told him when he was old enough to understand and keep secrets.

"Why can't he?" he had asked. "If he is my father, surely he should be able to do so as well?"

His mother turned to look into the street. There was a tall man standing there. There always was. His father had said it was to guard them, and he barely thought about it. A guard had always been there. And he felt safe knowing it.

"It's time you knew the truth about yourself," his mother said quietly, turning away from the window. "Keep your voice low. The guard shouldn't overhear what we're saying."

"Hear? Through the walls?"

He laughed. Mother must be joking. Her expression brought his laughter to an end, abruptly.

"You've already told me we are special..." he said.

"Shush! Whisper!" Mother put her finger on her lips.

To humour her, he continued in a whisper.

"You told me that we can breathe underwater and we shouldn't let anyone know that," he whispered, "and I haven't told anyone, Mum, I promise. Not even Father."

She was beautiful, his mother. She had long dark hair, features that never seemed to grow old, and tired, sad eyes. She rose now, and walked across to the window of the house she never left. Servants took care of everything. She only went out every Sunday to go to church with him, and the guard always followed at a respectable distance and sat on the bench nearest to the church door until the service was over.

"He doesn't want me to reveal to you what you are. He wants to impress you himself, so that you'll admire him and want to be like him."

He didn't understand.

"He told me that if I show you what you... what we are, he will change you into his likeness before it is your time."

He looked at his beautiful mother, understanding even less.

"But I have decided to let you know, so I can help you escape him," she said. "I will not live like this any more."

"I don't understand, mother," he said hesitantly.

"I will show you," she whispered, "say nothing."

First, she drew the heavy curtains. And then she opened her wings.

He was so surprised he fell on the floor in his haste to step back.

"Are you... an angel?" he finally managed to whisper.

"Not the kind of angel you hear about in church. But I – and you, are descendants of angels. And so is your father."

"Cain is an angel?"

"No. Cain is no angel. He is a descendant of the angels who took human wives. Have you not read the story in your Bible?"

He had.

"And now the other truth about yourself. You are not Cain's son. I was already pregnant with you when he killed your real father and abducted me into a life of imprisonment in this building. I had barely become aware of the fact, and I never told him, because he thought you were his son. If he had known the truth, he would have destroyed you."

"Why...?"

"You are the son of one of his worst enemies. He would never have allowed your real father's bloodline to continue in you. So I let him think you were his son. He would never kill his own son. His kind have trouble getting children."

"His kind? What do you mean, mother?"

And so she told him everything, in whispers he could barely hear. How the Nephilim were created, how the war of the Nephilim had started. Thousands of years of an invisible war of which ordinary people had no knowledge. How the evil Nephilim stole women of the pure kind in order to get children. When and how their wings opened. And how the enemy Nephilim were created through bites.

"Your wings should open soon – you're the right age. That's the moment he has been waiting for. He chose me as one of his wives because he believes my family line carries the ability to travel through time. There is a story the mothers of my bloodline have told their daughters for thousands of years – that our ancestors were a silver Nephilim couple. And not only that – but that one of them, the woman, was able to travel through time. Cain wants a child who can carry on this skill. A child he can call his own. You. He wants you to marry someone he believes is of another branch of my family tree. In time, he will try to abduct her too, to be your wife, if he hasn't done so already. To see if your offspring could travel through time – something the Nephilim have never been able to do."

"But why? Why does he want to travel through time?"

"He hasn't shared that with me. Everything I've told you, I have learned over the years, particularly when he has been careless in his speech while... visiting me. He loves to boast about his deeds and strength. Of how many Nephilim he has killed. He boasts about you, too. He believes you are his offspring, and he has had great difficulty to sire children... the traditional way. He was changed by one of the evil Nephilim before he had even opened his wings and it seems that is what makes it hard for the dark Nephilim to beget children and so they create offspring through biting them. He has tried to get more children, which is why he... visits us," his mother said, her expression stony, "but no more. I'm going to make sure you can escape to safety."

She had planned the whole thing for so long. She told her son that the servants were loyal to Cain too, and reported her every move to him. But she had managed to make contact with a servant outside the household, a laundress, who was not on Cain's payroll. And with her help, she had managed get a letter out of the house, to her own family. She had received a letter in response. And then more, through which they had planned the escape.

When the sun was setting, and the guard outside was being changed, there were a few moments while the servants were preparing dinner. He did exactly what his mother had told him. She remained sitting in the living room, by the window, reading a book. At her signal, he walked into the small back yard, and climbed into a sack placed on a cart. The laundry woman appeared with more sacks full of laundry, threw them over him on the cart and pulled the cart out of the side gate while the guard on day-shift was looking in the direction from which the night-guard always appeared. He paid no attention to the familiar laundress – old, bent, not of any importance at all.

And so he had escaped. The laundry woman let him out next to a fenced park, on a road where a light had been broken to create a spot of darkness.

A tall man was waiting for him. He gave something to the laundry woman.

"Get away. Now. You can't go back to your own house. The boy's father will kill you if he finds out you helped him escape. There's a train leaving in an hour – you have just enough time to get to the station. Don't pack anything. Just leave. Get off where the ticket tells you. Someone will come and take you to a cottage where you can live. There's enough money there for you to live comfortably for the rest of your life. Never mention this to anyone or the boy's father will hear of it, and you will die."

The laundry woman swallowed, curtsied and hurried off.

"And now, young man," the tall man turned to face him, "I am your uncle. I'm going to take you into hiding, take care of you when your wings open, and help you hide from Cain. Follow me."

"What will happen to mother?" he asked.

"If she isn't already dead, she will be very soon," he said tersely. "Cain does not tolerate disobedience."

"No! We have to get back and help her!" He turned, but the man gripped his arm.

"No. Then she would have died in vain. She's been planning this for a long time, to save your life. She wrote to me, telling me she considers her life a small sacrifice – if the silver family line continues."

"Silver family line?"

"Yes. There are several branches of our family tree, and the knowledge has followed us through centuries that each of these could give birth to children who will have silver wings. We live in hope that the legend is true. Cain has already killed every silver one he could find in the distant past. He doesn't realise that the silver line is still alive. He doesn't know that one escaped the killing he arranged, and had offspring. To keep the secret, we've chosen to give our children away, to be raised in ordinary families where no one has ever heard of Nephilim. We fetch them when it's time for their wings to open. Then they are old enough to keep secrets, and to hide."

"Has there been a silver... Nephilim, then?" he asked.

"No. But we hope there will be."

They hurried along the street, his uncle speaking as they walked.

"You mother suspected you could be a silver Nephilim, saying you bore all the markings of one – paler skin than normal, with strange bluish eyes. If your wings had opened when Cain was there, and they had been silver, he would have destroyed you on the spot. He believes in the prophecy that says a silver Nephilim will be the end of all his kind, and that's why he hunted down what he believes are all the silver Nephilim. You were safe as long as Cain thought you were his son, and as long as your wings remained unopened. When your mother sensed your time was near, she paid the laundress to deliver a letter to me. And I paid her so much for carrying our secret correspondence that she never dreamt of telling Cain about it. We had to get you away from Cain, in case your mother was right and you are a silver one."

The world seemed to be spinning around him. Only today, he had heard of the Nephilim, seen his mother's wings, learned what he was. And now because of this, his mother was already... dead?

He didn't know what else to do but follow this man, his uncle, tears falling.

They disappeared into the rising fog that muted their steps.

THANK YOU

Thank you for reading Nephilim Quest 3 / Amarna. I hope you enjoyed the book and it would mean a lot to me if you could leave a review. Reviews help authors gain more exposure and keep us writing more stories.

You can find all of my books by visiting my Author page at http://amazon.com/author/leenamaria

If you wish to receive free books from me and **join my reader team** you can do so at my website www.leenasbooks.com

LEENA MARIA'S NEWSLETTER

It's completely free to sign up and you will never be spammed by me. You can opt out easily at any time.

You can join my Readers' Club at
https://leenasbooks.substack.com/
leenasbooks@leenasbooks.com

MORE BOOKS FROM LEENA MARIA

NEPHILIM QUEST -SERIES

Nephilim Quest 1 Shadowhunter
Nephilim Quest 2 Moon Daughter
Nephilim Quest 3 Amarna
Nephilim Quest 4 The Khopesh of the Gods

Nephilim Quest Prequel: Angel. Only for the newsletter subscribers.

Space Witches 1: The Book of Witches
Space Witches 2: The Secret Library
Space Witches 3: The Mirror Witches

THE SEVEN SHABTIS -SERIES

Seven Shabtis 1: The House of the Morning Sun
Seven Shabtis 2: The Pillar of Death

THE CREATURE WARS -SERIES

Creature Wars 1: The Death of a Vampire

ILLUSTRATED CHILDREN'S BOOKS BY AUC PRESS IN CAIRO:

How I Became a Mummy

Mummies, Monsters and the Ship of Millions

Tutankhamun in My Own Hieroglyphs

***

If you wish to **join my newsletter** you can do so at my website www.leenasbooks.com or at my newsletter site.

ACKNOWLEDGMENTS

The research for this book took a lot of time. Readers wrote to me asking when the book would be out; they even commented on it in their reviews. Sigh. I sure wish I could write full time but as it is (when I write this), I have a day job and so writing happens in the evenings and weekends wherever I can steal a few moments.

On top of writing this book I was asked by the American University in Cairo Press to write and illustrate a book: "Tutankhamun in My Own Hieroglyphs". The book was chosen to accompany the official world tour of Tutankhamun's treasures beginning in 2018. That took a few months of my time as well.

So yes, getting this book out took a lot of time. Research alone was a challenge. Why did Akhenaten move away from Thebes? Who was Tutankhamun's mother? No one knows for sure. Perhaps new archaeological findings will enlighten us further about the fascinating Amarna period. But for now, I chose two possible scenarios for the above details, supported by the research as it currently stands.

As before I would love to thank my editor Miriam Bibby who worked her literary magic, pointing out the mistakes an author never notices...

I wish to thank Iris C. Meijer for proofreading and polishing the text.

Cathy Helms of Avalon Graphics surprised me with a cover I love - again. It happens so often I should not be so surprised but I am, every time I see what she comes up with.

And as ever I am grateful to my darling husband who has never-ending patience when I take every opportunity to write my books. His encouragement has been one of the reasons I managed to continue writing when the siren song of the couch in front of the TV almost won. And, conversely, I'm also grateful for the times when he knew flopping on the couch was just the thing I needed and made me leave the keyboard.

And again I wish to thank you, my readers, for asking me the question I hate and love the most: "When will your next book come out?". I hate the question because I feel guilty that I can't publish the books faster. And I love the question because it tells me someone actually reads my books and wants more! I have become friends with some of my readers and I cannot tell you how much I treasure that. Thank you so much for that encouragement.

Back to the old keyboard...

ABOUT THE AUTHOR

Leena Maria is the pen name of Leena Pekkalainen. She holds the MA in Egyptology from the University of Manchester. She is also an artist and has exhibited her Egyptological paintings in Tutankhamon's Golden Treasures replica-exhibition in Finland twice and her horse paintings have been exhibited in England and USA.

Her children's book Tutankhamun in My Own Hieroglyphs was chosen to travel with the King Tut: Treasures of the Golden Pharaoh exhibition on its world tour of 10 cities in 2018.

www.leenasbooks.com

Printed in Great Britain
by Amazon

61343631R00290